# BLOOD DRAGON

Also by Freddie P. Peters:

In the HENRY CROWNE PAYING THE PRICE series
# INSURGENT
# BREAKING PO!NT
# NO TURNING BACK
# SPY SHADOWS
# HENRY CROWNE PAYING THE PRICE BOOKS 1-3
# HENRY CROWNE PAYING THE PRICE BOOKS 4-6
# (COMING SOON)
# IMPOSTOR IN CHIEF
# RED RENEGADE

In the NANCY WU CRIME THRILLER series
# BLOOD DRAGON
# SON AND CRUSADER

# BLOOD DRAGON

## FREDDIE P. PETERS

NANCY WU CRIME THRILLER SERIES BOOK 1

# Glossary of Technical Terms

| Term | Meaning |
|---|---|
| ANPR | Automatic Number Plate Recognition |
| IDENT1 | UK central database for biometric identification, fingerprints, etc. |
| NCA | National Crime Agency |
| SOCO | Scene of Crime Officer |
| SO19 | Special Firearms Command of the Met |
| SFO | Serious Fraud Office |
| UVF | Ulster Volunteer Force |
| INTERPOL | International Criminal Police Organisation |

# List of French Expressions with English Translations

| French Dialogue | English Translation |
|---|---|
| *Absolument* | Absolutely |
| *Absolument mon cher* | Absolutely my dear |
| *Absolument, rebelle de la gauche* | Absolutely, left wing rebel |
| *Andiamo* | Let's go |
| *Bien entendu* | Certainly |
| *C'est vrai* | It's true |
| *Dès que j'ai fini* | As soon as I have finished |
| *En tête à tête* | Face to face (romantic and intimate) |
| *Ha, voilà. Parfait* | Ha, here we are. Perfect |
| *Je le sais* | I know |
| *J'ai besoin de vous* | I need you |
| *J'ai besoin de vous parler* | I need to talk to you |
| *Je suis très flattée, mon cher ami* | I am very flattered, my dear |
| *Ma chère* | My dear (female) |
| *Ma chère amie* | My dear friend (female) |
| *Mais je n'en doutais pas moins* | I had no doubt about it |
| *Messieurs* | Gentlemen |
| *Mon ami* | My friend (male) |
| *Mon cher* | My dear (male) |
| *Mon cher ami* | My dear friend (male) |
| *N'est-ce pas* | Isn't it |
| *Très heureux de l'entendre* | Very glad to hear it |
| *Une proposition irrésistible* | An irresistible offer |
| *Vraiment* | Really |
| *Vraiment désolée* | Really sorry |

# Chapter One

Cora hadn't called. She hadn't turned up at their rendezvous at the Groucho Club either. Nancy walked faster. She lifted the collar of her thick coat and rearranged the orange pashmina that kept her throat warm. She had made room in her busy diary to meet her young artist friend, but, somehow, she could not find it in her to be annoyed with Cora. Nancy was perplexed. Cora's voice message and text conveyed a sense of urgency.

Nancy recalled the words that had sounded out of place.

*I fear I'm going to lose Ollie if I tell him I know something is wrong.*

Nancy arrived at the top of Dean Street without having noticed she had overshot the turning that led to Chinatown. Shaftesbury Avenue was buzzing at 10.30pm. Theatregoers were in the streets, after the end of their shows. The cinemas on Leicester Square were emptying of their patrons and Chinatown in February was getting ready for the Lunar New Year. The energy of it all enticed Nancy. Milling around the crowd was what she needed to alleviate the evening's confusion. She crossed Shaftesbury Avenue and made her way into the mêlée of the streets. Lorries had started delivering their cargoes of exotic fruits, vegetables, and medicinal herbs of various kinds. She slowed down to watch the men unloading the crates and was almost knocked over by a young woman on her bike. The woman apologised with a smile and moved on.

Perhaps Cora had been distracted by the intense activity that often surrounded the food stores preparing for the Chinese New Year.

Nancy had invited her and her boyfriend Ollie to celebrate the event with her in a few days' time. Nancy had rarely acknowledged

1

the day in the past but the recent desire to reconnect with the country in which she was born, her father's country, had brought her closer to the Sleeping Giant.

The smell of food made her mouth water. She lingered for a short moment in front of a restaurant offering takeaways. She had tasted their food in the past and found it delicious… Not of course as good as her own Sichuan cooking, but still very enjoyable.

She looked at her watch. DCI Pole might still be at Scotland Yard. His latest case was proving challenging… but the chance of a late-night dinner with her might tempt him away from his desk.

The menu was stuck in the window. She dived into her handbag for a pair of elegant Chanel glasses. As she turned around, a shadow disappeared into the alleyway at the corner of the restaurant. Nancy frowned. So many people around her were walking, stopping, barely avoiding each other… She shrugged. Cora's missed rendezvous was still playing on her mind. Nancy shook her head and pressed number one on her iPhone speed-dial list.

His phone rung a few times. She was preparing to leave a message when Pole responded, slightly out of breath.

"Nancy… I was not expecting you to call tonight."

"I was not expecting to call either, but my little artist friend has been a no-show."

"The artist's bohemian life… she forgot because she was absorbed in whatever she was doing. I should know, my entire family falls into that category."

"Not her style, I'm afraid." Nancy glanced again over her shoulder. The sense that someone was watching her unsettled her again. "It's a little late but since I haven't had any food, would you care to join me for a late-night takeaway?"

"Takeaway… not a word I've ever heard you utter."

"I know. I'm a little snobbish when it comes to food but the restaurant I am standing in front of is very good. Even I have to admit it, and you know how picky I can be about Chinese food."

"I'm not complaining. I very much enjoy being on the receiving end of your outstanding culinary skills."

"No teasing… *trésor*. Otherwise, I might resort to the said takeaways more often." She heard the catch in his voice and sensed the slight blush of his cheeks in his response. "I'll be with you as soon as I can."

Nancy smiled; nothing was more effective than calling Pole 'sweetheart' in French.

She entered the restaurant still smiling. She placed her order and asked for it to be delivered to her Islington apartment. Out on the pavement again, she stood still for a moment. Despite the brightness of the neon lights, it was difficult to distinguish people's features in the constantly moving crowd. Young girls on their mobiles taking selfies with friends, couples snuggled together to keep themselves warm and men in groups celebrating something or other. Nancy shook off her renewed disquiet and hurried back to the main road to hail a cab. She would try to reach Cora once more on her way home.

* * *

Cora's mobile was ringing again. She bit her lower lip and tried to resist the temptation to move from her hiding place. The men's voices had faded away, and the noise caused by them rummaging around the loft she shared with Ollie had died down too. Nancy was calling her. She was sure of it. The very person she so needed to talk to was only a few yards away, but she couldn't be certain the men had left. Or, perhaps, they were laying a trap, waiting for her to appear in search of her phone. It was almost miraculous they hadn't found her yet. But there she was, hiding amongst the beams that supported the roof of her artist's studio. It would have taken an acrobat as agile as she was to reach her. She was a performance artist and suddenly grateful that her art and skills – of walking across almost any surface and at any height – had saved her life.

She pushed her small frame into the corner formed by the industrial-size beams that would have supported, in the past, heavy industrial machinery. The small factory had been converted into two lofts. The vast open space was ideal to accommodate her studio and house the various props she designed and used in her shows. The large lights she'd had installed, three massive LED theatre spotlights, also shielded her from view.

Her muscles were well trained when it came to holding a difficult position for a long period of time. Emulating Marina Abramovich's capacity for endurance had given her an unexpected advantage, even though choosing to follow in the footsteps of such a controversial artist had raised eyebrows amongst friends and family. Marina had once had a loaded gun pointed at her face by a member of the public…

The ringtone was now telling her that the person who had tried to call her had left a message. Cora had lost sense of time as to when she had taken refuge in the roof space of her apartment. Each second lasted an eternity, as she became certain the men who had invaded her home were going to discover her at any moment… She couldn't escape. But they seemed a lot more interested in Ollie. The expression on his face as he told her to hide had said so. Fear and urgency… He had to save her. From what, she had no idea.

He had grabbed her arm, squeezed it so hard it hurt as the banging on the front door turned into violent kicks. "Hide… don't ask why, please, please… just hide."

How had he known the men were coming for him?

Cora turned her head around carefully to avoid upsetting her precarious balance. She tried to gauge the time. She had been due to meet Nancy at 8.30pm. The men had arrived just as she was about to leave and they had taken their time to search the flat.

It had been violent and methodical.

Ollie had been taken away almost immediately, after refusing to answer their questions.

"Where is your girl?"

"She's gone… She forgot her mobile."

It hadn't convinced them, of course. But they kept searching in vain.

Cora attempted to relax the muscles in her back. Her body had started to complain. She brought her mind into focus and ignored the pain.

The men had taken Ollie away. He had hardly struggled. She wanted to scream, fight, escape… but the crashing of furniture being turned over and bookshelves emptied had created a thunderous, terrifying noise that had kept her hidden. As books fell to the ground and crockery was broken, she remained silent.

The ringtone of her phone was summoning her out of safety once more. Nancy was calling to check what had happened. Or perhaps the thugs who had taken her boyfriend were calling her to ask for what they wanted, to bargain for his release.

The thought punched Cora in the stomach. She shuddered. The urgency to reach her phone sent an electrical current through her stiff limbs. She stood up slowly on the top beam that crossed the entire structure of the roof, a massive steel joist. Her head swam a little. She grabbed the frame of the floodlight close to her. She could not rush her descent from this 20ft height. She sat down again, swung her legs astride the beam and stretched her back. She stood up again and started the perilous journey down. Her bare feet clung to the cold metal surface. Her arms were stretched out on each side of her body for balance. She moved at a measured pace, apprehensive to start with, then confidence returning as her legs responded to her command. She reached the centre of the joist. Climbing down from the central pillar she shinned towards the ground like a monkey.

The loft resembled a warzone. She took a small intake of breath, and steadied herself. She started looking for her phone, hoping the recall ringtone would guide her. The men had not bothered to turn the lights off, but she failed to see the small piece of crockery that suddenly lodged in her foot and almost made her scream in pain.

"Shit," she grimaced between clenched teeth. Sitting down on the floor amongst the debris, she slowly dislodged the shard from the sole of her foot. She hobbled towards the overturned sofa, leaving a trail of blood on the concrete floor.

Her pair of trainers were hardly visible amongst the cushions and randomly opened magazines. She quickly pushed her feet into them, wincing. She stood up in front of the wide lounge floor-to-ceiling windows and looked outside. A large man crossed the road, his silhouette looking familiar.

Cora ducked to the ground. The repeat sound of her phone announcing she had a message had stopped. She crawled towards the coffee table. The only piece of furniture that had not been toppled over. She fumbled around desperately, pushing aside cushions, blankets and broken pottery. Her phone had slid underneath the overturned settee.

She stretched out her arm as far as she could to reach it. She felt the tactile cover of the mobile under the tips of her fingers and clawed it slowly towards her until she could grasp it. As she looked at her phone, the picture of herself with Ollie filled the screen. Two grinning faces returned her gaze, with an unbearable display of happiness. She choked back a sob as she checked who had called her last. She didn't recognise the number and almost pressed the recall button, but a muffled sound stopped her dead. Cora half stood up, creeping as low as she could to avoid being seen from the window. She climbed the open staircase in her flat, ignoring the pain in her foot. Someone was coming down the corridor. Her phone rang again. She killed the call immediately and cursed.

Now, whoever was calling her knew she had the phone and was in the flat.

She dashed across the mezzanine and opened a side window overlooking the backyard. She yanked the window fully open. She was about to step onto the ledge when a male voice called her name.

He was inside the flat already.

Cora's mind focused... she breathed in deeply. She was a Chinese woman from Hong Kong. She was an artist... she knew what a government could do to those who expressed dissent, and she knew the sort of people they used to carry out their orders.

Cora ignored the 30ft drop that plunged below the open window and stepped into darkness.

Perspiration was running down her spine and yet she was shivering. Cora had reached the roof of her building after a perilous ascent, along a ledge that was barely 1ft wide. She continued along the pipes that ran along the building's façade, a remnant of its original industrial purpose.

She almost slipped but her athletic body regained its balance and held her in place. She crouched down as soon as she reached the flat roof, listening for sounds of movement.

Apart from the rumbling noise of London in the distance, she could hear noise at the front of the building. She half-rose, then dashed to the other side of the roof to reach the external fire staircase.

It was an old feature difficult to spot from the front of the building as it led into the backyard.

She risked a peek over the wall before starting her descent. Once she was on her way down there wouldn't be any escape if they spotted her.

What did they want? She pushed away the thought... Not now. There was only one thing she must focus on...

Getting away.

Cora stood on the wall, grabbing the iron bars that framed the stairwell. The icy cold shot through her fingers, reminding her she wasn't dressed for lingering around on this winter evening. She pushed herself onto the structure. It wobbled a little and she wondered whether it was strong enough. It hadn't been tested for years, a feature kept for show rather than function.

Too late to worry now though. She moved slowly, trying not to strain the steps with her weight. She must climb down four flights to reach the ground. The stairs groaned underneath her, but they held. Her mind was already racing ahead.

A thumping noise stopped her. Someone was trying to open the back door. It required a key, and the door was of solid steel. This didn't seem to deter whoever was trying. The kick of a boot against the door frame reverberated around the iron staircase. A gun discharge told her all she needed to know... in a few moments they – whoever they were – would burst into the backyard.

Cora forgot about a cautious descent. She stormed down now descending two steps at a time.

A second gunshot told her the door was about to spring open.

She darted across the yard, to a large stone that had been placed for effect next to the storage shed and used it to jump up towards its roof. She hit the flat surface and rolled over. Something had slipped from her pocket... her phone. The door burst open.

No time to pick it up. Cora rolled again over the boundary wall and jumped into the street. She groaned as a sudden pain shot through her foot. She hobbled along the pavement of the narrow alleyway that smelt of rotting garbage. She must find a cab before they found her.

\* \* \*

The box file still lay open on the coffee table. Nancy stopped in the middle of the lounge. She had not expected to be entertaining Pole that evening. Papers and photographs were arranged in neat piles, covering the glass of the table almost completely. They extended to one armchair and invaded the couch.

She walked over to the organised mess, lifted a few pages and stopped. Pole knew what these documents were. He had even sourced a large number of them for her.

Nancy reorganised the stacks, one on top of the other crosswise, to preserve their categories:

- Time spent with family in China
- Family in Paris
- Father returning to China

Nancy lingered over one picture and smiled. For a very long time, that picture had remained hidden in the small file Nancy kept about her family's history. But the pressing desire to reconnect with the past, to find out what happened in China more than 30 years ago, had forced her to pull it out of its faded envelope.

The black-and-white photo had turned a pale shade of yellow. A young man in his early 30s, sporting an elegant three-piece suit and a mandarin collar shirt. A young woman with long dark hair flowing freely over her shoulders, wearing a short dress with broad stripes of what Nancy recalled were vibrant colours.

*They are smiling, not at the camera but at each other. He has wrapped his arm around his wife's shoulders, and her hands rest in turn on the shoulders of a little girl called Nancy. Unlike her parents, Nancy is looking straight at the camera with a toothy grin. She seems to like the attention, or perhaps the person taking the picture is making her laugh.*

Nancy couldn't recall the moment, although she could remember her mother's dress. By then her parents had already left China as the Cultural Revolution of 1966 was taking hold. They had arrived in Paris after months of travelling through the Chinese countryside, escaping the communist regime, before reaching Hong Kong and finally France.

Nancy sighed heavily, glad that the pain of remembering had become more bearable. Pole was now there to help carry the burden. With care, she replaced the photo on the top of the appropriate pile. She should get it framed. It had been a moment of joy. Why keep pushing it away?

The ring of the doorbell told Nancy the takeaway delivery had arrived. She moved to the intercom, pushed the front door release button. "I'll be down in a moment."

She scooped up her door keys and mobile from the coffee table, and made her way downstairs. The lift door opened. The security guard was reading his paper. As she stepped forward into the spacious hallway, she looked around. There was no one there.

Nancy stopped in the middle of the large lobby. The broad modern table at its centre bore a vase of freshly cut flowers, a winter display of white, red and green.

She stepped towards the main entrance. The large glass doors threw back her reflection as she approached. She pulled her mobile out of her back pocket and dialled the takeaway number.

She came back inside and walked along the side of the building that looked out on to the gardens. She stopped for a moment, waiting for someone to answer. She gasped, stunned by the sight of a body slumped on the side of the building.

\* \* \*

The suit and tie had come off, replaced by a pair of dark winter jeans and the obligatory black rollneck pullover. DCI Jonathan Pole walked out of his office, a light rucksack and leather biker jacket slung over his left shoulder, a crash helmet in his right hand.

"I feel bad leaving you alone, holding the fort." Pole grinned at Andy... "Not."

Andy grinned back at his boss. "How's the new bike... sorry, Ducati Diavel 1260, behaving?"

"Splendid... and before you start making comments about my midlife crisis, I have ridden a bike before..."

Andy gave a sure-you-have nod and waved his boss off. "I'll manage… otherwise… I'll use this." He picked up his mobile and bounced it lightly in his hand.

"Exactly." Pole donned his jacket and slid the rucksack onto his shoulders.

"And if Superintendent Marsh calls…" Andy added as Pole was about to walk off.

"You deal with him like the outstanding DS you are," Pole said over his shoulder. He would not be running back to Scotland Yard for another debrief with The Super.

Pole rode his Ducati into the flow of cars as he arrived at the top of Northumberland Avenue. Victoria Embankment was almost deserted, the weather having turned much colder. Pole sat back, one foot on the ground, the other on the footrest, balancing the bike, as he waited for the set of traffic lights to turn green.

The Thames' waters were an inky black colour that reflected the lights of the buildings lining its banks. A few lights were still shining at the Royal Festival Hall… no doubt a crew of cleaners were making the concert venue ready for the next day's show.

He and Nancy would soon be taking their seats in one of its concert halls for a performance of music by one of her favourite Russian composers, Stravinsky. Classical music was not Pole's cup of tea, but he was making progress, appreciating more complex pieces in the same way that Nancy was slowly warming up to jazz.

The lights changed. Pole accelerated, giving the Ducati a gentle push. The road curved softly and he leaned the bike into the bend. The lights remained green for him almost all the way to Islington.

He parked his bike in a parking bay outside Nancy's building. Nancy's apartment was part of a restoration project that had transformed a grand old office building, once occupied by Metropolitan Water, into a luxurious accommodation complex. Pole jogged towards the side entrance.

He used his own key to enter the building and took a few seconds to take in the unexpected scene. Pole quickened his pace to a run… Nancy was crouching on the ground holding someone in her arms.

# Chapter Two

Logistics had called Jack Shield as soon as the cell trace had disappeared. One minute it was sending signals as expected from London. The next it had vanished, including the backup transmitter that was set up to operate even when the battery had been disabled.

"When did Wilson's mobile vanish?"

"At 7.46pm local time." Beverly had moved aside to let Jack take a look at the activity log. The route traced by the mobile had not shown any suspicious activity. From home to work, a quick break at lunchtime, from work back home to North London.

Jack grabbed the backrest of the seat next to Beverly's with both hands. His head slumped. No one, including Jack, had seen it coming. There were only two reasons why the mobile was no longer giving signs of life. It had either been completely destroyed or it had been placed in a special isolation tank that would not let radio waves penetrate its walls. Either way, this was a worrying development.

"Thanks Bev... let me know if the mobile comes online again."

Jack stepped out of the maze of offices on the fourth floor, where the logistics and surveillance teams operated. The elevator took him to the second floor. People got in and out, as it stopped twice before reaching its destination. Jack barely noticed them.

Had it been a mistake to throw Wilson so quickly into the deep end? He was not a trained agent, not the way Langley people were trained before becoming field operatives. He was just a smart kid who had noticed perhaps a little too much for his own good.

Jack arrived in his office. It was only 4pm in Virginia but already 9pm in London. However, Jack was certain that the CIA Station Chief would still be at his desk in the London office. He picked up his headset and dialled the London Embassy's secure line.

"Jethro… still around?"

"Just about to call it a day… what can I do for you Jack?"

Station Chief Jethro Greeney sounded suitably harassed when he picked up the call.

"A person of interest to us has, for want of a better word, vanished very suddenly, or at least his mobile phone has. It is a matter of concern."

"He's not an operative I take it?" Jethro's voice tightened a little… he didn't seem to appreciate having been left out of the picture, if there was indeed a new recruit in London. Jack also knew Jethro would rather avoid having to have a difficult conversation with his counterpart at MI6 about an operation he was not aware of, which was about to turn bad.

"Nope… nothing like that. He is a potential recruit, but for the time being he is providing information. It's speculative, connected to the US biotech industry but I believe there is something in it."

"But you're not certain yet… I get it. And you'd like me to send a team to check his whereabouts." Jethro was fumbling with something at his end. Jack could only imagine it was his other mobile on which he had stored a list of available agents and intervention operatives.

"Is this guy a Yank by the way?"

"Yes, he is."

"Good, that makes my life a damn sight easier in case this goes belly up."

There was a short silence. Chief Greeney seemed to have found what or whom it was he wanted. "I'll call you back when I have some news."

Jack thanked him and sat back in his chair. His eyes refocused on the file he had dragged from the depths of his filing cabinet. Its colour was a faded pink. It had a stain marking the top left corner, the leak of a coffee cup.

The topic covered by the file had been of concern to Jack in the wake of 9/11. The weaponisation of pathogens was always going to be a temptation for smaller malign organisations and terrorist groups. Yet what Wilson had stumbled upon did not quite fit the bill.

In Jack's experience, countries secure in their armament capabilities, showed interest in bioweapons of a more academic nature. They carried out extensive research to discover what chemicals or viruses were capable of… including how these could affect a population.

They sometimes also sought to enhance their preparedness at combating a rogue event with countermeasures, in the guise of specialist teams or anti-viral medication.

Wilson had computing skills in the biotech sphere that were of interest to the agency. The job he had recently landed at a new biotech company in London, with links to Asia, was an unexpected bonus.

Jack leaned forward and opened the bulging file with caution. He knew the contents almost by heart. Wilson had mentioned regular yet concealed contacts between his company and China. The details Jack needed, to assess whether Wilson's disappearance was linked to these secret contacts were lying somewhere in the slew of papers that had spilled out in front of him.

\* \* \*

"Help me…" Nancy cried as she noticed Pole running towards her.

She was holding Cora's head in her shaking hands. Pole dropped his biking gear, knelt and gathered the limp body of the young woman into his arms. Her face was a ghostly white and her breathing shallow. She was wearing only a light T-shirt over faded blue jeans. Oddly, she had no bag with her.

Nancy ran inside to the lift and pressed the call button. She signalled to the security guard not to be concerned as she returned to gather Pole's rucksack and helmet.

"Who is she?" Pole asked, looking at the young woman he was holding in his arms, once they were in the lift.

"The friend I was supposed to meet this evening." Nancy pressed the top floor button. "I tried to call quite a few times but there was no reply, and now here she is."

The lift doors opened. Nancy hurried to unlock her apartment door. Pole followed, carefully moving sideways to avoid the walls of the entrance corridor. He laid Cora on one of Nancy's sofas. She covered her friend with a blanket she kept in the lounge and started to rub her hands and feet to restore their circulation.

"She's been hurt." Pole pointed to the gash in her foot as Nancy took off her trainers. He disappeared into the bathroom to find the first-aid kit.

Nancy nodded without looking at him. Her attention was solely focused on her friend's face. "I found her like that, slumped outside... According to the security guard she didn't ring the main entrance bell, so she must have walked in when a car entered the car park."

Pole moistened a piece of cotton wool with surgical spirit and applied it to Cora's wounds. She moaned a little – an encouraging sign.

"Cora..." Nancy called softly. "It's Nancy... you're in my flat... you're safe."

Nancy pushed aside a strand of hair that had stuck to her friend's forehead. She returned to Cora's freezing hands and massaged them gently again until she felt Cora's left hand grabbing hers fiercely. The crush was almost unbearable. Nancy winced. Cora's eyes shot open, unseeing. Her mouth gaped open, and she gasped for air. Nancy squeezed back hard.

"I'm here... you're safe."

Cora half sat up. "Ollie..." She looked at Nancy and memories seemed to be coming flooding back. She brought her fist to her mouth, her eyes glittered with tears. Cora wrapped her free arm around Nancy's shoulders, fighting back a sob.

"They took him away..."

"Slow down... who took him away?" Pole had stopped tending Cora's wound.

"We haven't got time." Cora moved to untangle herself from the blanket that Nancy had wrapped around her. She tried to place one foot on the ground, almost kicking Pole in the process, and yelped.

"I know it's difficult and you want to rush to help him." Pole placed a hand on her other leg to stop her from moving. "But you need to focus on telling us the story so we can help you."

14

Cora noticed the man at the end of the sofa for the first time. She turned towards Nancy for reassurance.

"Inspector Pole, he's a friend… he will help you," Nancy said.

Cora nodded but remained silent for a short moment.

"Shall I make a cup of tea or bring you some water?" Nancy tried a reassuring smile.

"No, Nancy please stay." Cora reached out for her friend's hand. "Ollie knew they were coming, and I don't know why."

\* \* \*

"They were looking for something specific," Jethro said. "It was a professional job made to look like a possible burglary or debt collection of some sort."

"Why do you say that?" Jack asked.

"The jewellery box has been thoroughly and obviously ransacked, there is no jewellery left and the high-tech equipment has been taken… including of course any PC, laptop or even iPad, if they had them."

"But the search was processed methodically?" Jack ran his hand over his face.

"Exactly, no stone unturned."

"Shit. That is not what I was expecting."

"And what were you expecting, if I may ask?" Jethro fought a yawn down the line. It was almost 11.30pm in London.

"Biochemical warfare allegations are always a bit problematic when it comes to credibility. Since the debacle with Weapons of Mass Destruction in Iraq, management wants hard evidence not only suspicions… Especially when the person making the allegation is a young guy who has barely started in his first job in a new tech company."

Jethro took a moment to reply. Jack could hear him eating. "Sorry, I haven't had much food today."

"No worries." Jack carried on. "The problem for me is that Wilson was a little vague."

"So why did you persist?" The Station Chief had taken a bite of something crunchy.

"Because when China is mentioned, I pay attention."

"Now you have my attention too." The munching had stopped.

"This doesn't mean I believe what I have been told… but Wilson thought he had stumbled upon some illegal transfer of technology, including the development of bio-agents."

"You mean somebody's developing a controversial bio-agent on the sly, without the executive of the firm knowing? How big is the company?"

"That's the other point… not that big, 30-odd people."

"Then with a company that size, its executives are in the know…"
Both men fell silent. The munching resumed in London.

Jack in Virginia decided on his next step. "Keep me posted… Let's hope your people find him before something nasty happens."

"I have put a good team on the case. If he is still in the UK, they will find him."

Jack raised an eyebrow, but Jethro was right. Wilson might have been smuggled out of the country already and was now being taken to a dark site for interrogation.

* * *

Cora was still shivering. After a moment's hesitation, she finally accepted the tea Pole had prepared.

"Why do you think Ollie knew they were coming?" Nancy asked, still holding Cora's hand.

"He came into the bedroom as I was changing and asked me to hide." Cora sipped at her tea. "He looked so… scared."

Pole listened to the young woman's story without interrupting. Nancy had been her usual excellent self, warm and yet able to direct her questioning effectively… once a Queen's Counsel always a Queen's Counsel. She had stirred Cora gently, subtly probing her friend's account, making it coherent.

Pole was now certain it was time to call the Missing Persons Bureau at SOCA, to report Ollie missing and a possible kidnapping. The next 24 hours would be crucial if they were to find him alive.

As soon as she finished her tale, Cora slumped back on the sofa. She looked exhausted. Her attractive almond-shaped eyes had lost some of their sparkle. Dark rings had suddenly appeared under them.

Pole took his mobile out of his back pocket. "I'm going to call a contact of mine at the NCA. We need to issue a Yellow Notice for a missing person without delay." Pole scrolled down his contact list. "Do you have a recent photo?"

"I lost it when I ran." Cora looked even more upset. "It's in the backyard... I mean my mobile. Perhaps I could..."

"You won't be going back there tonight." Nancy shook her head. "I'll make sure the spare room is ready."

Pole was already in conversation with his National Crime Agency contact. He had walked away from the lounge and stood in the kitchen entrance. He ended the call and turned back to the two women.

"Rob is on his way. He'll contact someone at the Met." Nancy frowned; she seemed not to understand the links.

"The National Crime Agency is in charge of kidnapping these days. They'll establish contact with the Met for logistical support," Pole explained.

Pole took a few steps towards the sofa. His mobile rang again. He frowned, not expecting such a rapid call back. He moved out of earshot again and he turned away to answer. Pole listened to the information that was being relayed to him and hung up. He shook his head and took a short moment to face the two friends again.

"There is no easy way of telling you this, Cora. Your loft... in fact your entire building is on fire."

Pole stood at a distance from the burning building. He was glad he had convinced Cora and Nancy to stay behind.

"When did it start?" DCI Pole had found the fire brigade's senior officer in charge of the incident.

"An hour ago, maybe less. We were called immediately by the other occupants of the building. I have the call log if you give me a moment." Senior Officer Lord consulted her laptop. "At 10:42pm to be precise."

"I presume it's too early to tell what caused it?"

"Arson... plainly. Probably triggered by something as crude as pouring a flammable substance all over the floor of the flat. The only saving grace is that the walls of this former factory have been treated

17

with fire retardant paint. Otherwise, the other occupants might have had a tough time escaping."

"A professional job?" Pole zipped up his biker jacket. The wind had picked up and the charred building still showed a few incandescent spots that the firefighters were tackling.

"Too early to tell, Inspector… It does not take a pro to spill petrol over a surface and strike a match. But we'll know more once we have analysed the pattern of the fire."

"You mean, whatever substance was used it might have been poured precisely for maximum impact?"

"That's right."

A firefighter approached Senior Officer Lord. She nodded towards the smouldering structure.

"How many sources of fire left?" she asked.

"Only two small residual spots…" The young man's face was well shielded by his protective helmet, perspiration pearled on his forehead.

"Great job." Senior Officer Lord smiled.

"Thanks, Cap… glad the wind only picked up now."

"Always grateful for small mercies." The young man headed back towards the blackened structure.

"Is it possible to take a look inside?" Pole ventured. "Following one of your firefighters."

"Unless you are a fire expert, you won't gather very much from what you see."

"I just want to get a feel. But I wouldn't want to put anyone at risk."

Senior Officer Lord sized up Pole for a moment and called one of her men.

"Is it safe enough for DCI Pole to enter?"

The young man eyed Pole for a short moment.

"With breathing apparatus, that could work. But we turn back if I spot anything I don't like."

Pole nodded.

"Alright DCI Pole… but no heroics." She grinned. Officer Lord seemed to like a daring man.

"I have seen *The Towering Inferno*… I'll be as good as gold."

Lord squinted for a moment and burst into laughter. The film dated back to the mid-70s. Pole grinned in turn. She would have been born around the time it came out.

"The only reason I know that film is because I started an impressive collection of disaster movies when I was a teenager."

The young firefighter came back with a breathing mask, helmet and fireproof jacket and trousers. Pole dropped his helmet near his bike… "Now I feel like Steve McQueen."

"With this bike of yours, you're convincing… remember though, no heroics."

Pole gave the thumbs-up and followed his guide into the building.

The acrid smell of melted plastic and burnt paint seeped through the filters of his helmet. The stairwell was covered with a thick layer of soot that felt sticky to the touch. The old factory had been split into four lofts, only three of which were occupied.

Pole soon arrived at Cora's door. It was wide open, and he noticed that it had not been forced open. Whoever had set the place alight had entered the property after opening the door with a key.

Inside the loft the fire had ravaged anything that was combustible. Before that, however, the place had been gone through. The debris of broken pottery had not been caused by collapsing shelves. The bookcase had been thrown down, its contents spilling over the floor. Cushions had been scattered around, now blackened and half burnt. The coffee table stood on its side. Glass was shattered everywhere.

Pole's guide indicated he should be careful. The fire had started to eat through the structure of the building and a hole had appeared in the middle of the room. Pole suspected it must have been one of the combustion spots where flammable liquid had been poured. Looking at the room, Pole recognised the same combustion spot on the east side of the large lounge. Something to remember. The liquid had not been poured randomly but placed methodically at the chosen points. Not a random act of arson or a burglar gone mad. Someone had been seeking to cover their tracks.

Pole's companion nudged him suddenly. A faint glow had appeared near a spot in the floor that threatened to collapse.

"We need to go," Pole's guide said. He called the team and a couple of firefighters rushed through the main door as they were leaving the flat.

"The wind is not helping," he said, as they descended the stairwell in haste. Pole thanked him and let him return to his task of securing the building.

Senior Officer Lord had moved to the east side of the property.

Pole handed back his equipment and changed back into his biker jacket. He hesitated for a moment, looking in Lord's direction. She must have sensed him looking her way. She waved a hand and called him over.

"What do you make of it... if anything?"

"I'll answer your question if you answer mine first."

"Go on."

"Would a well-positioned number of fires around a room cause the floor to collapse rapidly?"

Senior Officer Lord looked surprised. This was an astute technical question.

"If you know what you are doing and you know the structure of the building... yes, that would be possible."

Pole nodded and ran his hand through his hair. "Then I know what I'm looking at."

# Chapter Three

Cora was still wrapped up in the blanket Nancy had thrown around her shoulders. She was hugging a large mug, the contents of which smelt delicious. Pole had announced himself with a short ring, then using his set of keys let himself in.

"NCA has been and gone." Nancy stood up and moved to the hallway to greet him. She managed a smile. It was good to have his reliable presence to share the load of a case. A few years ago, she would have been proud to carry the weight on her own. But she had learned to involve him and felt fresh joy in doing so.

"Good, Rob has a lot of experience," Pole said.

Cora laid the mug on the low table without having drunk any of its contents. Her eyes anxiously asked the question she could not bring herself to utter. Would she be returning to her home tonight?

Pole turned to Cora and added, "I'm sorry... The fire brigade caught the fire early though."

Cora brought her knees to her chest and let her forehead drop onto them.

"Those bastards managed what the Chinese authorities could not succeed in doing... destroying much of my work."

Nancy closed her eyes briefly, feeling the pain of her friend. She moved back to the settee and sat next to her. There was little she could say. She cast an eye at the box and files she had precipitously moved to another part of the room to make space for Cora.

"I want to know what you saw… please." Her face hardened as she lifted it towards Pole. She would not shy away from the reality of the assault on Ollie and their flat.

Pole sat down on the edge of the armchair that faced the sofa. He gave a detailed description of what he had seen to the two women.

"There is one thing I don't quite understand." Nancy took out a yellow legal pad she always kept at the bottom of the coffee table. "You said the room, or what remains of it, confirms what Cora said to us… the people who went through it were searching for something."

"Could be money, could be something else," Pole added.

Cora shook her head. "Bits of jewellery but nothing much, and nothing very expensive. And why would they have pursued me?"

"Because they needed to ask you the location of what they were looking for… It could still be cash or valuables." Pole hesitated for a moment. "Are Ollie's parents wealthy?"

Cora looked intrigued by the question and its implications. "They are well-off, but they hardly ever speak…" Cora pulled the blanket tighter around her. "I have only met them once in the past three years. Why?"

"Kidnapping for ransom is always a possibility."

"If that's what it's about… they won't pay." Cora stopped.

"We have to consider all possibilities." Nancy squeezed Cora's shoulder.

"I understand Nancy." Cora's voice was muffled and barely audible. "But whatever the reason, he certainly did not tell me he felt in danger."

Nancy turned to Pole. "Why the methodical torching of the place?"

"Either they wanted to destroy whatever they failed to find, and thought was still there, or else they found it and decided to destroy it on the spot."

"That is incredibly well organised… You need proper combustible liquid to burn down a place like the factory."

"That is why I think they are professional. They were organised enough to bring what they needed."

22

"Or rather something convinced them they needed to act quicker than they had anticipated. I'm not sure they had decided to torch the place initially, but something made them change their minds."

"That's a very good point." Pole frowned briefly and Nancy picked up on it. Ollie might have given them what they wanted or told them what they needed to know.

So why keep him alive?

* * *

It was still early but Nancy woke up just as Pole was preparing to leave. He had tiptoed around the bedroom at first and then sat on her side of the bed to wake her up with a slow kiss. "Got to go *mon coeur*... I'll call Rob as soon as I am in." Pole didn't move.

Nancy opened an eye and smiled. "I thought you were going." She wrapped her arms around his neck and pulled herself towards him, planting a quick kiss on his lips. "I'm sorry you had so little sleep."

Pole gave her a naughty smile. "And not for the hoped reasons."

Nancy sighed. "And to my own disappointment." Sleep had vanished from her face and she turned serious. "I'm concerned this story is not going to end well."

"I won't lie to you. After what I saw last night, try to keep Cora from returning home, until I know what we are looking at." Pole wrapped his arms around her slender body.

She gave him another quick kiss then pushed him away. "Come on Inspector Pole, the villains of London need to be brought to justice, and I need to check on Cora."

Pole stood up slowly, shrugged on his biker jacket and disappeared. Nancy let her eyes linger on the door Pole had just closed. His outfit not only made him look sexy but also adventurous and free.

Nancy slipped on a heavy silk dressing gown and tiptoed around the lounge. Cora had insisted she sleep on the sofa. Pole had succeeded in leaving without waking her up.

Nancy leaned over her young friend for a while, hoping she may notice her presence. Cora's face had disappeared into the soft blanket she had wrapped around her. Her spiky hair, part of which had been dyed purple, had flattened against the pillow. Nancy could just make out her balled fists against her chest.

The kitchen was still in darkness and dawn still a short while away.

Nancy moved slowly around the furniture. She opened a cupboard without a sound, took out her teapot, found the tea caddy in which she kept her favourite Sichuan tea, and started to prepare a fresh brew. The gurgling of the kettle almost sounded too loud.

When the tea was ready, she pulled out a couple of mugs and moved back into the lounge.

Cora was up. She had dragged the blanket all the way to the large window overlooking the gardens. The sky was becoming lighter, purple turning into a haze of blues and light pinks.

Nancy handed her a mug. There was no need to speak. It was still too early, and the quietness of dawn felt welcome.

Cora sipped the warm liquid. She nodded… a good Chinese tea… heart-warming.

She finally broke the silence. "I guess Jonathan will call if he has news."

Nancy smiled. "He will, and he will follow up with Rob as well."

She liked how her artist friends had warmed to DCI Pole and almost immediately felt they could call him Jonathan.

Cora continued sipping her tea. Nancy left her to her thoughts and returned a few moments later with toast and homemade jam.

"I'm not hungry, but you are going to tell me that starving myself is not going to help." Cora returned to her place on the sofa.

"And that would be correct…" Nancy pushed the plate of toast towards her friend.

"I need to replace my lost phone… and…" Cora picked up a piece of bread and nibbled at it. "…I need to go back to the flat… I know it will be bad." She added quickly. "But I need to see it for myself… please."

"I understand… it's better to see it as it actually is than to imagine a total disaster." Nancy ate a piece of toast.

"I'd like to do that alone." Cora swallowed the small piece she had been chewing. "I don't want to be scared. I don't want people to dictate to me what I should feel."

"Cora… please. As much as I understand why you may want to go alone… reconsider." Nancy dropped her breakfast back onto the plate. "The people who chased you, who set fire to your flat and who are holding Ollie, are still out there. They will follow you and they will get to you. They are dangerous."

"What are you suggesting then? Even if you are with me, what are we supposed to do against the bastards?"

"I'm not contemplating going on my own with you, but Jonathan will make someone available for protection, if we go."

Cora exhaled a short breath. She did not want to wait for security cover to arrive.

"And what are you going to do if you need to run away?" Nancy gave a quick nod towards Cora's foot, still covered in bandages.

"I have suffered worse injuries." Cora wiggled her toes and winced a little. "I have performed in shows that have brought me to the edge of comfort and safety… I understand physical pain."

"This is not a performance… You're not in control of your surroundings the way you are when you are putting on a show. I know you often push yourself to the limits, but trust me, the world of criminality is a very different kettle of fish."

"I need to check what the damage is to my artwork."

Nancy gave her a kind smile. "I know you do, and I also understand you are anxious, but it still doesn't mean you have to compromise your own safety."

"Please… the wait is unbearable." Cora stood up abruptly.

Nancy extended an appeasing hand. "I'll speak to Jonathan to organise protection for us."

* * *

Pole sat in his office, his tie hanging around his neck, undone. Rob Clark, his NCA contact had called back already.

"We've picked up a large SUV leaving the area next to Ollie Wilson's flat on CCTV. Its registration plate has no match on ANPR."

"Stolen vehicle… with fake number plates… that sounds like a good start. How far have you tracked the car?" Pole squeezed his mobile between his shoulder and ear, absentmindedly tying the knot of his tie.

"Not as far as we had hoped… we lost them in De Beauvoir Estate."

"I thought the cameras worked there; well, at least according to the latest internal report on policing in North and East London."

"They do usually, but either the route they took was the only one not covered or the cameras were not working."

"Or… they had been disabled." Pole sat at his desk and logged on.

"That crossed my mind. One of my guys is checking that out but it wouldn't surprise me. This is a professional job, not a simple kidnapping for ransom."

Rob kept quiet for a moment.

"I know what that means." Pole's lips thinned "If they get the information from him, he is dead."

"You mean when they get the information from him. These people will know how to make him talk."

"Unless he has been trained not to talk."

"So far nothing indicates this young chap is involved in anything bad… there's no police record connected with his name."

"But he's not British, OK… digging into his past is not going to be that easy or quick."

"INTERPOL has zero data on him. I used Veritone Identity – quite a good AI enabled software, nothing there either."

"Still… whoever wanted to speak to Ollie Wilson got some bad boys involved. That costs money and that means knowledge and access to the right network."

"I'm not disagreeing with you, Jon, but so far we have drawn a blank."

Pole obtained a few more details from Rob Clark, thanked him for his call and hung up.

Pole took a moment to consider his next move. He had spoken to Steve Harris only recently. Pole's involvement with the MI6 officer had borne fruit in the past, but it had also caused complications Pole could have done without.

Pole had come to an arrangement with him a couple of years ago. Pole had been leading the investigation of a high-profile case that involved the disgraced financier, Henry Crowne. MI6 had their eyes on the man as did Scotland Yard, but co-operating under the radar with the agency had pushed Pole to the limits of what he was prepared to do for justice. Pole had also learned during that time that Harris was not the sort of man who would do Pole a favour and ask for nothing in return. Then again, if young Wilson was involved in some undercover activities, perhaps Harris would know about them or know whom to ask.

Pole picked up his burner phone, his thumb hovering over the speed dial number. He inhaled deeply and pressed the key.

"Inspector Pole… that's a bloody good surprise." Harris's faint East End accent plunged Pole back into a recent past he'd rather not remember.

"Harris… I've got some information that may be of interest."

"So not about China and Miss Wu then?"

Did Harris really have to always be such a prick? "More about America… interested?"

"Fire away, mate… I'm all ears."

* * *

Nancy's jeans were a little too baggy on her, but she liked the jumper she had lent her. It was a sweater knitted in soft purple angora which matched the colour of her highlights. Cora brushed her hair vigorously to give it the spiky look she liked. She slammed the brush down onto the stone top that surrounded the wash basin.

Why had Ollie not confided in her?

She moved to the spare room that was adjacent to the bathroom and walked over to the window. A feeble sun now shone in the sky, clouds obstructing its glow intermittently. The few people who were leaving the building looked well wrapped up. Snow was coming… she could feel it in her bones. The sole of her foot still hurt, and she walked back gingerly to the bed.

A memory of Hong Kong compelled Cora to stop in the middle of the room. She was barely 16 years of age. It was her first march with the people of Hong Kong to demand democracy. She loved being part of such a massive movement. The organisers themselves had not anticipated the size of the turnout. Her parents were marching too, although Cora was sticking with her college friends. She was not staying with Mum and Dad. She disappeared into the mass of protesters and lost sight of them. She was a grown-up who could chart her own path.

Cora sighed.

She reached the bed and slumped onto it. She needed a new phone. She needed to get back to Hoxton. She needed to find Ollie.

She rolled onto her side, grabbed the pair of socks Nancy had lent her. The old trainers were a little tight, but they would do.

She walked out of the bedroom and called Nancy's name. Her friend was on the phone, talking to Jonathan no doubt. Nancy finished her conversation.

"We'll have someone with us in the next couple of hours. We can then go back to the flat and have a proper look at it." Nancy said.

Cora nodded... but two hours sounded like an eternity. "How about we go to buy a phone in the meantime?"

Nancy hesitated at first but after a short moment relented. "We buy the phone and then come back straight away."

Cora gave a big smile... butter would have melted. She had another plan.

The young man in the shop was all smiles. He expressed a suitable amount of concern when Cora explained she had lost her phone in a fire.

"Really tragic... but as long as no one was hurt." The shop assistant said.

Cora's face remained impassive. She just wanted the phone not some fake sympathy.

He downloaded the data saved under her mobile number and made sure it had all transferred smoothly. Texts would, unfortunately, be lost. She wouldn't be able to tell whether Ollie had tried to contact her that way.

Nancy presented her credit card. Cora thanked her and headed outside to find a secluded corner to place her phone call.

Ollie's phone rang and went to voicemail. Hearing his soft American accent as she listened to his greeting unexpectedly hit her. She pressed the phone against her lips to muffle a small cry.

She turned around. Nancy was still in the shop waiting for her receipt. Cora hesitated.

The pedestrian crossing light was green, it disappeared.

Cora ran across the road and vanished into the backstreets of Islington.

She ran all the way down to the canal that led from Islington to the River Thames. Her foot hurt but she ignored the pain. She found the stairs to the canal footpath, climbing down two at a time and almost slipped halfway. She stopped for a short moment. This was stupid, she knew, but she was not going back to Nancy's flat.

Cora started her journey again. She was alone. The bank of the Regent's Canal was deserted. With no money in her pocket, she could not hope to catch a cab or a bus if she left the canal further along.

The buildings along the towpath had been renovated and cleaned of graffiti. She recalled taking a similar walk with her parents. She was perhaps 10. Most buildings had been derelict, and she had squeezed her mother's hand hard. Her father had not been impressed with his wife's choice of setting for a family stroll, but she had convinced him that the artist they were going to visit was worth the extra effort.

"And anyway, it is broad daylight... It is unlikely we are going to be mugged," her mother had said.

"Unlikely" had not somehow satisfied her husband but it had all changed when they arrived in the studio of Yinka Shonibare.

The explosion of colours, the richness of the African fabrics he used for his sculptures stunned them. The young man in his wheel-chair had welcomed them with warmth and courtesy. He had showed them around the latest creations arranged on three mannequins... period costumes in batik fabrics.

Cora had wanted to touch the material, for it looked so beautiful. The artist had given her a couple of samples, leftovers from cutting out the garments. She had folded them neatly and kept them in her tiny rucksack for the rest of the trip.

The samples must still be in Hong Kong she thought, pressed into her first diary.

Inspired by the visit, she had immediately started to record the art she found so fascinating.

The towpath narrowed as she arrived at a bridge junction. Something distracted her from the memories of her parents. She felt a light pounding vibrate through her feet. The sound was muffled and yet distinct.

Its rhythm became more certain and the noise louder. Someone was running along the canal bank in her direction. She looked around for a way out... there was no escape. She couldn't go back and the next set of steps ahead of her was at least half a mile away.

She started running. Her injured foot pleaded for her to stop but she pushed against the pain. The cold air started to burn her lungs as she accelerated the pace.

One of the small boats near Wharf Road had left its mooring, entered one of the locks and was about to be on its way.

"Hey... hang on..." she shouted at the top of her voice. Her eyes were watering as the icy wind slapped her face. "Wait... please..."

She waved her arms, and the narrow-boat handler raised his head. The man turned around to check who was calling. He was wearing a thick anorak, a woolly hat that had seen better days and his dark stubble gave his face a rough unfriendly look.

But he smiled and shouted back. "Need a ride?"

Cora reached the lock gate and stepped onto it. The man moved to the front of the boat, offered a hand and she jumped onto the wooden deck.

"Welcome to the *Perfect Dreamer...*"

"That's very kind." Cora managed to smile.

"There's coffee downstairs... bring a couple of cups to the deck, will you?... It'll be two sugars and lots of milk for me."

She nodded, unfazed by the familiarity of the boat owner. The community of people who lived on narrow boats was carefree and welcoming. She had enjoyed taking pictures of buildings, waterways and structures she had encountered from their decks many times and enjoyed their travellers' stories.

Cora moved towards the rear of the boat. The jogger she had heard had almost reached the lock too. If he accelerated the pace, he might be able to board the small boat whether its owner obliged or not... and what if he had a gun?

She looked back. The woman at the helm had not moved from her position. She nodded to Cora. "Go on... don't be shy... get yourself and His Lordship a coffee." She eased the boat into the next leg of the Regent's Canal as the pursuer reached the back gates.

He had slowed down, the grey hoodie covering his face revealing nothing of his features, but Cora was certain he was looking at her. He slowed down further to a trot, digging his hands into his sport jacket's pockets.

Panic seized Cora. He was about to shoot her and the two people who had kindly offered her a lift. One hand retrieved an object from his pocket. A large mobile phone appeared, and he started taking pictures.

The lock… the boat… Cora… this was intimidation.

Cora's mouth ran dry, and the tightening in her chest was no longer caused by the running.

"Happens all the time." The woman at the helm of the narrow boat nodded. "People can't believe we can live a good life on such a small boat."

Cora ignored the woman for a moment. She was not going to be intimidated if this was the game these people were playing.

"I have got a mobile too," she muttered.

She took her newly acquired phone out of the pocket of the bomber jacket Nancy had lent her and aimed at the man. He had not expected this. Cora kept pressing the button. The jogger hesitated, turning back would give him away, walking further along the canal would give Cora plenty of time to take more photos. He stepped towards one of the small cafés alongside the towpath and disappeared into it without looking back.

Cora took a few pictures of the boat and its owners. She too did not want to give herself away. She disappeared below deck and returned with three mugs. The pursuer had not reappeared. She settled in the bow of the barge and pulled her mobile out again. It was time to make a much-needed phone call to apologise.

# Chapter Four

"I'm in a cab... On my way to her loft." Nancy said on her call to Pole, cursing herself for not having seen this coming. Cora wouldn't rest until she knew how bad the damage was to her flat and more importantly to her art.

She frowned. "Don't worry Jonathan... I'm not going to barge into a half-burnt building. I'll wait for the officer you've assigned for her protection to arrive."

Pole had been fast at rerouting the officer he had requested, from Nancy's flat to his new destination. Still, it would take a good 20 minutes before he reached Cora's building.

"Hang on... I have an incoming call..." The number did not correspond to a name, but she hoped she knew who the caller was. "I'll call you back shortly."

Cora's voice sounded contrite but also scared.

"I'm so sorry Nancy. I shouldn't have run away as I did but I had to know and now... I don't know, anymore."

"I am so goddam annoyed." Nancy sounded more severe than she'd intended. Had she been in Cora's place she might have done just the same. Not a fact to be disclosed to her young friend though. "Where are you?"

"On a narrow boat."

"On Regent's Canal? But why?"

"I think..." Cora breathed in and then released her breath. "...no, I'm sure someone was following me."

Nancy had created a map of the area she knew so well in her mind. The Regent's Canal was a good alternative for Cora to reach her flat without being detected.

How cunning and yet it could have cost her dear.

"Can you describe the man? I assume it's a man." Nancy's anger subsided at the thought of what could have happened to her friend.

"I took a couple of pictures of him."

"I'll be at Hoxton Docks before you are. Call me when you arrive. We'll drive to your flat and wait in the cab until the protection officer arrives," Nancy insisted.

"If you think it's best," Cora agreed without resistance.

"And please send me the pictures you took of the man who followed you."

As Nancy received it, she opened the attachment. She flipped through the photos... A tall man in a black-and-grey tracksuit, grey hoodie and gloves. With a sharp inhale, Nancy selected all of them, and forwarded them to Pole. There was only one word for it.

Menace.

The people behind all this must have found Cora after all and knew she had stayed at Nancy's. They did not seem to be put off by the police being involved either.

Nancy bent a little forward to check progress on the road. The cabbie had taken the backstreets, zigzagging through small lanes and a couple of nondescript estates. For a moment she had almost lost track of where she was, and doubt crept in... Was he going the right way?

They emerged near Haggerston Station, and Nancy relaxed. Only a few more minutes and she would reach her destination.

She sat back in the seat of the cab, watching the people of East London going about their morning business. The cultural and racial mix made her pay more attention. Without doubt it was the reason she had chosen to live in North London, dismissing the more select areas of South Kensington and Chelsea.

She had been a well-respected, perhaps even brilliant Queen's Counsel. Her legal career had been filled with high-profile cases – many controversial and often ground-breaking. She had represented war criminals. She had represented fraudulent bankers and CEOs.

She had done so because of the idea, or perhaps even ideal she had of justice and how it should be served. Yet ambition had taken over and she had almost lost sight of what mattered... almost.

The cabbie used his horn to warn a pedestrian on a mobile that crossing in front of his car might not be such a bright idea.

"We're almost there, luv… Do you want me to wait then?"

"Please, and could you stop as close as possible to the stairs that come up from the Regent's Canal?"

"Righto…" the burly chap nodded. His broad shoulders hunched over the wheel of his vehicle, almost dwarfing the front cabin. He indicated and parked his cab where he had been asked.

It took only a few minutes for Cora to ring back. A few more for her to emerge from the canal's towpath and come to sit beside Nancy.

"Sorry." She attempted her best smile and Nancy raised a don't-do-it-again eyebrow.

"I'll be very careful."

"Mmm… I hope so."

The cabbie swung his cab around in a perfect U-turn. A few minutes later, he deposited them in the small courtyard that stretched in front of Cora's building.

The charred windows and blackened walls needed no explanation.

The fire had ravaged the inside of the flat, and Cora let out a sob.

\* \* \*

Jack rose on his elbow and picked up his mobile. He slumped back into bed and brought the other elbow underneath his head. He listened to the long message the London Station Chief had left for him.

They had found the girl – Cora – and were watching her. MI6 had received a call from someone at Scotland Yard. "Shit. This is turning into a real cock-up."

Jack checked the bedside clock: 5.37am.

The alarm would ring in less than half an hour. It was hardly worth going back to sleep. He replayed the message he had received from London and gave a short, dejected groan. Not the start of the day he had been hoping for.

Jack grabbed an old fleece and put it on. He moved to the kitchen and started to brew fresh coffee. The laptop had been left open on the kitchen bar top the evening before. He sat on one of the bar stools and logged on. Ollie Wilson had stumbled onto something important. The question still remained, what?

Jack spent the next 10 minutes yo-yoing between the complex security vetting protocols on the laptop and his coffee machine that was not quite playing ball.

He sat down finally with a much-needed cup of Brazilian coffee and read the file he had been able to select once he had navigated the security checks.

Jack had taken a lot of time putting together the piece of research he was now reading, calling in favours from some of the best CIA analysts in the field. Biohazard and biowarfare no longer had, in his view, the reputation it might once have had. True, the large countries around the world – China, Russia, the US and some other European countries – had an interest in the matter. But he estimated that this was more to safeguard against an event than to initiate the release of a biological agent on foreign soil. The fear they were protecting against came from rogue states possessing and subsequently unleashing such an agent.

It was the growing power of the pharmaceutical industry that concerned Jack. The boom of the biotech industry was also on his mind. It was complex, and almost impossible to monitor all the discoveries small boutique firms were stumbling across... inadvertently or by design. Then they were only too keen to sell to the highest bidder.

Ollie had just started working for a new biotech firm in London. His novice, and perhaps still principled, mind had been disturbed. Ollie had not liked what he had seen, or what he had been asked to do.

Jack went back to his notes. Ollie had contacted Jack through the CIA website by first applying for a job. Jack had reluctantly listened to what Ollie Wilson had to say. There was always someone abroad who thought he'd come across another conspiracy or national security threat. Jack brought up the last email he had received from the young man.

*Must find a way to download latest findings. The next batch of research is crucial. What I'm working on is not what it seems.*

Ollie had previously sent Jack a long document – the thesis for the PhD he had received from Harvard Medical School. In many parts, it went over Jack's head, but he understood the thrust of it.

Using AI, machine learning and genome technology to design pioneering drugs... from antibiotics to vaccines.

The BIG Programme director at Harvard had been enthused by Ollie as a student, it seemed. Ollie's ability to generate ground-breaking ideas had earned him the exciting job of Head of Research in the small tech company he had joined in London.

Jack's mobile rang again. He recognised the London Embassy's number and picked up immediately.

"You'd better get to the office." Jethro did not sound pleased.

"There have been some further developments. I'd rather speak to you when you are back at HQ."

\* \* \*

"At least the other flats have been spared." Cora's voice faltered. Her head had dropped against Nancy's shoulder. They stayed there for a moment, contemplating the disaster, each engulfed by her own feelings. Nancy opened the door of the cab and stepped out.

"We should wait for Pole's protection officer to arrive," Nancy said, less to dissuade Cora than to postpone the moment Cora would walk back into her devastated loft.

Cora nodded, looking hesitant. It seemed she no longer wanted to know. Voices surprised the two women, and they turned around. Three young people were moving in their direction from across the road.

A young woman sporting long dark hair, braided with colourful extensions ran towards them, threw her arms around Cora and squeezed her tight.

Cora hugged her neighbour back.

"That was horrible... really spooky..." the young woman said.

"Were you in the flat?"

Nancy approached the two women with a warm smile.

"Sorry Nancy... This is Beth and Charlie."

Beth nodded. "Nice to meet you."

"Where is Ollie?" Beth carried on without giving Nancy time to reply.

Cora wrapped her arms around herself. She glanced at Nancy but said nothing.

"Nat was supposed to come but cancelled at the last minute. Johnny had just gone out for a takeaway..."

Johnny caught up with them and nodded at what Beth had just said, giving Cora a heartfelt hug.

"Any damage to your flat?" Cora asked him.

"Not much, just the smell and a bit of soot on the landing. Nothing compared with yours, my darling." Johnny reached out a hand to rub Cora's back.

"How is Ollie taking it?"

Cora's face turned pale, and she almost crumpled to the ground. "Perhaps we should get on with what we came to do. Sorry to interrupt." Nancy moved closer to Cora. The others took the hint, apologised for interrupting and disappeared through the entrance of their side of the building.

"If you need anything, shout," Beth said over her shoulder before disappearing through the glass doors.

Nancy waved an appreciative hand. "The protection officer should be here any moment. Let's make a move if this is what you still want to do."

"I don't want to meet any more of the neighbours... not yet."

Cora led the way, ducking underneath the yellow-and-black hazard tape that was still stretched across the left-hand side of the building and headed inside. Nancy half turned around. Where was the security officer Pole had promised?

She did not want to be a nuisance by calling him again. The cab driver was still there. She had asked him to wait and let the meter run. Cora had already disappeared into the property against all advice.

Nancy shook her head and hesitated for a short moment. She looked towards the yard's entrance. The police car that would deliver the officer assigned to Cora was nowhere to be seen.

Nancy cursed quietly and followed Cora into the building. She was glad she had decided to wear black that morning. The walls which were once white and spotless were now covered in a dark watery coating. The intense smell assailed her throat. The concrete structure had withstood the flames, but the windows had been shattered by the heat and a cold wind blew through the building.

The door of the loft had been left open so that the firefighters could gain access. Cora stood in the entrance. She was standing in front of the debris of her once happy life. Her stillness was absolute, a statue in a disaster zone. The scene could have been one of her own artistic creations and performances.

With every step Nancy took, she crushed either glass or China underfoot. The smell of melted paint, plastic and burnt fabric became even stronger in the apartment than in the corridor when she finally reached Cora.

"I don't know what to do first." Her friend's lips were hardly moving. "I want to yell. I want to cry… I want to catch the bastards who did this."

Cora picked up a blackened piece of pottery that had rolled to the door and stared at it for a moment. She seemed unable to work out what it once had been.

Nancy glanced at her friend and moved her head around slowly. She too was trying to recall what the loft looked like before the tragedy as a memory of their first evening there slipped into her mind.

*The Gallery has just closed its doors. Philippe is handing Nancy her last glass of champagne. They both decided to have dinner with the young artist to celebrate her first solo show.*

*"I'm working on a new project." Cora Wong's almond eyes are sparkling from the delicious beverage and from joy. The opening has been a complete success.*

*"Already?" Nancy too feels a little tipsy, just enough to be in a mellow mood.*

*"Ideas are buzzing in my head." Cora giggles… imitating the humming of bees. "This one is going to be a large-scale installation, that will also support a performance. I've had aluminium tubes cut to size already as props."*

*"And they are all stored in our flat." Ollie appears at his girlfriend's side. He is beaming too. "I'm so pleased to see her hard work pay off."*

*"Would you like to see them?" Cora says.*

*Philippe pours the remains of the bottle into a glass that may or may not be clean, but he doesn't care. He has sold most of Cora's pieces on the opening night… this bodes well for the young woman.*

*"Nancy may want to get back home… it is rather late," Philippe says.*

"Nonsense... I may no longer join revellers at 2am, in some remote derelict part of Hackney, but I would love to see more of Cora's work."

Philippe nods. Whatever he can do for his friend and one of his best clients. It's only 10pm after all.

Cora and Ollie jump on their bikes. The young generation is climate-change conscious.

Philippe and Nancy opt for a cab, less climate friendly but the only option at this time of night.

"I'm not surprised you like her work," Phillipe admits.

"I love the mix of craft, combining process and provocation... with that underlying sense of longing and nostalgia." Nancy settles in the back of the cab, her back resting against the window as she speaks to Philippe.

Philippe approves. "You share a similar quest I believe." He hesitates, the way someone realises they may have spoken out of turn.

Nancy frowns in a teasing fashion. "Come on, Philippe. No holding back amongst friends."

"Let's talk about that another day." Philippe beams his best smile at Nancy. He is a little tired and the days leading up to the show's launch have been hard work.

"A few words... then we'll talk about this another time, when you have recovered from the opening."

Philippe straightens up a little and Nancy senses he's now regretting the remark.

"It's about China. The research me and my assistant Aimee are doing for you."

"Surely, there can't be any direct connection between my father's disappearance and Cora. She could be his granddaughter..." Nancy frowns.

"Well, Cora's parents disappeared a few years ago, on the trip to mainland China. Their car was recovered, empty... they were never found."

Nancy's stomach tightens. The champagne's uplift disappears in an instant and the wound of the past tears at her once again.

"Apologies... I should have kept my mouth shut."

Nancy forces herself to be civil. She can't resent Philippe, a friend who has been helping her with tracing her artist father. He has had some success without regard either for money or his own safety.

"What happened?"

*Philippe seems now reluctant to provide an explanation, but they arrive at their destination.*

*"They're here." He almost jumps out of the car before it has stopped. Cora and Ollie are waiting for them outside their building's entrance.*

*"How did they manage that?" Nancy too is glad the subject can be dropped. Ollie winks. "Backstreets, wrong side of the road and jumping traffic lights." Nancy fakes indignation.*

*Cora has already opened the building door and she is calling them from inside. She then opens the loft door and a magnificent structure almost 12ft high engulfs almost the entire living space.*

*"The beauty of this piece..." Cora sweeps a hand through the air. "...is that I can rearrange it as I feel. The aluminium tubes are just props. They fit into one another in multiple ways... it's really neat."*

Nancy looked over Cora's shoulder, unable to spot any of Cora's art and said aloud, "The aluminium tubes... your props... where are they?"

* * *

Andy had worked his magic again. Pole never ceased to be amazed by his DS's ability with technology.

"Guv, I think I've been able to trace the hoodie guy."

Pole looked at his watch. Barely 40 minutes since he had forwarded the pictures that Nancy had sent him.

"Shoot."

Andy adjusted his thick glasses, cracked his knuckles and seized his computer mouse decisively.

"CCTV picks him up entering the Regent's Canal towpath at Saint Peter's Street. I backtracked and found another image of him on the High Street... interesting..."

"OK, genius. What is your point?"

"Right... a black SUV drops him at Camden tube. The driver must know what he's doing because I can't get a trace on the SUV either before or after. And as we know, the number plate doesn't exist."

"Same as yesterday, so... why not change car by simply stealing another one?"

"That's the thing, a black SUV looks very much like any other black SUV. Unless there is something distinctive about it, I won't be able to trace it. The other thing, of course, is that the windows are dark, and I can't see who's inside."

Pole dragged over an empty chair and sat next to Andy's desk, looking at the computer screen sideways.

"But something surprised me." Andy had isolated the hoodie guy as he was walking out of Angel tube station and towards the canal. Andy slowed down the movement of him walking on screen.

"I watch a lot of these, and I've learned a few things from hours and hours of CCTV deciphering."

"Are you telling me I am not being fair, getting you to do the tough work all on your own?" Pole crossed his arms over his chest. "You get the best CCTV footage there is, just for you... I selected it myself."

"Yes... you... did..." Andy was paying little attention to what Pole was saying. Pole could have served him his notice. He would not have heard him.

"Do you see the way he walks... legs close to one another, rather short strides?"

The image on the screen moved painfully slowly, one foot lifting from the ground and taking what seemed like forever to land on the ground again. Pole could see what Andy was getting at, the strides were indeed short.

"So, he has a problem with the way he walks... that's a good identifier."

Andy chuckled. "And also, the body looks as if it is bobbing up and down when he walks."

Andy used a highlight cursor to follow the movement with it to demonstrate.

"OK, I'm convinced. What issues does this man have with his legs then?"

Andy pulled a disapproving face. "Half the population suffers from it. I don't think it's a bloke... I think it's a woman."

"From a hoodie guy to a hoodie missus... well done," Pole said, casting an eye on his watch. Rob was due to call with an update and he was late.

# Chapter Five

"What about the props?" Cora asked.

"I don't quite know why they come to mind, but I just recall talking about them, the last time I was here. Somehow it feels relevant." Nancy stopped herself from mentioning Ollie, but Cora had read her mind. She remembered that glorious evening too. She ran her hand through her hair and grabbed a tuft of it.

"They are still there, stored at the far end of the room."

They both looked around the large open space. It had been cleverly designed to exploit the layout for maximum effect. A small entrance, leading directly onto an open kitchen with its long work top, a dining room and lounge area. At the far end, where the room turned a corner into the short arm of an "L", was Cora's studio.

"I don't think we can reach your studio." Nancy crouched down to assess the state of the floor. "I'm not even sure we should be walking on this floor at all."

"You can't but I can." Cora removed the thick bomber jacket Nancy had lent her and took off her shoes and socks. She started climbing the pillar that stood closest to the entrance.

Nancy opened her mouth but stopped herself from telling Cora to be careful. The evidence had been disturbed some time ago when the firefighters had trampled all over the place, and her friend was not a stupid young girl. She didn't need someone telling her off every time she decided to do something. Twice Cora almost slipped. The residue from the smoke that coated every surface of the flat was treacherous. Cora managed to reach the top of the column.

She moved up a little higher and swung her legs across the central beam of the room. She was now 12ft in the air looking as comfortable as if she were relaxing on a lounger.

"What do you see now?" Nancy craned her neck to follow Cora's eyes, but there was no way she could see round the corner.

"The props have been displaced but I'm not sure whether it is because of the heat of the fire, the water spray or someone trying to move them."

The soot that covered everything was clinging to her hands and feet. Cora stood up slowly. Her right foot slipped again. "Shit... this stuff is diabolical." She clung to the top part of the vertical beam she had used to climb up.

"I know you want to get over there and check, but we need to let forensic do their job."

Cora ignored Nancy. She was evaluating what it would take for her to walk all the way across the various beams of the room to her studio without falling off.

"I can shuffle all the way there." She was pointing to a central support beam.

"And then what?" Nancy's raised voice echoed around the loft.

"Then I can swing towards the furthest column."

"Please don't make me regret mentioning those props."

"Something prompted you, Nancy. You might remember if I tell you what I see there."

"If you even attempt to get over there, I will cross the floor myself."

Cora looked down and shook her head. "That is blackmail. You know I'll never let you do that."

"I don't care. As long as it makes you come down again."

The sound of broken debris being crushed underfoot stopped the conversation. Nancy turned around. The tall figure that was climbing the stairs towards the flat was not the police protection officer she was expecting.

\* \* \*

The little cul-de-sac in Camden felt damp and looked seedy. Despite the broad daylight, the lane remained in darkness, squeezed between two derelict buildings that never allowed the sun to warm it up.

Rob was standing near an opening that must previously have been a large door. It was now kept closed with a sheath of corrugated iron and discarded hard plastic windowpanes.

"You're sure it's him?" Pole asked.

Rob nodded, pulling a sorry face.

"Let's go then."

Pole moved aside the broken objects that served as a makeshift door, lit a small torch and entered cautiously. The smell that struck Pole when he moved inside made him retch, acrid and vinegary, but unmistakable...

Heroin.

Cooked, smoked or injected.

The den was providing shelter for those who needed a fix. Mattresses strewn on the floor, bodies limp, alone or in groups. People preparing their syringes, oblivious to whomever was around.

Rob shone his light on the mass of bodies. Nobody flinched... they couldn't care less. He fixed the beam of his lamp on the heap slumped near a pillar and started walking towards it.

"Hey mate... do you have a fiver?" a mumbled voice rose from a pile of garments that reeked of dirt.

Both men ignored the request, yet the voice persisted. More of the inert bodies that seemed asleep came to life. Someone that did not belong was intruding.

"We need to get out of here... I'm not sure I want to be in the middle of a heroin den when these junkies wake up and smell cash for their next fix," Rob said softly.

"I hear you." Pole tried to accelerate his progress towards Ollie's body. He almost tripped over someone's outstretched legs, eliciting a groan.

Rob reached the young man before Pole and flashed his torch into his face. It was ashen white, his lips were open, saliva had drooled down the side of his face and onto his T-shirt. Rob crouched, placed his index and middle finger on the young man's neck artery. He pressed hard.

Pole squatted next to him. "Alive?"

Rob pulled one of Ollie's eyelids open. The pupil had grown smaller than the size of a pin prick.

The sight of people gathering themselves to stand up as best they could alarmed Pole. He grabbed one of the young man's arms. Rob did the same on the other side and they lifted the inert body. The dead weight was astonishingly heavy.

"Come on mate, you don't want to finish up here."

Those who had managed to stand started to mutter some indistinct words. A skinny arm reached towards Pole. He tried to avoid it and almost dropped Ollie. Rob braced himself and Pole managed to steady the young man's body. Ollie's head was rolling from side to side. His feet dragged along the floor, starting to bump into the people lying on the floor.

"Fuck..." Pole looked around for an easier route. "It's impossible not to bump into people if we drag him like this."

Rob was also looking around. More mumbled words were coming from the crowd, but a few started to made sense... dosh, cash, dope.

"No, it's not going to work. I'll carry him... You clear the way." Pole braced himself and heaved Ollie's body over his shoulders, his torso lying across them. One of Pole's arms gathered Ollie's legs, the other his arms. Rob pushed people away as they approached the exit.

The grumble of those they were disturbing rose to a new level, some shouting, some swearing. Rob ignored them. The junkies were awake, and they needed to get out immediately. Pole accelerated his pace. Someone tried to stand in his way. Rob pushed him back and he fell down. The whole den had come to life...

Rob increased the brightness of the torch beam and shone it into people's eyes. They turned their heads away, yelling insults. Pole made a final push for the exit and within seconds they were out.

He didn't stop to relax, however. Some of the druggies were coming out in pursuit. Rob was calling for assistance when a beer bottle hit the back of his head. He stumbled forward almost losing his phone.

Pole was almost out of the small alley. His back screaming under the strain of the other man's weight. Two police cars, blue lights flashing, and sirens blaring, arrived from opposite directions, and screeched to a stop. Officers leaped out. The people who had come out of the den scattered.

Pole finally lowered Ollie's body to the ground as gently as he could. The ambulance had arrived too, and the paramedics took over. Pole slumped down onto the pavement against the door of one of the vehicles.

Rob joined him. "Well done..." Pole nodded and after a minute got up, still stiff. He walked towards the open back of the ambulance where one of the paramedics, a tall and lean black man, was busying himself over Ollie, fitting an oxygen mask over his face.

"How bad..." Pole did not have time to finish his sentence. An alarm sounded on one of the monitors. The paramedic pushed Pole away firmly, his colleague slashed open Ollie's T-shirt with one cut. The door closed and the ambulance lurched forward, siren screeching.

Pole stood... stomach clenched. The smell of heroin still floated around him.

\* \* \*

"Drug overdose... My chap on the ground says it's heroin." Jethro sounded irritated.

"You mean he has been injected by force and has OD'd on it," Jack asked.

"I don't know the details. Scotland Yard and the NCA are involved so I'm not sure we want to be that visible."

Jack stopped typing. Jethro awaited his reply. As far as he was concerned, he had done his best to find out what happened to Ollie Wilson.

"Why Scotland Yard and why the NCA?"

"Ollie's girlfriend seems to have the right connections, and she reported his kidnapping."

"It could still be a kidnapping that went wrong."

"Look... That's up to the police to determine. And if it is really serious, it will be up to the FBI to get involved. Maybe this kid got involved in some shady drug deal or borrowed money from the wrong people."

"The people who picked him up at his flat were pros... So not convinced."

"And the mafia uses pros when it comes to settling scores." Jethro had lost interest in the conversation.

"Any idea who the pros were?" Jack thought it was a longshot, but the London Station Chief for the CIA might know.

"We didn't get anything that helped ID them."

And there would be no attempt to do so. Jack continued typing his notes in frustration.

"Anything new... let me know," Jack said.

Jack stood up, put on this jacket. He walked out of the CIA head office building and ran across the open stretch of road that separated it from the cafeteria. The restaurant never closed. It catered at any time of the day or night for the agents and support staff that made Langley a centre of excellence.

A few people were there. Nobody he knew though. Just as well, Jack did not fancy an idle chit-chat with anyone.

Jack ordered pancakes with maple syrup and a cup of black coffee.

He picked up his tray and found a spot near the window. The cafeteria was a large open-plan room devoid of small corners in which to hide or eavesdrop. February's cold was seeping through the glass, but Jack did not mind. It would only take a few more mouthfuls of food before he returned to investigating Ollie Wilson.

Jack had to admit that so far there was very little evidence of a Chinese presence in what had happened to him. Jethro was right. The kidnapping could be anything... drugs, ransom, dirty money.

Yet the CIA profile of Ollie Wilson had not turned up anything suspicious... a little pot smoking at college, but no dealing. The information from his university was still pending.

The hunch that Jack had was based more on Ollie's uni background. His Bioinformatics and Integrative Genomics or BIG residency at Harvard Medical School made him part of an elite group of young men who would design the future. He had sounded articulate when they'd spoken on the phone. He'd wanted to be sure before presenting his case to the CIA... There had been no desire to impress, simply a genuine concern to share accurate information.

Jack pushed his half-finished plate away to concentrate on his coffee... the first of many.

Why could he not let this go? Experience?

The desire to see his theory about biohazards and the control of technological transfers in the field of pharmaceutical development vindicated.

Above all, the need to see what he had started through to the bitter end.

Jack sipped at his coffee and took out his mobile. His thumb hesitated. It fell swiftly over a name in his contact list... time to make a London call...

*  *  *

The silhouette stood on the long landing, neither rushing in nor walking away. Cora climbed down from her perch in haste. She landed softly amongst the burnt wreckage and moved to the door.

"Who are you?" Nancy looked around for some form of weapon. The helmet was still on the person who'd just entered with no indication it was about to come off.

Nancy picked up a piece of charred wood, once part of the coffee table. Cora moved next to her in full view, ready to make a stand.

The visor flipped open in one quick flick. "Cora?"

"Nat...?"

Cora started to pick her way across the floor, choosing her footing with care to avoid the glass. The other woman came forward and squeezed Cora in a light embrace. The helmet came off, dropped to the floor freeing up a mass of blonde curls.

"I'm so, so sorry... I've just been speaking to Beth." She squeezed Cora harder.

Tears welled up in Cora's eyes. Her nose started running, and she wiped it on the sleeve of Nancy's elegant sweater.

"It's really, really bad... We just arrived to see what's happened to the place." Cora bit her lower lip. "And also... Ollie." But she couldn't carry on.

Nancy stepped in, offering a hand to Cora's friend. "I'm Nancy... a friend."

Cora apologised. "Sorry Nancy, I should have..."

"Not to worry," Nancy interrupted. "What matters is that we are amongst friends."

Someone else was climbing the stairs in a hurry. The man arrived at the top of the stairwell and this time there was no doubt in Nancy's mind who the new arrival was.

"You should have waited for me," the man said, gruffly.

48

"And what took you so long?" Nancy shot back. The police protection officer was right of course, but she was not in the mood to spare his feelings.

"Traffic was murder."

"Even with a siren and flashing lights?"

"Not supposed to use them unless it's a code red."

Nancy focused on the new arrival. Male, white, a nascent beer gut and more hair on his badly shaven chin than on his head, and yet, sharp brown eyes that noticed everything.

Nancy breezed in. "Welcome anyway… I'm Nancy." She extended her hand in the direction of the others. "Cora and Nat."

"Michael Branning."

Awkwardness hung in the air for a moment.

"We are trying to reach the other side of the flat to check on my artwork." Cora nodded in the direction of the lounge.

"Before you ladies rush into doing anything clever, I'll check with the fire brigade. We wouldn't want you going through the floor, now would we?"

He took his mobile out of his pocket and turned around to make his call.

*Where the heck did Pole find this guy?* Nancy thought.

"Maybe he's right." Nat gave a small shrug. Cora turned to Nancy.

"Alright, let's get out and wait for our guardian angel to find out how safe it is to reach the other side."

Nancy knew what the answer would be. Neither did she relish going through Cora's props in front of an army of onlookers. She still did not quite know why she had mentioned them to her. The vague memory of Ollie standing next to them, talking about them, was not enough to warrant focusing on these, at least just yet.

Her mobile phone rang.

"Jonathan." Nancy moved away from the others onto the landing. "Michael has just arrived. Thanks for…"

"I'm not calling about that," Pole interrupted. "I'm on my way to A&E… University College Hospital… You need to tell Cora."

* * *

"Do you believe in luck?" Steve Harris, Jack's contact in London, was being mischievous.

Jack rolled his eyes. "Steve, you know I don't… We've been through that 1,000 times."

"Well, today you might change your mind."

"We've known each other for over 15 years… So far, you've never won the argument."

"Do you have any holidays left?"

"What has that got to do with anything?" Jack regretted for a moment calling his most reliable contact at MI6, a man he would also call a friend.

"Yay or nay?"

"Of course, when does a CIA agent *ever* take his full entitlement of vacation a year?"

"You mean the whole 10 days increasing to what… 14 after a 20-year-long career?"

"It's 15 days and it's 21 years."

"Pack your bag. You're coming to London for a well-deserved break. I know Jethro is not going to look into this for you because, as far as he is concerned, there is nothing obvious that smells of conspiracy against the United States of America."

"That's a bit unfair on the Station Chief."

"Hardly… Otherwise you wouldn't be calling me."

Jack grumbled an acknowledgement.

"And your own boss is not going to let you go on a hunch, when everyone is focused on the Middle East at the moment," Harris added.

"Still… If I'm going to sacrifice my 10 days' holiday, you've got to give me something to go on." Jack finished his coffee, now almost cold. "I've told you about Wilson… You barely asked a question about him."

"It's because a contact of mine at Scotland Yard has called about the possible kidnapping of a US citizen. I'm sure you can now guess who the victim is. Right?"

Jack stopped himself from taking the final sip. "That's impossible."

"But there it is… pack your bags… I'll see you in London." Harris hung up before Jack could ask his next question.

\* \* \*

Nat had offered to accompany Cora to A&E. She had thanked her friend for her kindness but declined. Nancy was the only person she wanted with her to visit the hospital. Nancy smiled to Cora and nodded. She understood.

DS Branning was driving Cora and Nancy through traffic at speed. Cora was looking out through the window, her eyes gazing into the distance, noticing very little of the journey. Nancy kept an eye on her friend, but there was little comfort she could offer until they knew what Ollie's medical condition was.

The strong smell of stale cigarettes didn't seem to disturb Nancy as much as it usually did. The unmarked police car stopped abruptly. Branning swore, reversed with dexterity and continued on the wrong side of the road for a short distance. Nancy braced herself but Cora, it seemed, hardly noticed.

*They are in an old truck that smells of tobacco, smoked or chewed. They have given up their bikes. It's the way everybody gets around in China, but her mother's distinctive European features are starting to attract too much attention. An old friend of her grandfather has lent them a truck, old, battered... perfect.*

*Her father is in the driving seat alone, in the front cabin.*

*Nancy and her mother are sitting in the back. The old tarpaulin cover has been fastened to the frame as best it can with bits of string in different colours.*

*They're driving down small country tracks. The main roads are teeming with national guards, and they don't want to be stopped. It's the last leg of a long journey that brings them closer to freedom. Nancy is tired. She has not slept properly for days.*

*Her mother has dozed off. She too has not slept since they left Sichuan to escape the Cultural Revolution. Some old rice bags have been thrown on the floor, barely cushioning against the rocking and bouncing of the truck. Her mother stirs from time to time, but Nancy is too scared to ask any questions about their journey.*

*The truck has stopped. Nancy hesitates to move but her father is already out of the vehicle. He lifts the cover after unfastening the strings on one side. His wife stands up, on full alert. A woman and a child appear at the back of the vehicle. Nancy's mother muffles a cry. The other woman jumps in and they hug each other fiercely.*

*Nancy's father lifts the little girl into the back and covers the rear of the vehicle again. There is no time for introductions. The two girls sit down next to one another, and the little girl takes out of her pocket a couple of turtle cakes… She offers one to Nancy with a toothless smile. "My last ones," she says. Nancy has found her best friend forever.*

*The journey starts again. Her father is still driving alone. His back is tense, shoulders hunched. The daylight is fading and soon they will rely on the moon to guide them.*

*The truck comes to an abrupt stop. Nancy and her friend are thrown against the steel side panel of the cab. The roar of a vehicle coming the other way grows and headlights illuminate the track.*

Nancy closed her eyes and fists tight.

DS Branning frowned, misinterpreting Nancy's expression. "I know what I'm doing."

Nancy managed a smile. "I'm in no doubt you do." There was no time for the past yet.

# Chapter Six

"He is stable now. We need to run a battery of tests… Go home and get some rest." The University College Hospital registrar was sitting on the chair next to Cora's. Nancy was sitting on the other side of her, listening intently too. The doctor warned them the tests would take some time.

Ollie had slipped into a coma after resuscitation proved successful. There was nothing more she could do but wait for the results.

Cora was holding an untouched cup of tea in both hands. She was nodding at what the doctor was telling her, still not wanting to accept the consequences.

The man she loved was no drug addict, not the sort of person who would end up in a heroin den, or perhaps she did not know Ollie at all.

The thought stabbed her heart, and she squeezed the cup hard; a little tea slopped out, wetting her fingers.

Nancy too had looked shocked at the news. But less so than Cora would have expected her to be. The world of criminal law she frequented as Queen's Counsel had shown her the dark side – often hidden – of human nature.

Cora was yet again on the brink of losing someone she cared for. Eight years earlier, she had suffered a great loss. Both her parents had disappeared during a visit to family in mainland China. Now, history seemed to want to repeat itself in an unbearable loop.

"You're very welcome to stay at my place… The spare room is already prepared." Nancy said, gently laying a hand on her forearm, her eyes made a little fuller by concern and kindness.

Cora shook her head.

"I don't want to seem ungrateful after all you and Jonathan have done for me, but I'd prefer to stay with Beth and Johnny. They'll say yes, I know."

"You'd like to be close to your home." Nancy nodded.

"It's strange but I feel I need to be there… Somehow to be able to look after it, even if I can't just yet."

Nancy searched Cora's face with an intense look Cora had never seen before. It made her recoil a little. Nancy pulled back. "Alright… But please stay out of trouble… If anything comes up, you must call me."

"Promise… And there is Officer… Branning."

They almost managed a smile. Cora wondered how her protection officer would fare in the midst of an artist community that did not care very much about rules and conventions.

"What about your friend Nat?"

"Natalie… She'll be there for me too. She lives in Camden, but with her motorbike she can come round in no time. We see her almost every day."

The beep of the doctor's pager told him he was wanted for another emergency. Cora grabbed the sleeve of his white coat before he stood up.

"As soon as you hear the results…"

He nodded as reassuringly as he could. "You will know the minute I know."

The pager sounded again, and he disappeared in a slow jog around the corner.

It had been good that he had spent time with her, but she couldn't help wondering whether he was preparing her for the worst.

Pole had appeared at the far end of the corridor. He slowed down, and Cora noticed his hesitation. She waved him in with a small gesture, almost childish. Pole joined them and sat in the chair the doctor had just vacated.

The kind-man-chair. Cora sighed. "What have you decided?" Pole asked.

"I'm going back to the building… Staying with friends. Nancy's met them."

Pole leaned back to look at Nancy. She nodded. "And I'll have the protection of DS Branning."

"It's your choice, of course…" Pole let the sentence hang. Cora shook her head.

"I've got to be there."

"Fine, I'll speak to Branning."

"Inspector Pole…" Cora hesitated, and Pole raised an eyebrow. She had seldom trusted anyone in the police, but Cora felt she could for once let her guard down.

"How did you find Ollie?"

"When someone goes missing, the NCA activates a number of channels… someone on one of those channels came through."

"So, it was a tip-off?"

Pole thought about it for a short moment. "You could call it that."

"So, it was a tip-off," Cora murmured, wondering why someone had wanted to save Ollie after all.

\* \* \*

Nancy stood up first, followed by Pole and Cora. Cora was about to leave the hospital. Nancy hugged her and Cora's thin, yet athletic body slumped in her arms. Pole stood aside, giving the friends space to say goodbye. Cora was just managing to keep her head above water, but returning to friends and the community of artists she felt close to was what she needed.

"Do you trust DS Branning?" Nancy asked Pole, as both Cora and Branning disappeared down the corridor. She didn't need to pretend with Pole.

"You mean male, white, a bit pudgy and a tad misogynistic?"

"You know me too well, Jonathan."

Pole smiled. "Do I?" He extended a hand and gently placed it on Nancy's back. "Branning is good at his job despite all his other… attributes."

"Won't take no for an answer or be deterred easily?"

"That's the sum of it."

Nancy turned towards him. "I'm not hugely hungry but I could do with something small."

"There is not much around here, unless we try the Wellcome Collection Cafe?"

"Normally I would say that's a really good idea and we could perhaps have spent some time wandering through their temporary exhibition, but today I'd rather go somewhere quieter."

"The British Library members' room?"

"Too busy…" Nancy opened the clasp that held her jet black hair together. She let it fall loose onto her shoulders. She took a fancy little lemon beret out of her coat pocket and fitted it onto her head.

"Let's try further afield then." Pole bent to pick up her handbag which he then handed to her. It was an attractive cross between a fashionable bag and a rucksack, matching the colour of her hat.

"How about the Renaissance on St Pancras?"

"Too grand…?"

Pole rolled his eyes. "Rotunda at King's Place, near the canal?"

"Excellent." Nancy adjusted a pair of grey gloves in supple calfskin that fitted her elegant hands perfectly.

"Shall we walk there?" Pole started towards the lifts. "I sense you need to unwind."

Nancy smiled, moving a little faster to catch up with him. Pole put on his jacket as he walked.

The cold hit them both as they went out through the rotating doors of University College Hospital. Despite it being midday, the sky was grey and lowering, and darkness would come soon that evening. Pole turned up the collar of his jacket against his cheeks. Nancy stepped closer to him, and he wrapped his right arm around her shoulders.

"Do you want to talk about it? It's been a tough 24 hours that's bound to have stirred up the past."

Nancy did not seem surprised at the question. Pole had made a successful career as a DCI, reading people well on a first encounter. There were few places to hide in the presence of Inspector Pole and he knew she did not mind his gentle probing.

She nodded, her yellow beret bobbing a few times against Pole's shoulder.

"The flashbacks are happening more often now."

"You are delving into your past... With both hands." Pole gently stroked her forearm with his fingers.

"But it's so strange it never used to happen so frequently until very recently. Then again I never dealt with cases that were so close to home... the people who suffered were never friends."

"Would you have allowed the past to trouble you like this when you were at the height of your career anyway, or even on the way up there?"

Nancy slowed down a little. "I never thought about it that way. But to answer your question, yes, you are right. The past was buried deep, and I certainly did not have any desire to revisit it."

"But now you do?" It was a question that Pole asked regularly. Nancy was grateful he had agreed to help her on the road to discovering the missing parts of her past. But that process had to be driven by her desire to find out what had happened to her father almost 30 years ago. Pole was not the sort of man to ingratiate himself by producing the information she needed unprompted.

"I'm not turning back now... I need to know. Although I have to admit that what I may find at the end of the journey or even, what I may find on the way is scaring me."

They walked for a little while in silence. Pole would not pretend the path to the truth was going to be easy. It would have been dishonest to say otherwise.

"This time... I mean the memory, was about the last part of our journey to Hong Kong. I had completely forgotten about it."

"You spent months being scared on the way to reaching safety. I'm not surprised that as a seven-year-old girl you chose to shut it away. Even adults do that when faced with the prospect of torture or death."

Nancy shivered. "I know... and yet, the memory is disturbingly fresh."

They arrived at the Euston Road crossing that led to the British Library. The little green man at the crossing disappeared and they both sped up to reach the other side.

Nancy slowed to a stop. Her eyes moved to the imposing Paolozzi statue that stood on a high plinth in the British Library piazza. It was of a man, sitting on a block, bending forward and, as he did so, measuring the universe with a set of dividers.

"I'm never completely sure about this sculpture, you know..."

"You prefer the original watercolour of Isaac Newton measuring the universe, by William Blake?" Pole asked.

"I suppose I do... I like Blake's uncompromising way of telling the stories he believed in."

"Which was unfashionable at the time. Sticking to your own version of the way the world worked which didn't conform with Newton's was risky."

"That's right... Newton was a dominant figure and well-respected scientist."

"But Blake thought Newton's attempt to measure the work of God was... futile."

Nancy cocked her head, still looking at the imposing piece. "Perhaps we too are limited in what we see."

A gust of wind reminded them that it was the middle of the winter and that they needed to find shelter. Pole wrapped his arm around her once more and urged her gently towards their cosier destination.

The Rotunda restaurant was almost full. Pole spotted a table that was being vacated and called the head waiter to secure the place for them.

Within five minutes, they were comfortably settled and had ordered their food. Nancy removed her beret and let her eyes roam around the room. She looked with interest through the floor-length windows past Pole's shoulder.

The Regent's Canal looked almost welcoming, despite the grey water. It reflected the colourful narrow boats that were moored there, and a few evergreen trees provided some foliage along the canal. Pole followed her gaze.

They both chatted for a short while about the new King's Place building and the improvements it had brought to the area. It was a gentle way to ease into the more serious conversation they would have once the food had arrived, and they were sure of their privacy.

The appetising dishes they had decided to share arrived.

Grilled broccoli, poached duck egg, truffle oil and hazelnuts. Pole absentmindedly picked up the pepper mill and gave it a few turns over the egg. Nancy would almost certainly pick at his dish. He knew she would enjoy the additional spice.

Braised beef ribs and skin-on fries with garlic herb butter. She had forgotten all about a small something for lunch after all. Nancy moved the small dish holding the fries between the two plates, ready to share.

They both took a mouthful and groaned with pleasure. The food had the anticipated effect on Nancy. She relaxed into her chair, and she felt herself mellow.

"Thank you for not pushing me." Nancy looked affectionately at Pole.

"There is no need for me to be impatient."

"Still, you have given me a lot of your time, and hard-earned information of course." Nancy toyed with a piece of broccoli that looked inviting, but she had lost her appetite. "I expected to discover that my father had completely severed his links to the Chinese Communist Party. But come to think of it, it makes sense. He always was a politically engaged artist and the prospect of a new, more liberal China might have lured him back."

"I suppose he never spoke about his continued connections with China when you were in France though?"

"That's right. After we had escaped from China and settled in Paris he never said anything about the people he knew back there… He spoke with me about China as a country, about its art and history, but not about its politics. I never realised that until now. Perhaps he commented on what was happening there with the artist friends he engaged with and talked politics with, but I would not have been party to those conversations."

"It's heart-breaking to leave the country one loves and to leave everything behind, especially friends and family." Pole stopped eating and waited a moment. "There was perhaps an element of guilt."

"There must have been… Survivor's guilt is sometimes stronger than…" Nancy chewed and swallowed her mouthful of food before finishing. "…the blood ties of love and family."

"You are making assumptions now… as I am, and I apologise. We still don't know what his motivations were for returning to China."

"You are right, and I have always assumed as a young woman waiting for him to return that his departure was a selfish act, but I'm not so sure now."

Nancy clenched her fork a little too tight, the sinews of her hand prominent under the strain.

"Is this what is linking you so strongly with Cora?" Pole reached across the table and picked Nancy's free hand up.

She gave Pole a faint smile. "Cora is so very young and yet, I saw something in her that inspired me to keep looking for my father and stop assuming."

Pole raised his eyebrows. "What was that?"

"She could have been angry too at her parents for visiting mainland China as they had become prominent political activists, but she wasn't. If they made a mistake, so be it, she just wants to know whether they are still alive."

"You mean that Cora's parents took too much risk and should have measured the consequences better."

"Exactly and I can't just keep telling myself my father was so blinded by the desire to believe in a democratic China that he didn't see the repression on free-thinking coming. Still, I can't deny I don't like the idea of my father having resumed his contacts with China's communist party."

"Perhaps he hoped that China would soon become a better place and that he would be able to return with you and your mother… and reintroduce you to your country of birth," Pole said, squeezing her hand gently.

"That's a hopeful interpretation, Jonathan." Nancy gave Pole a kind smile. "I fear things are not going to unfold in a way I am going to like but I have to give my father the benefit of the doubt and accept that his motivations might have been influenced by what he saw when he got there."

"I'm still holding out for that interpretation."

"I now need to learn a lot more about my family and the friends he spent time with."

Pole was about to renew his offer of help, when Nancy interrupted. "You have done so much already. Let me see whether I can gather some information from my own contacts."

Pole could not argue with that, not yet anyway. Perhaps this was a way for Nancy to slow down the process she had found painful from the very beginning. She'd felt abandoned, but had she truly been and was there something bigger at stake that validated her father's decision not to return.

"Always happy to help and…" The ping of Pole's smartphone interrupted Nancy's reply. A text had arrived.

Superintendent Marsh needed him urgently.

\* \* \*

Cora had offered DS Branning a cup of tea and a biscuit, which he accepted gratefully. He hardly stepped into the flat to retrieve the beverage and disappeared outside for what appeared to be a much-needed fag.

"You think we should offer him one of ours?" Johnny flopped onto one of the old sofas they had rescued from a junk shop and revived with patterned throws and colourful cushions.

"I doubt DS Branning smokes pot when he's on duty," Beth said, bringing in the tin of biscuits from the kitchen. Cora was balancing their cups of tea on the large green chopping board that doubled up as a tray. She hadn't said much since offering Branning his tea, but it was good to be amongst friends.

"Do you think he'll be able to smell it?" Beth asked.

"What… the grass we smoke or the plant that we grow on the rooftop?" Beth plonked a mug in front of each of them. "Cora da'ling, you've said nothing since you arrived." Johnny extended his arm towards his friend and laid a bejewelled hand over her forearm.

"Don't be a dick… she only arrived a few minutes ago." Beth took her mug and retreated deep into one of the armchairs.

"Not true… it was…" Johnny consulted with a great flourish his brand new Patek Philippe watch. "A whole 20 minutes ago."

"Sorry guys, it's just that everywhere I look, I'm reminded of Ollie," Cora said in a low voice as she sank into her favourite armchair.

Everybody went quiet for a moment.

"We'll help in any way we can." Johnny had dragged the old leather chair he favoured next to Cora's.

She straightened up and gave a short sigh. "Thank you… I know you are his friends, and you are missing him too." She leaned forward to pick up her mug and blew on the hot liquid that was sending curls of steam into the air. She managed a smile. "And you even remembered which is my favourite cup."

"Of course, my lovely, we gay men are good at that stuff." Johnny gave a little wave of the hand, mocking the conventional wisdom on gay mannerisms.

A ring of the doorbell interrupted their conversation.

"DS Branning must have finished his smoke and his tea." Beth stood up slowly. Her pink corduroy overall and matching striped pullover brought out the colour of her dark skin. She had just returned from Guyana where she had unashamedly enjoyed the sun, ignoring her mother's complaints about her skin tone.

Cora's thoughts were transported to a happier time. She had shared a holiday with Beth, still remembering the quiet argument with her mother. "So, what, Mum... I'm black and black is beautiful. And I don't need strange creams to make it look lighter."

Johnny indicated to Beth she should stay with a wave of the hand and went to the door. Beth took the opportunity to switch chairs.

The voice that came from the corridor told everyone that DS Branning must still be on his break.

Nat walked into the flat wrapped up in an emerging designer winter coat, created by one of her friends.

"No bike today then?" Johnny eyed the coat with envy.

"I didn't feel like biking with a box of cupcakes balanced on my handlebars."

"Ooo... Hummingbird cakes, my favourite." Johnny helped Nat with the distinctive purple-and-black cardboard box Natalie was carrying with caution across the floor.

"No," Nat interrupted. "Cora's favourite."

Cora stood up slowly whilst Johnny was already opening the box. "You're too good." Cora wrapped her arms around her friend.

Johnny started naming the cakes, pointing a famished finger at them.

Cora looked at the mouth-watering selection. She stretched a hand forward and stopped herself in mid-air. There was no vanilla flavour, her favourite... perhaps there were none left in the shop. She chose salted caramel, Ollie's favourite.

Everybody gathered around and chatted about this and that.

Cora was no longer listening. She took out her mobile from her pocket and checked for messages.

Nothing.

She placed the phone back in her jeans pocket and forced herself to eat another mouthful of cake.

Beth had grabbed a bright orange beanbag and dumped it next to Cora's leather chair. She sat there; a cupcake half-eaten in her hand. "How can we help?"

The cheerful atmosphere disappeared. Everyone chewed their cupcakes in silence.

"I just don't want to get anyone into trouble," Cora finally said, after clearing her tight throat.

"Nonsense." Beth leaned forward, pressing her upper body sideways into the chair, an arm outstretched towards her friend.

"We're here for you just the way you and Ollie have always been there for us."

A murmur of general agreement spread amongst the others. Cora ruffled her spiky hair. "I don't know... It's about what I've seen. These people... they are..." She recalled what Nancy and Inspector Pole had said. "They are professionals."

Everybody looked at each other. It sounded... impossible. "You mean... like... hitmen?"

"Johnny, that is not helpful." Beth's frown was more serious than usual.

"He's right..." Cora nodded. "That's exactly what I meant. They searched the flat methodically... I was hiding... then they chased me... and then..." Cora stopped herself dead. Should she be telling her friends all this?

"Then what?" Nat asked. She had hardly touched the cakes herself.

Cora struggled to make up her mind. Talking to her friends seemed to make matters clearer in her head. The permanent fog in which she had been living since Ollie's disappearance might start to lift.

"...then they set the flat on fire."

Her friends were involved whether they liked it or not. Who knew whether those men might come back and finish the job by setting the entire building alight?

"But why?" Beth asked.

"They must have been looking for something…" Nat ventured.

"That's silly… You don't set something you're looking for on fire." Johnny shrugged his shoulders.

"Maybe they found what they were looking for… and destroyed the place afterwards to hide whatever it was they had taken." Beth's thoughtful face looked more focused than ever.

"Perhaps." Cora abandoned her cake.

"But where could Ollie have hidden anything?" Nat had chosen to settle on the floor, cross-legged.

"I honestly don't know…" Cora's mind went back to the odd conversation she'd had with Nancy.

"You're thinking about something?" Johnny encouraged her.

"Did you remember anything when you were back at the flat with your friend Nancy?" Nat finally grabbed a salted caramel cupcake. Her sleeve rode up her arm, revealing part of her forearm. She pulled the fabric of her sweater sleeve down with a sharp move that almost made her drop the cake.

Cora remained silent for a long moment, and no one thought of interrupting her. "I need to think this through." Perhaps there was something amongst her installation props and Nancy had somehow picked up on it, but she needed to be sure.

Still, it was good to share with true friends.

# Chapter Seven

"You really have a knack for it." Harris's voice bounced around the inside of Pole's car. Pole was on his way to Scotland Yard.

"Coming from you that can't be a good thing." Pole glanced into the rear-view mirror of his car and changed lane. Today he had exchanged the motorbike for an unmarked police vehicle.

"Admit it, Pole. You enjoy dabbling with MI6." Harris's grin could be heard in his voice.

"You've got news about Ollie, I presume." Pole slowed down as a set of traffic lights was turning red. He was in no rush to meet Superintendent Arthur Timothy Marsh.

"I have… You are not the only one who is interested in this young man."

"That's a bit of an understatement… He is lying in ICU, breathing through a respirator. The flat he lives in has been torched to a crisp and his girlfriend has been followed and intimidated… Someone is most definitely interested in Ollie Wilson."

"A good friend of mine from across the pond called me yesterday."

"About Ollie?" Pole's voice sounded incredulous. "What's the chance of that? Are you the only agent at MI6 that the CIA contacts when they need information about the UK?"

"By the looks of it I'm the only agent one step ahead of everyone else…"

Pole was now speeding down the Victoria Embankment along the River Thames. The few pedestrians walking along the stone pavement were hunched forward, collars up and heads down against the cold winter wind. The Thames was at its low watermark revealing its banks of sand and mud. Pole joined a short queue of vehicles that were preparing to turn right. In the distance the London Eye, carrying tourists packed into small pods, was slowly revolving.

"What can you tell me that's helpful to this case?" Pole had learned, whilst working undercover alongside Harris, that the man kept his cards close to his chest but that occasionally he was prepared to share valuable information.

"Keep an open mind about what you think you see and what the evidence tells you."

"That's a tad cryptic... You're not the Oracle."

"Agreed... To be frank I'm not sure I know anything more myself." Harris's voice took on a serious tone. He was not holding back this time, or perhaps not as much as he usually did.

"What's in it for you, Harris?"

"You're pushing your luck... Let's say the biotech world is starting to interest me more, whether run by small firms or large pharmaceutical companies."

"Fine, I'll keep you posted... and I'm expecting you to do the same for me." Pole indicated that he was about to turn into a car park. "I'm just reaching Scotland Yard for a meeting with The Super."

"Is the counter-terrorist squad still sniffing around then?"

"What do you think? Crowne vanishing from Belmarsh Prison is a very large stain on their reputation. So yes, since I was the DCI who ran the investigation and the one who suggested Scotland Yard use him as an adviser, I am under scrutiny."

"The counter-terrorist squad are an ungrateful lot..." Harris had returned to his devilish self. "They managed to eliminate an entire terrorist cell... right in the middle of London... before they could wreak complete havoc."

"They would have done that in any case, Harris. My team knew where they were, and we would have got them regardless." Pole stopped his car at the entrance to the car park. An armed officer came out of his surveillance booth and checked Pole's ID, giving him a nod. The large steel bollards descended slowly into the ground, the iron gates opened noiselessly. Pole entered Scotland Yard's secure car park.

"But there was no damage done. I just needed a bit more time to infiltrate my assets into this new cell. That sort of work keeps me sleeping better at night," Harris said.

"I'm glad I'm talking to you from a burner phone," Pole grumbled. "You seem to forget about facilitating the escape of a high-profile city banker who had been an IRA operative for years."

"Minor detail, Inspector... You know it was for the greater good."

"Not sure Marsh or Ferguson would agree."

"Oh, The Super would agree if he had been involved... Marsh has a flair for drama. I suppose he is pissed off he can't involve Henry Crowne in one of your ultra-high-profile cases any longer."

Pole stopped the engine without replying. Harris was right and there was no point arguing otherwise.

"One last thing. Let's not get everything mixed up. Might be a good idea to keep Ms Wu out of this one," Harris said. He stopped Pole before he could protest. "It's going to be mighty difficult. But if matters involving MI6 or the CIA come to the fore, I'm not sure you want her involved since she doesn't know you and I are in contact."

"A threat... From which side?" Pole remained in the car to finish the conversation.

"Not from me if that's what you're thinking, mate." Harris grew serious again, his faint East End accent now a little stronger.

"Good to know."

"And when it comes to Marsh, keep me posted too. I don't want him to come anywhere close to our mutually beneficial arrangement."

\* \* \*

Nancy left the Rotunda restaurant on foot as Pole made his way back to Scotland Yard for his meeting with Superintendent Marsh. Marsh would be kept waiting but Pole, as ever, didn't seem to care.

Nancy didn't feel the urge to rush back and check on Cora. The young woman was safe, surrounded by her friends, and Pole had convinced Nancy that DS Branning would afford her more than adequate protection. Instead, Nancy was on her way to Philippe's art gallery.

Nancy turned into the small backstreets of Islington, not all of which had benefitted from the recent transformation that had changed the area from a mix of arty, showbiz and middle-class dwellings, to more upmarket contemporary apartments for the wealthy.

The few estates that remained looked sad and untended in comparison to the now up-and-coming Islington. Nancy cut through an old estate to the market she enjoyed browsing through at the end of each month and crossed into Camden Passage. She found herself walking through a mixed crowd of young people, chatting on their iPhones, at the top of their voices. They looked in their mid-20s, about Cora's age. The deep blue colour of one young girl's hair contrasted with the golden yellow of a long fleece. She was talking animatedly into her pair of headphones. Her friend was holding out her own phone, looking for directions... Perhaps trying to locate an undisclosed location for the private viewing of an art or fashion show.

Nancy arrived at her destination less than 10 minutes later. Philippe was waiting for her. He looked pleased to see her but perhaps a little more stressed than usual.

"How lovely to see you..." Philippe placed a quick peck on Nancy's cheek.

She smiled in return. "You do have a moment I hope?"

"Absolutely..." Philippe moved to the back of the long room used as the Gallery space. The office area at the back was neat and tidy. He offered Nancy a cup of tea, which she accepted, and they both settled onto the old leather couch that occupied the far wall.

"How is Cora? I heard about the fire from another artist who lives in the area." Philippe drank a little tea forgetting it was still very hot and grimaced.

"She's doing fine in the circumstances... Her young friends have rallied around her."

Philippe nodded. He took off his round, frameless spectacles and breathed onto the lenses. He started to clean them methodically with a cloth he always kept in one of his trouser pockets.

"Did you ever speak to Ollie... I mean at length?" Nancy sipped her tea with half closed eyes. Philippe always kept an excellent Darjeeling for his best clients and Nancy was glad she counted as one of them.

"Not really… I don't think I ever met him on his own. He was always with Cora and if we spoke it was always about her shows."

"I realise I didn't know Ollie that well either. Not in the way I know Cora, at least."

"I think he is happy to be the artist's other half." Philippe used his fingers to underline the word artist with air quotes.

"And yet he seemed to know a lot about art… And was happy to engage…" Nancy had almost finished her cup. Philippe stood up to get the teapot from the kitchen, refilling Nancy's cup. He placed it on the ground.

"It's so very upsetting. Cora has had a fair share of heartache with her parents' loss…" Philippe stiffened a little. He seemed uneasy speaking about loss in front of Nancy, knowing her own story.

"Don't worry Philippe… My own loss was a long time ago." Nancy smiled kindly. No need to make him feel uneasy even though she had rediscovered how raw the memories still were.

"How much has she told you about her parents' disappearance? It may be far-fetched but I'd like to understand what happened then," Nancy said.

"In case there is a link with the fire?" Philippe's eyes widened a little.

"That's right."

Nancy leaned against the side of the sofa. She brought her legs underneath her, having dropped her shoes to the floor. "Tell me."

He told her what he knew.

That Cora's parents, her father a lawyer and her mother a journalist, had gone to visit relatives in Guangzhou, in Southern China. And that they had never been seen again. The car had been found at the side of the road with their travel bags still in it, but their other personal effects had vanished. The police were called. They searched the area. They issued a missing persons notice…

And then nothing.

It was about eight years ago.

"Her parents were activists, if I recall correctly."

Nancy frowned. "They were. She hardly ever mentions that – as though she doesn't want to draw attention to it."

Philippe shook his head. "That's not quite what I meant... I'm sorry. Their activism is the only explanation for their disappearance, and she doesn't like discussing it."

"They disappeared a couple of years after one of the most well-attended demonstrations in Hong Kong." Nancy laid her cup on the floor and sat back. "A reaction against the Hong Kong government passing an anti-subversion law that might have restricted freedom of speech."

"You know more than I do about that, Nancy."

"I can believe that... There is a strong political stance in whatever she creates."

"And it has registered with a lot of collectors. She is on the rise." Philippe smiled. His round, amicable face lost all signs of concern for a moment.

"A well-deserved success. I'm glad it is happening so early in her career."

"Do you think Cora's past life had an impact on Ollie's..." Philippe was looking for the word.

"I'm not sure... I'm simply making sure that I don't overlook anything that could be significant."

"At least now you know everything I know."

"The worst thing for me is not knowing what happened to my father... the lack of closure. That must be even more so in Cora's case. She could have expected an investigation. But no bodies were found, which means no murder inquiry, no investigation, no difficult questions asked."

"A good thing Cora was not with them."

"That's a good point, Philippe... Perhaps that was not a coincidence."

"You mean they felt threatened?"

"I'm sure they knew they had been identified as troublemakers... But perhaps they felt they had to take the risk of going to mainland China for some other reason."

"What do you mean?"

"Something they needed to do or someone they needed to meet." Nancy moved from her comfortable position on the sofa. She leaned forward, as the conversation with Philippe became more urgent.

"I wish I could do more." Philippe sighed.

"You're doing plenty, and so is Amy."

70

Philippe sprang out of his chair, keen to dispel the dark atmosphere that had gathered in the room.

"Talking of which... Amy has discovered a rare article entitled 'Contemporary Art in China under Deng Xiao Ping'."

"How clever of her. And so kind to spend time looking for something that may help me with my own search."

"You will be very interested in that article, I think. It mentions the one name you've been looking for."

Nancy hesitated for a moment, stunned. "You mean... Mo Cho, the artist name her father used?"

\* \* \*

"What's the mood like?" Pole straightened his tie and ran his long hand through his hair.

"What do you expect? He hasn't had a high-profile case to boast about since last year." Marsh's PA rolled her eyes and gave Pole a grin.

"It's only February."

"And the head of the counter-terrorist squad paid him yet another visit yesterday evening."

"Ouch... Talking about the Crowne escape?" Pole inhaled and shook himself out, like a boxer entering the ring.

"Exactly." Denise picked up the phone and called Marsh. He responded through the loudspeaker. Pole could hear his angry voice though... Get Pole in.

"In you go then... Ready for a punch-up."

"*Un homme averti en vaux deux.*"

"Whatever." She nodded towards The Super's door. Pole entered without knocking.

Marsh as usual was in full uniform. He had left the safety of the seat behind his desk from which he liked to either terrorise or charm his visitors. A golf club in his hand, Marsh was practising with a series of swings with balls which had gathered around his feet.

"The next tournament is in two weeks. I'm damned if I'll let the boys from the rapid-response tactical squad win this time around."

"I'm sorry I can't be of very much help in that respect, sir."

Marsh stood up from his putting position, swinging his golf club as he walked back to his desk.

"Not to worry... You may be of help in another matter that has been bothering me for a while."

Pole nodded and came to sit in one of the chairs in front of his boss's desk.

"The head of the counter-terrorist squad and I have made progress on the leak that occurred last year... I'm sure you recall the event." How could Pole have forgotten?

A new terror cell in London had targeted a number of people... including one of Nancy's friends. MI6 had managed to delay storming the building where the group had gathered, to save two of its operatives... an intense few days.

"I do, sir." Pole's face remained expressionless.

"Commander Ferguson, whom you know very well, has come up with a plausible theory."

Pole pulled back a little, focused on hiding the somersault in his gut. He hoped that Ferguson's theory didn't involve a covert collaboration between MI6 and a certain DCI at Scotland Yard. Harris and Pole's work was strictly under the radar.

"Ferguson doesn't buy the argument that MI6 managed to find out the CT squad plans to storm the terrorist cell from external sources."

"Does he believe it was an insider job then?" Pole asked slowly his question.

"That's the sum of it... And he is also proposing to find out in a rather proactive manner. I didn't like the idea at the start but it has some merits."

Marsh had rolled his leather armchair forward, his prominent belly almost touching the desk.

"Ferguson is a determined and skilful officer." Pole knew what was coming next. Ferguson would investigate the communication trail within his team and ask Pole to do the same.

A lethal tactic that would track all calls and messages, including burner phone activity.

The Super confirmed Pole's fears. He had agreed on an unofficial inquiry, to be carried out as discreetly as possible. Marsh had not consulted him. Ferguson, whom he had known a long time, had not

72

communicated with Pole either. Ferguson was preparing himself to run a thorough review of what had gone wrong, and friendship would get in the way.

Marsh continued talking about how beneficial the exercise would be, but Pole was no longer listening.

*Pole stands outside a large vehicle that has been stationed a street away from the target they are about to storm. Steve Harris is showing a couple of pictures to members of Ferguson's SO19 team.*

*"These are my agents – do not engage." He repeats the same sentence like a mantra to each officer. They nod, and when he has finished with them, they roll down their balaclavas and adjust their night-vision goggles. Ferguson is the last to take a look, and signals to his men they are ready with a quick rolling gesture of the hand. Pole has not been shown the pictures, but he knows who one of the men is.*

*Henry Crowne, high-profile city banker, IRA operative, now inmate at the high security unit of HMP Belmarsh. But Henry is also a friend of Nancy's and the reason why Pole met her in the first place.*

*Ferguson enters the mobile control room. Properties have been evacuated around the target. He is pressing Control for quicker results. The element of surprise is key. The young woman in charge of OPS turns around abruptly. "We're all clear." Ferguson nods. "Roger that… Going dark in one minute." He moves past Pole. "OK lads… Let's go." His men are already taking positions around the small property.*

*"I hope they don't screw this up." Harris is nervous and has reason to be. The terrorist cell Ferguson is about to tackle won't care about their own lives and there will be no surrender. Harris has one operative infiltrated amongst the terrorist cell and he is set on recruiting Henry. He wants these two men alive.*

*Pole hears the young woman again. "We are clear to breach." The lights go dark everywhere in the street.*

Marsh stopped talking and Pole realised he'd stopped paying attention. He didn't know whether he was supposed to agree with something.

"I'll speak to Commander Ferguson and agree a way forward." Pole needed to make a quick exit before Marsh realised Pole hadn't heard him in the first place.

"Do remember what I said…"

"I'll inform you at each step of the way." An educated guess that proved to be right, Marsh forever wary of Pole's ability to make the right decisions without consulting him and possibly robbing Marsh of the kudos of another profile deal.

Pole left the room and stood for a moment outside the office after closing the door.

"That bad?" Denise had stopped typing and gave Pole a concerned look.

"Perhaps a little unexpected." He managed to smile and bid Denise goodbye.

A few moments later he was back in his office, and looked around the room, in its usual state of chaos.

It would be ironic if his involvement with MI6 were to herald the end of his career.

\* \* \*

The reply had come within the hour. Jack had applied for a five-day holiday online. He had rehearsed his arguments for taking a last-minute break.

Overworked and underpaid… his boss, John (Jack) Hunter III would reply that so was he.

Needed to clear his head for the next operation… Might need a psych evaluation… Not a good idea.

Spend time with family or friends… Do you have any there…?

He was not about to mention Harris.

Keeping friendly with Jethro, London Station Chief, a persuasive argument about team building, that would do.

The phone never rang, and the holiday was now confirmed. A hint of paranoia crept in. Was he no longer considered a worthy agent? He shook his head at the thought… He was in need of a holiday after all. Jack booked his airline ticket, open return to London departing from JFK at 8.15pm. He had indulged in a business class flight on British Airways.

Hell, he was not on a mission, strapped in the back of a Chinook helicopter, or in the hold of a large C-5M Super Galaxy that the US

74

Air Force used to transport people and supplies. Comfort was not a word that registered with the CIA OPS.

He bought his next ticket. One way to Boston, the return stop to New York.

The flight departed in a little less than two hours from Ronald Reagan Washington airport. Just enough time to nip home, pack up his toothbrush, and a few more bits that might come in handy... jeans, shirt, winter leather jacket.

He decided against a weapon. Customs at Heathrow airport might kick up a fuss, even with a valid licence. No need to attract attention. Above all he would take his second laptop, fully prepped already, as it always was for emergencies.

His mind drifted to a document he had recently received. Another piece of research comparing America's and China's military capabilities. The paper had been prepared by the military adviser to Senator McCain. The Pentagon had reviewed the thick document, recognising its importance.

At the CIA, the paper had landed on his desk. He did have a reputation for fighting lost causes and extracting unexpected data from information no one else was prepared to consider. Jack checked the length of the piece again, a whopping 857 pages. He hesitated, but sent it to his TO READ file nevertheless. He might get a chance to read it on the way back.

Another email alert came through, this time bringing a smile on his face. The head of BIG at Harvard Medical School had time to meet him early that afternoon... And he sounded excited to be talking to Jack about one of his most promising students in bioinformatics... Ollie Wilson.

# Chapter Eight

Cora sank onto the bed. Beth had dashed into her bedroom, rapidly tidied up the unmade bed and insisted Cora should not sleep in the lounge, but that she would.

Cora looked around Beth's bedroom and her friend's presence wrapped itself around her.

Vintage posters of French classic fashion designs by Chanel and Dior... Less conventionally, some sketches of clothes by JP Gaultier and Paco Rabanne. The large table taking up the space of half the room and on which Beth drew clothes and accessories, was covered with her own designs. Others had been pinned to a corkboard on a wall in clusters of different styles.

And of course, clothes were everywhere, hanging in the open wardrobe, from its doors, over the backs of a couple of armchairs that rested in the only free corner of the bedroom.

There must have been some on the bed, but Beth had done away with them by tossing them on top of a highly decorated silk screen she used to change behind. She liked to present the final picture of herself in whatever outfit she had chosen to whomever was in the room at the time... male or female.

The scent of lavender mixed with other floral perfumes made the room soothing and welcoming despite the creative energy that emanated from her drawings. Cora rolled on her side and brought her knees to her chest.

She took her mobile phone out of her jeans pocket. The screen displayed one of Apple's preloaded images and Cora's eyes swam.

The selfie of Ollie and herself pulling silly faces that had become her screensaver had vanished with her previous phone.

Tears started rolling down her face and she let them flow.

Her body shook, and she pressed her hands over her face to prevent anyone hearing her sobs.

"No more drugs... Not even weed," Ollie had said.

They were both at a party one of her artist friends had thrown, impromptu. The location had been chosen at the last minute, keeping the invitees guessing until a few hours before the start. The large derelict warehouse had been kitted up with DJ equipment; laser lights played around a monumental piece of art built out of recycled objects. Cora had hesitated. In her view it was old stuff and idea recycling. But Ollie had thought it might be fun. They had arrived shortly after midnight as the party was just starting.

The ripe smell of joints of various strengths and origins filled the air. Cora giggled... No need to buy any... You could just inhale. Ollie took a deep breath and laughed.

They grabbed two glasses of something sparkling and started looking for people they knew. Sure enough, a few art critics had turned up, some people in showbiz, actors of various calibres. It would have been a fine evening until a short, fat man who looked in his late 50s opened up a pill box full of various coloured capsules.

"Happiness in a gulp," he kept saying to the young girls and boys that had gathered around him. Cora turned away from him, intent on ignoring such a crass way of attracting attention or perhaps worse. But Ollie looked transfixed in horror.

"What is it?" She tugged at his shirt.

"Nothing... It's just... Bad stuff..." Despite the changes in light created by the laser-beam effects, Cora could see that his face had turned pale.

He looked away suddenly, twisting his head as if looking for air. "It's just too hot in here. Let's get out." He didn't wait for her response and walked towards the exit, barely noticing when he bumped into people.

*What was all that about?* She was not annoyed, more puzzled. Once home Ollie had told her his story... The escalation from a little weed... Then a little coke... to stay alert during his exams... The known risk of combination drugs supposed to help during his PhD and then the inevitable… dependency.

It had crept up on him without his noticing. He had convinced himself he could stop anytime… until he couldn't.

"Didn't your parents notice?"

"Too busy with their own business."

"How did you get clean?"

"My PhD tutor sent me to rehab." Ollie sat motionless on the sofa of their flat. "He got my parents involved by convincing them to pay for it, although he had advanced the funds to start with."

Cora brought her face next to his, brushing her cheek against his. "And now?"

"I'm clean, Cora. I promise. I've not touched any of that stuff since the US. That was years ago."

Cora rested her head on his shoulder and the weight of it brought him back to life.

"I promise," Ollie repeated, wrapping his arms around her tight.

* * *

"Certainly, Ms Butler." Officer Michael Branning was on a call to the senior pathologist. She was dispatching a SOCO team to Cora's flat and had argued with the London fire brigade that they should be first on site… It was a criminal investigation into whether or not arson had been committed. She insisted her team would go in first.

Branning was given a time slot for the team's arrival of 3pm, 4pm at the latest.

He grumbled when the phone went dead and heaved his heavy body up from the chair. He had been offered lunch by the arty gang, as he liked to call Cora and her mates.

Time for another intake of nicotine, and perhaps a better cup of tea than what that lot had been offering him. All those fancy fragrances did not cut it for him. He just needed a good, strong cuppa of honest builder's tea.

Beth was in the kitchen preparing the dough for some more cookies. He looked at the mix in the bowl with suspicion… The words 'organic' and 'free from' did not inspire much confidence. He told her he was just going downstairs to have a quick cigarette. She nodded and returned to her baking.

Branning lumbered down the flight of stairs. He tied his old woollen scarf around his neck – the only concession he made to acknowledging it was cold outside. He stepped onto the pavement outside the main door, lit a cigarette and inhaled deeply. It took a few more drags to do the trick but it eventually hit a home run. His neck relaxed. His shoulders dropped a fraction.

DS Branning looked up towards the flat and looked around for signs that might cause him to drop his plan. There was no one else around, and the cars parked in the small courtyard in front of the building had been there since he arrived. A police patrol car had driven around twice already that morning to show a police presence in the area, and an unmarked police vehicle would be taking up position within the hour.

He was almost finished with his fag. He moved swiftly towards the main road, crossed diagonally, and entered the small café he had spotted on his previous nicotine run.

And there it was… He could tell from the colour of the liquid in the mug that a large man in overalls was holding, sitting near the window.

A proper cup of English brew.

The woman at the counter eyed him with suspicion, then gave him a large smile. The broad cockney accent and the request for a cuppa and a sausage roll seemed to have convinced her that Michael Branning was an OK guy.

He dipped his lips into the burning liquid and smiled, perfect. Branning took a bite of his sausage roll. It was now pure heaven.

In the distance a large van had turned into the courtyard he had just left and parked in front of the building that was still cordoned off and sealed. He looked at his watch. They were early. He grabbed his tea and made his way across the road as quickly as he could.

Three people got out of the van and started kitting up in full PPE. "You were quick."

"No time to lose, mate." The tall man was zipping up his white protective suit and adjusting the hood over his head.

"Which lab are you from?" Branning stood a few paces away, relaxed, removing the lid of the cup in his hand.

"Yvonne Butler's lab." The sound of the man's voice was muffled by the mask he had now fitted to his face.

Branning nodded again. He looked at the other two men who had also completed their preparations. They lifted the yellow-and-black hazard tape. Two of them carried their SOCO kit inside the building and disappeared.

The tall man who had spoken to him lingered a little longer. He locked the van, and made his way to the first floor of the ravaged building.

Branning strolled through the other entrance to the building, climbing the steps quickly. He walked past the door of the arty gang's flat, straight to the back door that opened onto the old fire exit.

His mobile rang, a number he did not recognise.

"DS Branning, Nancy Wu speaking... I hope I am not interrupting."

He grumbled a no.

"Excellent... I wanted to check on Cora."

"She is having a rest."

"Good... Anything else?"

Branning almost asked why he should give her any more information but then recalled being told she was a consultant with the Met. Perhaps a little diplomacy would not go amiss.

"The SOCO team has arrived."

"Is that Yvonne Butler's team?"

"It is, ma'am."

"Splendid... Do you mind if I pop in to ask a few questions?"

Branning didn't mind as long as they didn't prejudice the integrity of the evidence.

Nancy assured him she understood the rules rather well. She was jumping in a cab and would arrive in less than 15 minutes.

DS Branning was waiting for her next to the van that had brought the SOCO team. They had not reappeared since he last saw them, then again he *had* nipped into the arty gang flat to check on Cora. "They started half an hour ago," Branning said by way of introduction.

"And still no evidence bag?"

"Not that I have seen."

"They probably came down without you noticing."

Branning squinted but did not reply. Nancy breached the new entry tape and turned back. "Are you coming?"

She walked into the property without waiting for his answer.

There was little noise coming from Cora's flat. The place sounded almost deserted apart from the soft sound of objects being moved around. Nancy stopped. Branning caught up with her. "What?"

She put a finger to her lips to stop him talking. They walked together towards the entrance.

The door had been shut. Nancy pushed against it and it opened. She ventured a quick glance. Branning shook his head. He was the one who should have gone in first.

They both stood in the entrance. There was no one in their field of vision. They moved further forward.

Furniture had been moved. A set of solid planks had been laid across a part of the floor that was threatening to collapse. One of the men was standing near the floor-to-ceiling windows and the other two had reached the far end of the room. Their face masks had been dropped around their chins and their gloves were black from the soot on the furniture they had touched.

The man at the far end seemed to be systematically going through the props for Cora's installation.

Nancy took one step forward, her eyes falling on the box that lay open. Its contents did not belong to the standard SOCO team equipment. Despite her caution Nancy trod on a piece of broken pottery. One of the men turned around. What he held in his hand had the glimmer of a gun.

* * *

The plane had been in the air for about 30 minutes. The ride was a little bumpy, but Jack didn't mind. He had chosen to purchase a first-class ticket, less out of a need for comfort but rather to ensure privacy. He had asked one of his analysts to gather as much information as she could about a subject that sounded more like sci-fi than a medical school study topic… Bioinformatics.

A number of emails had dropped into his inbox just as the steward had asked him to log off and shut the laptop down. Jack had indulged in accepting the snack offered by American Airlines... An excellent smoked salmon and cream cheese bagel and a cup of freshly brewed coffee.

He resisted the temptation to say yes when the tray of freshly baked muffins came through, poking with a finger at a waistline that had suddenly started to expand more than it should. He was going to London, and intended to taste the variety of culinary delights he knew he would find there... He was off on holiday.

Laurie had done an excellent job in the short time she had been allocated to gather the information Jack needed. Jack rested the coffee cup that had just been refreshed on the wide armrest of his seat. He opened the first email and started reading.

Bioinformatics was an interdisciplinary field that developed software tools to capture and manipulate biological data. It combined biology, computer science, information engineering, mathematics and statistics, in order to analyse large and complex quantities of data.

Jack sat back in his seat to ponder the information he had just received. He could understand why certain fields of biology, which had increased in complexity and relied on large volumes of data, might require computer science. The era of big data was reaching biology. The ability to treat a vast amount of information was now being used in that field. He was, however, amazed to read that computer science had reached the field as early as the 1950s. His face brightened up at the prospect of discovering a field he knew little about. He waved at the stewardess. "If you have a blueberry muffin left..."

She smiled the requisite "anything for a first-class passenger" smile and returned a few seconds later with the forbidden item.

The papers Laurie had unearthed were of good research quality, not dumbed down yet clearly presented. Jack created a new document to capture his notes. He thought it might be important to remember why bioinformatics was used in genetics to process information about genomes and observed mutations, and that it aided in simulating or modelling DNA.

The red light flashing on the panel above his head indicated that passengers were to return to their seats. The captain's voice came on the intercom to announce a period of turbulence. Jack's cup was empty, the blueberry muffin gone. And other passengers across the aisle had returned to their seats in a hurry from the WC, fastening their seat belts nervously.

Jack smiled amused and yet mellow at the pang of anxiety that the captain's message had produced. His fellow passengers had no idea what *turbulence* really means.

*He has just finished his training and his first mission has begun. Iraq's war is going well for the USA. The might of the American army has no rival on the ground, nor in the air… They are pounding the Iraqi forces relentlessly… Operation Shock and Awe.*

*Jack sits in the C-5 Super Galaxy aircraft that the US Air Force uses to transport its troops, munitions, and other essential logistical supplies. He has strapped himself in so tightly he can hardly breathe. The US marine master chief on the mission smiles at him with his usual amused yet good-natured smile.*

*"Your first trip to a war zone, son?"*

*"Yes, sir, it is."*

*Master Chief Hayes sits down next to Jack. The bulk of his upper body lands with a small thud against the metal frame of the aircraft.*

*"Are you joining the search for more WMD?" Hayes removes his US marine utility cap, slaps it against his thigh and folds it into a neat roll.*

*"Yes, sir, I'll be looking for weapons of mass destruction with the CIA team already on the ground."*

*"What's your gut feeling on that?" Hayes has now crossed his muscular arms over his chest. Jack notices a tattoo peeking out of his rolled-up sleeve. He doesn't know how to answer about what has become a controversial subject.*

*"Don't worry… I'm not interested in the official version. I'm just wanting to know what you think?"*

*"I haven't yet formed a clear opinion." Jack speaks slowly and Hayes drills into him. His eyes lock into Jack's. He's just told him he is not interested in official, and certainly not BS from a junior CIA agent.*

*Jack clears his throat. "I'm not convinced we're gonna find anything." There, he's said it. Jack feels his cheeks colour a little and hopes Master Hayes has not noticed.*

*Hayes drops his chin on his chest. His lower lip covers his upper, twitching slightly.*

*"Thanks for being honest," he finally says. "Although you know that it's not going to do you any good if you are too honest too often."*

*Jack nods. He knows. His CIA instructors have told him there will be plenty of occasions when he will need to be economical with the truth. He feels today is not one of them.*

*"For what it's worth…" Hayes is setting up his Invicta watch to local Iraqi time, ready for arrival when they land. "…neither am I."*

*Jack frowns. "You don't think they will find anything either?"*

*"Nope… We would have done already if there were any, and Saddam would not have held back from throwing the lot at us if he had the means of defeating the US."*

*"Even if it meant killing some of his own people in the process." Jack is not disagreeing but simply completing the picture.*

*Hayes settles back into his seat and closes his eyes. Jack is still waiting for an answer. Has the conversation stopped abruptly, or is Hayes waiting for Jack to say more?*

*"If you don't have anything valuable to say, don't fill the conversation with irrelevant crap." Master Hayes has not opened his eyes. Jack settles back into his seat and loosens his seat belt.*

*He would like to thank Hayes for the advice but it would be a piece of irrelevant crap.*

The plane dropped into an air pocket and the frame of the American Airlines aircraft shuddered. Jack glanced at his neighbour, eyes closed, shoulders to his ears and hands clasped white on his armrests. Jack shook his head…

Old memories of his first mission always greeted him whenever he departed from the usual routine of his job.

Perhaps this time it was also reminding him of how he had met Harris in Iraq. Neither he nor Steve had ever spoken again about the mission in 2003. There was no need for them to revisit a moment in their lives that would be engraved in their minds forever… The fall of Baghdad.

The captain's voice came back on the intercom. Half an hour to Boston Logan airport. Jack resumed his reading. He had finished the first paper and made some further notes.

This time it was the capability bioinformatics had to study how a normal cell might be altered by disease, and the mapping of the different stages in its progression, that attracted Jack's attention. Everything Jack had read so far indicated that bioinformatics would be a game-changing tool for a lab that was devoting their work to the discovery of new medications, whether these drugs were part of the fight against new viruses or old microbes.

Ollie Wilson would be in high demand. A newly formed high-tech company that entered the fray and wanted to make its mark would not hesitate to place Ollie at the centre of its research team, granting him full access to the high-profile projects the company was working on.

Ollie Wilson was right to want to dig deeper into what his company was up too… he had access to information that was worth more than a second look.

# Chapter Nine

"Where are you?" Harris's voice sounded more inquisitive than annoyed.

"Be with you shortly." Pole had parked his bike near Liverpool Street station and was finishing the journey on foot. He would not bring his brand-new Ducati to Whitechapel. It would attract unwanted attention and Pole did not need that whilst meeting with Harris.

He finally turned into the small alleyway Harris had indicated in a text. It had the requisite qualities of seediness ... Garbage strewn on the floor in various states of decomposition, discarded objects lying against the walls of the buildings or simply abandoned in the gutter. Harris certainly knew how to choose his venues to create the right ambience. "Hey... I like the biker look." Harris grinned, stepping out from the doorway in which he had been sheltering. The wind blew his untidy hair as he walked towards Pole.

"Appropriate to the area," Pole grunted.

"Except that you left your bike somewhere else... Very wise. I nearly had to headbutt a couple of little punks who noticed I was waiting for someone."

Pole gave him a look.

"I know... the old shabby leather jacket ain't worth any trouble... They probably thought I had some drugs on me," Harris said.

"Do you really meet your operatives in these crappy streets?"

Pole reached Harris. He was almost a full head taller and yet he wondered whether he could overpower him in a fight. There was something alert and unyielding about Harris that Pole had learned to be wary of. Pole could imagine that a disagreement with Harris could be settled by blows.

"We could have met at the Savoy but I'm not sure that would be as discreet as you might want it to be... Marsh goes there quite often."

"You've heard about the latest in the Ferguson inquiry?"

"Yep..." Harris took out a packet of chewing gum and popped a couple of tablets into his mouth. He started chewing. "Marsh won't get anything from MI6 and neither will Ferguson, I can guarantee that."

"I'm mildly reassured."

"But..." Harris kept chewing for a short moment, the muscles of his jaw working overtime on the piece of gum. "It will all depend on how careful you have been... Inspector Pole."

"What the hell do you mean?"

"Did anybody in your team notice anything? Was the delay in calling Ferguson when you had some data justified? Those sorts of questions."

Pole clenched his fists, but Harris was right. Was he now assessing whether he should throw Pole to the wolves if push came to shove?

"Don't worry, Inspector... I'm only telling you this because I find working with you pretty good on the whole. You deliver when I need it the most, and you don't mind taking risks without overdoing it."

"Now that makes me really anxious, Harris." Pole ran his eyes over the other man's face. "When was the last time you paid a compliment to one of your..." Pole hesitated for a moment. The word source stuck in his throat, and he would certainly never be one of Harris's operatives, whereas an informant... If Harris spoke the word Pole would most certainly whack him one.

"...contacts?" Harris suggested, pursing his lips in amusement. "When I need something from them, of course..."

"The Ollie Wilson case." Pole heard a noise coming from the top of the alley. He half turned to see what had caused it. Four youths had appeared at the corner of the main road and the small lane. They stopped for a moment, talking amongst themselves.

"Fuck." Harris frowned. "The little shits have come back with some friends."

Pole moved to face the small crowd head on. Their hoods were up. Two of them had their hands wedged in their trouser pockets, shoulders hunched forward. Pole assessed the alleyway quickly.

Derelict houses, squats, most of them occupied or boarded up. The top of the lane seemed slightly more promising. Still, there was little hope of getting the inhabitants to open their doors to strangers being chased by a group of angry youths.

"Where does that lead?" Pole jerked his head towards the top of the alley.

"One of the estates. You don't want to get lost in there… I can tell you." Harris had moved alongside Pole.

"This is the moment I perhaps wish I had a gun."

"Nah, if cops had guns, these guys would have more and better ones. The only thing I can see between them at the moment is a cricket bat and a lot of attitude."

Pole straightened up. Harris was right. The smallest of the group was holding something close to his leg. It rested on the ground and was half hidden by the baggy trousers he was wearing.

"So much for discretion." Pole muttered. It would be a little tricky to explain a black eye and broken ribs to Marsh.

Harris stepped back a little and looked around, getting his bearings. "When I tell you to run, just do as I say."

"Why?" Pole was deciding whether to use his bike helmet as a weapon or put it on for protection.

"Pole, just be a champ… and do as I say." Harris was not joking.

His focus was real. It galvanised Pole.

"Now…" Harris turned around and started to sprint towards the top of the lane, away from the gang. It took Pole only a fraction of a second to follow.

The shrieks that came from the far end of the alley told Pole that four young men had moved as one. The pounding of their feet on the ground reverberated between the walls of the shabby houses.

Harris almost reached the top of the street and came to an abrupt stop in front of one of the doors, the colour of which had disappeared under layers of grime and graffiti. He pushed the door handle and to Pole's amazement it opened.

They both dashed through it, slamming it shut and drawing the solid bolts across. Harris ran along the narrow corridor. Wallpaper had been pulled off the walls, some of it still littered on the ground. Pole hesitated. The force of the blows against the door and loud yells made him follow as quickly as he could.

He ran and found Harris going through another door at the back of the house. It led to a small yard. Harris walked over to the low wall that separated it from another street.

Pole could hear the slams against the front door; it would not hold for much longer. Harris climbed onto the wall that led to the street. He disappeared with one jump down the other side.

Pole followed. From a distance, he heard the front door break open and the thunder of feet and screams of anger engulfing the house they had just left. Harris was waiting for him on the other side of the wall. Pole jumped without hesitation. Harris was already moving ahead. He took a set of keys out of his jacket pocket and activated the release button.

A small beep indicated a car had just opened. Pole delved into the car and Harris drove off as soon as Pole closed the door, untroubled by what had just occurred.

"Did you know it would happen?" Pole had settled his helmet on his thigh, amazed he had not dropped it during the chase.

"Always a possibility in this neck of the woods…"

"Did you know the door would open?"

Harris smiled, looking straight at the road. He tapped his index finger a few times on the side of his nose. "I ain't gonna be defeated by the little gits that live in these parts… though to be fair I also feel sorry for them."

"Why… because they haven't been able to beat the hell out of us?"

"Nope… I could have been one of them." Harris was not being flippant. He stopped the car at the next set of traffic lights and turned towards Pole. "But not your concern… I'm impressed, Inspector Pole. You can get a move on when you have to."

"What do you take me for?" Pole rolled his eyes. "I'm with the Met and that means dealing with unsavoury characters just as much as you do."

"Not saying otherwise… still…" Harris drove through a few streets that Pole did not recognise to finally end up in Brick Lane. He relaxed a little now he knew where he was.

"Coming back to our conversation." Harris parked the car in front of an old sari shop. "Ollie Wilson has become of interest to me."

"Good." Pole half turned his tall body towards Harris. "And I need a lot more information about a certain Chinese artist we once discussed."

"I have given you a lot already." Harris frowned.

"What is it you said, Harris? You scratch my back and I'll scratch yours. I have a very sore itch that requires attention. I'm sure you can do a lot better than what you've delivered on Nancy Wu's father so far."

\* \* \*

DS Branning slowly placed his large hand on Nancy's shoulder, moving her gently out of the way.

He stepped in front of her and in front of the gun that was pointed at them.

The other two men had stopped rummaging through the props that Cora had stored in the studio part of the loft.

Nancy moved her head slightly to the side to measure the distance to the only exit route. She and Branning were not very far from the front door of the flat. She could certainly reach it but she doubted the police officer could.

The man with the gun was considering the options it seemed. He could gun them down now, but this would alert the other police officers guarding the entrance from the unmarked car he must have spotted when he and his mates drove in in their SOCO car.

On that basis, Nancy was making an educated guess he didn't want to shoot them. Then again, it would take a few minutes for reinforcements to arrive, and the only thing they would see was a van and its SOCO team.

Branning was not moving, and his calm manner seemed to have defused the situation. The man with the gun gestured with it a few times.

"Hands over your heads… kneel down, both of you." The accent was foreign, but Nancy could not quite distinguish its origin.

Branning raised his hands in slow motion and started to kneel down. Nancy followed. She cast her eyes around for something she could use as a weapon.

Ridiculous, of course... but she was not going to give up without a fight.

As she knelt, she noticed the proximity of the low kitchen wall that served as a breakfast bar. Before her knees touched the ground, she shuffled closer to it. Branning's eyes quickly slid towards her. She hoped he had noticed her movement.

The two men put down the props they were holding and made their way swiftly across the wooden planks. The charred wooden floor had started to cave in and the groaning of the broken wood under their weight made them hurry. The exit route led them dangerously close to where DS Branning was kneeling.

They edged their way past him, ready for a fight. The man with the gun had started to move too, picking his way carefully through the rubble.

Branning had not moved. His heavy body looked more like a sack dumped there to collect the rubbish than a threat to life. The two men had now disappeared. No doubt readying their van for a speedy departure... it would now take only a few seconds for Branning and Nancy to be gunned down. The gunman would make his exit swiftly and, as soon as he had entered the van, one of the other thugs would floor the accelerator before the police car could chase after them.

The gunman's phone rang. He nodded and raised his gun.

Nancy felt her stomach clench. She was about to die. It was ironic she had survived a similar assault so many years ago and yet.

*The man is laughing. His machine gun held against his side. His army boots only inches away from her knees. She can't see his face, but she can smell the stale odour of sweat and greasy food on his skin. She's kneeling next to her father, in the middle of the road. The doors of the old truck they have been driving in are wide open.*

*She doesn't know where her mother is.*

*Her father is speaking very fast, in a language she doesn't understand. She doesn't know whether it is the words she can't comprehend or whether it is a foreign language she doesn't know. But she knows he's pleading with the man who is still laughing.*

*She isn't scared, though she should be. Her father is still with her and he always makes things better.*

*Until a scream comes from the back of the van.*

*Her heart starts beating faster and faster. Someone is struggling back there. She can hear the thrashing of a body against the metal frame of the truck. She doesn't want to recognise the voice. She tries not to recognise the voice of her mother. Her father lunges at the laughing man. They are on the ground fighting for the gun. The screams have reached a higher pitch. She runs to the back of the pickup and all she can see is a man bending over a body and a pair of legs thrashing uncontrollably.*

*She looks around, picks up a rock that lays on the dirt track with both hands and strikes once, twice... so many times she can't recall... until her hands have turned red, and the screaming has stopped.*

The sound of two bodies colliding shook Nancy. She wasn't sure whether it was a memory or reality.

The speed of the rugby tackle had been vicious. DS Branning's lunge startled the gunman. The gun discharged when both men rolled onto the floor. The bullet shattered a piece of wood into splinters.

Nancy winced, diving behind the kitchen counter. The two men were struggling, thrashing about on the floor. A deafening noise reverberated around the room... another gun discharge.

Nancy stood up, seized one of the high stools from behind the breakfast counter and brought it down over the back of the gunman. He arched his back, groaning in pain. Branning threw a punch in his face. The man rolled onto his side towards the centre of the room.

Nancy stepped forward, raised the chair once more and hit him with all her might. The crack in the floor had widened with the screaming noise of wood being torn apart. She raised the stool once more.

"Stop." DS Branning was half standing. "Stop..." His hand stretched towards her.

92

Nancy dropped her weapon as though it had shocked her. The sound of crashing wood propelled Branning forward with just enough time to drag Nancy out of the room. The entire floor collapsed as the two looked on, staggered.

* * *

"When?" Pole had just adjusted his helmet and connected his mobile device to his earpiece.

Branning sounded shaken. It had been a near miss, but they were both unharmed, apart from a few scratches.

The Ducati sprang to life under Pole's angry foot. The bike lurched forward. He avoided with a swerve a couple of absentminded men crossing the road, as though they owned it. They shouted at him, but he was already banking right to turn into the main road.

He sounded his horn as he sped towards a pedestrian crossing. The traffic lights were on his side and 10 minutes later Inspector Pole parked his bike next to the police van that was blocking the entrance of Cora's building.

He flashed his ID card at the PC standing guard outside the building and ran to the ambulance parked at the side. DS Branning was holding a pack of ice against his swollen cheek. His jacket was torn, and blood had dripped over his shirt.

"She's safe," he mumbled. He made a quick move of the head in the direction of the entrance.

Nancy was sitting on the stairs of the building, wrapped in a blanket. She must have heard the two men talking. She lifted her face, swaying as she stood up.

Pole strode towards her, dropped his helmet to the ground and then wrapped his arms around her. "Are you hurt?"

"*Rien du tout...* Just a few bruises." She let her forehead drop against his chest.

Pole placed a kiss on the top of her head. Her hair smelt of Issey Miyake perfume and burnt wood. He gave a nervous laugh that caught in his throat.

"What on earth happened?"

Nancy clutched the leather of his jacket to draw him closer. She was not ready to talk just yet. Pole moved his hand around on her back a few times to keep her warm. He was in no hurry.

"*Desolée*..." Nancy pulled back a little.

"What for?" Pole loosened his embrace and gave her a kind smile.

"These people are your colleagues and I'm adviser to the Met..."

"You should know by now that it takes a lot more than that to embarrass me. I was not brought up in the stiff-upper-lip camp, remember... my family are a bunch of artists who wear their hearts on their sleeves all the time."

She let go of his jacket and ran her hands over her face. "I almost killed him... If DS Branning had not stopped me..." She started to cry. "...I would have finished him off."

* * *

The taxi dropped Jack in front of an impressive building in the centre of Boston. Large steps lead up to a series of white columns in ancient Greek ionic style. They, in turn, supported a massive granite portico. Jack climbed the flight of stairs quickly, reached a wide wooden door and pushed... The Harvard Medical School looked as impressive as its reputation merited.

Jack entered a spacious hallway decorated with old and new portraits of the pioneers of medical science. The receptionist, a young man in a dark jumper, welcomed him and informed him that Professor Park, the director of the BIG programme, was ready to receive him. Jack apologised. He was a little early.

The young man stood up and accompanied him to the lifts at the back of the entrance hall. He flashed his ID card over an electronic eye and pressed floor six. Professor Park was waiting for him as he alighted, the tall Asian man sporting an intelligent smile and the expected narrow-rimmed glasses.

They shook hands and Professor Park led the way. "Let's get settled in my office."

They exchanged a few casual words about Jack's journey, the cold weather and the Boston Red Sox scores.

Jack settled himself onto a small sofa that occupied one of the corners of Professor Park's office. He accepted a cup of coffee.

"So, it's bioinformatics that brings you here?" Professor Park sat down in the armchair across from Jack. He was drinking his coffee in small sips, cautiously and methodically.

Jack could not help but be impressed. The man must be in his mid-30s, without question much younger than Jack, and yet was running one of the most forward-looking programmes in Harvard's medical school.

"That's right... or more precisely one of your former students in bioinformatics... Ollie Wilson."

Jack had introduced himself as a member of the CIA. This was as much as he was prepared to disclose. It was not difficult to convince Professor Park that the agency was interested in the field and looking for an above average candidate from one of its programmes to perhaps join their ranks.

"Ollie Wilson was by far one of our most promising students... an unusual blend of creativity and scientific precision. I am not surprised he chose to apply his mind to virology and immunology."

Jack cocked his head. He had read the exhaustive summary that Laurie had compiled for him, but the topic of virology had not come up. "How so?"

"Applying bioinformatics to understanding viruses and their behaviours is critical to the development of drugs going forward. There is so much information to process when a new virus emerges, hypotheses about its mutations, its origin... it's a perfect application for bioinformatics, and Ollie was our first student to realise the potential." Jack leaned back into the sofa cushions and let Professor Park expand on the subject. He was without doubt thrilled about his student's project himself, willing to explain in detail why it was so significant.

"So, you think international labs would fight to employ Ollie?" Jack asked.

For the first time, Jack sensed slight reservation.

"He has a brilliant brain."

"But..." Jack placed his empty cup on the table at the side of his seat and waited.

Professor Park leaned forward, elbows on knees, hands clasped loosely together. "Look... I think it's a very personal matter to employ someone."

"Professor Park, whatever it is that makes you cautious... I will easily find out elsewhere."

The other man's lips twitched a little. "I guess so..." He exhaled slowly. "Ollie had a problem with addiction."

Jack frowned.

"Drugs..." Professor Park cleared his throat. "I know... because it was I who sent him to rehab."

# Chapter Ten

"Has everybody gone?" Cora closed Beth's bedroom door and came over to sit next to Johnny on the old sofa. He laid his laptop on the coffee table, stretched an arm towards her and smiled.

"C'mon da'ling... come and sit next to Uncle Johnny." Cora curled up into a tight ball against her friend's lean body. "They've all gone down to check on something..."

"That's a little vague," she murmured, but she didn't mind. She was desperate to rest her brain, to take a step back and make sense of the past 24 hours.

"He really loves you a lot you know..." Johnny stroked Cora's hair, flattening the spikes... She had not given a thought to gel this morning.

Cora was no longer sure she did know. "That doesn't sound very convincing." She buried her head in the sofa cushions.

"Sorry... I shouldn't be prodding. It's all been very rough." Johnny dropped his forehead against her back and they remained like that for a moment until they heard the sound of the door to the flat opening and voices coming through.

"I'll fix you a cup of tea." Beth sounded concerned.

Cora turned away from Johnny to see who was being invited.

"That would be very kind." Cora recognised Nancy's voice and jumped up from the couch, dashing to the hallway. Pole was there too. She heard him chatting to Beth.

Nancy was a sight. Her jacket was stained with blood. Her hair had been roughly pinned back and her face bore a number of fresh cuts.

"Someone tried to enter your flat again."

"I'm so sorry, Nancy. I should never have got you involved." Cora bit her lips to stop them from trembling.

"Nonsense... I've been through much worse."

As she entered the lounge, Johnny leaped up and threw his arms in the air. "Nancy... how wonderful." His arms stayed up for a moment, not certain whether they should embrace her or simply come down.

"Oh..." He just said when he spotted the blood on her jacket. He moved to one of the sofas that created an L-shape with the one he had just vacated and invited Nancy to take the more comfortable seat.

"How kind." Nancy walked over to the couch and lowered herself gingerly as though she needed to lessen the impact.

"Who were they?"

"We don't know yet... the floor collapsed underneath one of them." Nancy stopped. There was no need to let Cora have all the details of the fight.

"Did they find what they were looking for?" Cora asked.

"I don't think so... we disturbed them too early in their search," Nancy replied.

Cora sank back into the settee.

Pole had appeared with two mugs of tea whilst Charlie carried three more in both hands. The two men offered the drinks around and took a seat.

Johnny raised a quizzical eyebrow. "Jonathan Pole... Very nice to meet you." Pole extended a hand to Johnny, who hesitated, then stepped forward to shake it. "Likewise."

"Why would they come back after setting fire to the place?" Cora had already drunk half her cup of tea.

"Perhaps fresh information came their way and they decided they needed to take a second look," Nancy said.

"Did you see them arrive?" Pole asked.

"No... we haven't left the house yet." Johnny pursed his lips as he took a sip of tea, not to Beth's usual standard. "And Nat left quickly too," Beth added. She moved as quickly as she could towards Johnny, knowing what would come next... but too late.

Johnny knelt on the carpet to reach the large biscuit tin that lived permanently on the coffee table. He opened it and offered the contents round to the circle of friends. Beth's face froze, but Johnny thought nothing of it. Pole hesitated but said no.

"Something might come back to you later. If it does, give me a call." Pole finished his cup of tea, fishing something out from his jacket pocket.

Nancy bent forward to put her cup on the table and winced. "You need something to ease the pain." Johnny looked concerned. "I've got just what you need." He stood up and moved swiftly towards a long piece of furniture that decorated the far end of the lounge.

Cora opened her eyes wide and was about to make a comment. "I don't think that's a good idea." Pole managed a grin. He laid a couple of police business cards on the table. "If what I smell in the air is what is lurking in one of those drawers... I don't really want to know."

Nancy chuckled and winced again.

Johnny stopped dead, spun on his heels and cocked his head. "Just as well you didn't take a biscuit then... the stuff in the cupboard makes a very good flavouring ingredient."

* * *

Pole had given Nancy a lift back to her apartment.

"The one issue that is bothering me more than the identity of the people themselves is the timing." She had changed to a more casual winter shirt and black jeans.

"Agreed." Pole tossed his phone on the bed. He was surveying her with concern. Her face had recovered some of its spark but a small crease at the corner of her mouth told him pain was troubling her significantly.

"How is Ollie?" She sat next to him on the bed adjusting her shirt gingerly around her waist.

"The hospital is telling me there is no change. Police surveillance has been reinforced."

"Do you buy the drug connection?"

"I'm not sure. Rob at the NCA has not made any progress either. Andy and my team are looking into it."

"To be that serious it would have to be something to do with trafficking... a reprisal of some kind."

Pole nodded. He glanced at his watch quickly. He had a little more time to spare but soon would have to make a move. He had not yet spoken to her about the Ferguson inquiry.

Ferguson was due to visit Pole at Scotland Yard the following day, a meeting he was not looking forward to.

"Won't you talk to me?" Pole said.

"I am talking to you." Nancy tried to smile.

Pole cocked his head.

Nancy flopped back onto the bed and yelped. "Goddamn shoulder." Pole waited patiently.

Nancy turned her head towards him. "I have to think about what I just remembered... it's... terrifying."

"I can't imagine you escaping China's Cultural Revolution reprisals without having gone through some terrifying moments... you were only seven years old."

"I know and yet, the mix of helplessness and anger at myself is almost overwhelming."

Pole's mobile rang. "Andy... wait... I'll put you on speaker. Nancy is here with me."

"Good afternoon, ma'am."

"Good afternoon, Andy... I thought we had agreed you could call me Nancy."

Andy cleared his throat to hide his shyness.

"So, what have you got?" Pole asked.

"The SOCO team... I mean the real SOCO team was delayed because someone on a motorbike slid in front of their van. He wasn't hurt and legged it, but it took a good hour to get the van back on the road."

"Stolen bike, I presume."

"Correct." Andy rolled the rs with satisfaction.

"Do we know how they found out who we were using as SOCOs? They would have had to know it was Yvonne Butler's team that had been appointed."

"I thought about that, Guv... and it's not all that difficult."

"Really?"

"You're the DCI on the case and you almost always request Yvonne's... I mean Ms Butler's lab when the cases are complex. There

100

are two other labs that the Met works with on high-profile cases. If I wanted to know which one was going to Ollie Wilson's flat, I'd get the van of each lab followed when they came out and see whether they were going towards the target location. If they were... Bob's your uncle, I create an incident that slows them down without arousing too much suspicion."

"And I get a van that looks similar to wait near Hoxton Docks, ready," Nancy added.

"Exactly."

"Damn... are you telling me I'm too predictable?" Pole grumbled.

"Never... you simply like working with the best."

"Maybe... how about CCTV cameras?"

"On it... I've called the London Underground control centre and have been granted access to the CCTV cameras of all underground stations in the vicinity of the flat. One of the men disappeared into Holborn underground station. I've tracked him going south. He changed at Green Park, then Stockwell... But I lost him when he left the tube at Balham."

"But you are still going through the footage from the other over-ground cameras?"

Andy confirmed. "Although I'm less hopeful. There are quite a few blind spots near that particular tube station."

"And whoever is employing the man knows that."

"Or else he is a pro, working on his own but knowing his business very well when it comes to avoiding detection," Nancy wondered.

Pole thanked him and was about to hang up.

"Guv... before you go, Superintendent Marsh wants to talk to you again. He also mentioned Commander Ferguson."

Nancy raised an eyebrow and Pole cursed inwardly. So much for keeping the informal investigation away from Nancy.

* * *

The Delta flight from Boston landed at JFK on time. It gave Jack enough time to disembark and switch comfortably to the international terminal at JFK. As the holder of a business-class ticket, BA had given him the choice of having dinner in the lounge before departure, but he preferred to eat on the flight. As soon as he arrived on the plane, he settled into the seat that would soon be turned into a bed. He placed his order for dinner, indulged in a glass of champagne that he found rather good and stocked up with a couple of water bottles for the rest of the flight.

Professor Park had been generous, giving Jack a couple of books on the subject of bioinformatics and virology.

Jack yawned, more out of contentment than tiredness. He would read for another hour whilst he was having his dinner. This would leave him five hours' sleep before touchdown. Perhaps a little short but nothing he was not accustomed to.

He had pondered how Ollie had managed to find himself at the centre of what now appeared to be a large storm that was gathering fast. There was no doubt in Jack's mind that the biotech sector was a highly profitable and sensitive business. Some of the new products developed earned billions but also gave a company power when it came to the health of an entire population. If Ollie had discovered some form of fraud or worse, this could still cost him his life. And yet, Station Chief Jethro had not called him back.

No news might still be good news in this case. Or perhaps the Chief had decided the case was not worth his time or that of his people… just another junkie biting the dust.

The glass of champagne was almost empty. Jack shook his head. He had his sights on his goal, and this meant being clear headed when he landed at Heathrow airport. He took another sip, saving the last gulp for a little later.

Ollie's choice of job… a small, yet cutting-edge biotech company now made good sense. Jack remembered what he had read about Viro-Tech Therapeutics on the way to Boston.

Viro-Tech stood out as a leading young company, dedicating its research to the development of anti-viral therapies with a focus on respiratory tract illnesses that ultimately caused death in the most vulnerable. Its team of researchers was small yet highly qualified, and its pipeline of new drugs looked promising, with some already reaching advanced development phases.

A large pharmaceutical or biotech company might have carried out numerous background checks on Ollie. They would almost certainly have asked about drug abuse or drug dependency. A smaller firm, on the other hand, might not have enquired so closely, keen to snap up a talent like Ollie.

Jack reached forward for the book he had laid face down at the bottom of his extended seat. He caught a glimpse of the sky... Clear, stars shining unobstructed by pollution or clouds. The 747 had finished its ascent and reached its cruising altitude. This felt strangely comforting to Jack.

He was now out of reach of anyone for the next six hours. He spent a short time gazing at the view... trying to spot a constellation he might recognise. He gave up, and simply enjoyed a moment of relaxation.

The aircraft purser, a jovial-looking man, came along to check he was enjoying the flight so far. He also wanted to ensure Jack had been offered a choice of wine, mentioning the opportunity to taste a particularly good burgundy to accompany the excellent lamb they were serving. Jack could not help smiling. He could see why such attention and indulgence would be difficult for any businessman to resist.

Jack opened again the book he'd started reading. It made a compelling case for greater interaction between bioinformatics, immunology and virology. Whereas virology involved the study of viruses and their disease-producing properties, immunology dealt with the way in which the human immune system responded to infections through various lines of defence.

Professor Park had added to the books he gave Jack a couple of research papers Ollie Wilson had written whilst finishing his PhD.

One dealt with the issue of antibiotic-resistant microbes. In the research abstract and introduction, Ollie was critical of the lax attitude governments, as well as large pharmaceutical companies and food producers, had shown to the increase in antibiotic resistance.

The trend was in his view alarming... great enough to threaten the future of humanity. More and more bacteria that had once successfully been defeated by simple penicillin had developed resistance to second- and third-generation antibiotics. MRSA was all too common in hospitals and caused havoc. It was high time the warnings of the World Health Organisation were taken seriously.

The young man did not mince his words and certainly did not spare criticism of anyone in his analysis of the situation. But he also offered solutions, based on the potential bioinformatics had to accelerate ground-breaking discoveries and the development of new drugs.

Although he enjoyed the direct, easy to read and compelling style of Ollie's writing, the light sound of crockery being moved around as well as a rumbling stomach told Jack it was time to concentrate on something less academic.

A smiling stewardess served Jack his food tray and presented him with a choice of appetising bread rolls. The purser reappeared with the promised wine, which he let Jack taste before pouring a full... very full... glass.

Jack replaced the first of Ollie's research papers in the folder Professor Park had given him. He drew out the second paper and started reading. This time the topic dealt with virology. Again, Ollie Wilson did not refrain from asking the hard questions. Animal to human transmission had given rise to large-scale viral epidemics that did not bode well: SARS in 2004 and Ebola in 2014, although thankfully not experienced in America or Europe.

Ollie again made an impassioned plea in his research abstract. It was high time for animal to human transmission to be taken seriously. Human intervention in the food chain, the slaughter of endangered species and the trafficking and slaughtering of wild animals had to stop. Jack dropped the paper on his lap... impressed. Ollie Wilson not only had views. He also had a way of putting them forward that was compelling and perhaps... dangerous.

A shadow loomed over Jack's seat. "Is everything alright, sir?"

The purser's concerned voice surprised Jack a little. He gave him a smile... It was all absolutely fine. Jack had not touched his food and he thanked him for reminding him his meal was getting cold. The starter of lobster on a bed of curly salad and light lemon dressing reminded Jack's taste buds what good food was all about.

104

He attacked the lamb, cooked pink to perfection. The burgundy, an excellent Romanée-Conti, also hit the spot. Still, despite the quality of the food and drink, Jack's mind kept returning to Ollie's papers.

He interrupted his dinner and returned to the last document. In the methods section as well as in the discussion paragraph, Ollie was making a powerful case for the use of bioinformatics to deliver the rapid solutions needed to combat the problems he perceived.

Jack returned to his food and wine. He pushed into the comfortable back of the seat and moved the small pillow around to help his body relax in the large chair. One thing was now certain, Ollie Wilson had a knack for identifying thorny issues and championing proposed solutions. He would be a controversial employee who would not give up easily if he felt he was doing the right thing.

* * *

Pole's attempt to make light of the forthcoming meeting with Commander Ferguson had fallen flat. Nancy let him return to Scotland Yard with a promise he would explain what was happening as soon as he came back, which she hoped would be that evening.

Nancy could not help but smile. She enjoyed raising a quizzical eyebrow at Pole when she knew she was in the right, yet a nascent sense of unease had crept into her mind. She knew Ferguson. She had been involved in the terrorism case alongside Pole and knew the details of it, including the escape of a certain Henry Crowne. There was no reason Pole couldn't mention Ferguson's name to her unless something was amiss.

She stood in her lounge The place was still bearing the marks of Cora's overnight stay and this morning's rush. She started methodically clearing away cups, teapots, plates, rugs and pillows. For a very short moment she remembered an earlier time in which she had welcomed someone else, someone who had propelled her into the world of crime investigation.

Henry Crowne had entered her life unexpectedly and left it without a word. She understood it had to be that way, that he wouldn't be allowed to speak but she still often wished he had told her what he had decided to do to redeem his mistakes.

Nancy inhaled deeply as she loaded the last of the crockery into the dishwasher. Her new role as a Scotland Yard consultant was rewarding. She could finally use her talents as a criminal lawyer to help the Met, rather than defend criminals of dubious character to satisfy her ego.

Her iPhone rang. Nancy snapped out of her musings.

Philippe's voice sounded hollow. "It's Amy... she's not responding to her mobile. It's been more than 24 hours."

"I presume you've tried her hotel room and the gallery in Hong Kong?"

"No sign of her." Philippe's voice wobbled.

"Are you still at the Gallery?" Nancy closed her eyes to steel herself.

"Yes, I'm still in Islington."

"Don't go anywhere. I'll be with you in a few minutes." She hung up.

She ran to the bathroom to check the dressing over her face wound. It had bled a little but not enough to warrant a change. She returned to the lounge, stuffed her yellow ruled pad into a satchel and rang for a cab. Within five minutes she had hopped into it.

As she pushed the doors of the Gallery open, she found Philippe in the middle of a phone conversation. He was waving one arm in the air and for a moment Nancy hoped he had finally found Amy. The picture changed when he turned around. He looked dishevelled. His eyes were rimmed with red behind his round glasses.

He dropped into his chair and the phone fell from his hands, hitting the desk with a light thud. Nancy now knew Amy was missing.

"They found her bag and mobile phone on Victoria Harbour, near one of the ferry terminals from where passengers sail to Kowloon."

"Could they have been stolen?" An unlikely explanation. Amy would have called to let them know.

Philippe simply gazed at her in silence. The realisation of what had happened had just started to sink in. Nancy shivered. She recalled the previous conversation she'd had with him. Amy had found an article about China during the Deng Xiao Ping days. But who could be concerned about an article dealing with a bygone era? It had to be an accident... A robbery gone wrong.

Nancy reached Philippe and dropped into the chair opposite his.

"I'm going out there," Philippe mumbled. His body seemed to have lost all its energy. "I'm going out there," he repeated, hoping to convince himself he could spring into action.

"Is it safe?" Nancy stretched out her hand to reach his arm.

"Why should it not be?" He half turned his head towards her. He looked lost.

"I don't know yet." Her thoughts felt disorganised. She tried to focus on that question. Why would it be unsafe?

"What was Amy working on? Was she meeting any artists... controversial people, dissidents?"

Philippe nodded. "We are continually meeting artists... and all artists are controversial... what's different there?"

"No one new?"

"No... only the people we have been working with for months."

"What else?"

Philippe's face went blank for a moment. His eyes widened suddenly. He turned to face Nancy.

"The only new piece of research she was working on was a piece concerning..." Philippe's eyes blinked a few times.

Nancy's throat tightened. "...my father."

# Chapter Eleven

"Are you OK?" Nat asked Cora.

Her head turned round to the left. Nat had raised the visor of her helmet so that Cora could hear her shout. Cora gave Nat the thumbs-up.

The traffic light turned green, and she throttled up the motorbike. In a few minutes they would arrive at University College Hospital. DS Branning, the arty gang's new hero, was following in his unmarked car. He had grumbled, but reluctantly agreed Cora could ride with her friend when she had threatened to evade his protection if he did not let her.

Cora felt a little silly now, but it was so much nicer to ride on the back of Nat's bike than to share a car smelling of stale cigarettes. They reached their destination and Nat dropped Cora at the entrance to UCH. She walked the bike along the wide pavement to find the bike rack at the side of the building.

Cora quickly climbed the short flight of stairs that led to the large revolving doors. She walked in then turned around to wait for Branning. Now that she was on her own, she felt more exposed than she'd like to admit. But her protection officer appeared after a couple of minutes.

He was walking up the same stairs as she had, body bent forward, pushing against the cold wind that was suddenly blowing from the north-east. Cora shook her head... only a flimsy jacket but a thick woollen scarf to fend off the elements.

So British. They walked together to the lifts, heading for the floor where Ollie was being kept alive.

"You don't mind if I join you?" Nat managed to catch up with them just as the lift doors were closing.

Cora shook her head. It felt comforting that a friend wanted to visit, giving her hope that Ollie might yet recover. Perhaps it would do him good to hear a familiar voice apart from her own. She had read this online the day before whilst she was researching the impact of regular interactions on coma patients.

The PC who was watching Ollie's room stood up to let them in. Cora stopped at the door. She could hear the clicks and the rushing sounds of the monitors that had been plugged into her boyfriend's body. She turned towards her friend; no longer certain she wanted her to see him looking so vulnerable.

Nat had already moved into the room, her gaze running over Ollie's white shape underneath the bed covers. Cora could not make out her expression... fascination, remote interest... a furtive moment of cruelty. Whatever it was, it was not what Cora had expected. Cora walked to Ollie's bed, ignoring Nat and her strange attitude. She moved slowly as though she was approaching someone asleep. Her stomach tightened. She took her time to sit down and place her hand into Ollie's.

Nat walked over and put her hands on the bars at the foot of the medical bed. "He looks so peaceful."

"Ollie can probably hear us."

"Really? That's incredible." She kept gazing at Ollie as she responded. Cora adjusted her fingers around his, finding room amongst the various tubes and attachments. She wanted to talk to him, to tell him that she didn't care what had happened. That she would understand if he explained why he had got involved with drugs again.

But it was no use, the words didn't come, and Nat's presence made it impossible.

"Had he been using a lot?" Nat's voice felt too loud in the near silence of the room.

"I told you; Ollie can hear us," Cora snapped.

"Sorry... though I can't imagine Ollie being disturbed by an honest conversation."

She was right. Ollie liked honest conversations. He made a point of it. Still, Cora gave Nat a look that asked her to stop. But her friend did not seem to notice.

Cora squeezed Ollie's fingers gently and raised them to her lips.

She half stood up, bent towards his face and kissed his cheek. "We should be going." She would return later, on her own.

Nat's fingers slowly slid from the metal bars. She moved backwards without taking her eyes away from Ollie. Cora stayed bending over him for a moment, replaced his hand gently on the sheets and turned around to leave. Her eyes were wet with tears.

She turned around to face Nat in an awkward moment.

"We should be going," Cora repeated, more forcefully. Nat gave a quick nod, and left the room without a word.

"That was quick." Branning turned from talking to the other officer.

"Could you give me a lift back home… please?" Cora made an effort to control her voice. Nat was already halfway down the corridor.

"Did he say anything?" Branning asked almost mechanically.

Cora nodded. "He did."

\* \* \*

It was not the cold, harsh wind pushing against Nancy that made her eyes water when she left Philippe's gallery. She had done her best to keep a clear mind and help Philippe. She wanted to tell him that there might be hope of finding Amy alive, but she didn't believe it herself. It would have been too easy to play the hopeful card.

Philippe's accusations, although he had not spoken them aloud, shook her because they were so true. She had asked the people she knew for help – Philippe, Amy, Pole – with her quest.

Her father had disappeared over 30 years ago. She was only a teenager when he had left the safety of Paris and his family to return to China. At the time she had moved from hope to grief, and finally to rage. She had buried his image for years until now.

She had lived with false assumptions for far too long. She had to know.

She had to know what the true story was.

But it was she who needed to do the research and take the risk. Shame slapped her in the face. She needed help… that much was certain, but she also needed to be the one taking the risks associated with unearthing the past. Her father had been an artist and an activist. He had always been proud of his search for truth, whatever that might reveal. He had been a fierce supporter of Mao Zedong until he became a fierce critic, a catalyst that forced him and his family to escape the Cultural Revolution reprisals.

A car horn startled Nancy. She had started crossing the road that led to her apartment, ignoring the traffic. The woman driver at the wheel looked shaken. She pulled her window down, asking Nancy whether she was alright.

She was, thank you.

"Idiot," Nancy muttered, berating herself... She pushed open the heavy doors of the entrance to her building.

"Good evening," Nancy said, waving to the new security guard.

George waved back a friendly good evening.

The property had recently been equipped with enhanced security so that someone monitored the entrance and the gardens 24/7. Nancy did not like it much, but it had proved useful after the Henry Crowne affair had reached the papers. The journos were out there 24/7 and it was good to have someone who could stop their intrusions.

The lift took her directly to the top floor. She entered her apartment and dumped her coat onto the sofa. She stood in the middle of the room, torn between sadness and helplessness, and an overwhelming feeling of anger.

She had been a fierce lawyer, the youngest QC ever to take silk, at the age of 35. She had defended war criminals and international fraudsters as well as victims of international crimes.

But the review of her illustrious career did not help her to resolve the most important mystery in her life. Her link to China was of a different quality; personal, intimate... scary.

Nancy shrugged her coat off and sank onto the couch. She lowered her head into her hands and sat there for a while.

A text pinged on her iPhone. Pole was letting her know he was on his way...

*À très vite,* she replied and dropped the phone into her lap. The room was in almost complete darkness. She had not turned on the light and had barely noticed the twilight gloom deepen.

Nancy stood up heavily, walked to the wall and switched on a few lamps scattered around the room… she moved slowly back to her seat.

She had absentmindedly dropped the morning mail onto a coffee table. She started opening a large envelope and a document slid out of it.

The title page read:

Contemporary Art in China under Deng Xiao Ping.

Amy's covering note simply said:

Amazing.

\* \* \*

The voice of DS Branning calling Pole sounded muffled. Pole stopped his bike to listen to what his officer had to say.

Branning described the hospital visit. He had tried to prise a few words out of Cora, but her answers to all his questions had been monosyllabic at best.

Pole toyed with the idea of patching in Nancy, but if she became involved it would have to be official. The consultancy contract she had with the Met made provision for her to be called upon by a number of DCIs.

Pole would have to notify Marsh he was involving Nancy in a new case. There was little doubt Marsh would not object. If anything, he would be enthusiastic… even ecstatic.

Pole frowned. He would wait until tomorrow to make a decision on Nancy's involvement, torn between the desire to avail himself of her exceptional skills and the annoyance of having The Super try to woo his girlfriend.

Branning had finished his report and was waiting on the other end of the phone.

"Who is on night shift?" Pole asked.

"Helen McAdam, sir."

"Fine… brief her about what you know. She may get something out of Cora."

Branning grumbled an answer. "I'm not unsubtle, sir. I don't have to be a female officer to get Cora to trust me."

112

"I never said that, Mike." Pole smiled. "Since the SOCO team incident at Cora's flat, you're the arty gang's hero anyway. You caught the bad guy and saved Ms Wu."

"Maybe..." Branning grumbled back.

Pole arrived at Nancy's. He slowed down in front of the drive entrance, flashed his fob at the electronic eye and parked his bike in the garage for the night. All was quiet down there. The parking slots were all occupied apart from one.

Pole secured his bike and walked slowly towards the lift. He stopped for a moment in front of the empty parking space. Henry Crowne's car was no longer there and his apartment on Nancy's floor had been left unoccupied since he'd left to serve his prison sentence at HMP Belmarsh.

He had been condemned for financial terrorism as an IRA member, having worked in some of the largest financial institutions in the City of London. He had spent barely four years at the high security unit in Belmarsh before achieving a feat no one had ever managed before... escape. Pole knew why and how that had happened, knowledge which made him vulnerable.

Pole shook his head to chase away the memory. Nancy knew little of this and he intended to keep it that way. He had never spoken of the arrangement he had entered with Harris at MI6.

Pole let himself into Nancy's flat with his key. The lights were low and she was huddled on her sofa, a document resting on the seat next to her. Something was wrong and he wondered whether Cora had called with some bad news.

"*Comment vas-tu?*" French had always been the language of choice that brought them closer.

"*Une autre mauvaise nouvelle...*" Nancy raised her head and stretched a hand towards Pole.

"It can't be Ollie?" Pole asked.

"No... Although I really should catch up with Cora." Nancy wanted Pole to put down his bike jacket and helmet and come to sit next to her. "It's Amy... I'm not sure you remember her?"

"You mean Philippe's assistant?"

113

Nancy nodded. She squeezed his hand, hard. "She is missing..." Nancy gave a short exhale. "No... I should say it as it is. She is almost certainly dead. Her bag and mobile phone have been found on Victoria Wharf in Hong Kong, near one of the ferry lines that goes to Kowloon."

Pole frowned. "Was it an accident?"

"I don't know, Jonathan. It might have been, but I can't help thinking that her asking questions about my father might have something to do with it."

"You don't know that," Pole shot back, and Nancy gave him a sad smile.

"As much as I would so very much like to think that way... it's unlikely."

"People do get murdered for no apparent reason, or even have unforeseen accidents. It does happen." Pole's calm voice almost seemed to reassure her.

But after hesitating Nancy shook her head.

"She managed to unearth a very interesting and important document that creates a link to my father, an article that speaks of artists and their relations to the Chinese government in the 80s. He is mentioned in it under his artist's name."

She showed Pole the document. "Contemporary Art in China under Deng Xiao Ping". The title looked innocuous. Pole started flicking through the pages.

Despite the title and the conventional introduction, the contents of the paper grew more politically charged as the author developed his argument. He had gone to great lengths to identify those artists who, after the events of Tiananmen Square in 1989, had abruptly dropped their support for Deng Xiao Ping's socio-political reforms.

Pole speed-read the pages until he found the name he was looking for... Mo Cho, Nancy's father's artistic name. The fact that he belonged to a group of avant-garde artists was no surprise.

Pole had managed to gather information on this already with the help of Harris, but the article made an important point about the fierceness of the artists' criticism as they were still living in the shadow of Mao's Cultural Revolution. Her father had not only been part of the cultural push organised in February 1989 that supported the Tiananmen uprising, but he had in fact been one of the key organisers.

114

Pole sat back. He wondered why MI6 and Harris had not been more forthcoming about this aspect of Mo Cho's story. Not a point he would presently discuss with Nancy, but something he would soon clarify with Harris himself.

"I can see it is an important source of information, but it is also a research paper. Surely it is available freely on the internet these days."

"That's the point, Jonathan... it is not. I tried quite a few sites. I even tried a few French sites since the paper was originally written by a French student... I couldn't find anything."

"How did Amy come by it then?" Pole looked at the back of the document. He noticed that it had been photocopied, it had been done with care, seeking to capture as much of the document as possible. It was likely that the original was not available to the public.

"I don't know and neither does Philippe." Nancy shook her head again, rubbing her hand over her forehead mechanically.

"You need to be careful not to reopen the gash on your face." He leaned closer, a slow but careful move, concerned he might disturb some of her still weeping wounds.

"I'll be fine."

Pole saw it in her eyes. She could bear physical discomfort but not the emotional agony of losing her young friend Amy.

"I also need to determine whether this document is authentic," Nancy continued. "I haven't yet decided how I am going to do this... I have a few options."

"Which are?" Pole asked.

"To get in touch with my old contacts at the Sorbonne University in Paris and find out whether they know the author of the research paper."

"That could take forever."

"Agreed. And of course, I may again involve someone who doesn't necessarily realise the risk they might be taking."

Pole pushed away a strand of hair that had fallen awkwardly across her brow.

"You need to find someone who can research this in a protected environment."

"You mean someone who has access to a search engine that no one can trace?" Nancy asked.

"Something like that."

Nancy looked at Pole sideways. "You mean GCHQ or one of the other agencies?"

Pole almost flinched. MI6 and GCHQ were far too close for his liking. He had managed so far to produce documents that helped Nancy in her search without revealing their source. Pole had enough contacts at Interpol to justify the findings, but that argument was starting to wear thin.

Nancy's focus had shifted, and he recognised that she now wanted to own the research process fully.

This would complicate matters... a lot.

"If you have any contacts at GCHQ this might be the time to call upon them." Pole nodded.

"As you know, I don't... But I'm sure I'll find someone who does." Nancy smiled, the first smile she had given Pole that evening. She had a name in mind and Pole hoped that name would not lead her to Steve Harris.

\* \* \*

DS Branning's replacement for the night arrived. A woman in plain clothes, sporting a flannel suit and a neat haircut. Her smile was friendly, and Johnny warmed up to her immediately. Beth had not returned yet... She was almost certainly networking at one of the fashion events she attended almost every night during London Fashion Week.

Cora had retreated into Beth's bedroom. If she would not speak to Branning, she would not speak to the female officer either. She regretted having spoken to him about Ollie's words. She was no longer sure she had heard him speak. She thought he had murmured a word. Or was it that her desire to hear his voice again had deceived her?

Cora had almost finished clearing up Beth's bedroom. There were only a few garments now left hanging outside the large wardrobe. The makeup was organised in small jars and trays Cora had found lying around the flat. The books and magazines had found a place on the bookshelves, organised in stacks and by author.

"You're disappointingly organised for an artist," Beth always teased. Big Clearing Out Projects always helped her clarify her thoughts...

Boring, but there it was.

She moved a few books around on the shelves. She had decided that perhaps organising the magazines by theme would be an idea...

Was it true Ollie had broken his promise and got involved with drugs again?

The thought made her angry... Not at him, but at others and herself for believing this was the case so readily.

The full-length mirror that sat in pride of place in the bedroom sent back a sad picture. Her spiky hair had lost its edginess and the dark purple dye looked laughable. The clothes she was wearing were too baggy, too trendy. The fire had left nothing of her old wardrobe... If not destroyed by the flames, the smoke had left an acrid smell that had penetrated everything. There was nothing familiar to cling to. The only person she trusted who would believe in her instinct and give Ollie a chance was not there. Nancy was back home with Pole.

Yet, she was the only hope she had to help shed light on what had happened and why.

Against mounting evidence, she believed in the one word that Ollie had uttered.

Innocent.

# Chapter Twelve

The apartment hotel Jack had chosen had not changed much since his last visit. The Citadines, Trafalgar Square was ideally positioned... Central London, close to a number of tube lines and railway stations. St James's Park was around the corner, ideal for an early morning jog. Just as important, it was near enough to MI6 Vauxhall Cross but not close enough to be on their doorstep. He was on holiday after all.

Jack had repeated that sentence several times on the flight and again this morning, when he congratulated himself on securing the best apartment in this neat four-star hotel.

He was on holiday... but...

He walked around the room checking its layout. The inspection for any possible unwanted devices would come later. The safety deposit box was working but would not deter a professional. Still, it would do for the time being.

Jack yawned whilst unpacking his suitcase and, with difficulty, resisted the temptation to collapse into the crisp white bed sheets for a couple of hours' sleep.

But he was due to meet Harris a little later in Soho. An old pub Harris was raving about, and Jack was certainly game for it.

Jack took a reviving shower. He brewed a cup of coffee, from a surprisingly good range of coffee pods, using the small Nespresso machine that had been fitted into the kitchenette adjacent to the small lounge.

He made himself comfortable on the sofa and spread out the newspapers he had picked up on leaving the aircraft, *The Financial Times*, *The Times* and *The Guardian*.

An article about the UN Security Council passing a raft of new sanctions against North Korea attracted his attention. China had been actively involved in drafting the sanctions. A few days later, North Korea had withdrawn from the 60-year-old armistice that had been signed with South Korea. A truce that had ended the 1953 Korean War.

Jack poured himself another cup of coffee. The aroma filled the room, making it homely and welcoming. China seemed to be playing its part; did this signal a complete change in attitude towards North Korea? Did the Sleeping Giant suddenly feel confident enough of its power to no longer have need of the proxy war North Korea had helped to wield against the US?

He moved over to the floor-to-ceiling window and pulled open the net curtain. He had a full view of Northumberland Avenue and, from the far right-hand corner of the window, Trafalgar Square. Despite the traffic, the double glazing made the room quiet and comfortable. Jack finished his coffee.

Looking at his watch, he decided he had some time before he needed to make his way to meet Harris. He opened his laptop and started the lengthy login process. His smartphone indicated Laurie had forwarded more documents, including a new report on China's latest confidential conversation with the US about their proposed collaboration in biotech.

\* \* \*

Pole had relented and agreed Nancy should join the Ollie Wilson case in her formal role as consultant. Nancy would now be able to investigate whether he liked it or not, as he well knew.

They had woken up early and shared a quick breakfast. Pole had a meeting he was not looking forward to, she could tell, and yet he had been silent about it. She would find out what was troubling him even if it meant coaxing young Andy into telling her a little more than he should. Just enough for her to put the pieces of this conundrum together, but not enough to get him into trouble.

Her short list of names to call was lying on the desk. Her mug of tea was almost full and still warm. At the top of her list was the name of the woman she had befriended in the first investigation she had been involved in as a Met consultant… Yvonne Butler. Her lab was involved in the Ollie Wilson case but the favour she had to ask had little to do with it. Nancy checked her watch. Only 8.45am. Although she started early at the lab, Yvonne would not yet be in the middle of a post-mortem examination. She liked to run through the reports sent to her before starting the more gruesome work.

"Nancy…" She greeted her cheerfully. "It has been ages. Does DCI Pole keep you that busy? Day and night?" Yvonne's naughtiness made her chuckle.

"Well, yes… night and day." Nancy chuckled in return. "Anything I can do for you? Some new demanding case to sink my teeth into?" Yvonne's voice was eager. She enjoyed being involved in anything challenging and Nancy had provided her with plenty of perplexing puzzles since she'd known her.

"I hope you don't mind me calling to ask for a favour?"

"A favour… how intriguing… can't wait to hear what you need from me. How about 11.30am this morning? My coffee break, which I take religiously as you know, unless DCI Pole needs something urgent that is."

"Usual café, Borough Market?"

"The very same."

Nancy thanked Yvonne and returned to her list. She decided against calling another contact. One step at a time.

Nancy moved from the study back to her lounge. She moved the large book that sat on her coffee table, the latest publication by one of her artist friends who was retracing his career in sculpture, to make room for the other papers she'd brought with her.

She was tempted to flick through the pages but instead started arranging on the long glass table top the documents she had collected about her father's disappearance.

There was, to start with, the meagre set of papers she had kept from the past.

The black-and-white photo she had looked at only yesterday beckoned her again. An elegant young man in a three-piece suit sporting a mandarin collared shirt, and a young woman with long dark hair in a short dress patterned with large stripes. Nancy remembered the dress and its typical 60s colours. Both were smiling broadly. He had his arm wrapped around the young woman's shoulders, and she had laid her hands on the shoulders of a little girl called Nancy.

Nancy checked the date on the back of the picture. By then she and her parents had left China and there, the Cultural Revolution was biting hard. They had just arrived in Paris after months of travelling through China's countryside to escape the communist regime. A trip that had finally taken them to the shores of Guangdong province, leaving for Hong Kong from there and then reaching France.

Her hands were clammy. She pushed away the rest of the memories that had terrified her as a child. The nightmare that had lasted for years, only assuaged when she, at last, had convinced herself she would never have to go back to China.

The few official documents her father had gathered when they left were no longer relevant. They were written in Chinese, and she could barely decipher the ideograms on them. She hadn't spoken Mandarin for years... except occasionally to help some bemused tourists. The language she had learned as a child was now heavy with an English accent.

The next pile of documents neatly spread out on the table had been gathered recently. Pole assured her he had sourced them from contacts in Hong Kong as well as Interpol. Nancy sat back and pondered.

How careless of her not to have probed a little more as to how he got them.

She pulled the satchel that always lay to the side of the sofa and took the legal yellow ruled pad from it.

She had already listed the documents she had gathered in it. Her indecision and lax attitude towards a case, her own case, that she should have taken so much more seriously, irritated her. She had almost exclusively relied on Pole to source the information she needed. This would no longer do.

She stood up, took a few paces towards the large windows that overlooked the building's gardens. The sky was just starting to clear a little. The sun had risen only recently, and clouds were beginning to disperse. She turned back towards the coffee table and paper that lay on it. Nancy shook her head. There was not much point in castigating herself. She had to decide whether she truly wanted to keep digging into her past.

Amy had helped her, and she might have been hurt because of it, or perhaps worse. She owed it to Amy and to Pole to take the search seriously. She had succeeded in mounting some of the most complex defence cases, in front of both the British courts and international tribunals. She would approach her own case with the same professionalism, no matter how great the emotional cost.

She returned to the sofa and sat down again.

The documents Pole had gathered for her had confirmed what she had always suspected. Her father had become involved in the arts again after returning to China, trying to spur a new movement, introducing new ways of thinking and making, ideas and processes from the contemporary art world that had developed earlier in Europe and America.

A magazine called *Menshu*, printed in Wuhan, had published a small article written by him. The magazine had been censored in 1987, barely a year after her father had arrived back in China. She surmised he must have kept in touch with some of his old friends and been introduced to the new Chinese avant-garde, to be able to send an article from Paris shortly before he left France.

The few pictures, this time in colour, told her they would have been shot using a Polaroid camera and developed instantly. Her father was standing in front of a large poster. A circle in red and black, turning upon itself with a red bar across it, had been drawn at its centre. The new U-turn to the past was the sign used by the new generation of artists.

A few more pictures were now spread out on Nancy's coffee table. She had gone through them before with scant interest. She didn't know who these people were and had assumed they were part of her father's artistic crowd.

Nancy was about to tidy up the photos into a pile when she stopped. The Polaroid had faded considerably but there was a man at the back of the small group of people gathered in the picture she thought looked familiar. Nancy tilted the picture a little. She moved to the wall and turned up the light to full. It was still difficult to see but she now recognised him.

Nancy moved back to her study, opening a couple of drawers, rummaging frantically through. She found the magnifying glass she was looking for, returned to the lounge and looked at the photo again closely. It was him, unmistakably.

Deng Xiao Ping himself... the man who had been and still was the symbol of China's opening up to the world after years of communist introversion.

"Impossible..." Nancy shut her eyes and kept them closed for a moment. She opened them up again and returned the magnifying glass to enlarge the face she had been trying to identify.

There was no doubt left in her mind. Her father had gathered together a group of friends, presumably artists, and he was introducing them to Deng.

This confirmed what Nancy had both feared yet suspected... her father had re-joined the Chinese Communist Party wholeheartedly.

\* \* \*

"I'll tell him as soon as he has arrived." Andy was gesticulating to attract Pole's attention.

Pole looked at the clock on the wall. It was barely 8am. Someone was keen to get on with their day.

"Ferguson?" Pole balanced his tea on the low partition that divided off Andy's desk space.

"Spot on, Guv." Andy handed over the post-it on which he had scribbled the message. Pole glanced at it vaguely. He knew what the message was saying and was not keen to read it.

"Thanks Andy... how is the search for the mysterious man you lost in Balham going?"

"Nothing much, so far." Andy looked gloomy. He was rarely defeated by someone sneaking past CCTV cameras or other public recording devices. It seemed, however, that this individual had been well prepared.

"How about the gunman that went through the floorboards and is now lying on one of Yvonne's slabs?"

Andy remained gloomy. "Yvonne has not started the post-mortem yet... otherwise nothing has shown up."

Pole's eyebrows shot up. "You mean he has no record?"

"If he has one... it's very well hidden... the only observation Yvonne made was that he is almost certainly not British."

"I agree on that one."

"I'm in touch with Interpol and Europol. I've just received photos from the lab which have been forwarded to them."

"Something will give." Pole nodded encouragingly.

"Not so sure, Guv." Andy hesitated. "It is as though someone has gone to great lengths to erase all traces of whoever this chap is."

Pole grabbed a chair and rolled it next to his DS's desk. "That's an interesting theory."

"...and also, they are pretty well informed. Even if it was not too difficult to find out which lab was going to look after the Wilson case and intercept the real SOCO team, it's really ballsy." Andy had crossed his chubby arms over his chest.

Pole gave a shadow of a smile. His DS was getting much more confident in voicing his own opinions... he liked it.

"That's a good point too... and I suppose the next thing we need to ask is whether an informer is keeping close to Cora."

Andy pursed his lips. "How do we find out?"

Pole was fidgeting with the post-it Andy had given him. The idea of an inside job rattled him. At least MI6 was trying to fight the good fight. Harris would be helpful in trying to find out more about the group that targeted Ollie and Cora.

With Andy waiting for an answer, Pole shook away the unwanted thoughts.

"Let me speak to Rob... he may be able to help. His network is extensive, and I'd very much like to know who the person is, who gave the NCA the location of Ollie Wilson," Pole said.

"And I'll keep digging." Andy returned to his monitors.

Pole turned towards his office, keyed his pin code into the door lock and entered.

Ferguson had invited himself for an 11am visit this morning, that was if Pole didn't mind.

Pole very much minded, but that was not something to admit to one of the best counter-terrorist squad commanders in London.

\* \* \*

The doorbell ringing several times in short bursts made Nancy jump. She gathered together the photos that were still lying on the coffee table and, with nervous fingers, replaced them in the envelope they came from.

Nancy moved to the intercom. She immediately recognised Cora's voice. She took a moment to steel herself.

"I'll leave the door on the latch and prepare some tea."

She turned back towards the kitchen, barely missing the side of the door. She swore under her breath. She needed to get a grip.

Nancy heard the front door close. "Sichuan tea will do?" She turned towards Cora with a welcoming smile. "Although, dear DS Branning might not approve..."

Cora moved from one foot to the other. "He's not with me."

Nancy's measuring spoon stopped halfway in the air. "This is not on... really." But the sternness was not there. Why could she not be as severe as she should with Cora? "I'm going to have to call him and tell him you're safe."

"Please don't." Cora dropped her gaze and her shoulders followed. "Or at least give me a bit of time with you on my own first."

Nancy said nothing for a moment. She had made up her mind already, but just for good measure, she wouldn't yield to her friend's demand just yet.

"I'll give you a cup of tea and then I'll call him."

Cora nodded, relieved. She joined Nancy at the counter, and they made tea in silence, preparing the pot once the water had boiled, throwing in the right measure of leaves, covering it with a tea cosy.

"I thought DS Branning was the arty gang's new friend."

"It's not that." Cora stopped, holding onto the door handle of the pantry she had just opened to fetch some biscuits. "He is very nosy. He looks around the flat, and I'm always worried about Johnny's... you know..."

"Plant cultivation..." Nancy smiled.

"He does have green fingers." Cora giggled.

"DS Branning is there for your protection... I don't think he cares so much about your friend's smoking habits."

"I'm not going to complain, but I'm not always comfortable with all the attention."

"And if you give him the slip on every occasion… things are not going to improve." Nancy lifted the tea cosy, pouring tea into two mugs and replaced it to keep the pot warm.

"He probably won't even notice I've gone."

"How did you manage that anyway?"

Cora smiled. "There is a really handy drainpipe outside Beth's window and the flat is only on the first floor."

"Oh well then… you might as well have jumped." Nancy handed over a mug of the fragrant Sichuan tea, lips pursed yet amused.

"I hesitated." Cora drank some tea and exhaled in satisfaction. "So lovely… I don't know why I never think about buying this brand when I go to Chinatown in Soho."

"I only do because it's a family tradition." Nancy took a sip and gave a small sigh of contentment too. "One of the few traditions I can recall."

Cora sat on the sofa in exactly the same place she had occupied a couple of days previously, when she had been carried by Pole into the safety of Nancy's flat.

"I think Ollie said something." Cora left the mug on the coffee table, grabbed a comfortable blanket Nancy had left on the side of the couch and hugged it against her chest. "I was sitting next to his bed in hospital, very close… holding his hand… I was trying not to cry…" Cora bent forward to pick up her tea and took another sip.

Nancy moved next to her friend. She laid a hand very gently on her shoulder. "Is that possible?" Nancy recalled Ollie's image. The tubes and monitors, the gurgling and clicking of machinery around his bed making sure he was still alive. He had been given oxygen, but she couldn't remember whether his entire throat had been immobilised.

"He hasn't got a…?" Cora gestured with her fingers at her neck.

"Oxygen mask, then," Nancy added gently. Eyes soft, encouraging Cora to carry on.

"It was only one word." Cora held the blanket closer, fingers turning white as she dug them into the soft woollen material. "I might have dreamt it." Cora dug even deeper into the wool.

126

"I know how hard it must be."

"Innocent…" Cora turned her face to look into Nancy's eyes. She seemed torn between doubt and certainty.

Nancy held Cora's gaze. "How did his voice sound?"

Cora gave a little sob. Nancy decided she believed her. "Did he try anything else, give any other signs?"

"I felt his fingers trembling, but the doctor warned me about that. It could be an automatic reaction to touch. The doctor did not want to give me false hope." Cora closed her eyes, trying to remember the scene.

"Did you tell the medical team?" Cora shook her head. "But why?" It was important. This was not a reproach, just a concern.

"I was not on my own… Nat came with me." Cora hesitated. "I should have gone alone. It felt… intrusive. I can't explain better than that." She opened her eyes again. "I hoped another familiar voice might help, but she acted like she didn't care."

"How so?" Nancy slowly removed the hand from her friend's shoulder.

"She was detached. As though it was someone she didn't know lying on the bed."

Nancy waited.

"I didn't want to tell her what he said… it felt too…"

"…personal?" Nancy ventured.

# Chapter Thirteen

"You came alone?" Pole greeted Commander Ferguson at the lift but said very little otherwise.

"This is not an official investigation, at least not yet."

And it would almost certainly never be. Marsh would not want a scandal to erupt, and the head of the counter-terrorist command would not want that either. It was bad for both promotion and reputation. Pole moved the documents that had accumulated on the only chair facing his desk and offered it to Ferguson.

Somewhat reassuring… Pole would simply finish his career in a cupboard somewhere, perhaps not even in London.

Ferguson was speaking but Pole only managed to catch the end of the sentence.

"…been limited."

Pole frowned and it did the trick, Ferguson repeated the sentence Pole had not paid attention to.

"Don't you agree? The list of people who knew about the terror group location was small."

"But we are talking MI6. Their ability to find information should surprise us. Or perhaps I credit them with too much efficiency and power."

"I'm not denying it is their job to find out about these types of groups and their movements. But the way they interfered, asking for our assault to be delayed, is suspicious. They knew the location of that bloody lot almost as quickly as you and I had found out."

"Perhaps they knew it already," Pole ventured.

"If that's the case, MI6 should have informed CT command at the highest level."

"Well… I'm sure they are a little flexible with that obligation."

Pole's hands were spread wide over his desk. He did not want to start fidgeting with his iPhone or anything else that lay on his desk.

Ferguson pushed his stocky body into the chair. His cold gaze ran over Pole.

"You are not saying it is appropriate that MI6 should have interfered in our operation the way they did?"

"Absolutely not…" Did that sound a little too keen? Pole sat back. "I'm simply saying that we may be spending a lot of time on a wild goose chase."

"Listen." Ferguson's attitude softened a little. "I understand you trust your team, as I do mine. I can't imagine any of them tipping off the agency. Not their style. But if someone did, would you not want to know who that person was?"

"Yes… if there was such person, I would."

"And so would Marsh," Ferguson added, unusually keen to side with The Super.

Pole sighed. "I can't say I'm enthusiastic, but I think you're right… let's find out whether there was a leak in our teams."

Ferguson relaxed in his seat. He needed Pole's co-operation and Pole had gathered he would rather obtain it with his blessing.

"Let me give some thought as to who worked with me on the case," Pole said.

"And do try to think about who could have had access to the information."

"Ferg, I do know how to run an investigation!" Pole tried to sound humorous rather than irritated.

Ferguson ignored the remark. His mind was already elsewhere. "There was you, of course."

Pole stared pointedly. But the commander was simply drawing a list by order of seniority.

"Your DS Andy," Ferguson hesitated. "Your external adviser, Nancy Wu."

"She did not have access to the information, and the discovery of that terrorist cell was not discussed with her."

"Still, we need to be exhaustive... right?"

Pole nodded. Ferguson was right. No matter how much Pole wanted this inquiry to be over, he needed to retain control of it at his end.

"We need to add Yvonne Butler. She is the Head of Forensic at one of the labs we instructed on the case. I'll get in touch with her to see who else apart from her was involved," Pole volunteered.

"Good man." Ferguson crossed his muscular legs, and his face said it all. He was not moving anytime soon, at least not until he had discussed to his satisfaction the list of people they both knew to have been involved in the Mark Phelps case.

The high-profile case had cost people's lives and Phelps, a whistle-blower who had come forward to expose his employer's questionable dealings with the Middle East, had paid a dear price.

Pole ignored the clock and let Ferguson reveal his suspicions. For a man who did not suspect any member of his team, he had a particular view on each and every one of them. Perhaps it came with the territory, in an environment that handled extremists and in which each officer was equipped with high-performance firearms. Pole had worked with Ferguson before and he attributed Ferguson's success in extreme situations to the fact that he knew what each and every of his men was capable to do.

*Ferguson's team is doing a room by room sweep. On the ground floor a couple of targets are hiding in a place that controls the bottom of the stairs. The rattle of submachine guns is insistent. Ferguson has spread out his men... three of them are looking for the back door. Another crawls forward on the floor and throws two phosphorus grenades into the room.*

*Shrieks...*

*The man dispatched to the back of the house finds a way in.*

*Gunshots... the room at the bottom of the stairs is clear. Ferguson's team climbs the stairs and methodically cleans up each room as they enter.*

*Shots... screams... more gunshots... the sound of boots.*

*Pole is watching the screen from the safety of the control van, in which two operators are following the assault.*

*"Officer down."*

*"Shit." Harris swears as each room is cleared.*

130

*Pole does not utter a word. He is used to violence but not of this magnitude.*

*Ferguson's team is now on its way to the second floor. They ascend the stairwell without encountering resistance. The first door they try is locked. A machine gun burst, and the door explodes into splinters.*

*The window is open, a man in white robes is about to jump, a gun in his hand. A burst of bullets stops him before he can escape. He hesitates and then collapses back into the room.*

*Harris leaves the van before the operators can protest. He runs towards the backyard, pushing on his earpiece to keep it in place.*

*"They are in the backyard," he shouts. "Don't shoot... don't shoot... my guys are in the backyard."*

Pole should perhaps have paid more attention to Ferguson's ramblings, but the memories of Henry Crowne's escape a year ago still disturbed him. It had been carnage and he understood why none of the people who had been terminated, as Ferguson put it, would have given a second thought to planting a bomb in the middle of a crowded street, but the ferocity of the attack had left him numb for some time.

"Shall we fix a date for a debrief?" Ferguson asked.

"Excellent plan, three days from today?"

"Make it two. The head of CT command is getting impatient." Pole agreed. No need to drag his feet just yet.

Ferguson walked to the lifts and as he stepped into one of them, he turned around.

"I'll be asking for a list of all the mobile phones that have connected into or around my team's office at the time of the case..."

Pole gave Ferguson the thumbs-up as he disappeared behind the closing doors.

"Fuck." Pole clenched his jaw. His MI6 old burner phone would certainly show up in the logs and around his office at the critical time, telling Ferguson someone was indeed making some calls that were meant not to be traced.

\* \* \*

Jack crossed the road and stood in front of Nelson's Column in Trafalgar Square. Steve Harris had been right, and he had forgotten it until now. The Citadines Hotel was not only perfect for work, it was also the perfect place from which to enjoy London. He had an extra 30 minutes to spare before making his way to meet Harris.

He moved to the middle of the square, his eyes running over the façade of the National Gallery. An imposing building dedicated to culture, perhaps a little less impressive than the Smithsonian, but he was of course biased.

The fountains were filled but they were not jetting any water. In the top left-hand corner of the square, Jack noticed a splash of vivid blue. He had heard about the famous fourth plinth. Trafalgar Square was renowned for this large stone pedestal that stood below the National Gallery. Jack looked at his guidebook. It was fun to be a tourist for a while.

Circa 1840, the fourth plinth had been left without a sculpture as construction of the square had slowed down. It had remained so until recently when the space had started to be used to display contemporary, often provocative, sculptures, specially commissioned from leading artists. Jack made his way towards the spot. A five-metre-tall cockerel in bright blue stood there proudly.

Jack smiled... it looked a little mad, but he liked it. The search on his phone gave some details. The cockerel was, according to the artist Katharina Fritsch, a symbol of regeneration and strength. It was also rather humorous that on the place that celebrated the battle of Trafalgar a large cockerel, an icon to the French, should appear to defy Nelson himself. As if Napoleon had come for a visit.

Jack moved on, climbing the shallow stone stairs that ran along almost the entire side of the square. He fished out a couple of pound coins which he gave to one of the floating Yodas that inevitably attracted tourists to the place.

Jack made his way through the backstreets of Soho to the pub where Harris had suggested they should meet. In Covent Garden Jack again checked the address of The Lamb and Frog, a traditional Georgian pub with a reputation as one of Charles Dickens' watering holes and for its former (at least Jack hoped so) bare-knuckle fighting.

Harris had suggested a mid-morning meeting followed by lunch. Jack stopped at the top of the narrow lane. A few yards away in the distance he could see the name of the pub in faded yellow letters written over an old wooden shield.

Flower baskets of cyclamens and ivy had been freshly planted over the façade. The place looked suitably ancient, nestled at the corner of two alleyways. Jack reached the main door, old wood, thick glass and a cast-iron frame.

He stepped back again to take a better look at the antique building and spotted the date, circa 1623. This was indeed old. The *Mayflower* ferrying the Pilgrims to America had sailed in 1620, he remembered. Jack crossed the threshold with some excitement.

The smell of beer and freshly waxed furniture welcomed him. He nodded to the bartender who was polishing a glass absentmindedly and climbed to the first floor. He ran his hand over the worn wooden banister rail.

When he stepped into the room Harris had already arrived. He had settled into the far corner, choosing a table for two by the window. He stood up and walked towards Jack with an outstretched hand and an open smile.

"Good to see you again, Jack."

They shook hands. "It's been a while."

Harris organised a cup of coffee, which he assured Jack would be up to standard, and they settled at the table.

They made light conversation about Jack's trip until the coffee arrived. The waitress disappeared, leaving them alone.

"Does Jethro know you are in town?" Harris's eyes sparkled, amused.

"Sort of… the Station Chief usually likes to know when CIA staff visit, even when on holiday."

Harris chuckled. "Just in case you decide to go off on a tangent and get involved in some devious plot whilst on his patch."

"That's the sum of it." Jack raised the cup of coffee to his lips. His eyebrows shot up. It was a decent blend.

"It's your job to be devious. You're a snoop, not the Salvation Army."

Jack grinned. "I had forgotten what the English sense of humour sounded like."

"But onto some serious business. I had a call with my source. Ollie Wilson's case is starting to look more complex by the minute."

Harris told Jack everything he had learned. The kidnapping that ended up with Ollie being found in a heroin den, the ransacking of the flat, the fire, the fake SOCO team, the man Scotland Yard was trying to identify.

"The Scotland Yard team is good." Harris's arms rested on the edge of the table. He leaned forward to tell the story.

"I presume we can conclude that the people who are after Ollie are professionals," Jack said.

"Without a doubt, but they're not people MI6 has on its radar."

It was Jack's turn to speak about the meeting with the Head of BIG and to share what he had learned about bioinformatics and the world of viruses.

"Ollie's story is credible." Jack finished his cup of coffee. "But the drug addiction is of course an issue."

"And something to exploit, either to discredit him or to control him."

"Agreed… still we can't disregard the fact that all this may simply be drug related."

Harris frowned. "Perhaps."

"We need to dig around, find out who these pros are." Harris glanced at the wall clock. It was time for lunch. "Do you trust me?"

"An odd question… I wouldn't be here otherwise." Jack gave Harris a side look, his eyes narrowed.

"I'm talking lunch… shall I order a real East End dish for you? They do it really well here."

"Go for it." Jack had never regretted trusting Harris when it came to food in London.

Harris picked up his mobile and ordered over the phone "Two hips and ships, please."

Jack squinted at Harris but said nothing.

Harris was back to business. "Agreed on the pros. If they haven't popped up on our radar or Scotland Yard's, they've got to be top agency people."

"I used to think that… that we were, you know, the best. CIA, SIS, Mossad and the old KGB now FSB… but I'm not so sure any longer.

There are plenty of private organisations that are run by former agents from the East, ex-KGB. Officially they run information-gathering platforms, and at the same time they offer other 'services' of direct intervention under the radar. Hell... some of our own people have set up shop as well."

Harris stopped Jack abruptly.

Two pints of Pale Ale appeared on the table. Harris nodded his thanks and waited for a moment. He closed his fingers round the glass. "Perfect, nice and cool with a good head on the top." He raised his glass. "Cheers."

"Cheers." Jack took a sip of the golden liquid, yes... it was perfect. "If you are right, then whoever is employing the organisation has pretty deep pockets."

"Big pharmaceutical companies have very big pockets."

"But Ollie didn't work for big pharma."

"Some of the small biotech companies do have links with them, not through ownership, but through research sponsorship or through the top management staff." Harris stopped and waved the waitress carrying their food over towards their table. "Fish and chips, mushy peas and tartar sauce," he announced proudly.

"Hips and ships... fish and chips... is it because it sounds the same?"

"Yep... good ol' fashioned cockney rhyming slang, mate. You need to be brought up in the East End of London proper to understand. Hips because it rhymes with fish and chips, and ship because it is a ship with a sail... ale."

"Alright... it's like..." Jack was making an effort to remember. "Porky pie... lie."

"Hey, I knew I was perfecting your education when I taught you some of that stuff."

Jack tucked into the battered fish. It was surprisingly crisp on the outside with a succulent chunk of cod at the centre, the tartar sauce was light and tangy.

"But where does that lead us to?" Harris had taken a couple of bites, happy with his choice.

"Ollie was not specific about what was bothering him. He wanted to check out his suspicions carefully first, but the one thing he did mention was China."

"If he is concerned about technology transfer, he sure is spot on…"

Jack wiped his mouth and took a long pull of Ale. "I have access to some other information too."

"Information that gives you cause for worry?" Harris put his knife and fork together on his plate.

"It's an internal report… prepared for the Pentagon. I haven't finished reading it, but it puts forward the idea that the US military is about to lose its supremacy."

"China is no longer a sleeping giant." Harris nodded. "It's a dragon alright, and the Chinese will know how to rise to the challenge. After all they invented the art of war."

"I didn't mention China," Jack pointed out.

"Which other country could concern you that much? Russia? Not to be dismissed, despite what most world leaders think, but no… the main challenge to the US in this century is China. And they won't compete on a level playing field… they'll use technology and armament in novel ways."

"What do you mean?" Jack straightened up. MI6 had been doing their homework.

"China can only establish supremacy in one way. It needs to prevent the US from deploying its assets around the Pacific…" Harris waved towards the waitress. "Coffee?"

\* \* \*

"Are you sure?" Nancy asked as Cora jumped out of the cab.

Cora grinned in reply. She started climbing the wall to the first-floor bedroom window she had left on the latch.

The cabbie gave Nancy a quizzical look. "Should I be worried?"

"No need." Nancy assured him. "She is a performance artist. She likes to rehearse her number whenever she can."

"You mean performance, acrobats, like the Cirque du Soleil?"

"Something like that." Nancy waved back at Cora as she waved to her from the bedroom window.

The cab sped through the backstreets of Hoxton and hit one of the city's main roads. The traffic was surprisingly light. They arrived at

London Bridge shortly before 11am. Nancy thanked the driver, paid and finished the journey on foot.

The wind had changed direction, now blowing from the east.

Nancy raised her coat collar, took a pair of gloves from inside her small rucksack and put them on. She hurried along the wide bridge across the River Thames. The water looked grey and murky. Combined with cold, it gave a humidity to the air that penetrated even the warmest of clothes.

She walked quickly down a set of stone steps, trailing a hand down the stone rail for balance. Borough Market was busy. She slowed down a little to take in the atmosphere, walking along the street stalls, enjoying the appetising smells of the food on display. Her mobile rang. Yvonne had already arrived at the café and was asking what she should order.

Medium roast Colombian coffee, one sugar and a splash of milk.

She pushed open the door of the Colombian Coffee Company and waved. Yvonne waved back, eager it seemed for a catch-up.

Nancy indulged her friend when she fired a salvo of questions that had nothing to do with the inquiry... Nancy's sentimental life.

The coffee arrived, together with an assortment of delicious-looking pastries. Yvonne could never resist, thank goodness, and the conversation about Pole and Nancy was over.

She groaned. "I'm a romantic at heart... the fact that I cut people open, well dead people I should add, all day is just a way of hiding my true self."

"I'm glad that Jonathan is helping you connect with your true self then."

Yvonne roared with laughter. "Enough nonsense, though... so come on... what can I do for you?"

"It's not a matter that concerns an actual case." Nancy drank a little coffee. "It's more of a personal request." She was conscious of the slight hesitation in her voice and noticed that Yvonne heard it too.

Her friend grew serious. "Perhaps a little background might help as a way into it. If you feel it's appropriate, of course."

Nancy nodded; it was a fair request.

Her father had disappeared 30 years ago in Beijing, she needed to know why. Nancy elaborated whilst Yvonne listened without interrupting.

"The document, an article called Contemporary Art in China under Deng Xiao Ping, tells me a lot, or at least things that I've never been able to gather before, about my father. I need to establish it's authentic."

"How about the author?"

"The internet search didn't give me much... but I don't want people to know I am searching his name in any case."

"Are you being overly cautious?"

"Unfortunately not... someone paid a dear price for that document."

"Someone got hurt?"

"Someone died, I fear."

"Fine... I get it... you want help from someone in an environment that protects them from interference and danger."

"That's my aim... GCHQ perhaps?"

Yvonne pondered the request for a moment. "I need to know more about your father's disappearance."

"If you can spare the time and whoever helps really needs that information..."

Yvonne interrupted with a shake of her head. "Forget GCHQ... you need MI6, and I might have just the person."

# Chapter Fourteen

One of Yvonne's students had started the Y incision. Pole was standing in the observation gallery and Yvonne waved him in. He reluctantly donned a protective gown and overshoes. He grabbed a pair of gloves out of habit. There was no way he would be touching any part of what was coming out of the dead man's internal cavities.

Yvonne moved over to the door and released the lock from within. "I've just seen your good friend Nancy."

"Excellent." Pole was not in the mood to be teased, not that it would stop Yvonne. She chuckled and led Pole to the mortuary table. "I'm not going to tell you the obvious about our candidate on the table, but a few noticeable details... excellent teeth with zero work on them, which is a bummer because we won't be finding him with that."

She moved closer to the student who had finished the large frontal incision, exposing the internal organs.

"I think he had quite a few tattoos on his body. These have been removed, rather successfully, and probably a little while ago. The skin there is slightly different in texture, in particular this patch here, where the scar it left is still visible." Yvonne was pointing to part of the man's shoulder. "We have the same scars on the back."

Pole approached the body, to take a better look at the area Yvonne was pointing to on the man's torso. He walked slowly around the mortuary table, viewing the body from different angles.

"Can you recreate these tats by using some product or tool? Like ultraviolet light?"

"Good thinking, Inspector Pole," Yvonne noted, enthusiastic at the thought. "I'll have to check whether that is possible. I've not had to do it before."

Pole moved to the end of the table to view the man fully. He had only seen the picture the SOCO team had produced. As well as the one Yvonne had sent him when the dead man had arrived at the mortuary.

"Eastern European... almost certainly," Pole said.

"Well spotted, and the blood type we've found suggests that too. B blood allele is very uncommon in Western Europe but much more widespread in Eastern Europe and Central Asia."

Pole took a few steps back and turned towards her. "Let me know what else you find."

"As soon as possible and preferably yesterday... I know." Yvonne was already moving closer to her trainee. The stomach was about to be taken out and Pole decided it was time to go. Pole had left the bike at home. From the unmarked car he called Andy to check progress on the elusive Balham man. He plugged his mobile into the dashboard holder. The phone was ringing with no answer. Pole almost hung up.

"Sorry, Guv, was just on a call with London Transport Police. There was a bit of a scuffle with a chap whose description corresponds with the man we are following."

"Sounds promising." Pole had stopped at a traffic light. He engaged the siren of his unmarked car. He manoeuvred the vehicle around the queue waiting for the lights to change and sped away. "Keep going... why is that important?" Pole raised his voice to be heard over the noise of the siren.

"Someone in the crowd that witnessed the incident took a short video of it. They're just sending it to the London Transport Police and they will forward it on to me."

"More good news?" Pole swerved his car around a lorry that was double parked, swearing silently.

"Spot on... We can see the face of the guy under his hood."

Pole slapped the car wheel. "Well done, Andy. What comes next?"

"I've tried new software designed for facial recognition. I know it's not always accurate, but it'll give me a better image of the chap and then I'll broaden the CCTV camera search."

"Even if he has escaped from the Balham area, he might resurface in the neighbouring boroughs."

"Just my thinking, Guv."

"Anything else?" Pole slowed down to ease his car through a busy junction onto the Thames Embankment. "I'll be with you in 10 minutes."

"Perhaps we should discuss it when you get back."

"Give me a hint?"

"A request came to trace all mobiles that connected at or near Scotland Yard a few months ago. It coincides with the time we were working on the Mark Phelps case."

"Let's talk about it in 10 minutes."

Pole changed gear ferociously. He terminated the call and got out his latest burner phone.

"Harris… you'd better deliver," he muttered.

\* \* \*

"Have the forensic guys finished with my flat?" Cora turned to ask Branning.

She was in the kitchen, preparing a lunch of soup and freshly baked bread, one of Charlie's new culinary discoveries.

DS Branning shook his head. "They were still at it when I arrived this morning." He checked his watch and looked at the meal Cora was preparing a look of suspicion on his face. It looked a little too healthy for a meat and two veg man like him.

"I would offer you soup, but it may not be what you have in mind for lunch."

"Very kind, but I brought my own sandwich. Wouldn't want to cause you any trouble."

Damn, DS Branning had been efficient and prepared. He was not going to leave the premises. Or perhaps…

"You could get yourself a hot lunch from the café over the road, where you get your tea. I'm sure Renee wouldn't mind if you called her to order and pick up a bit later."

Branning straightened up… an enticing proposition. He slumped back a little. "Better not."

"She does a mean steak and kidney pie." Cora had not given up, anything to give her a few minutes on her own.

Branning folded the latest copy of the *Daily Mirror* he was reading. "I thought you were vegetarian." He rubbed the back of his neck with his hand.

Cora laughed. "I'm Chinese... you know what they say... if it crawls, I eat it, if it swims, I eat it and if it flies, ditto."

"Is that so?" Branning's eyes widened a little. "I had snails once... they were OK. Though I mostly enjoyed the garlic butter."

He stood up and fetched a carrier bag that had seen better days. He took out his sandwich, white bread, Cheddar cheese and pickle, wrapped in cling film. Either Michael Branning lived on his own or his wife had little imagination.

Cora wrinkled her nose at the sight. He watched her expression and shrugged. Cora picked up a mobile and waved it around playfully. "Last chance... I'll make the call to Renee..."

Branning hesitated. His stomach rumbled. "As long as it's ready when I arrive."

Cora gave him the thumbs-up. "It will be."


Cora saw him cross the small courtyard and turn into the road. DS Branning would be away for less than 10 minutes. Cora pressed the number on her frequent contact list as soon as the door had closed behind him. Philippe's phone was ringing.

"Please, please, please... don't go into voicemail." Her voice was low and anxious.

Philippe replied with a muffled voice.

"I haven't got much time... first of all though, are you alright?"

"I haven't slept much and don't know what to do."

"What is it?" Cora's voice tightened. "Have you not spoken to Nancy?"

Cora hesitated. She had better not talk about her unannounced morning visit. "Not yet."

Philippe sighed heavily. "Then you've not been told about Amy."

The hairs on the back of Cora's neck bristled. She uttered an inaudible "no".

"They found her handbag and mobile phone on the Victoria Harbour jetty in Hong Kong." Philippe's voice faltered. He muffled a sob. "She hasn't been seen…" There was nothing else to add.

Cora bit her lip to stop herself from crying. She dropped abruptly to the floor. It was impossible, Ollie, then Amy… But denial would not make the grim reality go away.

She recalled Amy's enthusiasm at helping every artist that exhibited at Philippe's gallery. She had been very excited about a recent discovery. For a moment Cora forgot she was on the phone to Philippe…

Ollie, now Amy. She wanted to scream… Why?

Just as she had a few years ago when her parents disappeared… she now asked herself why? Why them? The searing feeling of loss ignited again. Philippe was calling her name and she could barely reply.

"Sorry… sorry, Philippe." Cora stood up, grabbing the edge of the window for balance. She looked across the courtyard. DS Branning was still collecting his meal it seemed.

"I'm at the Gallery… I could do with some company."

"Give me half an hour." Cora hung up. Branning was crossing the yard with a large takeaway container. She returned to the kitchen. The soup she had prepared no longer looked appetising.

The door of the flat opened and the smell of food crossed the threshold of the kitchen before he did. She felt her stomach heave, ran to the window and opened it wide to let in some fresh air.

The soft sound of the box landing on the table told Cora Branning was in the kitchen. She took a few deep breaths. She rubbed the back of her hand over her eyes in a short wiping gesture.

A large hand gently landed on her shoulder. "More bad news?"

Cora nodded. She had not expected the question, nor in such a kind tone. She turned around. Branning looked at her with attentive searching eyes. He might not like her friend's cooking or the arty gang's way of life, but DS Branning seem to understand adversity when it came knocking.

He closed the window, moved to the kettle and started boiling water. He made two cups of tea in silence.

"It's a friend of mine," Cora eventually volunteered.

Branning placed a cup in front of her and came to sit opposite. The warm liquid soothed her throat a little.

Branning's hands had circled his mug. It had almost disappeared in his meaty grasp. Cora told him about Amy. He listened without interrupting.

When she had finished, Cora glanced at the takeaway lunch. "It's going to get cold."

Branning shrugged. "I'll whizz it in the microwave." He moved slowly around. "So, you'd like to see your friend Philippe?" Branning finished his mug, got up and placed it in the sink.

"That would be nice."

He nodded. "OK... let's go." He caught Cora glancing at his lunch again. "I need to lose a few pounds anyway."

DS Branning was smoking a cigarette outside whilst Cora and Philippe hugged each other for a long moment after she had walked through the doors of the Gallery.

"Any more news?" Cora finally asked.

"Nothing since I last spoke to you, but the Hong Kong police were pessimistic. Apparently, it's a well-known spot for suicides. The tide takes people out to sea in no time." Philippe slumped down at his desk.

"It's complete nonsense." The burn of anger had replaced the sorrow she felt earlier on.

"Of course, I said that to them."

"What have Liu and James at your gallery in Hong Kong said about it?"

"They are puzzled and in disbelief, just as we are."

"What did Nancy say?"

A flash of anger came and went in Philippe's eyes. "I told her I wanted to go to Hong Kong, but she was not encouraging. She thought it might be dangerous."

Cora came to sit next to Philippe. "I know this is not what you want to hear but... she might be right." Cora shook her head. "No... she is almost certainly right."

Philippe frowned.

"Amy told me a bit about the research she was doing for Nancy. She wasn't specific but she said she was helping her with her father's disappearance."

"She was not supposed to talk to anyone about that." Philippe's voice trembled.

"It's such an old story... 30 years ago. She didn't think it was a dangerous assignment." Cora sat back in her chair. "I didn't even think about warning her either and I should have known better."

They stayed silent for a while, both locked in thought.

"Why were you calling me in the first place, anyway?" Philippe asked.

"I wanted to check whether Ollie had chatted with you about anything in particular... anything that sounded unusual... worrying."

"Nancy asked me the same question... I can't think of anything." A shadow moved across Philippe's face. "Unless..."

Cora nodded encouragingly.

"He had asked Amy a lot of questions about Hong Kong and China."

\* \* \*

In the cab she had hailed whilst crossing London Bridge, Nancy called Cora and Philippe and had a short conversation with them.

Something had alerted her, she needed to find out whether Ollie had had any meaningful conversations with Philippe.

Ollie had always been curious about China. He knew that the disappearance of Nancy's father had created a strong bond between her and Cora, whose parents had gone missing eight years earlier in a fateful visit to the mainland. But his questions had become more searching.

How independent was Hong Kong now that the British had left?

What was the influence of mainland China and its political elite on business there?

Had Nancy ever done business in Beijing?

She hadn't detected the signs of someone concerned about the country. She had merely assumed his curiosity was motivated by the sympathy he had for Cora's past. But now she wondered why the place was so much on his mind. Pole needed to be made aware of that too.

Cora had given Nancy the address of the biotech company Ollie worked for. It would be a good start and she could investigate it on her own. Pole might not approve, but she wouldn't ask his permission. "Oi... blimey... careful where you're going!" the cabbie shouted, opening the window to give the other driver a piece of his mind. The traffic had now come to a standstill and cars were jostling, trying to move from two lanes into one.

"What happened?"

"Road works, luv... bloody idiots are opening up the road again."

Nancy decided to walk the rest of the way. She paid the driver and stepped out onto the riverside pavement. The Thames looked a little choppy as the wind had risen and the tide was coming in. A couple of small barges were cutting steadily through the water, the engines giving them an advantage against the flow. Nancy accelerated her pace as the wind became stronger and her coat failed to keep her warm.

She stopped at a set of traffic lights. The pavement ahead had been closed to pedestrians in readiness for more repair works. She needed to cross, however, and then resume her walk alongside Whitehall Gardens.

Nancy jogged lightly on the spot, waiting for the light to go green. A gust of wind pushed against her and she cursed. A car had stopped in the middle of the pedestrian crossing, preventing other vehicles from moving forward. Nancy stepped into the road to slip between two cars.

The roar of a motorbike startled her. She had almost reached the other side of the road when it drove towards her. She threw herself on the pavement and managed to roll onto her side, hiding behind the protective railings.

The bike mounted the kerb and the driver moved sideways, bending forward to grab Nancy's satchel. She dove over it but she wasn't quick enough. She clutched the handle whilst the biker got hold of the long strap. He changed tack, let go of the piece of leather and tried to run the bike into her body.

She rolled over again onto her other side, finding protection behind a metal postbox. She held the satchel against her chest with fierce determination. He tried again to grab the handle, but it snapped in his hand as Nancy pulled it towards her.

The satchel bounced against the railing and landed on the other side of the pavement. Now the biker would have to run her over to get to it. There was a moment of hesitation. A couple of people were yelling. Footsteps hit the road. The bike turned around and disappeared.

A woman was kneeling next to Nancy. A man was on his mobile. Nancy had just started to feel pain. Her knees were showing through her torn trousers. The cuts on her hands had started to bleed. She was sitting on the ground, still dazed after the attack.

A police car arrived. A young man in uniform crouched next to her to ask her questions, her name, how she felt... a paramedic was coming. The only thing Nancy could think about was her satchel.

She answered his questions in monosyllables... yes... no. The paramedic arrived on his motorbike and checked for broken bones. The young policeman asked her whether there was someone he should contact.

She asked for a phone and tried Pole again. His phone was now engaged. She called another number. A voice she did not recognise picked up.

"May I leave a message for Inspector Pole please?" She gave her name and asked to be called back.

The young policeman looked at her a little shocked. "Have you just called Scotland Yard?"

Nancy nodded. "And would you mind giving me a lift there please?"

They left the scene, lights flashing. Nancy clinging to the satchel she had defended so fiercely.

# Chapter Fifteen

"Langley confirmed it's a holiday." Jethro Greeney was sitting behind his desk in his embassy's office, a pair of half-moon glasses perched on his nose, rereading the email he had received.

"I haven't been to London for a while," Jack said, smiling amiably.

Jethro looked at Jack over the top of his glasses. His pale blue eyes glided over him with irritation. Who did he think he was?

"And it has nothing to do with the Ollie Wilson case, of course?"

Jack didn't budge from the comfort of the leather seat he had chosen when he entered the Chief of Station's office. "I'm meeting up with a few friends... people I spent time with in Iraq when I started the job."

Jethro stood up, moved around his large office desk in a leisurely manner, and joined Jack in the corner of his office which had been set up for more informal meetings.

"Your little trip to East London tech city is also completely fortuitous?"

"I'm not going to lie about that... I'm intrigued by the thought of the British trying to compete with the Americans when it comes to biotech." Jack gave a smug smile. Jethro might buy the argument that the Americans were the best in technology and always would be.

"You'd be surprised... London has become without doubt the largest hub for biotech companies in Europe. With a lot of competition from Oxford and Cambridge."

So much for the Chief's perceived narrowmindedness.

"I'm interested myself in what's happening in the biotech industry in this country, so if you happen to be in the area of Old Street

Roundabout… a place that is well known for traffic jams, its derelict central reservation and post war hastily built constructions, you should definitely pay a visit to some of the firms based there."

"I've never visited the East End as such… I gather that some of those areas are very hip now."

"Ask Libby, my PA, to give you details about the guided tour… I'm sure you'd enjoy that," Jethro said.

"What would I be looking for if I were to take a look at this famous roundabout?"

Jethro stretched his legs, sliding his heels over the thick rug. "How about delving a little bit more into a company that specialises in virology?"

"Like the one Ollie Wilson is working for?" Jack had found a Viro-Tech Therapeutics brochure on the internet and printed it out. He thought about pulling it out of his rucksack but decided otherwise.

"One amongst others." Jethro waved his hand, dismissingly.

Jack had found out that there were only two companies other than Viro-Tech to specialise in virology in the top 10 companies established in London that were worth visiting. Jethro almost certainly knew that was the case, so why play games?

"How many are there?" Jack muffled a yawn. The red-eye flight from the US was starting to catch up with him.

"Not sure… it's not the main thrust of the research… most of them are focusing on cancer cures or gene therapy."

"Is there a list available?" Jack rolled his shoulders slowly and straightened his back to get rid of the heaviness that had crept into his muscles.

"Nothing exhaustive… I'll get you what I have."

Jack would ask Laurie, his CIA research analyst, for information too. It was early afternoon in London and morning in Langley. She would already be at the office though and would as always be discreet about her research.

"Happy to help. I'll report if I find something of interest. It'll be fun to get to know London again," Jack said.

Jethro nodded and took his mobile out of his back pocket. "There is a number I need to give you. I'm sure you won't need it, but if you ever get stuck, you know… visiting the wrong pub in the wrong part of town whilst you're getting to know London again."

Jethro read out the number. Jack entered it on his phone. "Totally unnecessary, of course."

\* \* \*

Nancy had settled at the back of the police car. She looked a mess. She was in pain and no longer sure she wanted Pole to see her in such a state of disarray. At least not at the office.

The young police officer who had helped her was now trying to contact him. He was already through to the switchboard; no doubt the phone in Pole's office was already ringing.

"Excuse me. Perhaps it's not a good idea to disturb Inspector Pole after all," Nancy said.

The young man frowned. Had she asked him to disturb a DCI for nothing?

"We were supposed to have a meeting. I am advising Scotland Yard on a case… I didn't realise I look so…" Nancy cast her eyes over the torn trousers and soiled coat. "…unpresentable."

The female colleague driving the car gave Nancy an understanding look.

"Shall we drive you back to your home, ma'am?" the young woman suggested.

"Would that be all right?"

Her colleague grunted an OK. The young woman turned the car around with an expert U-turn, sirens blaring again.

It didn't take them long to arrive in front of Nancy's building. The young woman driving the police car offered to wait for her, but Nancy declined. She thanked the two officers and disappeared into the apartment building. The security guard gave her a bright smile that turned into concern.

"Not to worry, Mandla, I tripped badly on the pavement. I have been seen by paramedics though."

"You let me know if there's anything I can do, Ms Wu."

"I will." The lift arrived. She walked in and ascended to the top floor.

150

Back in her flat she threw her coat on the floor, dumping her broken satchel next to it. She climbed up the stairs to her bedroom, clinging to the banister with a wince.

"If you think you're going to scare me little man... think twice." She moved to the bathroom to discard the rest of her clothes, slipped into a comfortable dress and went down again to her study.

She moved aside the now growing file on her father to pick up the Ollie Wilson folder that was slim in comparison.

Nancy sat down at her computer, logged on and pondered.

What was it in her satchel that was considered so interesting it needed to be taken from her? The persistence of the assailant made her discard the idea it had been a straightforward mugging for money. She had barely made any real progress with her father's case until very recently. She wondered now whether the Ollie Wilson story was becoming entwined with her own. She needed to form a view before speaking to Pole. Although delaying meant that the assailant had more time to disappear. She drummed her fingers on the wood of the desk. No, she would delay calling Pole. The bike had probably not been captured on CCTV cameras. Whoever it was who attacked her had planned the assault well in advance. They would have chosen the optimal place to attack and escape with minimal traceability.

She pulled open the top drawer of the desk and took out yet another yellow pad.

Time to do some proper thinking.

From the Ollie Wilson file, she retrieved her notes from a couple of days ago.

Ollie's career unfolded on the page in front of her. His early education, a PhD from Harvard Medical School in bioinformatics. A first job at Viro-Tech Therapeutics as a Senior Researcher.

Nancy googled the name of the company. It had been founded in 2008 just before the financial crisis, but it was still standing and doing very well by all accounts.

She browsed the website; an excellent presentation, easy to navigate, with plenty of good quality pictures of people either doing research in labs or board members and management meeting in a smart boardroom. It was a mature company, even if small.

She moved to the page listing the pipeline of drugs being developed. Impressive.

Three of the drugs were doing extremely well, two of which had already reached phases one and two. The drugs had proved effective on non-human subjects and were entering patient trials to determine the optimal dosage and to assess their efficacy and side-effects.

The third drug was still in the discovery phase, with a single headline, genetic target. Nancy switched to another screen. She moved to the Companies House website and requested the latest Viro-Tech audited accounts. The company was privately held with an injection of venture capital.

Nancy smiled. There was plenty of scope for one of the participants with capital in Viro-Tech to make certain demands and to be linked to foreign fund investments. She picked up her mobile and called the offices of one of the best criminal QC's in London.

Nancy had finished her call with her QC friend and decided on her next step. The cab ride would last barely 15 minutes. Nancy placed her call, hoping he would be available.

Andy Todd answered before the first ring was over. She was in luck. "Good afternoon, ma'am, what can I do for you?"

"Andy, really… won't you indulge me and call me Nancy like everybody else? I'm not part of the Met's most notorious circle of women."

"Very true…" Andy chuckled.

"Good. Now… I have a delicate message you need to convey to Pole."

The tone changed at the end of the line. "Please go ahead." Andy was getting ready to take notes.

"At 13.07pm today, a man on a motorbike tried to run me over to steal my satchel. I was crossing the road in front of Whitehall Gardens when this occurred. I've reported it to the officers who helped me at the scene, PCs Doyle and Garth. I don't believe the aggressor was intending to steal the bag. It was much more personal… either a threat or a warning. I can't quite tell yet. You may want to take a look at the CCTV cameras around the area. The number plate of the bike is D 293 ACX. I'm about to go into a meeting. I will call Pole as soon as I am out... and before you ask, I am fine apart from a spoilt pair of tailor-made trousers and a few grazes here and there."

Nancy waited for a few seconds. "Are you still there Andy?"

"I... am." Andy cleared his throat. "I could try to find Inspector Pole."

"Sorry Andy, I've just reached my destination."

"He is not going to be happy." Andy spoke without noticing.

"I know. Just tell him not to shoot the messenger. I'll make it up to him..." She almost mentioned the evening but thought better of it. It might be a little too risqué although the thought was rather tempting.

"You will be fine... I must go now." She terminated the call, breathed in deeply and prepared herself. "Showtime... it's not a court of law... simply the CEO of a biotech company."

\* \* \*

"Enjoy the sight-seeing." Jethro was serious. He had asked his PA to prepare a list of the "Latest things to do in London". She had not insulted him by adding the Tower of London or Madame Tussauds, but the London Eye was high on the list, as well as the new Jack The Ripper tour.

Jack arrived at Barbican tube station. At least it would not be a lie if he said he had visited one of the landmarks of London... the Brutalist architecture of the Barbican Arts Centre had to be seen to be believed.

He found himself at a crossroads and at the end of what turned out to be a short tunnel, the famous ziggurat construction stood heavy against the skyline formed by other tall buildings. Jack crossed the road and entered the tunnel. The walls had been decorated with tiles, but the dust of traffic fumes had dulled their colours.

Jack turned away from the Barbican, towards his destination.

It took less than 10 minutes for Jack to reach the place he was looking for... Silicon Roundabout.

Jack enjoyed the stroll down the small streets that characterised the sector known as the City of London. The area had been heavily bombed during World War II and a lot of the buildings had appeared post-war, rapid constructions aimed at giving Londoners a roof over their heads. A few of the old buildings remained, and the curving streets conveyed the history of meandering lanes which had evolved to meet people's needs over centuries.

Old Street Roundabout appeared to his left as he emerged from one of these lanes. The desolated central reservation was as ugly as Jethro had described. A few larger streets radiated from it. Silicon Roundabout was no bigger than Central Park. Jack smiled. Unlike its better-known brother, Silicon Valley, which stretched over almost 100 square miles, the London imitation had a way to go.

"Got to start somewhere..." Jack grinned and walked towards Viro-Tech's location. He turned into an alleyway that looked like a dead end. The red brick building was suitably unnoticeable. Jack walked along the façade and turned into another part of the lane that housed a small car park. It felt cramped and, despite the cold breeze, the air was heavy with the smell of fumes and garbage bins.

A small door appeared on Jack's right as he retraced his steps. He stopped and checked the name on the doorbell. Viro-Tech Therapeutics' buzzer was at the top. The other bells had no names apart from the very bottom one that mentioned the Rainforest Foundation. Jack took a second look at the door, strong steel security panels fitted with specialist locks. The small camera that was fitted outside the door frame was also high spec.

Viro-Tech did not want any uninvited guests on their premises. Jack walked back along the front of the building. The windows had been placed high up in the construction. The frames looked solid, filled with what he thought was static-proof opaque glass.

If he wanted to take a look, unobserved, Jack would have to find a way through the back door. He stopped again at the top of the lane and checked the Rainforest Foundation on his smartphone. Unsurprisingly, the Foundation was dedicated to the protection of the Amazon rainforest.

The association of companies with such different interests puzzled Jack, but still, it might offer a way in. Jack pulled a black cap from his rucksack, flipped it onto his head. He retraced his steps, only slowing down when a black cab drove past him and stopped in front of the Viro-Tech door.

154

An Asian woman stepped out on to the pavement, paid the driver and rang the top buzzer. Jack was only a few steps away. She was wearing a smartly cut black coat, her silky dark hair pulled into a neat bun at the back of her neck. She looked professional, perhaps even severe.

He kept going at an even slower pace, hoping he would catch the conversation as the door was being opened.

"I have an appointment with Oliver Wilson," the woman announced.

The voice that answered the buzzer asked a question Jack could not catch.

"Nancy Wu." The door opened with a low clunk.

* * *

The door opened with minimal sound. Nancy recognised good quality security... strong steel doors with specialist locks, high performance surveillance cameras to scan visitors. The building inside did not contrast with the exterior.

The row of lifts looked plain. There was no receptionist and Nancy gathered most visitors could only ride to the top floor and not stop on the other floors, absent a security pass. When the doors of the lift opened, she was proved right. The swipe panel was flashing, prepped for a ride to the top floor.

The scene changed completely when she arrived at the top floor reception, cool steel and glass with a colour scheme matching the company website. A giant version of the Viro-Tech logo, which combined a stylised DNA strand with a woven textile, was hanging on the wall above the receptionist's desk. The young man in a black polo neck and jeans contrasted with the polished décor, setting the tone – smart casual with an emphasis on smart.

Nancy stepped into the reception area, and walked towards the desk with studied calmness to disguise her interest and a little apprehension. "Nancy Wu for Oliver Wilson, please." She forced a reserved, yet professional smile.

The young man acknowledged her with courtesy and without the slightest discomfort. He must have been well briefed. Ollie was critically ill in ICU, but it appeared to be business as usual, regardless of what had happened to him.

She walked over to the window and looked outside. The heavy skies had already darkened the day. Its inky colours were spreading on the glass, helping it reflect the brightly lit reception area.

A man arrived from within the offices. Dark hair with nascent grey at the temples… jeans and an open-necked shirt. Nancy turned around. She was about to meet the CEO of Viro-Tech Therapeutics Ltd.

Her expression was neither expectant nor inquisitive, it was simply business.

"Jared Turner." The man extended his hand to shake hers. "How do you do?"

Nancy feigned surprise whilst introducing herself.

"I'm sorry that Ollie Wilson will not be able to meet with you."

Nancy raised a disappointed eyebrow. "What a shame."

"But perhaps I can be of help."

"Well…" Nancy hesitated for what she felt was the right amount of time. "Why not?"

Jared Turner gave Nancy a corporate smile and gestured towards a part of the building which she surmised contained the meeting rooms. He waved a badge over the security eye and the glass doors opened. He stood aside to let Nancy walk ahead of him.

Alongside the walls that led to the meeting rooms, Nancy recognised a good display of contemporary art. Whoever was doing the buying had a knack for identifying up-and-coming artists, or perhaps the pieces were simply on loan through one of the ubiquitous art-for-offices schemes.

They entered a small yet comfortable room. She accepted a cup of coffee from the latest Nespresso machine. Jared Turner chose a coffee as well and settled at the small table in the seat opposite hers.

"I'm sorry about the inconvenience, but unfortunately Ollie has not been well recently."

"I hope it is not serious." Nancy steeled herself to sound mildly concerned.

"I'm sure he will be fine."

Nancy sipped her coffee and waited.

156

Turner clasped his hands on the table. "But perhaps you could tell me a little about the reason for your visit."

"Ollie spoke to me about the successful research in virology and vaccines Viro-Tech has undertaken over the past five years. And although I am not a scientist, I understand what the potential of a good outcome would be."

Turner's face did not betray any emotion. He was listening carefully, intent on not giving away any information until he was comfortable with the genuine interest of the person in front of him.

"I met Ollie through his partner, the artist Cora Wong."

Turner nodded, but still remained silent.

"Instead of spending substantial sums of money on contemporary art... which I normally do – incidentally I appreciate the quality of the small collection displayed around your office, including the early Grayson Perry – I decided I was ready to invest in other ventures. Ollie made a strong case for the future of biotechnology."

"An excellent suggestion. Ollie is right." Turner finished his coffee. His eyes had not left Nancy for a moment, assessing, weighing up the status and credibility of the person he was talking to.

"Biotech is a good long-term prospect, but investors must be prepared to wait sometimes years for a return... and, of course, to come in at the right level of investment. They have to be able to understand the complexity of the R&D process. It's not for everyone."

No sugar coating for the conversation. Nancy wondered whether it was honesty or chauvinism. Would a woman "understand" the nature of what she was getting herself into?

"Certainly. I am not completely ignorant about the world of business or patient capital for that matter. I have defended enough multinationals in the criminal courts to understand how the world of investment operates."

A dark shadow moved over Jared Turner's eyes. A lawyer of quality was not what he wanted on his company's premises.

# Chapter Sixteen

"The Northumberland Avenue crossing you say?" Pole was on his mobile to Andy. His hand squeezed the phone hard. He had almost shot the messenger when Andy told him about Nancy's attack, but instead he'd taken his jacket and walked out of the building.

What on earth was she playing at? She was not Jane Tennyson... come to think of it, Nancy would have been perfect as a tough female DCI.

The wind blew his tie into his face and he pulled it away to one side with a snap.

Pole crossed the road to he right-hand side of the pavement. He stopped and surveyed the scene. Skid marks at a right angle, made by a single motorbike which had stopped and mounted the pavement, were clearly visible. He squatted down for a moment. A few pedestrians gave him an odd look.

Someone stopped altogether and was about to comment.

"That's OK... I'm not going to have a crap... I'm looking for evidence." He took out his police ID card and shoved it in the direction of the onlooker without looking at them.

The passer-by scuttled off.

Pole called Andy back. "Speak to Yvonne... I want the skid marks on file... and find out who collected the evidence for the incident." Pole grunted, "...please." It was an afterthought, but he was not in the mood to be pleasant when he should have been told much earlier on.

Another gust of wind reminded him that he had just walked out in only a light jacket and that London in the middle of February required a little more than that.

He had spoken to PCs Doyle and Garth who, unlike Andy, had managed to get on the wrong side of him. DCI Pole did not think it was good police procedure to let a victim wander off alone... even if they had made sure she was safely at home.

Was it a good idea? No, sir.

Hope you learned from your mistakes. Yes, sir.

Pole surveyed the scene once more and called it a day. He hesitated, decided otherwise, and pushed his mobile deep into his pocket. He was damned if he would be the first to call.

He decided to pick up a couple of good coffees from his regular sandwich shop. As soon as he went in, the waitress started preparing his usual order. Pole managed a smile. "Times two please."

He returned to Scotland Yard and placed his peace offering on Andy's desk, but the young man only half noticed. His eyebrows were knotted into a scowl Pole knew well.

"What's up?" Pole started sipping his coffee, a welcome warmer.

"I'm not sure, Guv... I keep seeing a phone showing up in and around the office which I can't either explain or trace." Andy moved the data around several screens he had opened on his PC. He smiled a thank you, took a sip and sighed. Just what he needed, too.

Pole's hand squeezed a little harder around his cup. He fought the urge to check his jacket pocket. His latest burner phone was there. But this time he had switched it off. Harris had insisted it should change every month and for once he had to thank him for a good piece of advice. The phone Andy had traced was long gone. But the question would remain. What was this unknown mobile doing at Scotland Yard and, more importantly, who owned it?

"What do you make of it?" Pole took another sip, as did Andy.

"I'd say a pay as you go, therefore untraceable."

Pole nodded.

"I've just got to see where else this phone shows up."

"Keep up the good work," Pole managed convincingly.

As soon as he stepped into his office, the phone rang. Trouble always came in threes.

Superintendent Marsh was calling him.

Pole stroked his goatee. Letting one of his team pick up would only delay the inevitable. Marsh wanted an update. He sat down at his desk and picked up the phone.

"Good afternoon, sir."

"Afternoon, Pole... any news?"

Pole updated Marsh about the meeting with Ferguson, in detail. Although there was little that had been achieved, at least he could talk about the plan they had agreed on.

"Promising. How about the list of people who were working on the Phelps case?" Marsh said.

"I have finished my list and so has Ferguson."

A pile of documents had arrived with the mail. Pole picked up a large envelope at random.

"What does Ms Wu think about this?" The Super was almost meek.

"I haven't thought it fit to let her know about the informal investigation, sir," Pole replied smoothly. "She is after all on the list of the people who worked on the Phelps case."

Marsh cleared his throat. "I suppose..."

"I plan to review the data and interview the people on the list tomorrow. Commander Ferguson is conducting interviews on his side. I'll come back to you soon." Pole this time was curt... unusually so, and Marsh was silenced.

Pole hung up and picked up an old rubber band and played with it for a moment. He needed to place a call to Harris. The clock on his wall indicated 4pm... too early.

A text pinged on his mobile.

*You are fuming I know... BUT I do have very interesting information to share... dinner at 8?*

He toyed with the idea of not replying to Nancy. He needed the information though and, more importantly, a good explanation as to why she hadn't called him.

*Need to speak now... I too have information to share.*

An excellent excuse to leave the office and place the call he needed to make, away from the tracking devices Andy was now running continuously.

\* \* \*

Cora reviewed the information on screen. There were very few tickets available in economy class... Cathay Pacific was full, Emirates and Qatar Airways had a couple left, British Airways seemed a better bet, but prices had rocketed since she'd last booked a flight to Hong Kong.

Philippe brought two cups of tea and sat next to her.

"Crazy expensive. Emirates or Qatar with two or three hours' stop in either Dubai or Doha," Cora said.

"I've got to go there. The two other gallerists I work with don't know anything about Amy's search into Nancy's father's past and they are getting scared. The Hong Kong police are not giving me or them any information." Philippe ran a wary hand over his face. "The longer I delay, the more likely it is they will give up and not try to find Amy."

Cora rolled her chair away from the desk. "What are they saying? Suicide? Bad luck meeting a weirdo who pushed her into the water?"

"No, worse... they are not saying anything."

"Hong Kong used to be such a fun place," Cora said almost despite herself. She'd spoken to Philippe about her memories of the place she used to love. There was no need to explain. She simply wished she could have brought her grandparents to London with her when she left. Her mother's parents, so wonderfully supportive of anything she did even when she'd decided to train as an artist.

"I'm sorry I'm bringing back old..." Philippe's voice trailed off.

"That's OK, Philippe. It's not your fault." Cora drank a little tea to mask her trembling voice. "If it weren't for Ollie, I'd come with you." She was not certain it was time for her to go back, but Philippe knew nothing about the complexities of the place, and the underlying tensions between Hong Kong and mainland China.

"I haven't even asked." Philippe shook his head. "How is Ollie?"

"Nothing's changed." Cora's shoulders slumped a little. "I speak to him... I read his favourite poetry. It's a quirky little book, a volume of mathematical poetry celebrating the connection between maths and the arts. Just like the two of us."

She took the book out of her rucksack to show to Philippe. "I found it on the bookshelf in Johnny and Charlie's flat... isn't it strange sometimes how friends understand you beyond your wildest dreams?"

161

Philippe spent a moment not knowing what to say. He simply changed the subject.

"Nancy doesn't know I'm going by the way."

"Perhaps you should speak to her again before you go."

"So that she can get me to change my mind." Philippe shook his head. "She's very convincing when she wants to be and I don't want to cop out."

"It's not copping out if there is real danger out there." Cora turned her attention fully on him, his soft profile, the gentle droop of his often-dreamy eyes didn't gave Cora confidence he would manage to face Hong King's ruthless authorities. "If something bad were to happen to you, it would not help Amy."

"But sitting here in London is not going to help her either."

There was little to add to that. Her parents had fought against it and she spoke about it often… for years corruption had been creeping into the Hong Kong establishment, the police and even the judiciary. If Amy's disappearance needed to be forgotten or treated as suicide, it would be. It would take someone with resources, an understanding of Hong Kong government politics, and ruthlessness, to find out what had happened. Cora did not think Philippe was that person.

* * *

"The place is like Fort Knox." Jack found a table in the Barbican Centre coffee shop and was debriefing Harris. "I managed to squeeze in after someone entered the premises."

"I've opened up a map of the area showing the Viro-Tech building in 3D," Harris said. "How far into the building did you get?"

"I reached the gardens." Jack was looking out through the long window of the café. The pond area and its benches, tables and chairs were deserted. "There is another organisation in the building called the Rainforest Foundation. I claimed I was a new volunteer but didn't get very far with that argument."

"You mean they didn't trust your story?"

"No, they didn't believe my style… clean shaven… leather bomber jacket."

Harris said nothing for a moment. "I'm looking at a layers version of the map. What is that thing on the walls?"

"Plants. Different kinds of small evergreen plants that have been planted vertically up the wall… a new experiment apparently."

"Very clever. A good screen. No one can get through this wall, and it looks environment friendly."

"And the rest of the back of the building has the same security as the front… reinforced steel, specialist glass… high-spec devices."

"That makes me really curious." Harris's voice unexpectedly crackled on the phone. "I'll get my guys to find out more about Viro-Tech."

Jack took a sip from the bottle of water he had just bought. "You may call me paranoid but… a woman entered the building before me. She looked Asian, perhaps Chinese or mixed parentage; she had a meeting with Wilson."

"What's the chance of that happening? Did you get a name?"

"I did. Nancy Wu, perhaps…"

Harris's silence made Jack wonder whether he was still on the line. "You still there?"

"Yup… just sending my first email to the donut." Harris's fingers could be heard running over the keyboard.

"You mean GCHQ?"

"That's right… I work at the Cross and I get my information from the Donut. It's all very British, this use of nicknames."

Jack hung up on the call that had not given him as much information as he had hoped. He finished his water and rolled the empty bottle a few times between his hands. The Station Chief had told him to report. He would find out who Ms Wu was.

* * *

Someone else was trying to call. Nancy ignored the persistent buzz. Yvonne Butler was already on the phone with the details of a contact who could help, or rather who was willing to look into the origins of the document that named Nancy's father. The photos were now also part of the arrangement.

"I don't mind admitting it, Yvonne. I'm really impressed."

"Let's see first what the results are. Nothing intrigues a spook more than a piece of information that is contentious."

"I suppose there will be a catch to this." Nancy's voice shook a little.

"With MI6 there always is, I'm afraid. The deal is that if this is something important and the information is useful, my contact wants to be able to use it."

Nancy fell silent for a moment.

"You don't need to answer now. Think about it."

"Thank you, Yvonne, but I've waited 30 years for an answer... whether I choose to admit it or not, I need to take some risks to unearth the truth. We have a deal." Nancy laid her hands on the documents. "The documents will be on their way shortly, but the photos are rather old."

"Don't worry. You'll be amazed what these people can do with the information they receive."

Nancy thanked Yvonne and dropped the mobile onto the sofa. She winced as she tried to get up. More bruises were appearing on her body, but the excitement of finding a contact that could deliver certainty made her forget the pain. There would be no dithering hesitation from her any longer, no matter how perilous the process turned out to be.

Her mobile rang again. She had forgotten someone had been trying to contact her. Pole's name flashed onto the screen.

She cursed herself for not checking who had been calling. He hadn't left a voice message, but sent a text. Inspector Pole was mightily annoyed, and she couldn't blame him.

* * *

He ran across Victoria Embankment, making his way through static traffic and stepped onto the Millennium Pier. Pole's mac was hardly adequate for the plummeting temperature, but it would have to do. The River Thames' humidity crept onto the pier and Pole shivered as he reached the inside of the waiting room. People were huddled there, waiting for the river taxis, others were buying memorabilia from the little shop close to the river boat terminal. Pole chose a seat at the far end of the room, activated his MI6 burner phone, and called the only number stored there.

Harris answered almost immediately.

"The old burner phone has been traced."

"Relax, Inspector… it won't give you away. My team has been cleaning up that data. We always do this as a matter of course but we've done a lot more than usual to make sure the calls won't be traced."

"I'll only relax when Ferguson is off my back," Pole shot back. "If anyone is going to find out what happened, it's him."

"Ferguson has a reputation, I'm aware. But so far he has found nothing, and he never will."

"Don't be so goddamn smug, Harris." Pole's voice rose. He looked around, no one had noticed. "I'm also calling about China."

"Glad you are, because I too have news. But perhaps not what you might expect. It seems that Ms Wu is as incredibly efficient as ever at finding where the bad guys are." Harris was moving around, and Pole suspected he was finding a quieter place to continue the conversation.

"I'm waiting."

"She visited Ollie Wilson's place of work this afternoon AND was spotted by one of my CIA colleagues…" Harris sounded amused.

"Shit…" Pole slumped back into the plastic seat.

"A good summary of the situation. Needless to say, I have not told them who Ms Wu is but it's only a matter of time…"

"Hang on," Pole interrupted. "How did he get her name in the first place?"

"Valid question…" Harris chuckled. "She announced herself at the door of Viro-Tech Therapeutics as he was surveying the place… bit of bad luck."

"Which also means that those people, as you say, the bad guys, have her name too."

"Spot on… I can't imagine she wasn't aware of that though. From what I have seen in the short period of time I have known her, Miss Wu is not the sort to flinch when it comes to risk taking."

Pole groaned. "She doesn't need any encouragement, a motorbike tried to run her over this afternoon… and I don't think it was to steal her bag either."

"Don't take this the wrong way, Pole, but that's possibly a good thing... she's getting close to information that rankles with whoever is involved in Ollie Wilson's case and, as you and I know, sooner or later they'll make a mistake."

"What are you now, Harris... a detective at the Met?" But Harris was right. "I'd rather that did not put her in hospital alongside Wilson."

"But Wilson did not know how to go about protecting himself... or how to go about an investigation."

"So why has your CIA colleague, as you put it, come to London?"

"He's on holiday... he has an awful lot of days to use up."

"Harris, I'm your source at the Met and your CIA bod is getting information from me, so why don't you tell me what you know and cut the crap." Pole looked at his watch. He needed to get back.

"Point taken." Harris grew serious. "This is what I know."

Harris gave Pole the details he had gathered from Jack. Pole took in the information and made a few observations.

"The problem for both of us is to decide whether this is a matter personal to Wilson or a corporate matter."

"Or perhaps a bit of both... Biotech is a high-profile industry. No country is immune, if I can put it that way, to the impact it may have."

"I'll keep an open mind."

"And Pole... what about China?"

Pole sighed heavily. "Are you telling me the agency has finally found something about Mr Wu?"

"It's not my department that has gathered it... but..."

"Come on... what have you got?"

"Mr Wu survived the Tiananmen Square protest."

"You mean, despite taking part in the protest?" Pole asked.

"That's right."

"Which begs the question... which part was he on?"

# Chapter Seventeen

Pole's mobile was still going to voicemail.

"Come on... speak to me." Nancy was pacing up and down her lounge, following the large windows that overlooked well-maintained gardens. The streetlights had just come on and the orange glow gave the surrounding buildings a peaceful look.

Her text apology had been genuine, but she also needed to follow her instinct about the case. Her intuition was telling her that all the things she spoke to Ollie Wilson about when he had asked about China had spurred on the young man. She didn't know to what, but she was intent on finding out.

Pole had also been vague about the source of the information he had delivered to her. It had suited her at the time, but it had been careless of her. She should have been more insistent on finding out how Pole had managed to find the information he had brought to her. She now realised these details were giving her contentious information about her father and she doubted they would have been collected by the Hong Kong police 30 years earlier.

Nothing ever came for free, and Pole would no doubt have to reciprocate. He had convinced her the information he had obtained came from overdue favours he was now calling upon, but she no longer believed him.

She returned to her sofa and started spreading the documents she had gathered about her father yet again. She arranged the documents in chronological order as she always liked to.

Memories of a life spanning 45 years were reduced to a neat pile only a couple of inches thick. Nancy held back tears. These few pages were all that was left of an artist whose life had seemed so full. She had never bothered to track down any of the pieces he had worked on, or which had been sold. Her mother had talked about it once in the early days when she'd still been hopeful he might return.

"Every artist worthy of the name should have a catalogue raisonné," she would often say. She had started the process of writing an exhaustive list of what she recalled her husband had left in China. Then there were the pieces he had sold when working in Paris and that had been bought by a small group of collectors who enjoyed avant-garde artists like him.

But once he had sold a piece, her father had no interest in keeping a record... *I just wanted to let go.* It was an ideological stance. An artist was selfless, giving, art belonged to the world.

When her mother had finally cleared the artist's studio at their house, Nancy had saved some of his archives. They had first stored some of it in boxes kept with friends or distant relatives.

After her mother died, Nancy ruthlessly discarded almost everything that might remind her of a father who had never returned. The memory of her mother's death still brought much pain and anger.

Today, of course, she wished she had been less ruthless in discarding old papers. These documents might have shed some light on the journey her father had taken 30 years earlier.

The ring of her mobile made her jump. Pole's name flashed on the screen. Her heart swelled. She could not have found a better man to help her on her journey.

"Jonathan... I must apologise..."

"Later, Nancy... Someone switched off Ollie's oxygen and injected morphine into his drip. I don't know whether he will pull through."

A slap in the face could not have hurt her more. "Are you still there?" Nancy asked.

"Yes... so sorry... I'll pick up Cora and meet you at the hospital." Pole's curtness rankled. Though she understood there was no time for a chat.

She decided against calling Cora directly. Instead, she placed a call to DS Branning. He answered immediately.

168

"She is baking a cake with Charlie. Johnny is pestering them about how he would do it."

Cora's arty gang were doing their best to look after their friend. Thankfully, Branning was giving them enough space to huddle around Cora.

Good man.

"I'm on my way. There has been an incident at the hospital. Ollie is back in ICU. I'd rather she learned it from me."

"Understood, I'll go back up and wait."

Nancy heard Branning crushing his cigarette under his foot and going on his way.

When Nancy arrived 10 minutes later and entered the large lounge, the conversation stopped. Johnny and Beth stopped bickering. She turned off the TV that no one was watching, and Cora half stood up only to sit down again in slow motion, but eyes riveted on Nancy.

Cora closed her eyes. "Is Ollie..." Her voice faltered.

"No, but we need to go back.." Nancy wouldn't speak of the attempt on Ollie's life in front of the others.

Everybody's eyes turned to Cora, concern, anguish and kindness. She nodded. "I'll get my coat."

"You don't have a coat," Johnny piped up. Beth shushed him. "I'm just saying."

"I'll lend you mine." Beth stood up and returned from her bedroom with a long comfortable puffer coat.

Johnny had gathered up her rucksack. Beth helped her with the coat. She nodded to Nancy. Nancy put an arm around her shoulders. There was little she could say that would sound either reassuring or genuine.

DS Branning was already downstairs. He had brought his unmarked police car to the front of the building and left the doors open for them to get in.

DS Branning's unmarked vehicle stopped in front of the hospital entrance. The building was now completely lit up. The large, inverted V that supported the heavy overhanging construction cast a shadow over the pavement. Nancy and Cora got out of the car and Cora moved closer to her friend before entering the building. Her face was a mixture of dread and worry. She tried to be brave but knew she did not want to face ICU on her own, not again.

"I'll catch up with you." Branning pulled the window down and leaned forward to speak to them.

Nancy nodded and turned to Cora. She stood transfixed at the bottom of the entrance stairs. Without a word she suddenly started moving. She pushed the revolving doors, making her way through the crowd without waiting. Cora's agile body was moving fast. Nancy did not want to shout for her to wait, but almost missed the lift when the doors shut.

"So sorry Nancy." Cora shook her head. "It's unbearable."

The same diffused light and cubicles welcomed them when they arrived on the ICU floor. The same receptionist told Cora she wouldn't be able to see Ollie yet. Cora ignored her. She started walking towards the cubicles, checking each of them to see where he was.

Nancy caught up with her and grabbed her arm. "This is not going to help."

"I need to know."

"He's alive... otherwise they would have told you."

A female police officer stood up and walked over to them. "I too have been asked to wait."

"What happened?"

"One of the nurses came to do one of their regular checks. They're very good about that. The next thing I know is a doctor and another nurse are rushing into the room and doing resuscitation."

The short woman was holding her hat between two fidgeting hands. She kept opening and closing her fingers as she spoke.

"But he was doing so well." Cora's voice broke. He had spoken to her.

"I'm very sorry, ma'am. I don't know anything else."

The lift door pinged open. Pole stopped for an instant to get his bearings and made his way towards the small group.

The young female officer gave her side of the story again, adding a few small details about when she'd started her shift. She hadn't left her position since then, and everything had looked normal apart from the sudden deterioration in Ollie's condition.

Pole was about to ask more questions when the doors of the ICU monitoring room slid open. A woman in blue medical scrubs and operating theatre cap walked slowly towards them. She anticipated the question. "He is alive."

Cora collapsed on the nearest chair, holding onto Nancy's hand. "Let's all get ourselves a cup of tea." The registrar moved towards the vending machines and Pole took her cue. They disappeared away from Nancy and Cora. They spoke quietly as they organised teas for everyone. Pole made a face and ran his hand through his hair. Nancy followed the scene with interest.

Pole came back with the cups. The ICU registrar returned to her workstation. The doors slid open and shut without revealing what was happening beyond the frosted glass.

"The tests are going to take some time." Pole sat down next to Cora. "You may want to go back home. As you can see, the hospital is very good at keeping us informed and PC Craven will let us know if we need to return. DS Branning is waiting downstairs."

Cora slumped back into her chair. "I don't have a home." She ignored the cup of tea Pole was handing to her. He placed it on a coffee table nearby.

"I know it is hard for you. But you have my word, the minute I hear anything from the hospital, you will know."

"Jonathan is right, Cora. Staying here won't change a thing." Nancy moved closer to her young friend.

Cora relented. She looked exhausted and disoriented. Pole and Nancy tried to reassure her. She seemed to be nodding without listening.

After a short moment, Pole started walking back towards the lift. Nancy hesitated. PC Craven was also trying to convince Cora to go home. Nancy managed to reach Pole as he walked through the opening doors.

"If it is about this afternoon…" Pole's jaw stiffened a little.

"No." Nancy shook her head, releasing a strand of hair from a hairpin. "I need to give you some information which I gathered this afternoon."

Pole breathed in deeply. "Let's hear it."

"Ollie Wilson spoke to Cora yesterday."

His face tightened further. Why did she not tell him sooner?

Nancy replied before he could ask. "It wasn't a full-blown conversation… it was only one word… innocent."

She carried on. "I also spent a little time at his office. Before you tell me I'm a fool, I can assure you that the CEO of that organisation does

171

not want people getting too close to Ollie or whatever it was he was researching. He did not tell me he would not be around for a while, but simply pretended he was unwell. He equally did not welcome a lawyer asking questions, even on the pretext of making a substantial investment."

"Did he become suspicious?"

"Difficult to say. I offered to invest a large enough amount of money in his business. If he checks my credentials they will hold. Granted, it is a departure from what I usually invest in, but neither is it completely ridiculous."

They had reached the ground floor. Branning was sitting in the main lobby, leafing through a newspaper.

Pole's face was still closed. "Fine… I'll take note. We need to find out more about the type of work he was carrying out, I agree. But I can't just barge into Viro-Tech with a search warrant without good evidence."

"Which is why I wanted to ask those questions."

Pole looked at his watch. "I need to speak to Andy, but I can be at yours in a couple of hours."

Nancy sighed. It was going to take more than a good bottle of wine and an excellent dinner to assuage Inspector Pole's anger.

* * *

"I've asked the team to gather as much information as they can on the building." Jethro was on the loudspeaker. Jack considered whether he had invited the team to listen in, but no, it was just the Station Chief who was talking and browsing through his emails at the same time.

"Thanks for that." Jack had discovered a little café on Fleet Street, the street that once used to be home to all the major newspaper offices in London. He was on his way back to his hotel, having wandered around the City's business district for a while.

He settled at a window table in the Fleet Street Press café. The place felt cosy; old photographs that looked genuine, from the days when Fleet Street was the centre of the press industry, covered the walls.

"I'm curious to check whether the security in and around the building was included originally or whether it is an upgrade. And if it is, when they decided to increase their protection."

"I'll call you as soon as I have gathered the intel. And this Asian woman, Ms Wu, I'll see what I can do." Jack heard Greeney typing, already calling up her name in his database, but as a prerogative of his position, he would only tell Jack what he felt he could reveal. Jack hung up just as his coffee arrived.

He needed a couple of these to stay awake. Still, this would do as a start. He would simply take his time. And perhaps a call to Laurie wouldn't go amiss.

"You're on holiday..." Laurie was, as always, eating her lunch at her desk.

"I know, but I won't be able to have a proper holiday if my mind keeps coming back to the case I left behind."

"And how can I help with this high anxiety of yours, Jack? I would not want to spoil your fun." Laurie had stopped chewing.

"The office where Ollie Wilson worked looked rather well protected when I last looked at a picture of it... even more so from close up."

"Address please?" Laurie resumed her munching. Jack gave the address of Viro-Tech Therapeutics. "OK, I'm there. What do you want to know?"

"How secure is it?"

"Extremely secure... very little infrared penetration, a room with heavy plating security to avoid eavesdropping. High grade glass on the windows. An autonomous electrical system in case of breakdown, very fancy... what are they doing there? And in the middle of the City as well."

"I'm not sure yet. Now can you tell me whether the high spec of the building is recent or was it that secure when first built."

"It'll take me a bit more time to find out, but I'd be very surprised if a building in the middle of London came up to that spec to start with. It's the sort of security that exists in a scientific research park, not in regular offices."

"Even if this place is part of the so-called Silicon Roundabout?"

"Tech companies can operate without that level of security... it's usually their cyber security that matters. This smacks more of bio-hazard or unauthorised bio-research."

Laurie had given up on her food it seemed. "I'll do more research on how they dispose of their waste and rubbish. That's a very good clue as to what's going on inside a building."

"Brilliant... I'm much pacified..."

"That's it?" Laurie's voice rose a little, disappointed... couldn't Jack do better than that?

"Well, if you insist..."

"Today is your lucky day... I'm in the right mood. I'm all giving and compassionate."

"I am after a Ms Wu, who is presumed to live in London."

"Now we're talking... Wu is one of the commonest surnames in China but I'm lucky we are talking about London, the one in the UK perhaps?"

Jack chuckled.

"I'll call you with some results at the end of the day... I mean at the end of my day."

"Anytime... even after midnight."

"No, I wouldn't do that... you need your beauty sleep." Laurie hung up. Jack stretched and stood up. He was ready for a long walk all the way back to Trafalgar Square.

He was picking up his backpack when a call came through. Agent Harris too seemed to have news to share.

* * *

A couple of pieces of duck confit were slowly cooking in the oven. She had prepared a salad of lamb's lettuce and rocket accompanied by walnuts and seasoned with her own homemade vinaigrette. Nancy had chosen the type of comfort food they both liked. They would certainly need it after what was about to be an uneasy conversation.

She had asked herself so many times whether she should have done things differently, but how could she have? Her instinct had always served her well and she needed to be allowed to follow her intuition. It was true that she had taken a back seat when it came to investigating her father's disappearance. She knew why, but her days of letting people take risks for her were over.

Pole would not like that either. She sighed.

Her appetite for calculated risks. Her ability to push a little further than any of her colleagues at the Bar had made her the successful

QC she had been. Memories of past cases flooded her mind, but they didn't all bring a fond smile to her lips.

A presence in the room startled her. Pole had materialised in the flat. She hadn't heard the door. He looked harassed and she was shaken. Time for an honest conversation.

# Chapter Eighteen

"Thanks Laurie... I'll take a look right away." Jack hung up and fell back into the pillows of his large bed. He had organised a few of them against the upholstered headboard. His laptop lay open on one side and a couple of newspapers had been casually abandoned on the other.

Jack stretched his hand towards the bedside table. He had stopped at an off-licence on the way back. On the shop assistant's advice, he had purchased a bottle of Portuguese red wine, Quinta Vista. He had been dubious but decided to try something different whilst in London. The wine the shopkeeper had sold him gave off an intense aroma of black and red berries, with a hint of chocolate and vanilla... whatever it was he tasted Jack was enjoying this latest discovery.

He had also spotted a little deli shop adjacent to the wine shop. Jack had stopped there too, showed them the bottle and ended up with a couple of cheeses... one French Brie de Meaux and a British Kidderton Ash goat cheese. Jack stabbed a piece of Brie he had pre-cut on a small plate and placed it in his mouth... delicious. He took another mouthful of wine... heaven.

He was about to press a couple of keys on his laptop to check his email inbox but his eyes fell on the paragraph in the document he had been reading when Laurie called. The preliminary report, delivered by Senator McCain's senior policy adviser, had started on a grim note.

But Jack took the introductory words with a pinch of salt. It was not the first time that a report sought to attract attention by announcing the doom of the US military.

Jack reread the sentence that had attracted his attention and pondered again on the definition of 'kill chain'. It was a term that everybody in the US military used but seldom talked about in other circles, including the CIA.

On the battlefield, the kill chain is essential. It is the process by which the army command acquires an understanding of what is happening in the field, then decides what response is the most adequate, finally taking action to achieve the results it has decided upon. The name of the game, of course, is to break the kill chain of the adversary as fast and as often as possible to win the confrontation. Although acknowledging the technical superiority of the US army and its appetite for continuing to seek technical advances, the paper argued that there were other ways war should now be envisaged. It took, as an example, recent movements seen on the frontier between the Ukraine and Russia. Something was brewing but US forces seemed equipped against an opponent like Russia that was willing to use surprising tactics.

Jack's glass was empty. He considered whether he should indulge in another... he was on holiday after all. He refilled the glass and carried on reading, letting himself sink into the pillows that were propping up his back.

One of the report's conclusions was clear. The US army's technological advantage was fading fast and one reason for this was that the most important technical advances the military needed were being developed by the private sector.

These were issues that neither Russia nor China had. Both countries were quite prepared to requisition the technology they needed when they needed it, whether the owners and developers liked it or not.

Jack laid the laptop back on the bed. He folded the newspapers into a neat pile, swung his legs across the side of the bed and stood up. He was only a couple of feet away from the large window that overlooked Northumberland Avenue. The street was brightly lit and as he moved closer to the glass, he caught a glimpse of Nelson's Column illuminated.

The night sky felt low and heavy, making Trafalgar Square look bright and almost festive. Nelson's statue was bathed in a greenish light that gave him an almost fluorescent glow. Jack shook his head.

He wondered what the great generals and admirals of the past would make of the way warfare was evolving right now.

Jack leaned for a moment against the window frame. Despite the double glazing the cold had started to creep in. He shivered and pulled the curtains halfway across, still keen to enjoy some of the view's postcard quality.

He was about to grab his jacket and put on his shoes, to leave the room in search of a small restaurant for dinner, when he remembered Laurie's email. He had asked for a favour and she would be expecting some feedback. He slumped back onto the bed, turned the laptop towards him and opened the message.

She had sent him the details of the security measures that had recently been added to the Viro-Tech building. It was indeed as Jack had suspected, improvements over and above what Fort Knox might have considered impregnable.

\* \* \*

"Inspector Pole." His voice was formal, ready for any news the caller might give him. Nancy could hear him moving around, no doubt seeking a quiet place to take her call. If he needed time to decide how he wanted to respond to her lack of transparency, Nancy would give him that.

She had already taken the plates and cutlery out of the cupboards to lay the table for dinner. She started slowly to arrange them. Pole's voice floated in and out of the room, in small bursts. Questions she could not understand, followed by what seemed interminable answers.

Nancy went back to the oven to check the meat. Its nutty smell made her mouth water. She hadn't had much to eat during the day and her stomach was starting to complain. The salad was ready to toss. She uncorked a bottle of red wine, realising she should have let it breathe a little longer.

Pole stopped. She wondered whether he was still in the room. She waited a few moments and stuck her head through the door. Pole had dropped onto the large couch, elbows on knees and hands clenched in front of his mouth. Nancy moved to the armchair closest to him and sat down slowly. She didn't have to ask.

"Ollie Wilson will not wake up." Pole spoke in the neutral tone she knew he used to hide the sorrow he felt at times when his professionalism did not allow him to show his emotions.

They both sat in silence, struggling to come to terms with the news. "The UCH registrar called me to confirm what she'd suspected. It's not the result of his overdose in Camden..." Pole let his arms fall to his sides, his eyes fixed on the mobile phone he had dropped on the coffee table. "Someone injected him with a fresh dose of drugs... an opiate of some sort."

"But how is that possible?" Nancy's croaky voice sounded almost inaudible. "You mean... someone came into Ollie's room to administer it?"

"That's the only way it could have happened... it was injected into the drip they fitted when he first arrived." Pole picked up the phone and pocketed it. "Of course, I'll have to interview the two PCs who have been on duty the whole time he has been in hospital, but I'll be surprised if it has anything to do with those two."

"Then the only possibility is hospital staff." Nancy cleared her throat. She owed it to Ollie and Cora to focus on the matter. "Or, more likely, someone who managed to pass for a doctor or hospital nurse."

Pole nodded. "I'll get Andy to check the CCTV cameras. We should have a good record of who came in and out of the room." Pole finally raised his head. He briefly met Nancy's eyes. Some remaining anger flashed there, but he was no longer in the mood for an argument and neither was she.

Nancy stretched out a hand and gently squeezed his fingers. "I'm sorry I gave you concern, Jonathan."

Pole's fingers remained lose, hesitant. "I can't protect you if you won't let me."

"I don't always need protecting... it's also who I am, a risk taker, always needing to know how far I can push my luck."

"I'm aware of that, but by not talking to me, you have delayed what I could have done to investigate the assault."

"I had spoken to Andy." Nancy had laced her fingers into his. He almost pulled back.

"You know Andy will not query what you say. He is good, a very good DS, but he's still a little green."

"It felt right that I should not surrender to fear... I don't believe the bike attack was aimed at snatching my satchel. It was all about scaring me off, intimidation."

"But we don't know what the assailant was trying to scare you about. Is it the Wilson case? Is it your father's case?"

"And we won't know until I pursue both investigations with equal determination."

Pole looked surprised. He must have expected her key focus to remain on the Wilson case. But he had to know she would no longer rely on others to find out about her father's fate.

"I can't let people get hurt because they make enquiries about him on my behalf. And somehow China is a key player in what is happening to me, to Ollie and of course to Amy."

"What makes you say that?"

"I had a number of conversations with Ollie about China... At the time I thought it was all about Cora. Her parents' disappearance. Her upbringing as a Hong Kong Chinese. But his questions were very specific... corruption, the interference of mainland China in Hong Kong's affairs – those sort of things. But I no longer think that is the case. His questions were concerned not so much with the past but about the present, and I did not spot it at the time."

"Is that a good enough reason to go barging into his office?"

"You don't have enough evidence for a search warrant, as you said yourself. Not to search his office, anyway. You could just about justify requesting access to his computer, but the company will have removed any sensitive data by now and there is nothing you can do about it."

Nancy came to sit next to Pole. "You know I'm right. This case is made to look like a drug addiction gone bad, perhaps even a drug dealing transaction that went wrong... and nothing else."

"And we can't discard that as a possibility."

"You are right, we can't... I might be too..." Nancy hesitated but carried on. "...obsessed with China to think straight, but I'd like to follow my hunch."

"I don't mind you following your hunch as long as I know whether that puts you in danger." Pole moved his body round to face her.

"It's not always practical to do that."

He picked up his mobile. "This is switched on 24/7, as you know."

"But I know you too well... you'll try to convince me to stop."

"That's my job. I stop people doing stupid things all the time, so I'd like to stop you from doing them too." Pole dumped the phone on the table again, irritated.

Nancy smiled and leaned her head on his shoulder. "I need to be free to choose. I know I'm asking you to do the opposite to what you spend your career doing... very successfully I might add. I find solutions because I take enough risks to discover the right information."

"I don't want to change that, Nancy, I just want to be given the important information in time so that I can anticipate any problems."

"And I'm about to feed you exactly that."

Pole ran his free hand through his hair and left it there for a moment. "So, what have you got for me?"

Nancy moved more fully into the sofa, her back against the armrest, legs pulled underneath her. She gave a detailed account of her day without omitting the motorbike incident. Pole picked up one of her yellow notebook pads. He didn't interrupt. It felt more like a deposition than teamwork, but Nancy had decided not to worry if he felt put out by this.

"I'll check whether there is anything on record about Viro-Tech Therapeutics," Pole finally volunteered.

"And I'll get more information about the ultimate beneficial owner of the Hong Kong company that has invested in Viro-Tech... I have just managed to find the time to call the most suitable contact amongst my former criminal lawyer colleagues. I am sure he will help."

Pole thought for a moment. "The NCA has given me very little so far. I'd like to know how it was that someone spotted Ollie in the heroin den so quickly."

Nancy cocked her head. "Any idea? It is odd, as you say."

"Someone was very keen for us to find him... I just need to know who."

"Any other discoveries on your side? Andy has been sieving through CCTV cameras for two days solid."

"We've traced one of the fake SOCO men to Balham but after that nothing."

"And the other man?" Nancy asked.

"Eastern European, according to Yvonne… previously had lots of tattoos but they have been removed surgically."

"So, a keen desire for anonymity."

"Without a doubt… these people aim to operate without being noticed. They know all the blind spots of the London CCTV system. They have an excellent understanding of how the police operate."

"And they recruit people who won't mind being anonymised. It's a big deal for those Eastern European gang members to let go of their tats… they tell their life story."

"Is that so?" Pole moved forward a little.

"There is a code, and some tattoos will tell what crimes these people have committed, whether they have escaped prison, whether they are lifers and so on…" Nancy nodded. "The Russians in particular. The mafia and the prisoners themselves use it to signal reward or punishment. You get a tattoo that tells people if you are a snitch or a paedophile, and you are given that tattoo whether you like it or not."

"So, you think Eastern European or Russian mafia?"

"That's right… or an agency involved in this area, using former agents… ex KGB or ex FSB that have moved on."

Pole's jaw tightened. "Something we can't ignore either."

"I wouldn't. As long as we don't know what it is that Ollie was trying to hide, we can't discount anything." Nancy seemed to have hit an unexpected nerve.

"Shall we have some food?" Pole looked at his watch. He got up and moved slowly towards the kitchen.

Nancy waited for a short moment. She was not backing down and she had to try to make him see this was right. Whether the Russians were involved or not, she needed to keep investigating Ollie. She was now certain that Pole was himself taking risks he had not disclosed to her.

There was only one way to find out.

She stood up and reached the kitchen, as he was moving the tossed salad to the table, meticulously arranging the serving cutlery on top of the bowl.

"I almost forgot to say… Yvonne has found someone willing to help in the authentication of Amy's document, the article that mentions my father."

Pole slowed down a little. He considered the dish he had just brought in and rearranged the cutlery once more. "Who is that?"

"I don't have a name, but that person has the tools it will take... they work for MI6."

\* \* \*

"Ollie," was the only word Cora could utter when the UCH doctor called her. She had asked to be told as soon as the results came, torn between the desire to still have hope and wanting to know the truth.

He wouldn't wake up. He would never smile at her again. He would never...

The doctor was saying her name, asking questions. Was she alone? No.

Did she need help? No.

He could call back later to discuss things further. Yes.

Cora thanked him in a voice she barely recognised. She looked around, feeling at a loss. Beth's room that had felt welcoming and cosy now felt alien. She longed to be in her flat, in their flat, amongst their familiar things. She wanted to wrap herself in Ollie's ample dressing gown and smell the scent of his discreet aftershave.

Someone was knocking softly at the door. Johnny's cheerful face popped in through the door he had just opened.

"Dinner is..." He did not finish his sentence. In a few steps, he had reached her, knelt next to her to wrap his arms around her. There was no need to talk. Her friends knew about her last visit to the hospital.

Beth came in and sat on the bed next to Cora, hands on her shoulders.

"The doctor told me to speak to Inspector Pole." Cora closed her eyes for a short moment. She managed to steady her voice to tell her friends the news.

Crying would not bring back the man she loved. She needed to know what had happened. Whatever Ollie had been, he had no longer been a junkie.

"Why?" Johnny moved sideways to look at Cora, his voice tinged with anger.

"Because they found him in a heroin den and that looks bad if you don't know the guy," Beth said.

"That's ridiculous… I know a junkie when I see one and that was not him." Johnny shook his head.

"He didn't even want to try your excellent, crunchy cookies spiced with a hint of weed." Beth shrugged. This was almost incomprehensible.

"He had taken drugs though… at uni." Cora's voice trembled. Perhaps she was wrong after all.

"Everybody at uni tries a bit of everything… right?" Johnny looked at Beth for support. "That's what it's all about, try different things, find yourself… you know, that sort of stuff."

"And learn something…" Beth's tone of voice stopped Johnny. "… which Ollie did better than any of us… with a PhD from Harvard Medical School."

"What did Inspector Pole say about all this?" Johnny slid to the floor to sit next to Cora.

"I'm not sure he will want to discuss it with me. I suppose I could be involved… but I sense he is not ruling it out."

"That's his job." Beth spotted a loose thread on Cora's sweater and removed it delicately.

"He won't fall for it." Johnny shook his head with fierce determination. "For a copper he looks pretty enlightened."

"You just like the goatee and the fancy motorbike," Cora mumbled.

"Not true… I'm perfectly able to see a man for who he is, despite the goatee and the Ducati."

"Enough Johnny…" Beth snapped, and it silenced him. "What can we do to help, Cora?"

"Yes, tell us." Johnny grabbed Cora's hand and squeezed hard.

"I keep thinking that the answer must be in his office." Cora volunteered after a moment.

"Why?" Beth frowned.

"He was so involved in the development of this new idea, something that would revolutionise drug production… he didn't want to speak about it with me, because it was confidential… but I now wonder whether he wanted to protect me."

"What does Nancy say about it?" Beth was still frowning.

"I haven't had time to speak to her about it... it's just dawned on me... after the call from the hospital."

"Call her." Johnny was already looking for her mobile phone. Cora shook her head. "Not yet." She hesitated.

"Come on... tell us what you've got in mind." Johnny wiggled his fingers to coax an answer out.

"I'd like to pay a visit to Ollie's office first."

The others looked at each other. "Why not, you're entitled to collect his stuff from his desk aren't you?" Johnny proposed.

"I want to go now." Cora was already standing up.

# Chapter Nineteen

It was almost midnight. Jack's stomach had started to complain, and it was time he paid attention to it.

The file that Laurie had sent had triggered more questions than it gave answers. Ms Wu was not what he had expected. She was not a Chinese investor or biotech researcher and seemed to have little connection with that industry.

She was a retired QC, admittedly retired before her time, but nevertheless a lawyer. And a high-profile one at that. Her experience in criminal law and corporate fraud had propelled her into representing high-profile defendants. She had built a reputation for sagacity, perseverance, and an uncommonly sharp intelligence. She had given up the Bar at the height of a career when a possible appointment to the Bench was in the offing.

For many years now she had focused on mentoring young professionals and supporting contemporary art. Laurie had not found any questionable associations until the Henry Crowne affair popped up. Matters had changed abruptly for Ms Wu, it seemed. Henry Crowne, the disgraced financier, had spent time at HMP Belmarsh in the high security unit. He had disappeared however after a mere four years in prison, achieving a feat no one had before him... escape from HSU Belmarsh. No one had seen or heard of him since.

Jack had smiled at the information. If MI6 were not involved in this, he was no longer called Jack Shield.

The enigmatic Ms Wu had become, in the meantime, an expert adviser to Scotland Yard in London.

Jack had called Laurie a few times. She was still getting more information. According to her, the best was yet to come.

She was right. Nancy's father, Li Jie Wu, had been a well-known artist and activist. He had escaped the Cultural Revolution with his family before it was too late, and yet returned to China when Deng Xiao Ping had taken over the reins of the country. He had disappeared again, like so many dissidents had in the aftermath of the Tiananmen Square uprising.

His daughter, however, had never returned to mainland China after her father's disappearance. Jack was no longer certain what her link with Viro-Tech could be.

Still, coincidences were rare in his line of business. Whatever tenuous connection was there, he had to find it.

Jack had delved back into the McCain report in the hope that something might be relevant. So far, the document had not made him any the wiser, and by this time he also had to content himself with fewer restaurant choices when it came to dinner. Jack closed the laptop and placed it back in the safe.

He added a sweater to his shirt, donned his winter jacket and made his way downstairs to reception. The busy lobby was now empty, apart from a young couple who were enjoying their last drink. They sat next to each other, oblivious to the world. The receptionist was now an older gentleman. He gave Jack a friendly nod which Jack returned.

Jack pushed open the heavy entrance door and stood outside, at the top of the three steps that led down to the street. The temperature had dropped to freezing and he felt a few pinpricks of ice on his face. He lifted his head towards the sky. It might snow very soon. Jack stepped into the street and hurried up towards St Martin's Lane.

He walked at a brisk pace towards a row of old buildings with tall narrow frontages, red bricks and steep roofs. The streets were almost empty. The gift shops, casual eateries and pubs had already closed.

The pedestrian lane that appeared to his right looked dark and deserted. According to his guide, he was only a few yards away from the next passage in which he could find a restaurant that served dinner after 11pm. A place that had an excellent reputation for seafood and for accommodating latecomers after midnight.

The wind had become stronger. The small shards of ice he had felt when walking out of the hotel were now relentlessly assailing his face. He took refuge for a short moment underneath an overhanging roof. The theatre had closed a couple of hours earlier and the façade was now dark.

Jack took his bearings again. The pub opposite the theatre was also shut but the light inside the main room was still on, probably for staff preparing the place for tomorrow's customers.

A small group of people walked out of the restaurant he was looking for and Jack hurried towards its door. They looked happy with their evening and the weather seemed to have very little effect on their joviality.

He pushed the door open and a breeze of warm air welcomed him. A young woman in white shirt, dark waistcoat and long black apron smiled and took his jacket. "It will have to be the bar if you would like to join us for food and drinks."

Jack nodded. Any place would do as long as he could have some hot food. He took a seat on one of the bar stools. A couple sat at the corner of the long bar, a few seats away from him, enjoying the dessert they were sharing.

He ordered a crab bisque and seared scallops. The sommelier recommended a glass of Meursault. Jack couldn't argue with the sommelier's choice, a rich oaky palate was what Jack was looking for.

The waiter behind the bar brought him six opened Jersey oysters, on the house. An excellent ploy to make sure the first glass of the outstanding white burgundy would be followed by another.

The hostess who had welcomed Jack was about to lock the door for the evening when a small man slipped in. Jack cast an eye over him. He looked unremarkable, dressed in a black puffer jacket, a dark scarf wound tight around his neck and the lower part of his face. The hostess hesitated but allowed him in. He moved to the opposite side of the bar, taking off his scarf as he settled onto one of the stools.

Jack took out his mobile, checked on his emails, but decided it was too late to reply to any of them. One hour of rest to enjoy his food was well deserved.

He swallowed four oysters, enjoying with them the warm French bread that accompanied the dish. Jack cast an eye casually towards the latecomer. The man had taken his smartphone out too, browsing absentmindedly through its contents. He lifted his head to look at the last customers around the room out of curiosity and returned to his browsing. The fish soup came, and Jack tucked in, forgetting all about the man at the bar. The couple he had noticed a few seats away were readying themselves to go. The woman slid from the high stool, wobbled a little with a giggle. The man held open her coat and helped her to put it on. They were off; the night was still young for those two, Jack mused.

The scallops came just as he had finished his soup. The aroma of saffron and cream made his mouth water. The restaurant was now almost empty. Another couple of men at a corner table were also departing. Jack checked his watch, 12.35am. He stifled a yawn. It had been a long day.

The waiters around him were setting up the tables for the following day and yet there was no urgency in their movements. Jack finished the last morsel on his plate, mopped up the remainder of the sauce with a piece of bread and asked for the bill. The man on the other side of the bar seemed to have finished his food as well. He had settled the bill and downed the last of his beer. He zipped up his puffer jacket and rolled his scarf around his neck and face and made for the door.

Jack left a couple of £50 notes in the tray. He thanked the waiters who thanked him in return. He slid into his winter jacket and found himself out in the cold again.

Jack turned left, advanced a few yards and stopped. This was not the way he had come. He turned around to change direction. Two men started walking towards him from the top of the alleyway, and another man appeared from a recess in the wall of the adjacent theatre. Choosing a restaurant in a small passage hadn't been judicious. Jack had just walked into a trap of his own making.

* * *

The dinner had been more relaxed than Nancy had anticipated. Both she and Pole were surprisingly good at putting their differences aside over good food. She suspected that Pole's early family life, with numerous brothers, sisters and friends joining the family table, had given him a sense that a meal should be enjoyed to the full.

"You can always discuss and exchange, but never quarrel, around the dinner table," he once told Nancy when he started telling her more about his parents' arty household.

But dinner was over. Nancy had rustled up a dessert of vanilla ice cream, roasted almonds and melted toffee. Coffee had been brewed and she handed a cup to Pole.

"Yvonne is a source of unexpected help. I didn't realise she had connections into MI6."

Pole's face momentarily froze but he commented, "Yvonne has been in the game for a rather long time. She always drives herself hard to deliver over and above. I'm not surprised she has contacts in unforeseen places."

Nancy poured herself a cup of coffee, giving herself time before replying. They had almost quarrelled a couple of hours ago over her not reporting the attack. Did she want to make things worse? But she had taken matters for granted for far too long, ignoring what she was best at doing… asking the tough questions.

Now was the time to apply the method she was known for to her own case. Whether she liked the immediate results or not, she was confident that in the long run she would not regret it.

Pole drank his coffee in silence. Nancy refilled his cup without asking whether he wanted a top-up.

"I have always assumed that the information you gathered for me about my father's case came from the contact you have in Hong Kong." She lifted her own cup to her lips and took a sip. "But it was lazy of me, Jonathan. I should have asked whether…" She lifted her face towards Pole with a small smile of regret. "…whether these details came at a cost to yourself."

Pole's eyes closed briefly.

"I'm not talking about monetary costs, of course…" Nancy kept the conversation moving, hoping Pole would not clam up. "I have gone through all the data you have provided me with. It's a lot more than I ever had before, and certainly a lot more detailed."

Pole inhaled slowly and gave a short sigh before replying. "I can't always tell you where the information comes from. Not that I don't trust you, but it is also why the details are of such good quality… my sources know I won't reveal their names."

"Are your sources in danger?" Nancy abandoned her coffee. Her eyes searched Pole's face for signs that would tell her what she needed to know.

"No." Pole had almost finished his cup.

"Are you in danger?" Nancy grabbed his wrist as he was putting the cup back onto its saucer.

"I'm a police officer, *mon coeur*... that comes with the territory." Pole slid his hand over Nancy's and squeezed gently.

"That is not an answer." Nancy frowned, her eyes narrowing with concern. "Is the gathering of information about my father putting you in any serious danger...?"

Pole smiled at the well-formulated question... "Don't worry about your good friend Pole." He placed a light kiss on the palm of the hand he was holding.

"That is not an answer either." Nancy hesitated, her voice wavering a little. "If you are putting yourself in harm's way for my sake, please stop. The chances of my father being alive are minuscule. It is not worth endangering your life..."

"But finding out will give you some much-needed peace of mind." Pole grew serious.

"I'd have to find peace of mind in some other way. What would definitely not bring me peace is if something were to happen to you. I couldn't bear it."

Pole smiled again, a gentle smile. "Then you know how I feel when you go running after the bad guys without protection."

Nancy shook her head and smiled back. "I suppose I have to concede the argument, Inspector Pole."

"Very glad you do... at least for the time being. I'm sure I haven't won my case yet."

Pole had left a short time afterwards. It felt like a stalemate between them. Nancy knew now that he had committed to some unpalatable deal in order to find the information she needed. She almost succumbed to a moment of recrimination but thought better of it. It would not help her in her pursuit to find out what Pole had pledged he would do in return for information.

She went into her study. She had reorganised it earlier, and all the loose papers had been filed apart from the two cases she was working

191

on. The board she used to jot down messages to her cleaner had now been transformed into a tracking board any good detective would have been proud of.

It was covered with the relevant documents, photos and notes on yellow stickers. Her desk that was usually littered with books was now organised into piles of papers, and they were all about two cases, Ollie's and her father's.

* * *

One of the men turned back his head towards something on the ground. Jack recognised the scarf of the man who had just left the Atlantic Bar before him. So perhaps it was a mugging after all.

But the coolness with which the three men were closing in on him told him otherwise. He had heard the door of the restaurant lock behind him. By the time he went back and attracted the attention of the staff inside, the men would be upon him, leaving him little chance of escape.

Jack dug into his jacket pockets in search for something he could use. There was nothing in there except for a packet of Kleenex and what must have been the wrapper of an old chocolate bar. His best bet was to tackle the single man, but the moment he turned away the others would be in pursuit. The third assailant had to delay Jack for the others to catch up and he looked more than able to do that... large shoulders hunched forward, thick neck, the sort of man you imagined as a bouncer or butcher.

In the dark of the night something glimmered to his left. The Atlantic Bar staff had taken in all the tables and chairs that stood outside under the electric heaters. The lane looked a little broader than when he had arrived, and someone had left an empty beer bottle lying on the ground that the staff had not removed.

Jack took another step forward, crouched to the ground, seemingly to tighten up a non-existent shoelace. He measured the distance it would take him to run to the top of the lane. The big man who'd walked out of the shadows was now moving slowly, waiting for the others to catch him up. Still, he was advancing, and in only a few moments he would be upon him.

Jack leaped sideways, grabbing the bottle in one scoop, smashing it against the wall. The sudden move startled the man but only for an instant. Jack reached him in a couple of steps, avoiding the man's fist by a whisker, and planted the broken glass in his face.

The man yelled and pulled back. His colleagues sprinted towards Jack. Jack ran the few yards towards the top of the alleyway and dived left. He might as well try to make it back to the hotel, although he doubted he would be able to reach it before the other two had caught up with him.

The road was completely empty. Jack kept going, running in the middle of the street, hoping a cab might still materialise at this late hour. The resonant sound of pounding footsteps told him they were getting closer. He reached Trafalgar Square where the traffic picked up a little.

A few cars were waiting at the traffic light, ready to be funnelled into the one-way system. Jack changed direction and made towards the pavement running alongside the square. His foot caught on the kerb and he came crashing down. He contained the pain, rolled to his side and managed to stand up.

The men had almost caught up with him. He started running again, but it was too late A solid fist slammed into his back, sending him flying over the concrete ground. He rolled again onto his side with a yelp of pain, then managed a well-placed kick onto the kneecap of his assailant. Jack used the tree next to which he had fallen to stand up and shield himself from the next blow.

The other men had caught up with him and Jack stood back, fists at the ready, facing his two aggressors. One of the men lifted his hands, palms outstretched, left leg anchored behind him. The other started circling around Jack. These people had been trained in combat. The moves looked strangely similar to karate but had an edge that made them more like wrestling.

The shriek of a police siren went almost unnoticed. The man to Jack's right swung his leg in an impressive arc and caught Jack in the chest before he had time to swing his body sideways. The second slammed a semi-closed fist into his kidneys.

The police car screeched to a halt and four police officers ran towards them, shouting instructions to stop and pull back. The final kick almost got Jack in the face, but he parried the blow with a strong-arm defence.

The two men ran off with two officers in pursuit. Jack tried to articulate a sentence as the other two officers approached him with caution. He caught his breath and managed to articulate the words... Steve Harris.

\* \* \*

"Where is she?" Nancy was walking through her apartment, gathering a set of keys, her bag and coat. The voice at the other end of her mobile was getting more strained by the minute. "Beth, I'm on my way... just try to get her to wait somehow."

Nancy ran out of the door without locking it. She pressed the lift button a few times, hurriedly. She arrived in the building's garage less than two minutes later. Another minute and she was sitting inside her Aston Martin. It would not have been her choice of vehicle, despite its enviable reputation, but it had belonged to an old friend, and she was loath to sell it.

The key had started the engine by remote activation. She engaged the gears into drive and slid out of the car park, in the direction of the Viro-Tech offices.

She slowed down as she approached her destination. She had inserted her mobile into the hands-free holder on the dashboard and Beth was still on the phone.

"We couldn't stall her... she's gone into Martha's Buildings lane."

"Viro-Tech?" Nancy asked.

"I think so."

Nancy parked the car in a side street, got out and ran towards the lane she had visited earlier that day. Beth and Johnny were huddled together in a small doorway that could hardly contain them.

"She's gone mad." Johnny was flapping his arms. "She's trying to get in."

Nancy gave Beth her car keys. "Aston Martin a block away, wait for me there."

Nancy walked into the alleyway and stood still a few steps in... listening for the noise of someone moving around. There were no sounds at all, and she feared Cora had already started her ascent of the office building. Even if she reached the top, which Nancy very much doubted, it was unlikely that the roof would be any less secure than the rest of the building.

The office blocks in the small lane formed a continuous wall without any gaps. The streetlamps were providing very little light, some corners remaining in pitch-black darkness. Nancy recalled that the small street turned into a dead end on the right providing space for cars to park. She took a few steps forward. Then stopped again hoping of hearing a sound that would betray Cora's position.

Still nothing.

She scanned the façade of the building. There was no movement up there in the windows. Nancy judged that there was little chance a security guard would be patrolling the street.

"Cora…" she called softly. "It's Nancy… we need to talk. I have an idea."

No reply came. Nancy's eyes became accustomed to the dim lighting of the place. She spotted a few cars still parked at the top of the lane. She found it hard to believe people could still be working at this late hour… but perhaps they were. If so, she had to find Cora urgently.

"Cora… please." She took a chance and spoke a little louder. No answer.

Nancy scanned the front of the Viro-Tech building and squinted. Flat against the wall, a figure was stretched between two windowsills two floors up, paused in what looked like an impossible climb.

Nancy moved to stand below the figure on the wall.

"Cora, this is not going to lead you anywhere…"

Nancy was about to plead again with her friend, when a light came on in the small lobby. Someone had entered the lift and alighted at ground level. There was no way Cora could make it down before that person came out.

Nancy looked around. She dived into the recess of the backyard, hoping that whoever came out would be using a car facing in the right direction, away from her.

The door of Viro-Tech opened. Nancy ventured to take a look.

Jared Turner, Viro-Tech's CEO had been working late… very late.

He stood outside for a moment, uncertain, perhaps sensing the disturbance in the quiet environment of the secluded alleyway. He ran a hand over his face and walked towards one of the cars. He would need to turn around to reach the driving side of his car and was bound to spot Nancy huddled in the corner of the yard, and if Turner raised his eyes as he got into his seat, he would spot the figure attempting to climb his building.

Nancy spotted a tall rubbish container. She squeezed behind it, holding her breath and staying as still as she could. She could no longer see what was happening in the lane. The beams of two headlights swept the small courtyard in a semi-circle, paused and moved forward to finally disappear. Nancy waited for a few moments before extracting herself from her hiding place. When she reached the front of the Viro-Tech building Cora was already back on the ground.

"I can get into this building, you know." Cora was not being stubborn; she had seen a way in.

Nancy took a minute to consider what her friend had said. "You mean to say that you can access Viro-Tech from another building?"

In the semi-darkness a smile showed on Cora's face.

"If that's the case, we need to plan your visit a bit better than this." Cora's smile deepened. "You mean…"

"I'll help you."

# Chapter Twenty

His hand crept towards the source of the noise. Pole's fingers tried to make sense of what they were touching before finding the right button to press. He placed the phone against his ear without speaking.

"Rise and shine, mate..." Harris's East End accent was a little more pronounced than usual.

Pole blinked, finding it hard to focus. He rolled onto his side towards the bedside clock.

"What time do you call this?"

"Time to get out of bed and meet for breakfast... and before you complain, I've been up since 4am." Harris was almost cheerful.

Pole sunk back into his pillow. "Why should I?" Even though he was playing hard to get, Pole knew he would meet Harris. Harris was not a time-waster. Still, Harris could not expect to ask and be granted.

"Because I have some information about your case and because the CIA got a beating. Normally I couldn't care less but he is a pal and he's getting close to something people don't want him to find."

Pole threw the covers away. "Where?"

"Small caff, not that far from you... near the Oval cricket ground. It's called Kennington Lane Café."

"Seriously?" Pole was gathering his clothes in the darkness of his room. He remembered he was home and alone, sadly – no need to tiptoe around the place – and switched on the light.

"What's wrong with a greasy spoon at 6am in the morning anyway?"

"Everything..." Pole grumbled.

"And Pole." Harris chuckled. "Think twice about bringing that fancy motorbike of yours."

"It's true that if you park your shitty car next to it, it'll look a lucky prize worth nicking..." Pole killed the call and moved to the bathroom for a much-needed cooling-off shower.

He parked his Ducati along one of the steel bike racks. Pole removed one of the spark plugs, a trick he had learned from his father a long time ago when he had bought his first motorbike aged 19. The thought usually made him smile but today he resented having to go through this extra safety measure.

Pole looked around. The busy junction was starting to come alive; cars and lorries had begun to pile along its complex road system. The pavement was wide, with grey stones that looked surprisingly clean. The black-and-white frontage said simply Kennington Lane Café – all day breakfast, accompanied by a row of pictures intended to whet the appetite by displaying burgers, fries and various other breakfast options.

His phone rang. "Don't be shy... I'm in already... what would you like? I'll order for you whilst you brace yourself."

"Toast and tea." Pole pocketed the spark plug.

"Wow... choice is between full English with or without black pudding, and tea with or without sugar."

Pole rolled his eyes. "Without on both counts."

This was a really bad idea. His stomach would regret it for the rest of the day.

Harris had chosen a table near the window yet tucked away in the corner of the room. A cup of tea was already in front of his seat. It couldn't have been there long as steam from the hot liquid was still moving in hazy circles above the mug.

Pole sat opposite Harris, dumping his leather jacket, as well as his helmet on the seat next to him.

"This had better be good."

"So grumpy and it's only 6am."

"Cut the bull... what is it you have to tell me?"

Harris's lips kept the humorous curve but his eyes had grown serious.

"We spoke about the CIA interest in Ollie Wilson…"

"How can I forget?"

"The agent who is following the case got jumped by three men last night… actually this morning to be precise."

The breakfast plates arrived. Pole lost focus for an instant. He had not had a full English for a long time, and it smelt more than tempting. Harris stopped speaking as the waitress lay the food in front of both men. "Anythin' else lads?"

"Nah luv, that'll do." Harris nodded.

Pole picked up his knife and fork and let them hover for a moment over his plate; eggs, sausages, bacon, tomatoes, mushrooms, baked beans and two pieces of crisp white toast.

Harris was already tucking in. "My CIA contact doesn't think it was a mugging attempt… These guys were trained in some form of martial art." He shovelled in a piece of sausage and some beans, munched and smiled… heaven.

"And what is it your contact thinks he's getting close to?" Pole drank some tea, letting the tempting smell of bacon whet his appetite.

"He'd gone snooping around…" Harris grinned. "…the offices of Viro-Tech Therapeutics yesterday afternoon… managed to get in after the delightful Ms Wu."

Pole had cut into a piece of egg and was about to eat it. He replaced the fork back onto his plate with a small clunk. "He got in? How?"

"Just the old trick of not letting the door slam shut after someone goes in."

"Did he find anything of value?"

"Confirmation that the place is worse than Fort Knox… to quote the man himself."

Pole's face darkened. "It is a biotech company. I presume they will want to keep under wraps whatever it is they are developing… and isolate their research."

"Are you out of touch, Pole? Tech companies like this one don't do any dangerous stuff… I mean the viral stuff… on their premises anymore. They do research through other techniques, but when they come to the in-vivo phase – injecting mice or some other poor animal – they do this elsewhere… usually on a research campus dedicated to the purpose."

Pole still hadn't touched his food. "But surely, they must be protecting data… That sounds reasonable."

"There is reasonable and reasonable." Harris didn't mind Pole pushing back. "I agree that the protection of research is essential, but this is done through cyber security, not necessarily through upgrading the security systems of an entire building. The property is fitted with anti-spying kit MI6 at Vauxhall Cross would be proud of."

Pole swallowed the piece of egg and moved onto the bacon and toast. It was surprisingly good. Pole took a few mouthfuls, looking at the mounting traffic outside.

"You'd like me to get a warrant to take a look at the place? You're not the only one…" He was still looking outside. His conversation with Nancy still rankled. The sky had become lighter despite the heaviness of the clouds. "I'd like to take a look around myself as well, to be honest."

Pole faced Harris again.

"That's the spirit." Harris raised his cup of tea.

"I don't need MI6 to raise my spirits."

"But a bit of extra information from the agency doesn't go amiss." Harris had almost finished his plate of food, chasing the last few baked beans with a piece of toast.

"What's in it for you in all this?"

Harris pushed away from the table and settled back into his chair. "Just because it's you, Pole… I don't mind telling you I'm being opportunistic here. China is increasingly on the radar of my agency, and so is biotech."

Pole ached to know more, but it would be pushing his luck. "Going back to the drugs side of the Wilson case, my DS is following up the original line of inquiry."

Harris cocked his head. "That's not a bad idea. Search their offices for something less contentious than their research programme and gain access to the place that way."

"That's the only card I have to play at the moment." Pole finished his cup of tea. "I have absolutely nothing suspicious to go on otherwise."

"I'll see whether I can find out a bit more about the drugs aspect of your inquiry… You said you found it odd that the NCA was tipped off so quickly about Wilson's whereabouts in Camden. I agree, it's almost too good to be true."

"I need to know whether someone else had an interest in making us find Ollie that quickly." Pole stopped himself. Harris picked up on the idea and raised an eyebrow. "The last incident at the hospital is also a huge issue. Someone managed to get in… and knew exactly what police protection he had," Pole volunteered.

Harris placed his forearms on the table, leaning forward. "Another agency?"

"Perhaps… I need to know whether another agency or someone within that circle is involved."

"Is your DS looking into Wilson's background?… Uni, friends…"

"Why?" Pole frowned.

"You'll find that the drugs element is going to come back… and for what it is… though I don't want to tell you how to do your job…" Harris's voice trailed.

"Spit it out." Pole nodded.

"Wilson had a history… needed detox after finishing his PhD. Might have dealt a little too, but I don't buy the idea he was attacked because of a drug deal going bad."

"Noted… anything else?"

Harris grinned and then grew serious. "As you know, Ms Wu has attracted the attention of the agency, not mine, the one across the pond, and my contact is gathering information about her. If there is something I need to know about her in order to manage the CIA, now would be a good time, Inspector Pole."

Pole arranged his knife and fork together across his plate. "Then you'd better watch your back, Harris… Ms Wu seems to have found an introduction at Vauxhall Cross."

\* \* \*

"Too early." Nancy looked at her watch. Despite the late night, she had got up at 6am, made the first cup of tea of the day, settled in front of the Bloomberg news channel and ignored what the presenter was saying. She had convinced Cora to return to her friends' flat. Beth,

Charlie and Johnny had sworn they would take turns in looking after her, vowing to do a better job than even Scotland Yard could.

Nancy had been curious about how they had escaped the police car parked in front of their building for protection, and the protection officer in their flat. They all shrugged and told her about the fire exit at the back of the building... the alarm never worked so it could be opened without attracting attention. Nancy had given them a mild bollocking and made them promise to have it repaired, or else DS Branning would be told about it.

The fact that she was now contemplating using Cora's idea to get into Viro-Tech had not been discussed, and Cora knew better than to ask in front of her friends. Perhaps she did not even believe Nancy was serious.

Nancy couldn't help but smile. To the arty gang, she would look like a nicer version of their mums, a little funkier, a little more fun perhaps... but not someone who would take risks of the magnitude she was used to taking.

She moved back to her study, sat in the armchair at the desk and contemplated her handiwork. On the left-hand side, the details of her father's case, and on the right, that of Ollie Wilson. The connection between the cases was tenuous, and yet she had written China in bold letters on a sheet of paper at the intersection of the two.

Nancy picked up the yellow writing pad that she had left on the desk the night before and started jotting down the long list of questions she needed to focus on – the habit of a lifetime that had always paid off.

No question was too hard or too direct.

How far had Pole gone to source the information he had found about her father?

What would MI6 expect from her in return for their help?

How close had her father been to the Chinese Communist Party, more specifically Deng Xiao Ping?

As she penned the last question, she took a sip of tea. It relaxed her tightening throat. It was so much harder than she had imagined to remain dispassionate about a case that was so close to her. She stood up and walked back to the kitchen, refreshed her cup and gave herself a few moments before returning to her study.

She gazed outside into the gardens below. The trees stood naked and dark against the brightening sky. Another few minutes and she would call Pole's DS.

She returned to her desk and decided to concentrate on the Ollie Wilson case before calling Andy.

Was Ollie working on unauthorised bio-tech research? Where did the financial backing come from?

What was Viro-Tech CEO Jared Turner's background, and what were his connections?'

Nancy toyed with her pen for a moment, reluctantly added a final question.

Was Ollie Wilson still clean?

Her hand lingered over her mobile phone. It was only 8am but she nevertheless picked it up with a sharp move and dialled Andy's number.

"DS Todd." Andy's voice sounded young and keen on the phone. Nancy bade him good morning, amused.

"Good morning, Ms W... Nancy... are you calling for an update on the Wilson case?"

"Excellent guess, of course, and to thank you for updating Inspector Pole on the particulars of my misadventures. I hope he did not shoot the messenger."

"It got a little hairy." Andy chuckled.

"Oops... I owe you one then. I hope it's OK if you tell me a bit more about the Wilson case, though."

"No problem... Inspector Pole is not around. He's just been summoned to see Superintendent Marsh."

"The Super is involved in the case?" Nancy asked candidly.

"I don't think so." Andy hesitated and Nancy didn't push. There was very little Andy would not tell her, and certainly Pole had not mentioned Marsh. Not unexpected in itself, but the combination of Andy's reluctance and Pole's silence piqued her curiosity... another question to be added to the list.

"Never mind... what is the latest?"

"Still very little information coming through on the man in the mortuary. Yvonne, I mean Ms Butler, has confirmed that the genetics of our John Doe is Eastern European.

"But otherwise, we have nothing, no dental records, some broken bones, but nothing like a plate or a medical implant that could help in further identifying him. The other matter of interest is that he had tattoos removed recently. We can no longer see what these were, but we can see that the skin has regrown in places after the procedure."

"Tatts, Pole mentioned this. Can you tell me more, or perhaps send me a picture of what you have?"

"Sure, but you're not going to see much." Andy sounded more intrigued than reluctant.

"I know... you wonder what it is that I might be able to see," Nancy acknowledged. "I have met many villains in my time and quite a few of them came from the East. I've learned a lot about what these tattoos mean, and if you can still see some of their shapes... who knows?"

"Brill... I'll send you what I've got right away." Nancy could hear Andy on his keyboard, already sending an email with attachments. As he did so, he kept updating Nancy on progress.

"I've also gone through Ollie Wilson's bank accounts, and apart from the usual standard current account and deposit account, I have found an account in Jersey, set up a couple of years ago. It had very little activity until recently, and that's when it becomes quite interesting."

"You mean the regular payment and withdrawal of large sums of money?" Nancy inhaled, holding her breath until he answered.

"Not huge, but big enough, and ranging from a couple of thousand up to £10,000."

"Have you been able to trace the funds and the payee or recipient?"

"An account in Panama for the incoming payments, an account in Switzerland for the sums going out... It's a nominee account so we'll need to do a lot more digging before I can get the name of the ultimate beneficial owner."

"Typical money laundering structure," Nancy mused. "That sounds right. How about the biker?" She had to ask.

"Well, I lost his trace in one of the underpasses in the East End. The camera had been smashed. By the time we picked up his trail he had switched clothes and swapped number plates. I did a trace on ANPR... nothing."

204

"Organised crime... and they were well prepared." Nancy knew that. The question was where from and who was paying.

"Very much so." Andy's voice lowered a little. "I just can't pin these guys down... frustrating."

"I've got the pictures you sent me... let's see what we've got." Nancy opened the shots of the man's torso, arms and shoulders, back and neck. Andy was right, there was very little to see. She took her time to consider all of them.

Apart from the thoracic puncture that had caused death, the skin looked remarkably intact. Large patches of newly grown skin indicated where the tattoos had been removed. It must have been a long and painful process, and the requirement for anonymity must have been obligatory.

There was nothing left on the torso or the arms. She moved meticulously to the man's neck and shoulders. She enlarged a close-up shot and considered it for a moment.

"Look at photo #37... what do you see?"

The sound of fingers on the keyboard, a moment's hesitation. "A long object perhaps... not sure... a rod?"

"Could it be a dagger...?"

"Perhaps... I could ask Ms Butler to take more pictures and I could play around with the pixilation..." Andy's voice trailed off. His mind was assessing whether this was a possible route to an answer.

"And I'll pay Yvonne a visit. I'm sure she won't mind," Nancy said.

"Excuse me for asking, but what does a tattoo of a dagger mean?"

"It's a typical tattoo used by the Russian mafia or by people who have spent time in Russian prisons... A dagger through the neck means that the bearer has killed someone in prison, and they can be hired to kill."

"Wow... how did you..." Andy stopped short, hesitating whether to ask.

"I saw some pretty grisly things when I worked on war crimes in Eastern Europe. You learn to recognise who you are dealing with quickly."

She promptly finished the call. She had enough time for a quick call with Pole before making her way to the mortuary.

Her mobile rang. Perhaps he was calling her first, but the number on the screen was unfamiliar. She hesitated, pressing the reply button before the voicemail kicked in.

She recognised the voice of Superintendent Marsh's PA. They exchanged a few pleasantries before Denise asked her about availability. "He would like to see you on a rather delicate matter, I'm afraid."

"It always is." Nancy bit her lip. Marsh's keen attention was not what she needed at a time when she and Pole were at odds over her investigation methods.

"For once, it actually is a tricky situation." Denise meant every word she said. Nancy took note. Denise did not pander to her boss. Matters must indeed be tricky if she said so.

"What time did you have in mind?"

"Perhaps late morning… 11.30am?"

"I'll make sure I am available. Any inkling?"

"Perhaps you should speak to DCI Pole?"

* * *

"You're not as injured as I thought you might be." Jethro Greeney picked up Jack's health record that hung at the bottom of his bed without paying much attention to it.

"I've got two damaged ribs, a black eye and a split lip… what did you expect, to find me brain dead?"

"No…" Jethro replaced the chart. "But they left my other agent in a much worse state, I can tell you."

Jack straightened up in his bed with a wince. "The man that was having dinner at the same place as me?"

"Correct… I thought perhaps you needed someone to keep you company… I didn't think my guy was going to be beaten to a pulp, though."

"Those people knew exactly what they were doing."

"Evidently. My operatives are well trained but so were they."

"I can't quite put my finger on it, but it was a strange mix of moves. Something I have encountered before."

206

"There are only a couple of agencies that craft their own training when it comes to hand-to-hand combat… Mossad and the FSB, or rather, men with military training who join the FSB."

Jack pondered. It was not Mossad's Krav Maga. "I'd say boys from the FSB then."

Jethro pulled a face. He couldn't quite reconcile how the Russians might be involved in Jack's beating. "Whoever they are, your little escapade into the premises of Viro-Tech Therapeutics did not go unnoticed."

"I gather not…"

"Yep, the woman you spoke about, Nancy Wu. Former eminent QC, retired early, does a lot of pro bono for a university and collects contemporary art. She was involved in a controversial case… Henry Crowne, IRA operative turned investment banker… after that she was appointed as adviser to the Met in London. They must have been impressed with her work."

"Do I sense a but…" Jack said.

"A few of them, to tell you the truth. Her father was a well-known artist, Chinese… supported Mao Zedong, until the Cultural Revolution hit. He escaped with his family but returned under Deng Xiao Ping. We don't seem to have much about him after that."

"You said a few." Jack slid down the bed again to make himself more comfortable.

"She worked for a guy called Vergès, a French barrister… very controversial lawyer, very left wing too… she didn't stay long with him in the end. I'm not sure what her political affiliations are, but I'm looking into those."

"Back to her being a consultant with the Met, that's pretty high profile."

"You bet… so she has the means to find information, pass it on. The best part of the story about Henry Crowne is that he escaped HSU Belmarsh. No one had ever escaped the high security unit there before… although if you ask me the Brits are getting soft with their prisoners."

"You mean they should reintroduce the death penalty?"

"Might not be a bad idea… a terrorist is a threat, right?"

Jack thought better than to disagree with the Station Chief. "So, what's your take on all of this?"

"She could well be a player for a foreign power."

"What? After years in the country, she suddenly turns into a spy? The Met must have done their due diligence before recruiting her."

"Or someone managed to convince her. That's what we do when we recruit our informants."

Jack sank back into the pillows. Steve Harris would not like the way the Station Chief was going about the Wilson case.

# Chapter Twenty-One

Superintendent Marsh was standing in front of the large window of his spacious office. Pole noticed that his figure had grown a little heavier, the panel of his uniform jacket looked tight around his waistline. Too many networking lunches and dinners were starting to take their toll.

Marsh's eyes followed Pole as he walked in, headed straight to Marsh's desk and stood next to the single chair that awaited visitors summoned for interrogation.

The Super finally turned away from the grand view his office commanded... Westminster Bridge that led to the Houses of Parliament on the right-hand side, the London Eye straight ahead and the South Bank cultural centre on the left.

Marsh indicated to Pole he should sit with a short movement of his head. "I haven't heard any more news about the progress of your inquiry."

Pole pulled the chair further away from the desk to accommodate his long legs and sat down.

"I'm sorry, sir. The Ollie Wilson case has been keeping me busy, but we are making progress."

"The young man who was kidnapped and is now in hospital?"

"That's right." Pole didn't volunteer more information, hoping his silence might arouse Marsh's interest.

"Anything I should know about this case over and above what you wrote in your report?"

Between a rock and a hard place... the expression sprang into Pole's mind. Did he really want to attract his boss's attention to a case in which MI6 was involved, as well as the CIA, in order to deflect Marsh's attention from the Ferguson inquiry?

"Ollie Wilson is a US national." Pole waited. Marsh came to sit down at his desk. He let himself drop into his leather armchair a little too heavily, judging by the complaining sounds the joints made as he did.

The Super rolled his chair forward, elbows on the armrests of his seat, fingertips joined in front of his mouth. His mind was working on whether there would be anything to gain by being involved. He no doubt reminisced about the Henry Crowne days when Pole, in the space of only four years, had brought him some of the most high-profile cases of his career.

Marsh's eyes lit up, a mixture of renewed interest and mischief. "Is Ms Wu involved?"

Pole raised a quizzical eyebrow, odd that Marsh should find a case of interest solely based on the involvement, or not, of their consultant.

"Well, yes, as a matter of fact she is, sir."

"And what does the excellent Ms Wu think about the central question?"

"If you are referring to whether Ollie Wilson was involved with drugs in some extensive way, she's waiting for DS Todd to complete his research."

Marsh nodded. He swivelled from left to right in his chair. How far could he get involved without looking a little too obvious? The change of tack came as a surprise to Pole... he had not forgotten after all.

"And of course, you have notified her of our need to clarify her involvement in the Mark Phelps case?"

Pole's fingers tightened on the armrest of his chair. "Not yet, sir."

It was now for Marsh to raise a quizzical eyebrow. "Are you dragging your feet?"

Pole managed a lukewarm smile. "No... I'm simply trying to do this sensibly and with sensitivity." Pole remained serious. "It is always rather difficult to question people's integrity. I am seeking to approach Ms Butler, one of the best pathologists in the UK, and Ms

Wu, a former QC of impeccable stature, in a manner that does the job without alienating them."

Marsh rolled the chair closer to his desk.

"I'm not suggesting otherwise, Pole." He sounded irritated that DCI Pole might think him unsubtle.

"Commander Ferguson, an excellent officer... may become a little impatient, but I am carrying out the informal investigation as fast as I can."

"And what is the outcome of your findings so far?" Marsh leaned forward, his eyes searching Pole for a physical reaction he might not be able to hide.

"We have found logs of a number of burner phones, active at or near our offices." Pole exhaled slowly. "But we haven't tracked down the owners yet."

"Isn't the idea of a burner phone that it is untraceable?" Marsh retorted.

"That's the general idea. However, sometimes we can trace them back to the place they were sold, and with the help of CCTV cameras find out who the buyer was."

"Who is dealing with this?" Marsh pursed his lips.

"DS Todd."

"But did he not work on the Mark Phelps case himself?"

"That's right." Pole's words almost stuck in his throat.

"Don't you think that amounts to a conflict of interest?" Marsh pointed out, satisfied to have found a weakness in Pole's approach.

Pole sat back in his chair. "That would be the case, sir, if this were a full formal inquiry. In fact, I would certainly not be allowed to conduct it myself, since I too would be compromised. But if we are going to keep this investigation informal, and prevent it from raising unwelcome attention, we need to limit it to a small number of people." Marsh tapped his fingers on the desk. Pole knew he had a point, and that Marsh did not want the Ferguson inquiry to get out of hand.

Marsh had been involved in the case himself, and if it came to a formal inquiry, he too would be on the list of staff under suspicion.

"Then perhaps we should introduce a four-eye procedure?"

Pole froze for an instant. "You mean..."

"Well, yes… let's make sure that each individual finding is reviewed by two people. Since I was the senior officer on the case, why don't I be the second pair of eyes?"

Pole nodded slowly, lost for words. Marsh would be looking over one of his shoulders and MI6 the other.

\* \* \*

"Fresh cup of tea?" Johnny was telling, not asking. No one around the table looked their best. Johnny and Beth had dark rings under their eyes. Whereas it could be expected of Beth, who was now sleeping in the lounge, and Cora who was understandably feeling the trauma of the past few days, Johnny also looked a little fatigued after their eventful night.

Johnny had opted for a good dose of concealer that seemed to have gone some way towards hiding the shadows under his eyes.

The doorbell rang and everybody straightened up. Perhaps Branning had forgotten his keys. Johnny decided he looked the most presentable and went to open the door.

"Darlin' we missed you."

"Obviously not Branning." Beth grinned.

Nat entered the kitchen, holding her bike helmet awkwardly and did the rounds, kissing everyone on the cheek. She bent over Cora, holding her a little longer. She too looked pale. Beth offered her some tea.

"I'm just popping in really quickly to see how you are all holding up." Her eyes rested on Cora for a moment.

"Won't you stay and have a cup with us then?" Beth had already taken a mug out.

A shadow crossed Nat's face, but Cora could not quite make out why it was.

"All right… Just a quick one." Nat took the mug and leaned against the worktop, gulping the hot liquid down.

"Isn't it a bit hot with your leather jacket?" Johnny asked.

"I'm fine." Nat moved away from the counter. "I'm sorry I can't stay for very long."

She held back from finishing her cup, waiting for the conversation she had interrupted to resume it seemed. Cora hesitated. She wanted to share the crazy evening she had just had, but wondered whether perhaps she should be more careful.

The front door rattling as someone tried to open it interrupted her thoughts.

DS Branning had finished smoking yet another cigarette. The whiff of it came through the door as he opened it. He announced himself to the crowd of friends by banging the door shut.

Nat downed the rest of her tea and made her excuses. Branning took no offence. As Nat left, Cora sensed her departure had lifted the atmosphere.

Beth took another mug from the kitchen rack, a cheerful polka dot Emma Bridgewater. She refreshed the pot and poured a second round.

"I'm off to the grind…" Johnny yawned nonchalantly. "I'll be back at 1pm, as agreed."

Branning frowned. "Working part-time now?" He sat in the designated spot he had been assigned by Beth. It was an improvement on the previous one… the "as far as possible from everyone else's seat". He was making progress with the arty gang.

"Nope, giving moral support to friends in need." Johnny pursed his lips and gave Cora a little nod. She wouldn't be climbing up or down any walls without one of them trying to stop her.

When they had returned from their Viro-Tech expedition, Johnny had indulged in one of his famous meltdowns; surprisingly, Beth had joined in too. Nancy had arrived just in time to drum some much-needed sense into her… Otherwise who knows… Cora might have been thrown into jail for a very long time or trapped in a building without being able to leave… or even used by the evil Jared Turner for his own medical experiment.

Cora had pointed out the building was neither a labyrinth nor the hideaway of Doctor Frankenstein. She had omitted to mention, though, that Nancy was not at all unhappy about her efforts. But she had looked contrite, and this had worked. They remembered why she was doing all this… Ollie was their friend too.

Cora moved to the lounge. Morning TV did not appeal. She could not go back to her own flat.

The sky was becoming a little brighter, but the thick clouds were still too dense for the sun to shine through. She stood up again and moved to the window seat. It was cold but she didn't mind. Beyond the courtyard, she could see people hurrying along the pavement, a couple of men in shabby tracksuits and orange hazard jackets were crossing the road towards her local café.

Cora smiled, remembering DS Branning's face when Johnny had first offered some of his more exotic teas. He had since corrected the choice of tea available and bought extra strong PG Tips, much to Branning's delight.

The postman, pulling a large red trolley, walked into the yard. Cora crossed the room towards the hallway. Beth and Branning stood up.

"Don't panic... I'm just going down to check the mail."

Branning nodded. "I'll come down with you anyway."

"Time for another fag, no doubt," Cora grumbled. Beth joined them for good measure. Branning made his way downstairs first and Cora slowed her pace. "What was that all about? Why couldn't Nat stay for a bit?" Cora whispered.

"Branning makes her uncomfortable."

"That's silly..."

"Perhaps not." Beth slowed further and dropped her voice. "Did you notice how she keeps pulling down her sleeves?"

Cora shook her head.

"And how she downed her tea so quickly?"

This time Cora frowned. "You're not going to start seeing drugs everywhere? I know she used to smoke a bit of dope, but so what?"

Beth shook her head. "She did a lot more than that, but I agree, it was a few years back."

They reached the bottom of the stairs and stopped for a moment.

Cora hadn't known about the hard drugs Nat had been taking and this worried her.

The young postman was standing very still. He had not delivered post to the building for a few days and the site of the charred walls and broken windows made his jaw drop.

He recognised Cora and shook his head. "I'm sorry... what happened?"

"Not sure yet." Cora shrugged.

He opened his trolley, picked up a wad of letters and a large heavy envelope.

"I'll take next door's as well." Cora smiled.

A gust of wind reminded her she had walked out of the flat in a light sweater. She pressed the post against her chest and walked back in quickly. Beth had already disappeared back to the warmth of the flat. Branning's cigarette was only halfway through.

"Anything interesting?" he said.

"Don't know, haven't looked yet." She hurried up back into the warmth of her friends' lounge.

She sat back on the couch that faced the large window. Beth joined her with two steaming cups of tea. Cora started leafing through the mail. The predictable assortment of bills and junk mail ran through her fingers. She set aside the pile of correspondence that was addressed to her friends. She absentmindedly dropped the large envelope onto their pile, picked up her mug of tea and held it for a moment, warming her fingers. Charlie had disappeared into his home office. He was on a call to a contact about the latest story he was compiling for *The Guardian*. He liked being a freelance journalist; it was hard work and the living sometimes precarious, but it meant he was also his own boss.

Beth picked up the post in turn, looking for something that might be addressed to her. She turned over the heavy packet to read the address and frowned. "This is addressed to Ollie."

They both froze. Ollie sometimes received magazines through the post and the occasional bill, but most of what he read he read online.

She had never seen him receive a packet of that size. Cora extended her fingers towards it.

Beth stopped her. "What if it is dangerous?"

"What do you mean? It's too small to be a bomb."

"Something chemical perhaps… I've read that somewhere. Politicians in the US are sent letters with poison in them all the time."

Cora shook her head. "Not all the time… sometimes… and frankly, I'm almost sympathetic when it comes to certain politicians." But she didn't open the packet. Beth slid her eyes towards the kitchen.

DS Branning had returned from his cigarette break and was reading a newspaper.

"How about talking to him about it?" Beth whispered.

Cora shook her head again. If she told him, she would never get to see the contents of the envelope, even if they were important to her. It was evidence…

She tiptoed to the bedroom and returned with a pair of gloves. She sat down again and pulled the envelope towards her. The stamps were UK stamps, and the date of postage was three weeks earlier. Ollie's name and address were on the reverse of the packet, but the original address was in Hong Kong, a name she had never heard before… Randy Zang. The parcel had not been delivered and was being returned to sender.

She examined the flap of the envelope. It did not seem to have been tampered with.

Cora took a small breath, held it and started to open the flap, trying not to tear it. It resisted to start with. She took her time to coax it open and finally managed. Beth's face had followed the operation, forehead creased, one eye on the kitchen.

Cora tilted the packet, her heart pounding. Perhaps an explanation about the horrendous events of the past 48 hours would be contained in the package.

The top of a stack of printed papers appeared.

She read the titles in a low voice as they came out one after the other.

Human Intervention in the Food Chain: Animal to Human Viral Transmission, an Increased Risk, by Ollie Wilson.

Antibiotic-resistant Microbes – the Future of Pandemics, by Ollie Wilson.

There were a few more papers written by him on similar topics… arguing how vital proper research was in areas that might not yield immediate monetary results, the impact of bioinformatics on data harvesting and how it could accelerate the initial phase of research in the fields of virology and immunology.

Cora pushed the papers around cautiously with her gloved fingers.

She found a transcript of several of Bill Gates's interventions on the subject of epidemics and pandemics.

Finally, she tried to make sense of a document that had been folded on itself. She hesitated, reaching deep into the envelope to pull out the item. The meetings schedule of Jared Turner over the past year, with dates circled in red and marked 'China', emerged.

* * *

Her mobile was ringing again. Nancy's meeting with Superintendent Marsh had been postponed to 2pm, pushing it back a little. She grabbed her phone, half hoping it was Denise, Marsh's PA, proposing a new date or, even better, cancelling. It was not Denise, but the name of the caller made her smile.

"Yvonne... What do you have for me?"

"To be more precise... what does my contact have for you. I've got to say the turnaround time rather surprises me. I was bracing myself for a long two weeks and a few calls from me reminding my contact we were expecting an answer soon... but here we are."

"Which means?"

"Whatever – or whoever – the document you received from your contact Amy deals with is very much on their radar."

"That's rather strange." Nancy could not decide whether she was pleased or concerned. "It's a very old case and apart from me, I don't see who at MI6..." Her mouth ran dry. She had just been handed the answer to a question that had been puzzling her for a couple of days.

"Well, it seems this file is red hot at the moment... don't ask me why, they wouldn't tell me but the document you sent me and the photos are authentic."

For a moment she was lost for words. She had suspected this to be the case, but she needed to be certain. All she knew about her father, or thought she knew, was being overturned by the revelation she had just received.

Who had her father really been?

Yvonne waited for a moment. "Won't you tell me who it is we are talking about?"

"I'd rather not Yvonne, a few people have been hurt in the process, so perhaps the less you know..."

"So very kind of you to be protective but let me worry about my own safety." Yvonne had once demonstrated her ability to defend herself when an ill-intentioned thug had tried to steal her bag as she and Nancy were coming out of a small bar, next to where she worked. The knee into his groin and the fingers in his eyes had done the trick.

"On the other hand, Nancy, if you'd rather not talk about it for other reasons, it is fine by me. I'm not insisting, I'm just trying to help."

"And it's very much appreciated." Nancy fidgeted with a few pieces of paper that lay on the coffee table. "How much detail is your contact able to give me? Reasons why they think the documents and photos are authentic, for example."

"Funny you should say that… my contact is prepared to be generous about the information they have gathered," Yvonne said.

"And what does your contact want in return?" There would never be a free lunch with MI6 and she had accepted it.

"As I mentioned before, whatever you discover during your investigation using this information, whatever it is, they want to know."

"I still don't quite see the benefit to the agency. Do they have something specific in mind?"

"If they have, they haven't told me, and I can't imagine they will. But my experience is like yours. There is some valuable intelligence they are going to extract from this."

"Fine, when do I get the information?"

"If you come to the lab later on, the USB key should be with me by then."

"I'll see you then."

Nancy sat still for a moment. Her father had suddenly become a stranger. But perhaps it should not have been such a surprise.

She was only a young girl when they'd left China and a mere adolescent when he left Paris. He had only showed to her the side he had wanted to, the artist, the man of skill and knowledge. She had discovered him through her own eyes but also through her parents' artist friends. After he had left, she had retained this image of him, until she had decided to stop remembering.

She glanced at her watch. It was almost time to leave for an appointment she did not want to attend. Denise had been apologetic about the short notice, but the Super had insisted on meeting her. She had not managed to speak to Pole to prepare herself.

Never mind.

It was not the first time she would have to improvise.

She went up to her bedroom and en-suite dressing room. She pulled out a severe black suit she had not worn since she had gone to court for the Henry Crowne trial. She added a plain white blouse and chose simple black pearls as jewellery.

In the bathroom, she applied a little makeup and twisted her jet-black hair into a low-sitting bun.

She had time to check on Cora.

"Oh my God… Nancy, your call startled me." Cora's voice was almost inaudible on the phone.

"Are you OK?" Nancy would cancel the Marsh meeting if Cora needed her.

"I'm fine… it's just…" There was movement around her that Nancy could not make out. "Something has happened, or rather, I've received something important."

A door closed and Cora started speaking a little louder.

"I've received a parcel or rather… there was a parcel that has been returned to Ollie undelivered. It was addressed to someone in Hong Kong. Someone I don't know. But that person never received it so it has come back here."

A shiver ran down Nancy's spine. "Have you opened it?"

"Of course I have. I did it with gloves on, though."

"What was inside?"

"Academic papers written by Ollie, on biology… immunology… pandemics… a lot of complicated research, I think. Then transcripts from some of Bill Gates's lectures… again about epidemics and pandemics. Then something odd… the timetable of Jared Turner's meetings on a trip to China."

"Do you have a photocopier or scanner in your flat?"

"We do."

"This is what you are going to do. Photocopy the documents. When you have done that, speak to Branning and apologise for opening the envelope... Tell him you didn't notice it was redirected to Ollie... Or whatever you think he'll buy. I'll drop by after my meeting. Don't show the documents to anybody else."

"Shall I do a bit of research in the meantime?"

"On what?"

"I could find out more about the documents themselves."

"If you do, do it incognito in your search engine."

Nancy could hear Cora smile. "Not the first time you've sailed close to the wind, then."

"Indeed, and not the last time either."

# Chapter Twenty-Two

The stairwell resounded with the weight of his footsteps. Pole ignored the lift and climbed down the four floors that separated Marsh's office from his own. He had almost missed a step at the beginning of his descent, his focus still on his latest conversation. He was now concentrating on the stairs, pounding them in anger. But truly, who did he have to blame but himself?

Another colleague had started his journey upstairs. He greeted Pole with an out-of-breath smile and carried on. Pole stopped on the third floor and took a moment to gather himself. Would he have handled the investigation differently though?

Almost certainly not, and that answer bothered him.

He walked into the open-plan office, straight to his DS's desk. Andy was concentrating on his work, oblivious to Pole hovering over him.

"Anything you need?" Pole asked.

"I'm examining the payments received by Ollie Wilson. The Swiss account is a numbered bank account, with no name associated with it... yet." He was tucking fervently into a packet of jellybeans. He offered it to Pole without shifting his eyes from his screen. "Have some, Guv..."

Pole considered the packet, took it from Andy and grabbed a few beans. A little sweetness in this moment wouldn't go amiss.

"How long before you know?"

Andy rotated his chair to face his boss. "A few hours maybe. I have a call with a federal police colleague in Switzerland. They've contacted the bank that holds the account. Anonymity is no longer what it used to be in Switzerland... but we shall see."

He looked into the sweet packet, ready to seize one of his favourites. "But I'm certain there will be yet another account somewhere more difficult to reach, such as the Cayman Islands or Lichtenstein," Andy added.

"But what would that tell us?" Pole asked.

"That whoever is paying is a fishy customer."

"That's right." Pole dragged over a chair and sat down. "Remind me when the payments started."

"Four months ago."

"And when did Wilson open the account?"

Andy returned to his screen and checked a different document from two years earlier, according to the Jersey bank records.

"The opening is legit. His father opened the account with him, when Wilson moved to the UK. His father sent him some cash then. If I compare it with movements on his London current account, the cash was used for renting the flat, furnishing it… stuff like that. Before you ask, I've also checked the opening of the current account. It's with a well-known UK bank."

"Nothing unusual there?"

Andy shook his head. "But suddenly, four months ago, Wilson starts receiving payments into and making payments from the Jersey account."

"Didn't the Jersey bank ask any questions about why that was happening? Isn't that part of the anti-money-laundering rules, that you investigate sudden changes in patterns in a particular bank account?"

"I raised that point with the bank and they are coming back to me with an answer." Andy crunched a couple of jellybeans between his teeth.

"Sooner rather than later would be good, otherwise I might be tempted to speak to the financial authorities about this lapse in judgement."

"I'll relay the message." Andy chuckled. "Firing on all cylinders this morning, Guv."

Pole couldn't help but smile… his new bike seemed to be inspiring his team of late.

222

"It's very convenient don't you think… suddenly, questionable transactions start showing up in Wilson's account, fed by what is almost certainly dirty money?"

"Perhaps he was made an offer he could not resist?"

"Perhaps…" Pole looked at his watch. "I'll give Yvonne a call… We need to know what drugs were given to Wilson, and whether we've made inroads with the identity of the guy lying on the mortuary slab."

"He's almost certainly Russian." Pole cocked his head surprised.

"Because the tattoo on his neck… the only one we can still make out the shape of has a knife through it," Andy continued.

"One of those mafia tattoos that tells you about the con who wears it?"

"That's right, and apparently it means the man has killed in prison and is available for hire."

"May I ask where you got that information from… a reputable source I presume?" Pole said.

"Ms Wu has a reputation."

"I'm aware," Pole grumbled. He appreciated the fact that Andy had not qualified which way that reputation was going.

Pole left his DS's desk and went into his office. He navigated his way through the piles of files that he had rearranged the day before. He stood in front of one of them and extracted the folder he was looking for, from a dangerously high tower of papers. He dialled Yvonne's number from his landline, whilst removing his jacket and loosening the tie he had knotted awkwardly for his meeting with Marsh.

"Pole… what's up?"

"You tell me. I hear we've made progress on the ID of our John Doe."

"Da… that's the extent of my Russian. But yes, I've photographed the wound left by the tattoo-removal procedure again and I'm convinced it is a knife or dagger that goes through his neck. The tattoo was pretty intricate and its removal tricky, which was helpful for us."

"Anything else?"

"I've asked the team to find out from the list of the most wanted on Europol and Interpol whether we have a match. I ran his fingerprints through AFIS and there's nothing there."

"Are we dealing with one of those ghosts that the old KGB produced?"

"Quite possibly. On second examination, I noticed his fingerprints had been damaged, probably using some caustic substance like acid. It's a well-known technique."

"Is he old enough to be KGB?"

"A man in his mid-40s, so yes. He would have been young but he could have been KGB, then FSB... and then recruited by the mafia."

"You seem to know quite a lot about that."

"I know a lot about many things, Inspector Pole. I have seen dead bodies from all walks of life on the slab of this mortuary, and spies are no exception."

Pole did not welcome the news... Harris was going to want to know more about the man on the slab if he was to provide Pole with the information Pole needed, and Marsh was likely to start easing himself into what might become a high-profile case.

"What about the drugs injected into Wilson?"

"I was coming to that... patience." Yvonne was moving around her lab. "Right... heroin produced from poppy seeds grown in Afghanistan."

"Anything else about how the drug was produced that could help us identify the people who administered it?"

"Good quality. It's the amount that was given that caused the damage, not the way it was produced."

"Any trace of that batch in the UK?"

"Nothing I have previously identified, but I'm asking other labs for a comparison check. And you may want to speak to the NARCS. They will be able to tell you whether they've encountered the same batch or quality in one of their raids."

Pole thanked Yvonne and hung up. Harris had mentioned Ollie's past involvement with drugs. It had almost cost him his PhD. Harris did not buy the connection and on balance neither did Pole, but he could not fight the evidence. A Russian connection in the biotech world... why not?

\* \* \*

"Thank you." Jack took his time to get out of the car. The Station Chief had sent a car to drive Jack back to his accommodation. His face was now turning an unhealthy shade of yellow and blue, and his limping completed the picture of a man who'd had a rough night. The receptionist who had welcomed him a day earlier opened her eyes wide and left her desk to check he was alright.

"I'm fine," he managed to say through a sore jaw.

"I hope you don't mind my saying, sir, but you don't look it… is there anything we can do?"

Jack appreciated the thought but said he could manage.

"I'll send some ice packs up." She was not taking no for an answer.

The driver had accompanied him inside and left a number for him to call in case of need. Jack hobbled towards the lift with as much dignity as he could muster. A couple of other guests emerged from the opening doors and took a surprised look at him.

A few moments later, Jack entered the small cosy lounge that was adjacent to his bedroom and looked around. The room had been cleaned and the bed made. It was tidy and welcoming, but he would no longer have time to relax in it. He turned towards the safe and retrieved his laptop. He checked on the arrangement of objects he had positioned to detect whether the safe had been opened. They indicated that no one had tampered with it in his absence.

He went back to the lounge, laid the laptop on the coffee table and logged on. Time to check what Laurie had found out for him.

In a sea of unopened emails, he found what he was looking for. *Call me*, was all she had to say.

This was not what he had anticipated. He had no means of screening his room for eavesdropping devices. He could ask Jethro for help, but the Station Chief would want to know more. Harris, on the other hand, might be more accommodating.

Jack replied, but looking at the clock on the side table, he realised it was only 5.30am in Langley. Laurie was almost certainly getting ready for work, but it was perhaps a little too early to call.

He moved to brew a fresh cup of coffee and when done, made himself comfortable on his bed to finish reading the McCain report.

The young man who had helped prepare the report was incensed about the loss of technological intellectual property to China. Billions of dollars had been forfeited by private companies that were keen to do business with the emerging power. A market of more than one billion people was tempting.

Yet each company knew the price it would have to pay, compelled to relinquish some of its technological advances and allow China to steal its research and development. For years the US had turned a blind eye in the belief that, since the fall of Mao Zedong and the market opening fostered by Deng Xiao Ping, China would eventually embrace the world of free trade to become a strong economic partner. What was a little R&D thieving amongst friends?

Except that China had not seen it that way, or at least not according to the report. Jack read the chapter devoted to the illicit transfer of technology and sat back, coffee in hand. He had heard some of his colleagues lament the lack of influence the military had over the private sector. The schism had occurred a while ago. The intellectual property in the technology the military needed to maintain its advantage over other competitors no longer belonged to the military. The CEOs of these firms did not report to the army chief but to boards of directors concerned with the returns to company shareholders and not with the might of the US army.

Jack could see the argument, and although the report applied to large tech corporations, there was no reason why a smaller company would not do the same, as long as the market it was targeting was worth it.

He checked he time. It was almost 6.45am in Langley. Time to make his call. He dropped a text to Steve Harris. *Need to discuss a theory. Will meet you in the lobby at Vauxhall Cross.*

What better place to make a secure call than from the impregnable building of MI6?

\* \* \*

Yvonne waved at Nancy from inside the mortuary room. Another day... another cadaver, she liked to quip. The young woman with whom she was working had finished sewing up the Y incision. It was time to tidy up and Yvonne could leave this to her. She approached the bin next to the sliding door of the room and removed her gloves with a precise movement, folding them in such a way that she would not be exposed to any of the residue staining them. She removed her visor and gown and put them in a large bin. She washed her hands as meticulously as she had removed her gloves and finally made her way to greet Nancy.

"I have an envelope for you," Yvonne said.

"And I'd like to see the man who died in the flat incident…"

"Something I missed?" Yvonne grinned. She enjoyed rather than resented Nancy's acute mind.

They moved to another room, distinctly cooler than the one they had just been in. A middle-aged man was closing one of the drawers and turned around.

"Nick… do you mind showing us RG-734-A?"

Nick nodded and moved to the far end of the room. They followed and he pulled open the square door of one of the drawers. He slid the slab halfway out and left them to it.

Nancy froze for a moment; the images of her crashing a chair over the man's back, the ferocity of her attack assailed her. She blinked a few times to will them away.

"Are you alright?" Yvonne murmured.

"Fine… I'm fine." Nancy approached closer to the gurney and Yvonne removed the white sheet.

"It is a dagger…" Nancy concentrated on the man's neck and then his shoulders. Yvonne stood on the other side and started nodding. "Absolutely… I took a few more pictures with better resolution."

"Russian prisoner… probably a contract killer."

"Anything else?" Yvonne waited and Nancy shook her head. It was enough. There was nothing left there for her to glean. Nick reappeared to roll back the gurney and close the drawer.

"Let's get a coffee somewhere." Yvonne walked out first and made sure Nancy was following closely. They walked into her office and Yvonne handed her the envelope which Nancy put in her bag.

The place was new and cosy. They were waiting for their order when Nancy pulled out the envelope from her satchel.

"Are you going to open it?" Yvonne's brows were raised, her eyes slightly larger than usual.

"It would be rude not to share with a friend." Nancy smiled.

227

"Exactly so…" Yvonne leaned forward. "The suspense is killing me… I know, it's a bad joke considering the circumstances."

"I'm afraid you hit the nail on the head, and I worry that may not be just a metaphor."

"Come on… indulge my nosiness."

"You're not nosy. You're resolutely curious."

"…must remember that…" Yvonne's eyes had not left the package. The order arrived.

Pain aux raisins and black coffee for Nancy. Triple chocolate muffin and espresso for Yvonne. Both took a bite of their pastry and approved.

Nancy could delay no longer; she slid a finger underneath the flap and lifted it carefully. When this was done, she tipped the contents carefully into her hand. A USB key appeared together with a couple of photos. What looked like a very old photocopy also slid into her hand. Nancy brought her other hand to her chest for a short moment.

She slowly put the pictures on the table. Her father had again been photographed with Deng Xiao Ping, but this time another man was also present who looked the same age as Deng. The picture had been taken in China before they had left. There were characters written at the back, but she could not decipher the Chinese ideograms.

The second photo was of her father looking older than when he'd left Paris, an aged man photographed somewhere that looked like a public space, but she couldn't tell where.

She looked at the first photo again, replaced it on the table and took a sip of coffee.

"The same man in both these photos is… was… my father, Li Jie Wu."

Yvonne smiled kindly. "A trip down memory lane is sometimes hard."

"This one is particularly…" Nancy hesitated. "…challenging."

"Is Pole helping you?"

"He is… but what can he do? It was China, 30 years ago."

Yvonne nodded without asking more.

Nancy was glad her lie had been accepted so readily by someone as astute as Yvonne.

She resisted going through the other documents in detail, but speed-read the conclusion in what turned out to be an article mentioning her father.

It had been written by a French academic 20 years earlier when China was beginning to open up and reveal the activity of its contemporary artists. A period when key people like Ai WeiWei were starting to emerge. It didn't say whether the author Emmanuel Licot was still alive, or where he could be found. But the report indicated that what he had written had been well researched and rang true.

"The document I was concerned about has been validated. It also gives me the name of the author."

"Any way of contacting him?"

"There is no address, or name of an institution or publication, but I could try a few contacts in Paris." The final document looked more official. It was arranged in neat paragraphs and had been rubber stamped a few times. The photocopy was of good quality and one paragraph had been highlighted in yellow.

The Chinese language remained opaque to her. Nancy forced her mind to recall the construction of simple characters. She couldn't. She was about to shove the document back into the envelope when she noticed some words written on the back of the page.

Two sightings of the man, Li Jie Wu, both in Hong Kong, on 27 July 1989 and 18 August 1989.

Nancy raised her hand to stifle a cry.

Her father had been alive after the massacre of protestors in Tiananmen Square in Beijing on 4 June of that year and yet why had he never given a sign of life after the event?

# Chapter Twenty-Three

"Jack Shield," the man repeated into his earpiece. He gave Jack another look, neutral yet watchful. The heavy steel door, covered with a criss-cross linear pattern, was wide open, but the NO UNAUTHORISED ACCESS written in bold letters on the wall behind him was ominous. Jack's black eye and swollen lip didn't do anything to enhance his credibility. Then again, would an ill-intentioned suspect turn up to the gates of MI6 looking so beaten up? The guard listened to the reply that came into his headset. He gave way to Jack, moving aside his heavy bulk of muscle, clothed in a bulletproof jacket.

Jack nodded his thanks and made his way through the entrance of Vauxhall Cross. He lifted his head to take in the view of the interior. The exterior of the building had always impressed him, with its mix of heavy cream-coloured stone blocks, the towers and turrets, and the light blue steel that gave the place a futuristic look. He was not sure that Legoland was an appropriate nickname for the postmodern construction.

A second guard was waiting for him at the revolving doors. He repeated his name and the man went through the same procedure. The guard released one of the gates. Jack pushed against the bar and went through.

He had visited Harris before, but their contact had usually been in areas of conflict, working on joint Middle East operations in Iraq, Afghanistan and Syria.

Jack entered the main reception area. It was less imposing than the entrance might suggest. It was comfortably furnished with black leather sofas, glass coffee tables and a choice of that day's newspapers. One could have been entering any corporate building in the City.

The receptionist stood up, printed out a badge and handed it to Jack. Beyond yet another set of turnstile gates, Jack caught a glimpse of two sets of lifts. The rest was solid stone blocks and blue steel again… a fortress, as might be expected in a building housing one of the world's finest intelligence agencies.

Harris was on his way, the receptionist had told him. Jack got out his mobile phone and dialled Langley.

"Not too early, I hope." Jack said.

"Just because it's you." The voice was not flirtatious, unfortunately, Laurie genuinely enjoyed working with him as a colleague but not more.

"What is it that you couldn't write to me about?"

"I presume you are in a secure location?"

"The reception area of the MI6 building in London."

"That sounds good enough… even if they listen in on our conversation. Wait a moment, I'll switch us onto a secure line."

Laurie's voice returned. "I did a search on that company, Viro-Tech Therapeutics, and its CEO Jared Turner."

"And…" Jack had started pacing up and down. He stopped and sat down.

"I've been told to lay off the search."

Jack took a moment to comprehend what Laurie was implying. "Yep, I know… so I did what I do best, not take no for an answer." Laurie took her time. "This is totally off the books etc, etc… you know the drill."

"Go on."

"Viro-Tech is part of a group of companies helping the US government to put together a taskforce of virologists, epidemiologists and immunologists who will be tasked to fight the next global epidemic, or even pandemic. The countries involved include the Europeans of course, but also a number of other players such as China."

"What's the idea behind it? Fighting the next SARS type virus?"

"Must be, and the significant thing is that the Chinese seem to have agreed to an exchange of researchers with other countries to strengthen co-operation if and when it happens."

"Let's hope it's if not when."

"The Gates Foundation and WHO disagree with you, Jack… according to them the world is due a global pandemic in the next 10 to 20 years."

"Where is the catch in all this?"

"I don't know. It's been hard enough to get as much information as that."

Jack sensed a shadow looming over where he sat. He lifted his head. Steve Harris was standing next to him.

"Thanks, Laurie… if you could…"

"I know, keep digging."

Jack stood up and shook hands with Harris.

"Bad news?"

"Not sure… call me a cynic, but I'm always wary of news that sounds too good to be true."

\* \* \*

Rob's contact at the NCA was going through his own files. Pole could hear at the end of the line the distinct click of a computer mouse moving documents around a screen, looking for answers.

"Afghanistan produces 95 per cent of all European opium-based drug supplies. So, you need to be a lot more precise. Your lab should be able to give you an idea of the province it comes from… poppy production from each area has specific characteristics. If the drug is of such good quality as you say it is, it won't have too many additives, so the identification should be easier," Rob said.

"Have you seized any substantial shipments recently? Anything noticeable from the Russian side?"

"We've had a couple of good hits, but not on the Russian mafia. A Lithuanian gang has been partially dismantled and a German gang, originating from East Germany, has lost a lot of its members."

"East Germany? You still make that distinction?"

"It helps where gang members are concerned."

"Could there be a link to Russia?"

"That's a possibility. There was nothing indicating that when we intercepted the guys, but that was not what we were looking for."

232

"What was the origin of the drugs they were importing? Did you find out?"

"We systematically analysed the drug we picked up before destroying it so that we can trace the area of the supplies."

More clicking on the other end of the phone... Pole was taking notes of his own.

"The heroin came from the Herat region. That's not a usual provenance. Poppy cultivation there is not intense. Helmand province is the most prolific..."

"Any reason why the Herat province?" Pole kept typing.

"It's a good quality production and the land on which it is farmed is near the Turkmenistan border."

"In short, easy to export."

"That's right."

"What's the route from Turkmenistan?"

"Across the Caspian Sea, into Georgia... across the Black Sea, and into Europe through Romania."

"A well-known route?"

"Well known but difficult to close... the local police don't have enough resources and the drug traffickers are often better equipped than they are."

"Without forgetting the usual bribes and blackmail."

"That's the sum of it."

"Any chance you can send me the exact molecular composition of what you lifted from the East German traffickers? It might..." Pole was interrupted by the sight of a uniform that had stopped short of entering his office. The bulky frame of Commander Ferguson was waiting to enter, his face drawn and dark.

"Apologies... I'm going to have to go. Do you mind emailing me the rest of the info?"

Pole hardly heard the other man's reply. He thanked him anyway and hung up.

Ferguson came in and closed the door.

"What's up, Ferguson?" Pole stood up.

"My team and I have been reviewing the data your DS sent us."

"Good, and he told me he had also sent some information about mobiles and associated usage in and around Scotland Yard."

"We extended the search a little wider."

Ferguson removed a pile of documents from the chair in front of Pole's desk, and sat down, his chunky body filling it.

Pole sat down again and nodded his approval about the search.

Ferguson took a piece of paper out of a file he was carrying with him. A list of numbers and locations had been compiled, together with relevant dates and times.

One line had been highlighted in red and the location of where the burner phone had been activated circled several times, also in red.

Islington – Rosebury Avenue – 173 New Riverhead... Nancy's address.

* * *

"This is all I have." Cora handed over a thick A4 envelope to Nancy. They were sitting in the little café opposite her flat. DS Branning had agreed to cut the ladies some slack. He was at the table outside the little food shop, smoking a cigarette and drinking a cup of tea. Branning had wrapped his scarf twice around his neck, a sign the weather was getting colder. Nancy wondered whether a winter coat might be more efficient.

Branning had been convinced when Nancy asked for privacy to discuss female issues. At first, he looked at her rather blankly. Then he nodded slowly. Perhaps it was best not to be too inquisitive about which female issues Nancy had in mind. Here they were: Branning on the outside and the ladies in the inside.

Nancy took Cora's envelope and placed it cautiously in her lap. She retrieved the one document she was interested in the most. The research papers she would read later, but Jared Turner's schedule was immediately intriguing.

There had been a clear increase in the frequency of travels to China.

First Hong Kong, then mainland China and then always Beijing. The Beijing address seemed at first obscure, but when Nancy typed it into her iPhone, the organisation that resided there came up immediately.

The National Institute of Biological Sciences, a strategic Chinese government initiative, according to its website. It housed over 500 scientists working on life science related issues. Nancy sat back in the small wooden chair and looked around the café as she digested this information.

The owner of the café came up and offered a top-up. Cora nodded and Nancy smiled. Nothing better than a good old-fashioned cup of builder's tea to clear one's mind.

"Did Ollie ever mention these trips?"

"Never... he kept asking more questions about China, but I assumed it was because of my background, and about my interest in Ai WeiWei's work. Perhaps I should have been more inquisitive."

"No one could've known... I fell into the same trap. Ollie spoke about China, and I gave a pretty grim description of what I recalled, but it was such a long time ago, and the only place I praised was Hong Kong. Setting foot on the shore of Hong Kong Island felt like reaching the promised land."

Nancy stopped, concerned about where the sudden flood of memories might take her. This conversation was not about her.

"We need to find out more about the NIBS in Beijing. I'll make some enquiries."

"And I'll find out who Randy Zhang is."

"I have spoken to Ollie's PA and arranged to pick up his personal effects from his office." Cora drank some tea to stop her voice from trembling. She ran a hand through her spiky hair that no longer looked like a bristling hedgehog, more a puffed-up sparrow.

"That sounds good." Nancy took a sip of tea and smacked her lips. It had the right rich aroma that reminded her of late-night work at Chambers, slaving over a complex case.

"Did someone come and pick up the documents once you gave the originals to Branning?"

"Within 15 minutes of him calling. A police car was sent by Inspector Pole. They must be with him by now."

Nancy replaced the documents in the envelope and slipped it into the satchel that had almost cost her a stay in hospital. She patted it with affection. The strap had been torn during the incident, so she was now just using the handle. It was as hardy and resilient as its owner.

"I have an appointment at Scotland Yard soon... I'll let you know what I find out about that Chinese research institution."

Cora gave a small exhale. "I hope you won't mind me coming back to this…" Her eyes searched Nancy's face for a short moment. "But I believe in Ollie's innocence… I mean, I believe he was clean."

Nancy squeezed her hand. "I know you do… and I intend to find out the truth about what happened. I promise."

\* \* \*

The persistent ring of his landline and the knock of his DS on his door gave Pole the breathing space he needed. He apologised to an increasingly irritated Ferguson.

"I need to take this." Pole didn't wait for an answer. "DS Branning."

Branning updated his boss and was given swift instructions about collecting the evidence and taking statements from whomever had been in contact with the envelope.

Ferguson grumbled his goodbyes in the middle of this activity, firing a resentful look at Pole. "We need to clear this up, Pole. I don't believe in coincidences."

Pole nodded and waved Andy in. Andy had called Yvonne to tell her the new piece of evidence in the form of an envelope was on its way to her, but not before Pole and he had been able to take a look at it.

"Perhaps we should take safety measures before opening the parcel?" Pole said.

"Why? Do you think there will be something dangerous in it?"

"Ollie Wilson was targeted twice."

"Anything dangerous in it would already have done its damage. Unfortunately, the envelope has already been opened by Cora."

"Bad news, Guv?" Andy asked.

"Always a little tense these days when Ferguson's around… Nothing to worry about."

"Yvonne is expecting the package as soon as we can deliver it to her."

"Anything else?" Pole's mind was still drifting back to his conversation with his counter-terrorist colleague.

"I've made progress on the account in Switzerland. It's held by the owner of another numbered account in Malta."

"Malta… a known platform for East European mafia activity."

"Including Russians, of course."

"And the man on the bike?"

"Disappeared… I don't think I'm going to find anything." Andy pulled a disappointed face. He had not yet admitted defeat but was edging closer to it.

"Although…" Andy hesitated. "You're going to think I'm a little obsessed."

Pole smiled. "Come on, tell me what crazy idea is brewing in that great mind of yours."

"I'm not sure it was a man."

"What?" Pole chuckled. "Another woman?"

Andy raised his podgy index finger. "No Guv, the same woman who chased Cora on the canal, according to my latest gate software."

\* \* \*

"Am I troubling you?" Nancy had pushed her mobile into its dash-board case.

"Never… I'm just finishing a lengthy report and the chit chat with a friend is just what I need." Yvonne didn't bother to stifle a yawn.

"I am now seeking information about a biotech organisation called the National Institute of Biological Sciences, they are located in Beijing."

"Beijing… difficult… but Hong Kong, I can do. A friend of mine worked for the Biotechnology Research Institute there. I'd be sur-prised if he doesn't know a thing or two about that organisation."

Nancy accelerated the Aston Martin's engine to go through an amber light. It responded with perfect obedience. No surprise that Henry had loved driving this car.

"You will shortly receive a set of documents relevant to the Ollie Wilson case via email."

"And you'd like to know what my take is on them?"

"If you're offering…"

Nancy thanked Yvonne and concentrated on the approach to Scotland Yard. Victoria Embankment was packed, and she realised too late that it was madness to take a car into Central London at this time of day. She had no choice but to crawl to a standstill until she arrived at the spot where the motorbike had tried to run her over. Nancy tightened her grip on the steering wheel. She looked straight ahead. In a few seconds she would leave the place behind.

The traffic eased off and she succeeded in brushing the memories of the encounter away.

She finally turned into Scotland Yard's car park. Marsh's PA had been good enough to arrange for a space in which to park her Aston Martin Vantage. Mentioning the car's make had also done the trick. The Super did not yet own one of these.

A police officer in full body armour with a machine gun at his side walked towards the car, whilst his colleague stayed behind, observing.

Nancy's name had been added to the list of visitors. She presented her passport for the officer to scrutinise. He took his time to do so thoroughly and instructed someone in the control room to open the gates. Movable bollards started to slide into the ground to give her access, and she parked her car in the space which had been allocated. As she approached the building the heavy metal doors slid open. Ten minutes later, Nancy was walking into Superintendent Marsh's office.

Predictably he was standing at his favourite spot in the corner of his office. He turned around with a broad smile to welcome her.

"Ms Wu, how good of you to make the time."

"Always delighted to be of assistance, Superintendent." Nancy extended a slim hand, elegant in the black Dior suit she had chosen for the meeting. "The Ollie Wilson case deserves all our attention."

She walked over to the corner where she could see tea had been laid out.

Marsh caught up with her and courteously moved a seat for her. "I'm sure it does, but the reason I have asked you to meet is a little more…" Marsh sat down as she did. "…sensitive." Nancy sat down, raising a quizzical eyebrow.

"The counter-terrorist squad commander and I have decided to conduct an informal investigation into what we presume is a leak of key information in the Mark Phelps case."

"A leak?" Nancy's voice managed to remain neutral. "To whom do you think the information was leaked?"

238

Marsh settled, and almost hesitated. "MI6."

"Don't the agency and the Met usually work together?"

"It is sometimes a little more complex…"

"Then I assume you have made a list of all the people who were involved in the case, and I am one of them… hence the meeting."

Marsh's body jolted forward. "I would not want to imply we are in any doubt about your integrity."

Nancy gave him an affable smile. "But you need to do the right thing, Superintendent Marsh… I would not want to be treated in any other way."

The Super looked much relieved, extending a hand towards a brewing pot. "Of course, every person who has been involved in the case will be questioned… tea?"

Nancy managed an agreeable nod.

She now knew the trouble Pole was in.

# Chapter Twenty-Four

The tedious meeting with Marsh had yielded results. Nancy had patiently answered all his questions. Despite his arrogance, the Super was not a narrow-minded man... The combination of intellect and ambition was a potent and dangerous one. There was a rationale behind the diligent interrogation... Timeline, contacts with the victim and the SFO prosecutor, contacts with Pole. Whether Marsh was aware of their relationship, he didn't say.

Marsh seemed to be content with her answers. It was time for Nancy to turn the tables a little.

A fresh pot of tea had arrived, with a clean set of cups. He poured without asking. Nancy smiled encouragingly, eyes focused. "Commander Ferguson is a very thorough officer. It is worrying that he himself has concerns."

Marsh nodded whilst selecting one of the small pastries that had been brought with the tea, after offering them to Nancy.

"Indeed, one of the most successful officers in the counter-terrorist squad... It is good that he and Inspector Pole know each other."

"It must certainly help when it comes to discussing difficult situations."

Marsh settled back into the sofa he had chosen to sit on. He chewed thoughtfully on the chocolate brownie he had just put into his mouth, an expression of pleasure on his face. "It helped contain the burner phone issue... the calls made in and around Scotland Yard."

"And I'm sure Inspector Pole came up with a plausible answer about its presence."

Marsh raised his eyes from his plate, as Nancy looked down at her own. "Not as convincing as we had hoped."

"How unfortunate… but sometimes the explanation can be… complex."

"In this instance, though, there is nothing complex about the questionable locations of the burner phone." Marsh gave Nancy a condescending smile. Pole had not come up with any plausible explanation.

"But I presume Commander Ferguson has found a possible explanation?" Nancy forced herself to nibble at the madeleine she had chosen.

"A hypothesis…" Marsh's rapacious finger hovered over the table and then chose a new victim in the form of a chocolate éclair.

"May I be frank with you, Superintendent?"

"You needn't ask." Marsh gave Nancy a surprised look.

"Would I be right in thinking that the phone was detected close to my home? It would explain the in-depth questioning." Nancy's face remained smooth… a single question coming from a consummate criminal QC.

"An excellent question, of course, that might have to remain unanswered for the time being." Marsh was enjoying the forwardness of the question.

Nancy noted the compliment, her fist clenched over her napkin. She had her own theory about who owned the mobile and there was no time to lose. She needed to speak to Pole.

\* \* \*

"Let's cross the river." Harris slapped Jack on the shoulder.

Jack winced as he got up and Harris shook his head.

"Man, you've got through quite a few tight spots unscathed, and now you come all the way to London to get beaten to a pulp."

"Don't rub it in, Steve," Jack grumbled through his swollen lips. Despite the sun that made the River Thames look almost inviting, a cold wind was pushing against them as they crossed Vauxhall Bridge. Harris raised the collar of his short winter coat and drew his neck into his shoulders. Jack wrapped his scarf over his face; the icy gusts cut into his wounds and made every step a struggle.

They crossed the road as they arrived at the end of the bridge and turned left.

"Just a few yards and we are there," Harris said.

"Another of your favourite pubs?"

"Not this time... a bit of culture my dear fellow... a bit of culture." Harris's imitation of the English upper-class accent always made Jack laugh. He put a hand to his face. "Don't, I can just about talk, let alone laugh."

"I know..." Harris chuckled.

They stayed silent for the rest of the journey until they arrived at Tate Britain. Jack looked up at the neo-classical entrance and stalled.

"I'm not sure I'm in the mood for a gallery tour."

"Neither am I, but the restaurant is excellent, and it won't be full of other eavesdropping colleagues. We've got a table in a little corner I usually book."

"Have you recently turned into an art buff?"

"Nope, but one of my operatives is, and he likes the wine list too." They settled into the comfort of the Rex Whistler restaurant. A table had been set apart from the others, it seemed, for the purpose of accommodating guests who required a little privacy. Jack sat down and rubbed his hands together to shift the cold away. His eyes drifted over the mural that spread around the walls. He frowned and Harris noticed his surprise.

"I know... not a politically correct painting by a long shot. It's called *The Expedition in Pursuit of Rare Meats* and was painted in 1927... according to my guy."

"Was the British Empire not on a steep decline by then?"

"Ten out of ten, mate. Yes, it was."

"How can they keep that on the wall then?"

"I suppose it's a part of history and British heritage... Tate remained silent on the point though..."

The menus arrived, they ordered, and waited to talk business until the food arrived.

"News on your side?" Harris tucked into his shellfish ravioli.

"How much is the UK government monitoring biotechnology for IP theft?"

"A question answered by a question is disconcerting." Harris took another mouthful.

"Agreed... but I'm trying to assess where this Ollie Wilson story is going."

"You mean, how much you can disclose to me without compromising another CIA project." Harris squinted. "No hard feelings, I would do the same if I were in your shoes."

"And what is your answer?" Jack gingerly took a sip of his smoked haddock soup.

"There is something brewing on that front. I've been assigned to a new MI6 project involving the Far East."

"And would you say the UK has extended its field of interest to the Far East?"

"A good way of putting it. The UK has realised that for about 20 years we've been obsessed with the Middle East and that we need to focus our attention further afield."

"The US is doing exactly that, and I can't imagine it's a coincidence. China and North Korea are at the top of the list."

"Hong Kong is also a priority for the UK. The Chinese government has tried a few times to tighten up the regime around that enclave's attempt at democracy... so far Hong Kong has resisted, but it can't last forever."

Jack drank a little more of his soup, deciding how much more he was prepared to tell Harris about the McCain report that elaborated on the threat China truly represented to the West.

"Do you see a large divergence between the UK military and the private sector in your country?"

It was a curve ball Harris had not expected. He put down his fork, to concentrate better on working out the answer he was prepared to give.

"Yes... in short." Harris's fingertips rested on the edge of the table, as if holding it for balance. "And with it the lack of control of what technology goes where."

"It's happening on a large scale in the US." Jack stopped eating as well. "And I'm sure you can guess where the technology goes."

"China." It was not a guess but a statement of fact.

"Which is the reason why I'm increasingly interested in Viro-Tech Therapeutics."

"But it's one of many companies working in the field." Harris drank a little white burgundy and resumed his eating.

"Ollie Wilson saw something important. I'm not sure what it is that he found, but it must be worth finding out."

"I'll see what I can learn from my sources."

Jack nodded, resuming his eating. "Have you been able to find out more about Ms Wu?" he managed between two bites.

Harris lifted his eyes and met Jack's for a moment. "Will you believe me if I say you are looking at the wrong person?"

"I'm going to need a little more than that to be convinced."

Harris took another sip of the excellent wine, undecided. "She was close to a person of interest, so we carried out an in- depth check."

"You mean the banker who helped launder money for the IRA, Henry Crowne."

A faint smile brushed Harris's lip. "The very same."

"How about her communist father?"

"Her Chinese father disappeared 30 years ago, and she has not been back to mainland China since she was a child."

"Yet she's looking into that story again, as well as the Ollie Wilson case."

Harris looked surprised.

"If you didn't know that, perhaps you should revise your views about her," Jack said.

"How much of an interest is she taking in the Wilson case, then?"

"Between enquiring about what happened to him, getting a friend to contact your agency and visiting Viro-Tech Therapeutics? I'd say she's getting pretty proactive."

"Point taken. Though of course Ms Wu may simply want to know a little more about her ancestry... or what happened to her father... that does not make her a Chinese agent."

"But she has a perfect background... people take years before they decide on their true allegiance."

Harris pursed his lips. "That's very true, but so far we have found nothing." A phone was buzzing. Harris took out of his pocket one of his burner phones and stood up. "I have to take this call."

"Your source?" Jack took a sip of the burgundy.

244

Harris maintained a poker face and left the table to take the call outside. The answer Jack was looking for was tantalisingly close.

* * *

The cold wind blew a strand of hair across her face. Nancy pushed it back into the clip, her fingers fiddling to find a way to make it stay there. She stood outside Scotland Yard, underneath the iconic triangular logo. There were too many moving parts she needed to consider before attempting to build a coherent picture, and it was too early to speak to Pole.

She secured her yellow pashmina around her neck, fastened the belt of her black-and-white chequered Chanel woollen coat and started walking.

Pole had taken unimaginable risks and, although she loved him more then she had anyone else, she hoped it was not solely for her sake. The thought made her so uneasy she had to stop for a moment.

Marsh was an egotistical bully who, like all bullies, liked to have it his own way. But as long as the high-profile cases kept coming, and his thirst for fame was assuaged, he could be kept under control.

The ping of her phone told her she had a message. She took a cursory look. Philippe had sent her a text. She hesitated, but decided she would pick up the message once she had returned to her car. She turned to the left out of the car park, following a red asphalted lane. She followed it for a while and the thought of the text awaiting her reminded her of China.

Everything seemed to converge on the awakening dragon. The Ollie Wilson case, her father's last sighting in Hong Kong, Amy's disappearance.

She had passed through Hong Kong many times in the past on her way to other destinations but had never spent much time there except on business, always keen to avoid awakening old memories.

Nancy sat down on a lonely bench before returning to her car. The wind made her shiver. She was giving herself another 24 hours to obtain as much information as she could from Yvonne's various contacts. She would need to convince Cora to stay put. She needed to go to Hong Kong as soon as possible.

Nancy doubted Jared Turner was the sort of man who left sensitive files lying around, or even inside a locked desk and she didn't believe much would now be gained from interrogating him or raiding his office.

Nancy placed her elbows on her knees in a sudden move and let her head drop into a hand. "...Jonathan... why?" Why had Pole worked with MI6 and not told her he did? Information about Nancy's father wasn't worth his career.

Was her next move the only way she could diffuse the tension... send the hunting dogs on another trail?

The gusts of wind became more vicious. Nancy stood up and resumed her walk around the desolate lawn. She slowly returned to the car park. There was still time to change her mind.

She reached the Aston Martin and sheltered into it, happy to be able to call on an efficient heating system. She placed her phone in the dashboard holder and dialled Philippe's number.

The phone rang and after a few moments a muffled voice answered. "Nancy, this is so timely. I'm about to depart."

"Are you going home early today then?" Nancy reversed her car and slowly moved towards the exit.

"No... I'm on a BA flight to Hong Kong. They are about to ask us to switch off. I'll call you when I arrive."

The phone went dead. Nancy stopped the car suddenly. The officer manning the gates took a step back at the abrupt movement of her car.

Nancy squeezed the car wheel and inhaled deeply. She resumed a more sedate course towards the gates, lowering her window and apologising.

As she eased the Aston Martin into the flow of traffic, she thought about her latest plan. She did not have 24 hours to prepare her trip for Hong Kong. She dialled the BA booking line from her mobile. She needed to find a flight that left that evening.

* * *

"I'm sure one box will be enough." Cora was standing in front of Ollie's desk. She bit her lip.

246

His personal effects had already been transferred to a cardboard box... to make Cora's task easier. She didn't believe this was just thoughtfulness on the part of his company.

She tried not to imagine Ollie eating at his desk, calling her to tell her about small things... forgetting to put the laundry into the washing machine, or wash his breakfast plate... or to spring a surprise dinner *en tête à tête* in a nearby restaurant.

Cora quickly cast an eye over the items in the box, not noticing what they were.

"Do you mind if I take a look in his desk to make sure I've got everything?" Cora asked Nikki.

"Of course not." Nikki's fair skin turned a little paler. She was not enjoying the task. Cora sat down at Ollie's desk, her feet barely touching the ground. She opened the drawers to look inside.

"How long did you work with Ollie?" She was now reaching towards the back, checking to make sure nothing had been missed. Nikki stood a few feet away, looking unsure.

"Almost three years. It's been... it was..." Nikki's voice caught in her throat and she couldn't finish the sentence.

Cora found a few pieces of stationery, plastic ballpens, yellow post-its. She fingered them and her throat caught her too.

"Jared... I mean Mr Turner made an announcement about Ollie's health yesterday."

"Ollie spoke a lot about his colleagues here and in Hong Kong."

Nikki nodded. "They too are aware." She was twisting a crumpled tissue.

"Do you think I could have a cup of tea, please?" Cora was not faking her need for something to ease her tight throat.

Nikki nodded and disappeared down the corridor.

Ollie's office was small but light. His desk and PC had been set up so that he could see both the corridor and his door, and still benefit from the window view that looked upon the small garden that was growing up the walls of the building. The office seemed quiet. Cora had seen only a couple of people walking past his door. They had made an effort to avoid looking in on her.

Cora's fingers coursed over the keyboard. Ollie always made

sure Cora had his up-to-date password in case of an emergency. She thanked him mentally for it.

The screen came to life and the screensaver gave Cora a shock. A picture of her and Ollie, taken on holiday in Bali... the first big, expensive holiday they had looked forward to for so long. She had argued against it, unhappy to be spending thousands on luxury hotels. But he had been so keen to treat her with his first bonus that she had relented.

Much to her surprise, she had enjoyed the beautifully presented rooms at the Raffles Hotel in Jimbaran Bay, and the spectacular Four Seasons in Ubud, with its breath-taking entrance that invited guests to walk over a bridge suspended over the jungle treetops.

It had been perfect. Everything had unfolded as Ollie had planned, and Cora had resisted the urge to introduce a little chaos into his well-organised trip.

Cora straightened up... her fingers clicked the mouse, checking folders and their contents. There was no contentious data stored in what she was opening. She methodically tried all the folders that looked promising. Those could not be opened.

In the distance, Nikki's silhouette was moving along the corridor, reflected in the glass partitioning of the offices that lined the L-shaped passageway.

Cora attempted to open Ollie's calendar. That too had been locked. She promptly logged off and diverted her gaze towards the garden outside.

Nikki knocked at the open door and walked in hesitantly. Cora's face must have looked distraught as she stopped in the middle of the room.

Cora nodded her in. Nikki placed the tea in front of her. She laid it on a small paper napkin with a stirrer, a couple of sugars and a small tub of milk. "I was not quite sure how you take it."

"That's very kind of you." Her fingers still shaking after her failed incursion into Ollie's computer, she managed to prepare the tea slowly, pouring in the sugar and the milk in a controlled manner.

"I forgot to ask. There was a gentleman Ollie mentioned a few times when he spoke about his Hong Kong colleagues... Randy Zhang. Do you think I could perhaps contact him? It would be lovely to speak to someone that Ollie knew so well."

248

"Mr Zhang no longer works for the company." The answer came out like a shot. Nikki's cheeks turned deep red, the flush spreading to her forehead and neck.

"Oh." Cora opened wide watery eyes. "Never mind… it would have been nice."

Nikki looked around as though someone was about to materialise in the room. She hesitated, then bent forward towards Cora.

"I'm not sure what happened, but he was asked to leave very suddenly."

Cora didn't take her eyes off Nikki's face.

"But he came from the Biotechnology Research Institute in Hong Kong… maybe they have an address for him."

Cora nodded her thanks and finished her tea. She had the information she was looking for.

# Chapter Twenty-Five

Pole lashed out at Harris without any preamble. "Who the fuck do you use to clean your data, Harris, and don't bloody well tell me to calm down."

Even Harris could not argue with this. Letting the calls of Pole's burner phone register next to Nancy's apartment was poor practice, unforgiveable.

"If you want more information about the Ollie Wilson case, you make the burner phone issue disappear," Pole said.

"Consider it done." Harris already had a plan in mind, or so he suggested.

"What are you proposing?" Pole had left the Scotland Yard building, crossed Parliament Street and ended up next to the Churchill War Rooms. There were plenty of tourists there and his burner phone would mix with other similar devices.

"That doesn't need to concern you. I have an idea."

"It does concern me very much. I'm not giving you one more bit of intel until I understand how you are going to get me out of this mess."

Harris remained silent for a while and Pole wondered whether he was still on the line.

"Fine... this is what's going to happen. You recall that it was a woman who tried to gun down the SFO prosecutor?" Harris said.

"How can I forget... I ran after the little cow across Kennington and couldn't catch her."

"Then you will also recall that she is no longer of this world after an unfortunate encounter with the bullets of Ferguson's squad, so I intend to associate her with the burner phone you used."

Pole weighed up the idea… plausible. She might have done a reconnaissance of her next target's residence, or hovered around Scotland Yard to track down either Nancy or the SFO prosecutor.

"That's a credible idea… how are you going to create the link?"

"I'm sorry, but from there on you will need to trust me, and yes, I know what you're going to say." Harris interrupted Pole before he could vent his still simmering anger. "We could have done better and we didn't. I'll deal with it personally, in any case. For what it's worth, I too do not want you to get caught."

"How touching." Pole's jaw clenched again and he felt the desire to hit something, anything. He started walking again along Horse Guard's Road.

"It's pure self-interest. You are an excellent source and I trust your judgement."

The genuine compliment silenced Pole for a short moment. Harris was infuriating for most of the time, his assurance and cockiness sometimes unbearable, but he was also capable of being straight.

"If you have something to tell me, now is the time. I'm having lunch with the US contact we spoke about… And it would be good to convince him he should concentrate on somewhere other than London at the moment."

"Why?"

"Because he is getting a little too interested in Ms Wu."

Pole almost regretted the kind thought he had just had about Harris. Harris was a cocky little git. "I have just received some documents which I need to go through thoroughly with my team. But in a nutshell, they were sent by Ollie Wilson to one of his colleagues at Viro-Tech in Hong Kong, a certain Randy Zhang."

Pole gave a list of the documents that had been returned to Ollie. Harris did not comment until Pole mentioned Jared Turner's diary extract.

"Regular meetings in China? Whereabouts?"

"The National Institute of Biological Sciences in Beijing."

"The name is familiar… I'll look into that too." There was no point in telling Harris to let him do his job. He might as well avail himself of the MI6 and GCHQ research capability.

"Anything else about Ms Wu's search?"

"She's been given details of her father's whereabouts after Tiananmen Square. She now knows he was alive after the June massacre."

"Are you controlling the flow of information that goes to her?" Pole shot back.

"I'm not the person she used. Yvonne Butler has been her go-between with a contact at MI6, but I still can find out what is going on."

"What else does she know?"

"That the document she was shown about her father's links to art events during the Deng Xiao Ping era is genuine."

"Don't hold back on me Harris... I'm not in the mood."

"And that her father, at least for a while, was in close contact with Deng Xiao Ping himself, China's leader at the time."

*  *  *

"Slow down... where are you?" The Aston Martin was now gliding smoothly through traffic. Cora's breathless voice made it almost impossible for Nancy to understand her.

"I'm... back... at home."

"You went to Viro-Tech?"

"Yes." Cora's voice changed and Nancy detected a tremor.

"I'm sorry I'm not with you. Call me back if you want to take a moment..."

"That's OK," Cora interrupted. "I want to tell you now, it's important. Randy Zhang, Ollie's colleague, no longer works there."

"He was sacked?"

"Yes, I believe so... Nikki told me. She was Ollie's PA. I could see she was not supposed to talk about it, but she did. She also told me where we might find him."

"Perfect... I'm on my way."

Another call was coming through, Nancy switched caller. "I have news for you."

"You're a mine of information, Yvonne."

"First, I have found a couple of contacts at the Biotechnology Research Institute in Hong Kong. I'll send their names via text, and secondly, my MI6 contact has come back with an address for Emmanuel

Licot, the author of the paper that talks about your father. He lives in France, but he regularly lectures in Southern Asia…"

"In Hong Kong?"

"Correct." Nancy could picture Yvonne stabbing her desk with her index finger whilst she rolled her rs.

"It seems that all roads lead to one place at the moment."

"Are you going to buy an air ticket?"

"Perhaps…" Nancy would play that card close to her chest. "I'm surprised how incredibly helpful MI6 are being."

"Don't be, she wants something… I don't mind telling you it's a she. There is an angle for her, but of course she won't tell me what it is."

"I'll bear that in mind." Nancy hung up. A set of traffic lights turned green and she pushed the car a little more whilst the roads were clear. Nancy found a parking spot and stopped abruptly. She took the iPhone off its cradle and typed in the name that had been surfacing in her mind too many times now for her to ignore.

Deng Xiao Ping's profile materialised on the screen.

The traffic was now whizzing past the door of her car. She scanned his profile, scrolling down the page until she found a place name that caught her eye… Sichuan province, the same province her father and his ancestors had come from.

Nancy nudged the Aston Martin back into the traffic.

She accelerated, overtaking a few cars that objected, sounding their horns in protest. She kept going until she was forced to stop abruptly, barely avoiding the boot of the car in front.

The window of the BMW she almost hit came down. A bearded man leaned out of the window, shouting insults that she, no doubt deserved.

She eased her clenched fingers off the wheel and sat back for a few seconds, numb.

When the traffic started moving again, she resumed the drive towards Cora's flat at a more civilised pace.

\* \* \*

The CIA Station Chief in London had called Jack. Jack had left Harris after he had gathered fresh information from his source.

Apparently, Ollie Wilson had sent several documents to a contact in Hong Kong. He had squeezed as much as he could out of Harris. He could not expect to be given everything. After all, he too had not disclosed all he knew about the Wilson case. He hadn't felt able yet to discuss a possible research co-operation between the US and China. This was too sensitive to be entrusted to just anyone, even a close professional colleague and friend such as Steve Harris.

Jack hailed a black cab... One of the great joys of London. He loved riding in the back of these quirky vehicles, with their cramped cabin for the driver and the spacious passenger compartment with five comfortable seats. He enjoyed even more the chattiness of their drivers.

"You on holiday?" the driver asked.

"That's right." Jack quickly surveyed the cabbie, an older man in his 70s, white thinning hair underneath a tweed cap. His leathery hands were relaxed on the wheel, and his manner confident yet courteous.

"Did you enjoy the Tate?"

"I have to confess; I've only been to the restaurant... But I'll go back."

The old man nodded appreciatively. "I like to visit the gallery meself. We do that on Thursdays with me wife, Di... Not too many people then."

They continued chatting. The cab entered Grosvenor Place. The tall garden walls of Buckingham Palace stretched on their right. Jack recognised the place he had once visited under very different and less relaxed circumstances. He changed seat, sliding to the left, ready to disembark when they arrived at Hyde Park Corner.

The glimmer that flashed next to the right-hand side window caught Jack's attention in an instant.

"Stop the cab... now!" His shout worked. The cabbie applied the brakes as though he was about to hit an obstacle. Jack opened the door and rolled onto the pavement, sheltering behind the heavy metal frame of a van.

The sound of bullets hitting the open door of the cab, and breaking glass, made Jack crouch even lower. There was nowhere else to hide. The wide pavement was a simple straight line; anyone venturing there would be too exposed. He had counted five shots. There were still plenty more in the gun's magazine, whatever its make. Jack crept around the body of a van that stood on the opposite side to the shots. He tried to open the rear door. It was unlocked. A person was coming towards him from the road.

He waited for his assailant to come nearer and slammed the door into his face. The figure staggered, Jack slammed the door closed and stood in the road to face the gunman. The man was wearing a helmet and the crash of metal against metal had stunned him.

Jack threw a back-leg kick into the man's side. He dropped his gun, staggering. Jack made for the gun before his aggressor could retrieve it. The aggressor forgot about his gun. He turned around, jumped on the back of a waiting motorbike and the two men roared off.

Jack hesitated for a short moment. He had a clean shot but the risk was still too great. He pulled back, remembering the taxi had been shot at and suddenly remembering the cabbie inside it.

The old man had dived sideways, hands over his ears. Jack worried he had been hit. He opened the door in one swoop and leaned over the driver.

"Are you alright?" Jack touched his shoulder lightly.

The cabbie shuddered and removed his hands from his face. He sat up slowly. "Fifty years I've been driving a cab... 50 years... never been shot at."

"I'm very sorry about this..." Jack was genuinely upset for the old boy. "I'll make sure the damage is taken care of."

"Fifty years..." The cabbie kept shaking his head in disbelief.

Jack could almost hear it. Bloody Yanks... come to London and think it's Chicago.

"I know... I'll make sure you're not out of pocket."

The old man's face broke into a smile. "Wait until I tell Di..." He chuckled. "Never... in 50 years." He pushed his cap back on his head still smiling.

Jack just managed to catch what the Chief of Station was saying, the memories of the incident still a little too fresh for him to fully concentrate.

"That's the second time in less than 24 hours, Jack." Jethro had poured himself a coffee and Jack had opted for water. "Don't you think it's time you got back to work? Clearly holidays do not suit you."

"Or perhaps I need a change of destination."

Jethro Greeney raised a quizzical eyebrow. "If you're not safe in London, where else in the world are you going to be safe?"

Jack pursed his lips. He did not need to be safe, he needed answers. "Anyway, we'll take care of the cab once the police have received your statement. The British are going to want some answers. It's one thing being set upon by some thugs late at night. It's another when you have a gunman targeting you in broad daylight in the middle of London."

"I'm a CIA agent. I'm sure you can convince them I've made a few enemies in my long and distinguished career."

"That's the problem. The Brits don't want to have a high noon gunfight on their doorstep, and frankly, I can't blame them."

"I'd love to give you the name and address of those guys, but I didn't get a chance to ask for a business card."

Greeney did not dignify Jack with a response.

"Seriously, I really have no idea who they were."

"I hope not…" Greeney drank some of his coffee and scanned Jack with a doubtful eye. "And unfortunately, we have to let your boss know."

"I'll take care of that." Jack cleared his throat and drank some water.

"You have until the end of today to do that, after that I'll make the call myself."

Jack said back in his chair, nodding an OK.

"Now, about this Nancy Wu you've been talking about. I've made some progress."

*You mean your team has made some progress.* But Jack shut up. He simply wanted the information.

"She has just booked a ticket on today's last BA flight to Hong Kong."

\* \* \*

Nancy parked the Aston Martin in one short sweep and opened the door. She bent forward over the gutter. She was about to be sick. The taste of bile in her mouth felt acrid. She gave a few gasps and slumped back into the car seat.

256

What had she been thinking?

The complexity of the search for her father, the Ollie Wilson case and Pole's dangerous position had created the perfect storm. But she was damned if she would let herself drown. She was a survivor, and a seasoned one too.

The clock on the dashboard of the Vantage indicated it was 2.30pm. The flight departed at 9pm from London Heathrow.

She had booked business class. First class seemed too ostentatious and might attract attention. In business, she would merge with the crowd of businessmen and women who regularly commuted between the two countries.

She needed to be at the airport an hour beforehand, she would allow herself another hour's journey time. It might be cutting it fine, but she was used to travelling on a tight schedule.

Back in her apartment, Nancy moved straight to her computer. She resumed her search and within seconds found Deng Xiao Ping's profile again. Nancy read a few times the small paragraph which told her that Deng's ancestors and family had come from Sichuan province. His father, a mid-level landowner, had studied in Chengdu, at its Law University. He was by all accounts a prominent local man.

Born in 1904, Deng received a traditional education and joined the Communist Party of China in 1923.

Nancy's heart was racing as she read the text once more.

*The garden is immaculate, and she has been running around the white pebbled alleys. The famous Sichuan pepper trees form part of a row of trees that define the borders of the narrow paths. There are orchids and other flowers she can't quite make out. Bamboos taller than the house lean against the garden wall. She plays hide-and-seek with her mother. Her father is calling them, yet they are having too much fun.*

*He is trying to sound annoyed, but his heart is not in it. He would much rather join them in the giddy race.*

*But someone else is in the house.*

*Her mother finally catches her and tickles her. He can hear the laughter. "We'd better go… Grandfather is visiting, and he doesn't like to be made to wait."*

*The house smells of spices... she is now sitting on a chair with her mother. Her father is speaking to a man that looks so very old... she has been told not to stare but she can't help it.*

*Her mother squeezes her arm to make her stop and she drops her gaze. She doesn't quite understand what they are saying. Her Chinese is good, but the conversation is too complicated. There are lots of words she still doesn't know... grown-up words.*

*Her grandfather calls her Bo. It's her Chinese name and he asks her to approach him. She looks at her mother who nods at her and mouths, "It's OK."*

*The old man bends forward. She can smell his breath, and she almost recoils, but has learned to be polite. The serious face comes closer to hers and breaks into a smile. He takes something out of his pocket and hands it over to her. It's the most exquisite carving and she is struck by its beauty.*

Nancy hadn't recalled this early memory for years. She never discussed it with her father nor her mother. All that might have helped her trace her ancestry she had thrown away. Anger had not been a good counsellor. Most of the papers that her father and mother had carefully saved on their perilous trip to escape China had been burnt to a cinder. It had been reckless but there it was.

She looked at her watch, another three hours to go before she must leave.

Was it all worth it? Discovering whether her father had been an ally of Deng? But the anxiety of not knowing who he truly was would not disappear until she had the answer.

She gave a short exhale and returned to the screen.

She browsed a few websites. After all, everything was on the net these days, and, nevertheless amazed, she found a web page dealing with Chinese ancestry. It was written in English since it was targeted at the Hong Kong market.

She inputted with feverish fingers the name of her father, Li Jie Wu, his birth date and Chengdu, the main city of Sichuan province, and pressed the return button. The English page remained blank, but a link appeared to two pages written in Chinese.

Nancy thumped the desk in frustration and abandoned the search. She hadn't spoken Chinese for years, let alone read it. She went to the small box in which she kept some of the older papers. A couple of them were written in Chinese. She had kept them because the calligraphy on the finest rice paper was exquisite.

She tried once more to recall the meaning of the characters, but it had been too long.

It felt hopeless. She needed more time. She would need to expand the search when she reached Hong Kong.

There was a more pressing matter that needed her attention. To convince Cora not to follow her on the trip. She was going alone. She had to.

# Chapter Twenty-Six

"I have spoken again to the Jersey bank that holds Ollie Wilson's bank account. I've investigated their track record and called the FCA to check their credentials. Nothing major to report, a few incidents like in any other bank. The guy I spoke to on the phone was helpful. He was cautious but I didn't sense he felt guilty about the transactions we discussed. He is coming back to me with an explanation as to why they didn't query the flows when they started happening regularly," Andy said.

"But was he the person in charge of Wilson's account?" Pole was sitting at his desk, toying with the mobile phone that lay on it.

"No, he runs the team of advisers who speaks to the clients direct."

"So could the person who authorised the transactions have left of their own accord or even been sacked?" Pole had hung his jacket over the back of his chair and rolled up his sleeves, tie loosened from around his neck.

The cold spell outside had pushed the office temperature to almost tropical… the women in the office loved it, but the men not so much… so far, the women were winning.

Andy scrolled through his iPad. "Ollie Wilson's account has been allocated to a new person… you're right. His predecessor took early retirement."

Pole stopped playing with his phone. "He's been paid off."

Andy removed his thick glasses from his nose, fished a well-used tissue out of his pocket and dabbed his eyes. "That's a good point, Guv… he could have been offered good money to keep quiet about the regular payments."

"Once the first payment is authorised, and as long as the other payments are for a similar amount, they don't trigger the money-laundering alert."

"That must be what happened here." Andy was meticulously cleaning his glasses with the corner of his shirt. He replaced the spectacles on his nose with a smile... much better. "And no one is going to do another check on the origin of the funds or the identity of the account holders."

"What about the banks making and receiving the payments?"

"Some progress there... from Malta we've reached an account in Estonia with Deutsche Bank."

Pole loosened his tie a little more. "We are getting closer to identifying the owner of the account?"

Andy nodded.

"Check again with Yvonne, about the composition of the drug that sent Ollie Wilson over the edge. Rob's NCA contact sent me the molecular composition of what they intercepted from the Russians. She's already got that."

"You think there might be a link?"

"I'm not a betting man, but if I were, I would say yes... That would link Wilson to a Russian drug cartel."

"You don't seem to be convinced, Guv."

"I might have been convinced if Cora hadn't received the documents Wilson sent to his colleague in Hong Kong. Wilson seemed to be a damn sight more concerned and involved with China than the Russians..." Pole's attention was diverted by a voice he seldom heard on his floor... an excellent thing in his view.

Marsh walked from the lift onto the open-plan office. He stopped, as he always did whenever he honoured them with a visit, to speak to some poor sods who were trying to do their jobs.

At least Pole had the advantage of knowing he was on his way, his booming voice carrying across the space.

Andy began to look a little nervous. Pole for once shared his DS's feelings as he remembered Marsh's plan for a four-eye review of the evidence found in the Ferguson inquiry.

"Wait to go back to your desk until he's walked into my office, otherwise he'll insist you go through the burner phone evidence from A to Z with him and I won't be able to divert his attention," Pole said.

261

Andy looked truly alarmed at the thought of discussing any evidence with The Super. Marsh did not like details, which Andy revelled in. Marsh liked speedy conclusions; Andy preferred to take his time.

"One quick question before the Super comes in… the burner phone we identified, you said it was on the premises, but could it simply have been very close by? For example, across the road on the banks of the Thames Embankment opposite the building itself, or even near the reception area?" Pole spoke with a sense of urgency.

Andy's head was turned towards the door, surveying Marsh's progress.

"It would have to be closer than the embankment, but the pavement outside the building or the entrance next to the reception area would work…" Andy started to stand up. "Or perhaps the back of the building… there is a little garden that very few people use."

Pole nodded encouragingly. "Someone outside surveying the building from close up, for example, and using a burner phone."

"That's possible."

"How sure are you about that?" Pole's voice became insistent.

"Yes, yes… that is definitely possible."

Marsh stood in the doorway, waiting for Pole to welcome him with the courtesy owed to his seniority.

"Sir, how good of you to pay us a visit." Pole stood up.

Andy made his excuses, muttering something about Ollie Wilson's account.

Marsh moved out of his way to let him through. His lunch with Nancy had gone well. The Super was in a good mood.

"Has your DS made some inroads into the burner phone issue?"

Pole invited Marsh to sit. He needn't have bothered, because Marsh had already grabbed the back of the chair to place it at an angle to Pole's desk.

"We were just talking about that."

Marsh squeezed his heavy frame into the seat, resting his elbows on the armrests. He was all ears.

"It might be tempting to think that the burner phone was on the Scotland Yard premises, but it is equally possible that the phone and its owner were outside the building."

Marsh cocked his head. "You mean someone undertaking surveillance, keeping tabs on the place and the people inside?"

Pole had to give it to Marsh; he was not a complete dickhead.

"That's a real possibility."

Marsh moved his head forward. His fingertips had joined in front of his face, lightly touching his lips. "There are hundreds of CCTV cameras in the area... We should be able to see something."

"That's what Andy is going to do next. Although the Ollie Wilson case is starting to gain traction."

"Any new developments worth mentioning?"

"Nothing that requires your attention, sir."

Marsh pursed his lips, disappointed.

"Well, I have news of my own... I spoke to Ms Wu."

Pole sat back in his seat, bracing himself for a lengthy account in which Marsh would give a blow-by-blow of their lunch.

"As reluctant as I am to admit it, I think Ms Wu is not quite telling us the truth."

* * *

Cora rested the book slowly on the immaculate white sheet. She had heard it was good for coma patients to hear familiar voices, voices of the people they loved and who loved them. Johnny had run to the bookshelf and brought back a small compilation of Yeats love poems. Cora had found the words that Ollie used to recite to her when they had first met... All to show her he was not a soulless biotech geek... It had worked. She had only put up a resistance, because she'd been too frightened to let him know how much she already cared for him.

"The rose in the depth of his heart," she murmured and sank back a little into the chair, still holding his hand. The rhythmic noise of the instruments now attached to Ollie's body permanently had become almost unnoticeable.

From time to time his hand twitched, raising her hopes, but the doctor had been very clear that this happened with most patients, a simple reflex of the nerves to touch.

Her mobile phone buzzed in her jacket pocket. She hesitated but dragged it out, prepared to ignore it. Nancy's name was flashing on the screen. She stood up in a small jump. A call from a friend was exactly what she needed.

"Cora... how are you? Can you talk?"

"I'm at the hospital. It's good to hear your voice... it's so bleak here."

"Perhaps I could call a little later."

"No, that's fine... please tell me what's on your mind." Cora had gently laid Ollie's hand back on the sheet, and moved to the window. Perhaps a warm drink would ease the tightness of her throat. "Wait a moment if you don't mind, I need to fetch a drink."

She walked through the sliding doors and almost bumped into a tall nurse. Her face looked somehow familiar, but the woman turned around and disappeared into another patient's room.

Cora hesitated but parked the thought. She approached the vending machine, ordered a tea and when it was ready moved to a row of empty chairs.

"Sorry, Nancy, I'm with you now."

"I've made some progress in researching possible contacts with Randy Zhang."

Cora's heart jumped up in her chest. "That's great. Do you have another address?"

"Not as such, but I found someone at the same institute in Hong Kong... and I also spoke to Philippe."

"I should have called him... it's been so strange and difficult."

"He understands better than anybody else... but you would not have been able to speak to him in any case... he's gone to Hong Kong."

"He's mad... what is he going to do out there on his own? Let me call him now."

"I've left messages already." Nancy's voice trailed off. "I won't try to justify what I'm about to do, but... I too am on my way to Hong Kong."

"...but you have barely lived there... how will you manage? Let me come with you." Cora was pacing up and down the corridor.

"Please don't." Cora was about to protest. "Please listen... you are all that Ollie has left. And I too need you to stay in London. You are the only person who knows the details of the evidence gathered and you can speak to Inspector Pole, if need be. He will listen."

"It's not fair. I need to find out what happened to Ollie too. I want the truth to come out…"

"Just as I do. You need to try and catch up with Nikki again and see what else you can find out, but please… no more climbing up walls and trying to get into Viro-Tech on your own."

"I'm not promising anything…" Cora had stopped in the middle of the corridor, feeling stubborn.

"That's your choice, of course, but it won't help either Inspector Pole or me to uncover the truth, if you end up behind bars."

Cora looked down at her cup of tea. The beverage looked unappetising. She took a sip anyway, pulled a face and walked over to the nearest wastebin.

"Is there another reason you're going out there on your own?"

"I won't lie to you. More information has come to light about my father, and I need to find out what has happened for myself, without getting other people into trouble."

Cora understood. "But you must let me help you… Hong Kong has got its different communities, and there are ways of making sure you stay under the radar of the authorities."

"Yes, I'd be grateful for that, thank you." Nancy's tone sounded heartfelt. "I haven't had time to speak to Inspector Pole about your conversation with Nikki at Viro-Tech. Perhaps you could give him a call."

"Consider it done… does he know about your trip?"

Nancy paused. "Not yet."

* * *

"Randy too comes from BIG at Harvard." Laurie had been in touch as soon as she'd received Jack's mail about Randy Zang, Ollie's contact at Viro Tech. "I'll send you a detailed map of Hong Kong. They knew each other well… Randy joined Viro-Tech soon after Ollie."

"So, he trusted him, what else?"

"The most interesting part of the story… Randy has completely disappeared. He was let go of by Viro-Tech a couple of months ago, and he's bailed out of his flat as well. He has closed his bank account… vanished," Laurie said.

265

"Spotted anywhere else?"

"No… the man has literally become a ghost."

"I suppose his tech abilities make disappearing a little easier," Jack added.

"Perhaps, but it still takes a lot of doing to stay completely under the radar, particularly in Hong Kong."

"He may no longer be in Hong Kong… he may no longer be alive." Jack had been dropped back at his hotel by an armour-plated car the embassy used for high-profile dignitaries. He did not enjoy the attention, but at least it provided him with a secure place to make his call.

"That's entirely possible… and if he has been dispatched in Hong Kong, and dumped in the bay, the sharks have cleaned up after the guys who did the job in the first place," Laurie said.

"I am not going to get much help from the Station Chief in London. I need to find Randy though."

"You're on holiday, Jack… no one said you had to stay in London."

Jack smiled. "I might take up your idea. London is colder than I remember at this time of the year."

"How about you-know-who?"

"I just dropped him an email… I need to tell him about the latest attempt on my life."

"High risk strategy… You-know-who is not going to like it."

"He never likes anything anyone does… and it'll just mean I won't be able to take a holiday for the next 20 years."

"You won't have the support in Hong Kong that you found in the UK… I know Jethro is a bit full of himself, but he does come up with the goods."

"I'll just have to introduce myself to the Station Chief there and see what he can do for me."

"It's a real political minefield, and if what we know about the planned co-operation agreement between the US and China to combat the next epidemic is right, there will be even less desire to rock the boat in Hong Kong."

"I'm not asking anyone to scupper the negotiations. I'm just making sure we understand why Ollie Wilson was so concerned about his CEO's involvement in mainland China."

266

"But if Jared Turner is one of the negotiators in this highly sensitive conversation, it is going to be pretty tough to get at him."

"Not unless he's up to—

Laurie interrupted. "Jack, are you for real? You know how politics works. Jared's needed to help close this high-profile deal. He is too valuable at the moment to be got to. A few misdemeanours like making money on the sly or being awarded highly lucrative contracts will not matter."

"Unless it's a matter of national security... I get that. And perhaps attempted murder might do the trick, too." Jack bent forward to look through the window. For once, he was grateful for traffic. The gridlock around Piccadilly was giving him more time to speak to Laurie.

"And you won't get to that level of discovery on your own... you'd need a properly mounted operation."

"Are you trying to convince me to come back to Langley?"

"No, I'm not. I'm just pointing out the rather steep hill you're going to have to climb, if what you think is happening is actually happening."

"Much appreciated." Jack checked his watch. He had a little time to pack.

"Since you mentioned him... what did you manage to find out about Jared Turner, in his role as CEO of Viro-Tech Therapeutics?"

"Very well-connected guy."

"It's not surprising, given he's landed the job of go-between to help the US and China come to an agreement. He has to be."

"But more remarkably, across the political divide, both Republicans and Democrats are prepared to work with him."

"Two possible reasons for that in my experience." The car had started moving again, and they would soon arrive at Trafalgar Square. "Either he has some real dirt on those people, and could indulge in some good old-fashioned blackmail, or his business connections are second to none."

"Or a bit of both..." Laurie was weighing up the idea. "But to be fair to the man, no matter how unpalatable it may seem, I would say the latter. He has some very high-profile connections in the tech world. He seems to know Bill Gates pretty well. Yes, connections in the small biotech industry as well as with the big pharmaceutical companies, and a whole host of smaller companies in Silicon Valley."

"Whom does he know amongst the big pharma companies?"

"Pfizer, AstraZeneca… and he also has good connections with Johnson & Johnson."

"Why isn't he working for one of the big guys, if he has such good contacts?"

"That's not the way he operates. He makes a lot of money by developing new drugs in small companies or start-ups, and then sells them on to the large pharma companies once he has a prototype bio product that works."

"How many times has he sold his start-ups?" Jack asked.

Jared Turner, the man he had seen in the picture attached to the file Laurie had sent, did not look that old.

"Three times, and that is pretty impressive at the age of 37."

"So, Jared Turner is gifted when it comes to research and development in the biotech industry… That doesn't mean he's not involved in some dodgy deal."

"Agreed… he must be pretty ruthless to finance his companies through private equity and then sell to the big groups. He knows how to play the financial game, and he's no pussycat."

"I'll bear that in mind. Anything else on his background?"

"Yep… his father worked on Wall Street until he retired a few years ago. He worked in asset management and in the same pharma sector. Now running a consultancy practice and sitting as non-exec director on the board of large companies in the NASDAQ."

"Still involved in pharmaceuticals?"

"Good question… let me see." Jack heard a few clicks of the mouse before Laurie returned. "A couple of pharmaceutical firms… one medium, one very large."

"I'm not surprised Turner Junior can get a deal done, then."

"I agree it helps to have dad sitting in the right boardrooms."

"Can you email me the information?"

"Done," Laurie interrupted.

The car had arrived at his hotel. Jack moved swiftly through the lobby and called the lift.

268

"Going to Hong Kong?" Laurie's cheery voice lowered. "BA flight tonight at 9pm from London Heathrow."

"Is it not the flight…" Jack wondered.

"…on which Ms Wu is flying?" Laurie replied. "It is."

# Chapter Twenty-Seven

Nancy hesitated when Charlie, her limo driver, called to say he was waiting downstairs and would she like him to help with her luggage. But there was no point in procrastinating, she had to go to Hong Kong. She slowed down when she presented her British passport at passport control, yet the sense that she would find answers made her last doubt disappear.

Now that she was sitting in the first-class BA lounge courtesy of her gold executive card, she stood at the floor-to-ceiling window overlooking the runway in a secluded corner of the lounge.

Nancy checked her watch, only 30 minutes to go before boarding for business class, and 45 minutes before departure. Charlie had been, as ever, efficient at driving her to the airport in record time.

She took a sip of the champagne an affable stewardess had deposited on the low table next to her seat. The bubbles did not produce the lift in mood they usually did. It was time to call Pole.

The mobile phone felt clammy in her hand. She had been holding it ever since she settled in the lounge 10 minutes earlier. Nancy took a slow intake of breath and pressed recall button number one. The phone rang a few times. Pole's voice sounded pressed. "Could I call you back please... or, even better, shall we speak tonight over dinner?"

"Jonathan..." The tremor in her voice surprised her. "I'm at the airport. I'll be boarding in 20 minutes."

The silence at the end of the phone was deafening. She cursed herself for not giving him more notice, hearing his muffled voice giving instructions and sounds that indicated he was moving around.

"Are you flying to China?" His voice was hardly recognisable, blunt, unemotional.

"Hong Kong."

"Why?"

"Philippe has already gone. I can't just leave him there on his own." She stopped herself. Whether Philippe was there or not wouldn't have made much difference. She would have gone anyway. "And because too many things have surfaced recently... concerning Ollie, my father..."

"Can't you wait a day, so that we can at least discuss it?" Pole interrupted and she interrupted back.

"...and also concerning you..." She grabbed the glass of champagne, almost spilling it and took a large gulp. "You've been so helpful..." She hoped she was choosing her words carefully enough. "*Peut-être trop...* I feel my absence may give you a break."

Pole was now walking outside. She could hear traffic in the distance. "I'll call you back from another number."

The line went dead, but within seconds her mobile was ringing again.

"This line is secure... What do you mean? What are you saying?" Pole's voice had an urgency she had only heard when he sensed danger. "Are you sure?"

"Certain... *S'il-te-plaît...* I know where you have been getting your information from and I suspect that is also the reason why Ferguson and Marsh are running this damn inquiry on the Phelps case."

Pole remained silent.

"You can't tell me, of course, but I have a feeling from my meeting with Marsh that some piece of information has perhaps moved a pointer in my direction... and my trip to Hong Kong will also serve that purpose."

"I'm not using you as a decoy." Pole had recovered his voice and his pent-up concern had turned into anger.

"Why not? After all I have benefitted from the information you gathered on my behalf without asking too many questions, which as you know is not like me at all."

Pole tried to interrupt but Nancy carried on. "I could have been much more suspicious about that. Instead, it suited me fine to be taking a back seat with the investigation into my father's disappearance."

"So now you're taking the front seat, by making yourself a suspect with Marsh and the counter-terrorist squad?" She imagined Pole, striding along the banks of the River Thames, not having bothered with a coat like most of his colleagues.

"Now that you put it like that, it sounds very dramatic, but at least it will give you and your... contact... time to sort out something that can exonerate you."

"What if it doesn't work?"

"I'm not an expert in these matters, but the little I have seen of MI6 tells me they are pretty resourceful when it comes to protecting their sources."

There, she had said it, and it was a weight off her shoulders to be telling it how it was.

Pole had stopped walking, it seemed.

"You have more faith in them than I have."

"I don't have faith in them, Jonathan. I have faith in you."

"But can't you at least delay your departure so that we can talk about it... make a plan?"

The thought of being back in her flat, speaking to Pole about her next step made her stomach churn. She could still change her mind, claim an emergency of some kind... BA could unload the luggage... there was still time. "Please, only by one day." She heard in Pole's voice he had sensed the shift.

Nancy gulped down the rest of the champagne, warm and acidic now.

"If I don't do this now, I may not..." She hesitated, felt the pressure in her stomach again. "I may never do it. And in any case, Philippe has gone, and he needs someone to shepherd him around, if he is going to find out what happened to Amy. One day can make a big difference in Hong Kong."

Pole must have been holding his breath. She heard a slow exhale. "I'll try to join you as soon as I can," he finally said.

"No way... that would defeat the object of the exercise. You are needed there to look after Cora, please. And you also need to be in London to keep gathering the information I need."

"Ollie Wilson's case might well require me to fly to Hong Kong."

Nancy thought about the documents Cora had shown her, but perhaps now was not the time to tell Pole she knew about those too.

"As long as Marsh is on your side."

"Since when do I care about Marsh's opinion when it comes to solving a case?"

"Since you became the subject of an inquiry led by the counter-terrorist squad."

"You may have a point," Pole grumbled.

Then she felt a presence, polite but hovering at her side.

"I'm sorry, ma'am, but you should think about boarding the aircraft now."

Nancy turned towards the young man who had approached her and nodded a thank you.

"The flight is boarding now…"

Pole's voice held back his goodbye for a short moment. "Safe flight then… call me when you've settled into your hotel. I'll text you a new number to use."

"I'm staying at the Mandarin Oriental."

"Do I need to say it?"

"I'll be careful, *mon coeur*, promise."

"That does not fill me with the warm glow of certainty."

Nancy started walking towards the gate. Only a few people remained. She presented her boarding pass.

"But the one thing that should convince you I'll be careful is that I want to come back to London and to you."

\* \* \*

"I could ask Nikki for a drink or a coffee… see what she has to say," Cora suggested.

"As long as it does not involve doing a Nancy Wu and getting into trouble. And as long as DS Branning is in the vicinity… why not?" Pole sounded more concerned than she had expected. It did not fit the relaxed and self-assured image she had of him. He was the second person to make her swear to be careful with Viro-Tech, perhaps she should listen.

"Call me if you remember anything else." Pole's warm baritone voice soothed her. Cora felt a little guilty. She knew about Nancy's imminent departure to Hong Kong, and yet had said nothing.

She imagined Nancy settled into her business-class seat. She had loaded the information she needed to review on her laptop, and taken the documents Cora had photocopied with her

Cora pulled the soft blanket up to her shoulders and snuggled into the bed. She was still squatting in Beth's bedroom. The latest from the builders who had visited her flat was a minimum of six months to clean and rebuild after the fire. A specialist firm had started removing the furniture, and the personal effects that could be salvaged.

She was staggered at the amount of stuff she and Ollie had accumulated. She was grateful she had digitised all of her photos. It was not the fire that had caused such damage, but the smoke that had penetrated and covered everything with a thick coat of black soot. Nothing had been spared.

She still hadn't been able to reach her artwork and the props she had stored at the back of the large L-shaped room where her studio once was.

Some of her work was still at Philippe's gallery. At least she had saved some of the more recent print editions she had created.

Her mind shifted back to her conversation with Pole.

She had described in detail the visit to Viro-Tech. The reluctance to speak about Randy Zhang. Nikki's eventual disclosure that he had left under a cloud of suspicion. Pole had been grateful for the information. She could sense it in his voice. He was perhaps gathering enough information to justify a visit to Ollie's former company.

She had never shared Ollie's blind appreciation of Jared Turner, too cordial to be honest, too keen to praise people to be genuine. She didn't like the man, perhaps because of the condescending way he looked at women when he thought he was not being observed. People were a means to an end, yet he seemed good at running a successful company, supporting his employees in their research endeavours.

Pole had found it interesting that Ollie's electronic files had been locked so quickly. But perhaps the attempt on his life had spooked the people in charge of keeping the company secure against industrial espionage and cyber-attack.

Someone knocked at the door. A small gap opened and Johnny's head popped in.

"I saw some light underneath the door. Just wanted to check you had not fallen asleep with candles burning around the room as Beth usually does."

Cora waved him in. He was holding two mugs of chamomile tea. "And what do you do then? Extinguish the fire hazard by throwing herbal tea over it?"

"I wouldn't, but Beth might." He had changed from his work clothes into a brand-new pair of designer jeans and a tight grey T-shirt that showed off his well-exercised trim body. "I saw you talking to the builders when I left this morning... not that we don't want to have you around. But what did they say?"

"Six months... and I still haven't been able to access the back of the room."

Johnny sighed, put both cups down on the bedside table and picked up her hand.

"You tell us if we can do anything to help. Perhaps help you find a new studio or something until you can safely go back in."

Cora squeezed his hand and grabbed the mug with the other, bringing it to her lips. She blew off the steam and sipped the hot liquid. "Thank you."

"You're not thinking about giving up the flat I hope? You've been here for as long as we have... and the studio part is ideal. Where else are you going to find high ceilings like these and... and... climb the beams of the flat to rehearse your performance?" Johnny's arms were waving around, like a windmill.

"Don't panic... I'm not done yet with it." Cora straightened up when she spoke the last words. Some of the hot beverage spilt over her hands. She pulled a face and put the mug back onto the bedside table. She disentangled herself from the blanket with difficulty, jumped out of the bed onto the floor in a single leap and stood next to Johnny. "I need to get back to the flat."

"In the middle of the night… with no electricity and holes in the floorboards… never! I gave my word to Nancy."

"I just remembered something… something I discussed with Nancy and that we never thought on."

"And what would that be that requires you charging out all of a sudden? Without mentioning the cops at the bottom of our building, or the fact that you will have to use the old fire exit stairwell…" Johnny had crossed his arms over his chest. The tattoos stretched as his muscles tightened.

"There is something Ollie might have left for me there."

Johnny's face switched from doubtful to inquisitive. "You mean like a clue… you mean like evidence?"

"I don't know, Johnny. I can only find out if I go there and check."

He rolled his eyes and threw a pair of dark jogging bottoms and the matching top to her. "Well then… I'd like to come with you if you're going to break your promise to Nancy that fast."

* * *

The email from his boss had popped into his mailbox just as he was on his way to the airport. Jack ignored it. He could always argue reception on the Heathrow Express was not at its best.

Jack was cutting it fine. He ran all the way from passport control to the gate. Boarding was almost complete. He crossed the threshold of the plane as the door was closing.

Jack found his seat and settled just as the crew was going through the usual preparation ritual… the captain made his announcement… the safety demonstration followed. Jack was glad he had chosen a seat in the Boeing 747 bubble at the top of the aircraft.

It had been a good move. Nancy Wu was sitting only three rows in front of him. She had chosen the window seat and for some reason the place next to hers remained empty.

The aircraft pushed back from the docking bay and started rolling slowly along the lanes that led to the runway. The seat-belt sign came on and within a few minutes they were airborne. The smooth rise of the plane almost made Jack uncomfortable. He had experienced the same discomfort on departure from JFK to London. It was different to

276

the usual rough lift of the large army planes he was used to. The man sitting next to Jack changed into the light jogging suit BA provided for its business-class customers. He got himself organised, ignoring Jack as he extended the partition that separated the seats to give privacy. He put on a set of headphones and started browsing through the channels provided for entertainment.

Jack sat back in his armchair. He would have preferred to be by a window rather than the aisle but there was enough room for him to read the documents he had scanned without being overlooked. He took out his laptop, pulled out the table from the holder in his armrest, sat the device on it and started logging in.

From the corner of his eye Jack registered the drinks trolley approaching. He chose a cool beer and returned to his laptop. He hadn't had time to go through the documents that Harris had forwarded from his source. Jack went through the titles of the papers, assessing which documents were the most relevant. Predictably, Jared Turner's timetable of meetings in China came top of the list.

He cast an eye towards Nancy Wu's seat; she seemed to have settled. Laurie had completed a schedule of meetings too, coinciding with the tracking of Turner's mobile phone. Jack called up the two documents side by side. There was no discrepancy with regard to dates, but the locations seemed to diverge.

Turner's mobile drifted out of Beijing on almost every visit he had made to China in the past six months. His mobile reappeared in Chengdu, in Sichuan province.

Laurie had made further inroads in identifying the location of his visits. She had found a small industrial estate on the outskirts of the city. She would be drilling down into the site details to find out what was being produced there.

In itself, visiting an industrial site for a company head was acceptable, but why not record it on his business planner?

The aeroplane encountered a patch of light turbulence. This might provide him with the perfect opportunity. Jack left his seat and went towards the bathroom. The plane started shaking even more when he was on his way back. He lost his balance and fell into the back of the seat next to Nancy's.

Her face was illuminated by the light of a laptop... fine regular features, high forehead, and beautiful slanting eyes. Jack noticed the quirky notepad she had placed to one side, yellow with ruled pages.

He took a moment to recover his balance and apologise just as Nancy lifted her eyes to check what the commotion was. The disgruntled businessman sitting in the seat behind mumbled a complaint. Jack apologised again and returned to his seat to take stock of what he had just seen.

Ms Wu was perusing the same document as he was... Jared Turner's schedule of meetings in China.

* * *

"Rubbish..." Pole threw a cushion across the room and leaned back further into his lounge's favourite armchair. Andy had sent a flurry of emails.

The bank account trail had gone cold. In the chain of accounts Andy was trying to identify, the last account had been closed. No doubt everything was being done to wipe out records of who had opened it.

The other email he had received from Yvonne Butler's lab confirmed the drug used on Ollie Wilson came from Afghanistan, Herat province. Tomorrow he would have to call the drug squad and let them know.

All this was neatly leading to one conclusion: Ollie Wilson had been involved with a Russian trafficking gang and had paid the price for it. It was very tidy, evidence rolling in, one piece after another, wrapped with a bow.

His gut thought otherwise, but the only possibility to counter the argument was the pile of documents from Cora which Branning had delivered to him. There was, of course, Harris's opinion, but Pole was in enough trouble with Ferguson to mention industrial espionage or the sale of sensitive biotechnology research to a foreign power.

For all they knew, the biotech Viro-Tech was researching and selling to China was completely legal. Unless national security was endangered by the research or sale, the company was free to deal on the market as it wished.

Pole poured himself a large glass of red wine and took a mouthful. He had not yet allowed himself to dwell on Nancy's decision to leave for Hong Kong. He had witnessed her resourcefulness first hand, but when it came to her father's story, her brilliant mind often succumbed to a whirlpool of emotions. His best plan of action was to push Harris to produce more evidence and persuade Marsh that he had to take a trip to the former British colony.

His burner phone rang. He let it go to voicemail.

"Pole... I know you're listening. No, I don't have cameras in your home. Call me back. It's about Ms Wu and her Hong Kong trip." Harris sounded unusually serious.

There was no point in delaying the inevitable... Pole snatched up his phone.

"Harris... to the point, please."

"I presume she told you she's on her way to Hong Kong?"

"Why, yes."

"That's a good move... Ferguson is going to jump at the fact she's gone, and Marsh will follow his lead, because he has no other choice."

"I'm not sure I agree to..."

Harris interrupted. "It gives us a bit more time to tell our story about the burner phone."

Pole remained silent. As predicted, Nancy had become the bait and he was not happy to fall in with Harris's suggestion.

"Besides, she won't be on her own in Hong Kong. My CIA contact is with her on the same flight."

"What?" Pole sat up. "She's already got the counter-terrorist squad after her. I'm not having the CIA involved too."

"Relax, Jack is a good guy. He's not the sort to shoot from the hip and ask questions afterwards. He's got me out of a tight spot or two in the past."

"Does he think she's involved with Viro-Tech?"

"That's the premise... I've tried to indicate he might want to reconsider, but..."

"...but you bloody well haven't because you need something else from him."

"It's a bit more complicated than that. He hasn't told me what he knows about Ollie Wilson... so I need to bide my time."

"I thought he was a trusted friend?"

"And he is a good spook too, but I can't expect him to disclose everything to me. Hell, I wouldn't either. That's the way it works, and don't tell me the different teams at Scotland Yard always work together like a happy family."

"So, is that all your news? A CIA agent is chasing Nancy across the globe, believing she's involved in some goddamn conspiracy when all she's trying to do is find out what happened to her father?"

"Not quite... her good friend Yvonne Butler has facilitated a bit of information gathering from my service, and MI6 has been happy to oblige. At the moment, Ms Wu is aware of a possible connection between her father's family and Deng Xiao Ping. They share the same Sichuan ancestry and, surprisingly, Chengdu in Sichuan is also of interest to a certain Jared Turner, CEO of Viro-Tech Therapeutics."

"This is ridiculous."

"But it's true. I have been doing a little homework on Turner's schedule. So perhaps a visit to his offices would not go amiss. I have sent you the list of visits he made, complete with the airline bookings. If your DS Andy looks a bit more closely, he should be able to find the same information. Don't tell me I'm not a nice guy."

# Chapter Twenty-Eight

She had been extravagant in booking two seats in business class for the sake of enjoying a little extra peace during the flight. Nancy moved the food tray to the adjacent table. She pressed the remote control and the seat started to slowly unfold underneath her. It was gradually transforming itself into a bed. Another hour of work and she would get some rest.

It was already 6am in Hong Kong and her prior experience of jet lag told her she was better off adjusting straight away to the local time of her destination.

She had connected her laptop to the onboard Wi-Fi system. A great improvement from a few years back when in-flight mode meant no internet access.

Her fingers coursed over the keyboard and the information appeared on the site she had discovered a few hours ago. It was a simple genealogy research tool, a record of family and ancestors. Something that had taken China by storm.

The previous site she had visited was of little help. But it seemed that this one, designed to be used by the middle classes looking to evidence their lineage, was easier to navigate.

She had struggled to filter the large number of hits her father's name had generated. It seemed that Li Jie Wu was a rather common name, generating results in the thousands, but adding his birthplace and date of birth had whittled them down to a manageable number.

Nancy sat back on the comfortable bed, brought a cup of tea to her lips, eyes closed. She had ordered chai without milk, since she doubted she could ask for traditional Sichuan tea. She inhaled deeply the scent of spices and let her mind wander down the alleyways of the past.

A few images slid into her mind. She caught glimpses of her grandfather. A small man, dry as a stick, so proper... he wore the typical round glasses encircled by a gold frame that most educated Asian men wore in the 1940s.

There was nothing else to remember, apart from the exquisite gift he had given her on one of her birthdays. She couldn't recall which. She couldn't remember his name either. She must have been told but it was just out of reach.

She returned to the site and continued narrowing the options, searching each possible name and, so far, following dead ends.

She had revisited the page that gave her a more in-depth account of Deng Xiao Ping's life. The Sichuan and Chengdu connections were strong, despite a period of absence. Deng's family had spent most of their lives there until he started university.

Nancy jotted down a few names that she needed to investigate further. The site was good enough, but the absence of pictures held her back. She had managed to find a way to translate the Chinese, but progress was slow.

She stretched her arms overhead and yawned without holding back.

One of the stewardesses was clearing the trays. She offered Nancy a fresh cup of tea which she accepted with a smile. She stood up and walked to the galley at the back of the 747 bubble. A man in the last row had passed her a few times when using the restrooms at the front of the aircraft. She could have sworn he had leaned heavily on purpose over the back of her armchair during a spate of turbulence.

She walked past him, slowing down a little. The stewardess was coming her way with her fresh tea.

"I just needed to stretch my legs." Nancy smiled again.

The man lifted his head. He looked at the interaction between the two women in a neutral way that displayed neither interest nor annoyance.

Nancy walked back to her seat. "Can't become paranoid just yet... I'm not even in Hong Kong," she muttered.

She settled back in her seat, brought the blanket over her legs and sipped her tea. The light had gone off in the cabin. Passengers across the aisle were turning on their seat lamps. She lifted the window shade which she had lowered when the light had started to disappear. The aircraft had reached its cruising altitude a while ago.

There was not a single cloud in the sky and the starry night felt restful. She had kept herself busy until now, putting off the inevitable moment of reflection.

She had made a rash decision using her intuition, judging it was the right thing to do. Unleashing the counter-terrorist squad against her was almost reckless, but she would never let Pole down. Getting the CT squad to focus on her rather than Pole was the right thing to do. She wondered why MI6 had been so keen to help Pole collect information about her father. But there was Henry Crowne's escape from Belmarsh. How much had Pole known about that?

Yvonne had warned her that MI6 would want something in return for the information she had requested. It was clear that Pole's own contact had already received his dues since Pole had been given plenty of information. But if they had wanted help only for Henry's escape, then the flow of information would have dried up. But here they were, still feeding Pole information.

Whatever they wanted, she was somehow a part of it… she couldn't fathom why the search for her father was still of interest to them. Had he been involved in something that continued to be worth their while investigating?

It would have seemed unthinkable only a week ago, but what Nancy had learned about her father's political involvement now made it more plausible. She remembered him with a mixture of awe, respect, love and excitement. She had buried her feelings in the months following his departure. The attempts her mother had made to talk to her about him had fallen on deaf ears. As the year passed her mother stopped talking about him, until his existence had become shrouded in silence.

Nancy's mind drifted again towards the vast expanse outside her window. She brought her face up to the acrylic double glazing. The world below was plunged in darkness. There was no sign of light or life. She closed her eyes for a moment.

*Whatever it is MI6 want, they're not having it until I am sure Pole is safe.*

\* \* \*

*Call me.* Those two words felt like a shot across the bows. Jack knew he was in trouble. His boss, Robert (Bob) Hunter III, was usually rather more forthcoming in his emails. Short was not his style. Thankfully, the 12-hour time lag meant that he was probably still fast asleep at 4am.

Could his boss in fact be waiting for his call though? Jack hesitated and pressed the call button. Hunter III was indeed waiting for him.

"Where are you?"

"Just landed in Hong Kong, sir." Jack was in the queue for passport control. The line was moving swiftly.

"Call me when you've gone through immigration." How did he know?

"You're going straight to the consulate. I want a call with you from a secure line," Hunter said.

The phone went dead. Jack had barely had time to press the recall button after walking through customs. He pursed his lips… certainly he would be going to the consulate, but not before he had followed Ms Wu and secured a room in the same hotel.

Waiting at the conveyor belt, Nancy's suitcase came up almost first. Jack cursed that she would be gone within seconds. But he was in luck and his case was spewed out by the system, just as Nancy had loaded hers onto a trolley.

It was easy to follow her to the taxi rank. There was nothing curious about that. They had made eye contact, but why wouldn't a business-class passenger find himself in the same five-star hotel… he hoped it was a decent place she had chosen for her trip.

Nancy's choice did not disappoint him. The Mandarin Oriental had been rated the best Hong Kong hotel for the past 20 years and none of its competitors had managed to shift it from the top spot.

The receptionist did not bat an eyelid when Jack arrived without a reservation. She found a couple of options. The suite he was first offered was ridiculously expensive, but the deluxe bedroom, overlooking the Peak rather than Victoria Bay, suited him fine.

Jack dumped his suitcase in his room and jumped into another cab, direction – the US Consulate General. The taxi driver shrugged. It was hardly any distance he said. Jack took out a $20 bill from his wallet and the driver made his way swiftly through traffic.

Within minutes of having arrived at the consulate Jack was being ushered into one of the basement rooms. A polite Asian woman had led him to it without any explanation. There was a table, a couple of chairs and several phones and computers. Clocks on the wall indicated the time in New York, Hong Kong and London.

"Jack Shield." A voice boomed from behind him. The man was tall and stocky. He threw a large hand in Jack's direction. "Adrian Wong... Bob tells me he needs a chat with you on a secure line... always happy to oblige."

Adrian didn't seem to have been told what it was about. He might not even care, as long as it was not him on the receiving end of Hunter III's wrath.

The phone rang only once. "Where have you been?" was the only preamble to the conversation.

"There was a lot of traffic," Hunter grunted.

"What have you got yourself involved with? And I don't want some bull about a case of mistaken identity, or some pissed-off agent resurfacing from the past."

Jack considered his options. Telling the truth, at least a simplified version of it, might work. He spoke about Ollie, his suspicions and the two attempts on his own life.

"The problem is, Jack, that Viro-Tech's CEO Jared Turner is a no-go area."

"Why would that be, sir?"

"Let's say he is central to some delicate negotiations... and the US government has given those negotiations top priority."

"What if he is abusing his position?"

Hunter considered his answer for a moment. "It would have to be a pretty sizeable breach..."

"What if it threatens national security, and involves a large foreign power? And how about attempted murder?"

Hunter was almost thrown by the comment.

"You have 48 hours, after that I want you back home. Otherwise, your next mission will be to a desert island in the middle of the Pacific."

* * *

The alarm rang a long time. Pole had woken up at 4am, just as Nancy's flight was touching down in Hong Kong. He had pretended he could go back to sleep but simply drifted in and out unsuccessfully.

A text pinged on his new burner phone. "Settled at the Mandarin Oriental in a room overlooking the Bay. *Tout va bien.*"

She was 12 hours away with an eight-hour time lag, in a country with which he had few connections. Pole threw off the duvet but didn't get up. The long list of to do's had started to churn in his mind, but he was most preoccupied with the way Ferguson and Marsh were going to react. How far would Ferguson go? Marsh was more of a containable problem... for once his soft spot for Nancy might stop him becoming more than an irritant.

Pole shivered. He swung his long legs over the edge of the bed, running a hand through his hair. He left it there for a short moment, then grabbed his new burner phone and typed a response. "Glad all well. Call me if you need anything, anytime."

He had once resented owning a mobile phone, but here he was juggling his professional mobile and two burner phones... ironic.

Pole threw his rucksack underneath his desk, as soon as he reached his office and grabbed a pile of documents relating to a case he had just closed successfully. He added them to an already dangerously high stack of papers on the table next to his desk. He poured a cup of tea and started munching on his brown toast with Marmite. He retrieved the Ollie Wilson documents from the filing cabinet closest to his desk.

The research papers Ollie had written were clear and made grim reading. He feared the risk of antibiotics no longer working to combat a list of known bacteria was not just a problem of the future. It was happening now, and the threat was imminent. The pharmaceutical companies had simply not spent enough money on that type of research.

It simply did not yield enough income in comparison to the highly lucrative research on drugs for cancer or other diseases. As long as the old antibiotics that had been developed in the 1950s still worked, why bother? These were now produced in China or India in order to further reduce costs and increase profits, to revive what had for many years been a cash cow.

Ollie's second research paper was of a very different kind, but equally chilling. He had investigated how the constant human interventions in nature – displacing animals' natural habitat – would trigger more occurrences of animal-to-human-transmitted diseases.

He quoted Ebola, and the avian flu that spread in Hong Kong in 2003. In the first case it was bat to human transmission; in the second, a chicken-to-human propagation had been the trigger point. Viruses adapted. He feared some of them would mutate and develop into deadly diseases transmitted to humans and become unstoppable.

Ollie had included in the set of documents a paper written by a research company specialising in biological and medical topics. The Bill & Melinda Gates Foundation had requested a paper on the threat of epidemics. The document had aimed to gather sufficient evidence to show how quickly an epidemic of a viral nature could spread from one country to reach the entire globe... a pandemic was due in the next 10 to 20 years.

Pole wondered how Ollie had managed to obtain the information for the paper. It looked tailored to fit the Gates Foundation request. Perhaps he had used the advantage of being a member of the Harvard Medical School Alumni group. Perhaps it had opened doors and allowed access to information that few other people would be able to obtain.

Another study looked at the increased transfer of manufacturing power from the US and Europe to China and India. It covered a small number of industries but included pharmaceutical companies. The production of drugs and medical equipment had been moving steadily between these two countries over the previous 10 years. The scale of the migration was astonishing, ranging from simple painkillers to start with, to the full range of antibiotics more recently. China produced 90 per cent of the penicillin-based antibiotics consumed by America. Key medical equipment was also on the list.

Pole noted the alarm in the tone of the papers. Ollie had attempted to raise issues concerning the location of pharmaceutical production, as well as to highlight neglected areas of research.

Pole's conversation with Harris was taking on another dimension. The Viro-Tech CEO's regular visits to China had worried Ollie. Pole was certain he had been a long way from finding out what the company was up to... but perhaps Ollie had discovered enough evidence to unsettle Jared Turner's plans.

A formal visit to Viro-Tech might rattle Turner further and give Pole an edge.

More people had arrived in the office. Andy had appeared at his computer... Danish pastry in his mouth, balancing coffee, documents and rucksack... looking somewhat of a mess. But he was a brilliant mess and Pole could always count on his DS to come up with the goods.

Pole's attention returned to the papers on his desk. He wished he could have discussed them with Nancy. Her precipitous departure still bothered him. He would decide later whether to send the documents to her. His decision about Marsh was clearer cut. Marsh would not resist another high-profile case brought in by Pole... a China conspiracy of international dimensions. It was time Pole played his joker.

* * *

"Breath-taking." Nancy stood at the large floor-length window that took up a whole wall of her room. She had requested a room with a view on one of the upper floors. She got exactly that.

She had been worried as she entered the limo that the hotel had sent for her that the past could spring back from nowhere. Hong Kong had never been a destination of choice for her, but the new airport, built on land reclaimed from the sea, with its futuristic structure and high-end shops, had made the arrival almost pleasant.

She was a world away from Big Wave Bay, the place she had first landed in Hong Kong so many years ago.

She was in her comfort zone, surrounded by an environment that looked business-like and luxurious. Identical to the surroundings she had been used to frequenting when instructed by corporate clients.

Nancy checked her watch. It was almost 6.30pm. She had just enough time to take a quick shower, change into a lighter dress and make her way to the Hong Kong Academy for Performing Arts. Professor Emmanuel Licot was giving a lecture on contemporary art and performance. The panel discussion would be followed by drinks. Nancy had sent a text to Philippe about the conference, and he had in turn secured two tickets to the lecture.

Shortly before 7pm, Nancy stepped into the building, asked for the ticket Philippe had left for her at reception and walked into a foyer where the audience were starting to pour out from the lecture theatre. She wove her way through the crowd and finally spotted Philippe.

He looked tired and on edge. Philippe usually managed to strike up a conversation with complete strangers but today he was standing alone. Nancy made her way over to him. His face lit up as soon as he saw her and he looked relieved.

"I'm so glad to see you." He bent down to kiss her cheek.

She squeezed his shoulder. "And I you..."

She steered him towards a quieter place. "How have you been?"

"I won't lie to you, terrible. Can't sleep. Can't rest. The Hong Kong police have been a wall of silence." He stopped abruptly. "I'm sorry. I know you're here to speak to Professor Licot."

"Don't apologise. I'm here to help you too." A cloud passed over her face and they remained silent for a moment. She hadn't forgotten the reason why Philippe had left London in a hurry before her.

"Licot has just arrived." Philippe gave a small nod in his direction.

Nancy had only seen a picture that she thought would be out of date. She would not have recognised him now... a long and thin face, surrounded by thick white hair cut in a Beatles-like bob.

As he walked into the foyer, Licot was mobbed by a crowd of young men and women seeking his attention. He was the star of the event. His writings about the connections between modern and traditional art had propelled him to the pinnacle of academia.

Nancy grabbed a couple of glasses of what she hoped might be decent champagne. She handed one to Philippe and made her way towards Licot.

Her assurance and seniority over the young people surrounding the professor did the trick. Unlike their counterparts in Europe, who would have ignored her, the Hong Kong students made way for her to move closer.

When the moment felt appropriate, she extended her elegant hand. "Nancy Wu, delighted to make your acquaintance Professor Licot. *Enchantée de faire votre connaissance.*"

Her perfect French caught Licot's attention. All smiles, he extended a friendly hand towards her. "*Le plaisir est pour moi.*" He shook her hand with a surprisingly firm grip.

"Would you have a moment for us, please? This is my colleague, Philippe."

Philippe had just arrived at Nancy's side. He did his best to appear keen and interested.

"Absolutely." Licot moved away from the crowd still gathered around him, towards one of the large sliding glass doors that had been kept shut. He slid it open with ease and walked with his two guests onto a spacious terrace overlooking the gardens.

"We've been lucky. The weather has been the warmest I've ever known it to be since coming to Hong Kong for the winter."

"It's a magnificent building."

"And despite the academy's traditional background, the Dean always welcomes different perspectives about the arts."

"A different perspective…" Nancy echoed him. "That is precisely what I'm interested in."

Professor Licot nodded approvingly. "Contemporary is my bag, as they say, for that very reason."

Nancy opened a large folder and came alongside him so that they could look at its contents together.

"Contemporary Art under Deng Xiao Ping." Her voice sounded loud in this wide-open space. "It is a piece that is exceedingly well researched you wrote about the Deng era."

Despite the sparse lights that peppered the terrace Nancy noticed colour rising on Licot's face. Philippe stepped closer.

"My assistant, Amy Grant, came across the paper in her research. I'd like to know whether she contacted you about it at all?"

Licot cleared his throat. "It's a very old piece. I haven't revisited its contents for rather a long time."

"But it's a piece that makes important assertions about how contemporary art had managed to grow and break free from the Chinese government's claw. Your research must have meant you met some of the artists of that generation."

Licot turned towards Philippe. "I recall an Amy Grant contacting me, but unfortunately we never managed to meet." Licot's voice had become strained. Nancy was now turning the pages of the document, arriving at the section she wanted to read aloud.

"To answer your own question, I met a lot of people who had moved to Hong Kong, including artists who had vowed never to go back." Licot started moving towards the door. No one was coming in their direction.

"In the paper, you mention an artist called Mo Cho. Could I please ask how you knew his work, and who had introduced you to him?" Nancy forced herself to stay calm.

"I would have to refer to my notes." Licot ran his hand over the back of his neck. "Is it important?"

"It is."

"Why?"

"I am his daughter."

Licot's face changed in an instant. He looked into Nancy's eyes and nodded.

"Let me say my goodbyes and wait for me outside the main entrance, we need to talk somewhere else."

# Chapter Twenty-Nine

Pole and Ferguson almost bumped into each other. Ferguson's thundery face thrust forward. "Did you know she'd gone?"

Pole managed to look shocked. He had expected Ferguson's reaction barging into his office as he almost always did when arguing about a point he felt strongly about. But this time Ferguson was enraged. His lips twitched and his nostrils flared.

"What are you talking about?"

"Wu, she's left for China."

"Are you sure?" Pole's voice caught in his throat. His shocked face and look of incomprehension did not convince Ferguson.

"Of course I'm sure. And can you tell me why she bothered to book two seats rather than one?"

This time Pole was genuinely at a loss. "I have no idea." He detached each word to give himself time to think.

Ferguson pushed past Pole, the bulk of his presence sending ripples around Pole's room. Pole moved back into his office and closed the door.

"She has been trying to retrace her father's steps before his disappearance." That much he could divulge. Yvonne Butler was also involved and she could support him in that statement.

"We are in the middle of a bloody internal investigation... People who are subject to that inquiry don't up sticks without telling us."

"An informal investigation..." Pole moved behind his desk and leaned on the back of his chair.

"But why not tell us? She knows the drill. And, more importantly, why not tell you?"

Ferguson had seen how closely Nancy and Pole had worked together on the Phelps case. He didn't seem to care whether they were involved as long as they delivered the goods. Today, however, Ferguson was not prepared to turn a blind eye.

"I don't know, Ferg..." Pole pushed his chair away from his desk, in a sharp move. His anger was not faked. "I'll call her as soon as we finish this conversation."

"Why don't you call her now?"

Pole's jaw clenched. Ferguson was right, if it was a simple professional call, why not now?

"You have a point." Pole bit his tongue before he could make a comment about time difference. "What part of China is she in?"

"Hong Kong." Ferguson had dragged a chair right up to Pole's desk. "She landed an hour ago."

Pole took his mobile out of his trouser pocket and pushed speed dial number one.

Ferguson was following his every move. Pole could feel the intensity of his gaze. Nancy's phone was still switched off. He left a short professional message.

She would know from his tone that her prediction had come true.

Ferguson and the counter-terrorist squad were on her trail.

"I hear from Marsh you have a theory about the burner phone that registered both at Scotland Yard and near Ms Wu's apartment." Ferguson's abrupt question was directed more at someone he considered a suspect rather than a colleague.

Pole settled into his chair and spun his mobile in his hands a few times before replying.

"That's correct. I have a possible theory... I said so to Marsh yesterday evening." His face had become expressionless. He didn't have to share his findings with the Commander until they were more substantial. He had to give Harris a little more time to produce his decoy.

"Is that it? A hunch?"

"It's a little more than a hunch, but I'd like to make sure I'm right, before I share with you."

Ferguson sat back. He had not yet finished, but Pole could tell he had not unhinged Pole as much as he had hoped. Pole waited. He hadn't had time to think about the motives for launching this informal inquiry relating to what Ferguson perceived as a leak. After all, Ferguson had dismantled a new terror cell in London, eliminated its members after a brutal assault, despite the delay caused by MI6. Pole had known Ferguson a long time. He was a relentless, determined officer who deserved his successes.

"What's your beef with Steve Harris?" Pole's question came out of nowhere and surprised even him. It had been an obvious point he should have thought of right at the beginning of the inquiry.

Ferguson pulled back a little. "What do you mean?"

"I've gone along with this inquiry because I'd like some clarity too, but why move heaven and earth, when at the end of the day, no one was hurt, and you eliminated the terrorist cell as you had set out to do?"

"It could have cost us a lot… the delay engineered by Harris to get his operatives out."

"But it didn't… don't we all have better things to do than to hunt for some hypothetical mole?"

"The mole isn't hypothetical, Pole. You and I both know that."

"OK then… this mole of yours, have they done any more damage recently?"

Ferguson's eyes narrowed in anger. He sized up Pole for a moment, but judged it was not worth a fight… at least not yet. He took his time to rise, hands gripping the armrests of the chair he occupied. A slow motion that told Pole… you haven't seen the last of me.

\* \* \*

"Forty-eight hours. Shit…" Harris was on the phone to Jack.

"At least he hasn't asked me to come back to Langley straight away."

"Would you have done so?" Harris had a smile in his voice, showing he knew the answer.

"What I need from you, pal, is all you have on Randy Zhang." Jack still hadn't unpacked the suitcase he had hurriedly left in his room at

294

the Mandarin Oriental. He hadn't had time to check the whereabouts of Nancy Wu either. He would catch up with her tomorrow morning and then do a bit of good old-fashioned trailing.

His focus was now on Zhang.

"He left Viro-Tech a few months ago with little ceremony. One day he was there… the following day he was gone." Harris had turned serious. "This is not the UK so no employment law requiring consultation."

"How about the Biotechnology Research Institute?"

"He was employed as a research assistant there too. It seemed that Viro-Tech liked the thought of him being able to access the research facilities as well as the lab capabilities. He hasn't been seen there for a couple of months either."

"Has anybody filed a missing person's report?" Jack opened his laptop, firing it up. He wanted to check Laurie's latest input too.

"Nothing. So, either he's not missing and simply lazing around or managing to keep people concerned about him happy that he is still fine."

"Randy is an American Chinese; he's lived all his life in California. San Jose to be exact. He moved from Hong Kong with family because this is where his grandparents come from. He only moved back to Hong Kong three years ago to join the research arm of ViroTech there."

"But we can assume he is in touch with his folks in the US?"

"I'd say he's lying low. Laurie was unable to find any evidence of a girlfriend, and Harvard doesn't describe him as a loner."

"How do you know that?"

"The same way your agency would know about someone who had studied at Oxford or Cambridge."

"Perhaps you should check the YMCA… A lot of students stay there when they visit Hong Kong. It's a place where young people mix socially, and he may have had friends staying there too."

"Good point, will do." Jack hung up and started scrolling down his emails.

Laurie had not been as productive as he might have hoped. Or, more likely, Hunter III had put an end to her freewheeling co-operation. He hesitated but he only had 48 hours before being recalled to the US. Jack dialled her number. Laurie replied before the first ring had ended.

"I'm in the doghouse, Jack."

Jack was about to apologise but Laurie carried on. "But I don't care… I'm with you on this one. There is a lot more to the case than meets the eye."

"Where are you?"

"Not at the office, this is my day for working from home. I'll be looking after the kids this afternoon. Their father will be dropping them back from an overnight stay."

"Are you sure this is OK?"

"Don't even ask again… as long as you don't mind hearing screaming kids in the background, let's keep talking."

Harris's information cross-checked with Laurie's. She gave Jack details of her research so far, which all came down to one important point. Ollie and Randy had technical capabilities that complemented each other. They had both graduated from Harvard at the top of their year. They had both written about the dangers of misusing biotech. Laurie had traced the address of Randy's family in Hong Kong. It seemed that Randy had not had much contact with them during the past three years he had been in Hong Kong.

"The other interesting point about Randy is that he has been very vocal about the status of Hong Kong," Laurie said.

"Is he an activist?"

"I would say so… He has joined quite a few protests in the past."

"How about the YMCA?"

"How about it?" Laurie was trawling through some data from the file she had compiled so far. "Hang on… Oh, I see… That's a good idea."

She moved to another screen. "The YMCA is in Kowloon, Salisbury Road, very close to one of the ferry routes between Central and Kowloon."

Jack scribbled the address on the notepad picked up from his bedside table.

"Guess where I'm having dinner tonight?" Jack said.

* * *

The taxi ride from the arts centre towards the residential part of Hong Kong was silent. Professor Licot was sitting at the back with Nancy. Philippe had insisted he should sit at the front with the driver.

296

They had driven through Hong Kong Central to arrive at the Peak. Densely populated streets gave way to a leafier environment.

Nancy gripped the handle of the door and did her best to conceal her panicked breathing. She needed to keep her mind calm.

The dense forest with its jungle of tangled tropical trees and shrubs revived memories of her arrival in Hong Kong so many years ago. She was amazed that the feel of nature on the island had not changed since then.

*She has two missing front teeth that make her resemble a gentle vampire. She has managed to hold onto a couple of marbles from an old game. Despite their parents asking them to keep quiet, the two girls giggle almost the entire journey.*

*Everything is easy when her friend is around. They chit chat about what they see along the way. What is this tree? What is this flower? Why do they speak so low? Why, what... it's a fun game even though answers don't come often, and they are only whispers.*

*They have been walking for a long time, she thinks. She's not quite sure. She's only seven. They have stopped in a small clearing. In the distance, Nancy thinks she can hear the sound of waves. Her friend thinks it's spirits ready to take them away... She doesn't really believe that, but she likes spooky stories.*

*Their fathers have gone ahead. They've left the women and children alone. For once the girls are quiet, holding hands tightly. They huddle together like two sparrows on a branch in winter.*

*The light fades away. It will soon be dark, twigs and branches crack in the woods nearby. Everyone holds their breath. The mothers have moved next to their children, ready to flee. But a low voice calls them. She recognises her friend's father. The road is clear. It's time to go. They make their way in stillness towards a small cove where a flimsy boat awaits them. Their fathers lift them into their arms. But they are separated. Nancy wants to cry but her father puts a hand over her mouth gently. "Silence." They board the boat for a crossing.*

Nancy shook the memory from her mind. She didn't want to remember any more. A hand on her arm made her jump. Professor Licot activated the gate of the residence where he lived. Nancy searched his features, but, in the darkness, she couldn't make out his face.

"We've arrived."

The car glided into an elegant courtyard. The apartment blocks were lower than the skyscrapers in Central, two storeys, modern and spacious. The walls that surrounded the eight buildings were of good height, protective and robust. It was a place that felt secure and welcoming.

"I moved here recently." Licot led the way, now that they'd left the taxi. "I suppose I'd had enough of fighting the air conditioning and cockroaches in downtown Central."

"Is this an expat building?"

"No, when I first came to Hong Kong, it was to live amongst its people, down in Central. But now is a little different, some other residents share the same profession as me... quite a few academics and some lawyers too."

Licot pressed a sequence of buttons on the keypad and one of the entrance doors opened.

Nancy breathed in the cool air. February nights were chillier in Hong Kong, and she welcomed the soothing effect of the breeze.

Licot pushed open the door and gallantly stood aside to let her walk in first. Nancy noticed a camera above the door recording people's comings and goings. The glass door was heavy and, she suspected, bulletproof, judging by the strange glow it emitted in the corridor's light.

They climbed one flight of stairs and walked into a modern apartment. It faced the mass of an untouched forest and, in the far distance, the sea. Modern and contemporary art covered the walls. It felt deliberately cluttered. Nancy and Philippe couldn't help going up to a couple of pieces, both noticing an Ai WeiWei print.

Licot smiled. "Contemporary art is my passion... as you can see." He moved into the back of the large open-plan room, offering drinks of wine, white or red, and came back with some savoury snacks.

"When did you land?" Licot asked.

"Earlier today." Nancy didn't feel the need to disguise her eagerness.

"Oh my... you must be starving. I'm afraid I have little to offer you."

"Don't worry…" Nancy managed a smile. "I'm here for something much more important."

Licot sat across from his two guests, gathering his thoughts. "Your father."

* * *

"I need a good rope… that's all." Cora and Johnny were having breakfast at the kitchen table. It was late and DS Branning had disappeared for his first cigarette of the day.

"You're nuts." Johnny had cooked a couple of eggs and he was sliding them onto two pieces of well buttered toast.

"I have managed a much more complicated performance than this… it's not difficult."

"Why won't you ask for proper help… Inspector Pole seems a very reasonable guy?"

"Because I don't know what I'm looking for."

"And what if you find something you don't want to find? Then what?"

Cora slumped in her chair. "I don't know." She shook her head.

"That's not the right answer, darling." Johnny pushed a plate towards her. He was going to be annoyed if she didn't eat what he had cooked for her.

"I wish Nancy was here," Cora moaned.

Johnny took another bite of his food and sighed. Even his favourite breakfast did nothing to alleviate the strain of the past few days. "Me too."

"Have you heard from Nat?" Cora changed the subject.

"Not a squeak… Beth and I were discussing that. We're worried she's…"

The door of the flat opened. Someone coughed heavily, a drawn-out rattle that threatened to end badly. DS Branning walked into the kitchen, straight to the kettle.

"Cup of tea?" Branning asked.

Cora and Johnny nodded. They hadn't noticed their breakfast preparations hadn't included tea.

Branning just got on with it, filled the kettle with water, warmed the pot, threw some teabags in.

The gurgling of the kettle was for a moment the only sound in the kitchen. Branning had made the tea. He poured the liquid into three different mugs.

The polka dot for Johnny, the red-and-white stripe for Cora, and any odd mug going for himself.

"I'm sure, if you ask Inspector Pole nicely, he might let you enter your apartment again..." Branning brought his lips to the cup, advancing them gingerly to taste the liquid and finally took a sip, satisfied it was the perfect temperature. "Whatever the reason." Branning leaned towards the biscuit box, opened it and offered it around.

Johnny gave Cora an alarmed look. He hesitated. "They're probably a little stale for you, officer. Why don't I make a fresh batch this evening? In the meantime, I'm sure I can find something nicer in one of the cupboards." Johnny was already rifling through the larder.

"Not to worry." Branning pushed the box away. "I need to lose weight anyway and you never know... the service may want to test me for illegal substances..."

Johnny's back stiffened. He slowly closed the larder door.

Cora could not help but laugh. It seemed that DS Branning had sussed out each of their little secrets. Cora's night-time investigation, as well as Johnny's pot-laced biscuits.

"The truth is..." Cora slid her finger over the rim of her mug. "I'm not sure I want to know what is hidden in my flat."

# Chapter Thirty

His feet were pounding the red asphalt. His rucksack swayed from side to side on his back. The ferry to Kowloon was departing in three minutes and they would be closing the doors in less than one. Jack pushed his way onto Central Ferry Pier 7. The crowd that had disembarked 15 minutes earlier had not yet left the shops set out along the side of the pier.

"Wait…" Jack shouted at the top of his voice.

One of the mariners lifted his head. He was loosening the ropes whilst one of his colleagues had started to raise the metal sheets of the ramp to board the boat. He gave Jack a distant look, neither man acknowledged him. Jack started running faster. He didn't hesitate and jumped upwards to clear the top of the metal doors. The men leaped sideways and gave Jack an earful in Chinese.

"Sorry, pals… I've got to get to the other side now."

The men shrugged angrily, moving the ropes faster to complete the manoeuvre.

A few other passengers had raised their heads from their mobiles but soon returned to them.

Jack moved around the seats of the lower deck, checked the stairs and found a space to sit near the bow on the upper deck. In less than 15 minutes he would be disembarking in Kowloon. From there, it was a five-minute walk to the YMCA. The sea breeze now blew cooler than at the Central Piers. Jack shivered and drew a light jacket out of his rucksack. He took out his mobile phone and saw on his screen a couple of pictures that Laurie had sent him. Randy Zhang smiled in a photo taken at his graduation. Another more recent shot at a conference showed him looking tired and strained. His face had changed, looking thinner and older. Laurie had sent Jack a few extra details. She had used one of her facial recognition apps to produce a picture in which Randy had grown a beard, another where he had changed the colour of his hair. Jack committed the pictures to memory, replaced his iPhone in his bag, and sat back. For a few moments he would simply sit still. Getting a little rest whenever possible was a trick he had learned during his tours of the Middle East.

The green-and-white painted Star Ferry docked in Kowloon. Jack waited for the other people to disembark. He was keen to reach the YMCA as soon as he could, but he also knew the value of being patient. If anyone was trailing him, his follower too would have to wait until his target left the boat. The crowd that had gathered at the doors spilled onto the causeway and into the night. Jack looked around. He was the last person on the upper deck.

He stepped down the metal staircase. A few other people were also taking their time. A couple, looking amorous, were walking towards the gates in a leisurely fashion. An elderly man with a large bag that seemed too heavy for him was following them.

Jack crossed a couple of busy roads. Skyscrapers of various heights were jostling for space. The car exhaust fumes reminded Jack that Hong Kong Kowloon was a city that never slept. He didn't need to wait for the light to go green at the crossing. The traffic was at a standstill.

He moved in the direction of a building that looked under repair. As Jack got closer, the YMCA façade came into view. Sheets of plastic resembled billowing black sails in the light breeze; others had come loose and were floating along in the air. Jack increased his speed. He reached the front of the building that read in bold letters – YMCA – NO ENTRY.

"Shit…" His shoulders sagged at the discovery. Part of the entrance was obstructed by a heavy tarpaulin cover.

"It's not completely closed, if you're looking for somewhere to stay." A young Asian man was moving towards the building, slowing down to speak to Jack.

"Do you live here?"

"Just got a room a few days ago... they're renovating a few floors, but the rest of the building is pretty decent. And the price has come right down."

"Much appreciated..." Jack gave the young man a thumbs-up. He carried on towards the building. Some of the floors were plunged into darkness whilst others looked inhabited.

Jack made a mental note of the floors still under repair. He continued walking towards the building and stepped into the reception area, lifting the tarpaulin door. The space was more welcoming than he had anticipated... light stone and cream-coloured walls. The reception desk, a long slab of tropical wood, looked brand new. Two receptionists were waiting for guests to arrive. One of them moved towards Jack from behind the desk with a smile.

"I need a room... just for a couple of nights." Jack looked around him as he spoke.

He was presented with a choice of options and prices.

"Which floors are under repair? I wouldn't want to be below one of them," Jack asked.

"Floors one to five, sir. How about floor 10?"

"Floor seven would be better." No need for an explanation.

Jack grabbed his key but didn't go to his room immediately. He walked outside again, looking for somewhere to sit in the small garden that spread in front of the entrance. He could see the building well enough from there. He bought a beer from the little shop that sold drinks and snacks. Jack settled down to survey each of the YMCA floors that were not taking any guests. He had time to check them for movement before he needed to decide on his next move.

"If I had to live somewhere anonymously... that's where I would go."

\* \* \*

"Inspector Pole of the Metropolitan Police."

The door opened with a click. Pole's team, headed by DS Andy Todd, walked into the Viro-Tech Therapeutics building. Two PCs were left downstairs to ensure no one either entered or left the premises.

The rest of the team took the lift to the first floor where a flustered receptionist awaited them.

Andy showed him the search warrant and the search team fanned out into the premises, with Ollie Wilson and Jared Turner's offices as the site of primary interest.

Jared Turner, the CEO, was at a meeting elsewhere in the City, the receptionist advised. Turner's office did not disappoint; the requisite expensive desk, expensive ergonomic armchair, the luxurious sofas in a corner to huddle with guests. Despite a sense that the office was in use, the place felt perhaps too clean. Pole noticed the absence of files or even filing cabinets.

The people working and running Viro-Tech belonged to the age of virtual everything, no paper scattered on desks, no note of any kind hidden underneath piles of documents… no document, apart from those parked on a cloud and protected by the latest cyber technology.

Pole moved slowly around the room. It had been rearranged recently. The furniture had left dents in the pile of the deep carpet. He crouched next to one of the couches and managed to move it a little, despite its weight. Another piece of furniture had been standing there, but he could not quite make out what it had been.

Pole stood up and resumed his systematic search. The desk had a couple of screens plugged into a laptop docking station… a ThinkPad laptop. Pole ran a gloved hand over the equipment. There was no dust and, unless their cleaners were unusually efficient, the computer had been either replaced recently or deep cleaned.

The choice of a Lenovo ThinkPad, the only laptop certified for use by astronauts on the International Space Station, spoke volumes.

Viro-Tech was keeping its research well under wraps.

Turner's PA arrived to announce her boss would be back any minute now.

Pole thanked her. She stood there almost certainly under in-structions not to let the policeman out of her sight. He smiled. "A glass of water would be welcome if I can trouble you with such a request."

She shifted from foot to foot uncomfortably before making her way to the nearest water cooler. Pole returned to the sofa, trying to make sense of the mark on the carpet, and finally took a seat to wait for Jared Turner.

Turner's PA came back with the water but felt too embarrassed to stay any longer. She left Pole to his thoughts and a review of his day so far.

Ferguson had left his office glowering.

Andy had come in as soon as he had left to find his boss still deep in thought.

"I've got a little more information about the Eastern European connection."

"Let's hear it," Pole said.

"The drug squad has given me information about the group they are targeting. They managed to catch a couple of these guys, but they turned out to be only couriers... not the senior bods, or even middle-ranking gang members. Their theory is that the top men are ex KGB or FSB people. They have recruited agents they worked with in the past."

"Is it a large organisation?"

"That's the theory... well, a bit more than that. The problem is that not a lot of people are talking about them, and those who do don't live long afterwards," Andy said.

"Apart from the obvious drug link, any other information that could be helpful to us?"

"That's what I wanted to talk to you about. They have a small team of assassins they use to ensure everybody toes the line. The drug squad has a bit more on them, because when they target a victim, they make it very obvious. It's like a code that tells other members of the gang why that person has been executed."

Pole perked up. "Those assassins." He air-quoted the word. "Are they for hire too?"

"That's the thing, Guv... the squad doesn't think so. That's not part of what the gang offers... However..."

"...for the right price, which must be pretty high, they might make an exception."

"That's what Ted, my contact at the squad, said."

"I wonder how someone gets to know this Russian gang well enough to hire their hitmen... or rather to be allowed to hire their hitmen."

"I wondered that too and I think the point of contact is drugs."

Pole frowned. "You mean…"

"An illegal substance is only illegal because it's not used to manufacture medications. Opium is used to create all sorts of drugs, approved and regulated, sold around the world to hospitals, and used under strict medical supervision."

"If you're in the drugs business…" Pole rolled his chair towards his desk. His fingers were running over the keyboard. "You sent me a file on Turner, I believe."

"I did, and I also sent you details about his father."

"Turner Junior is a repeat CEO of biotech companies… He buys, builds and sells, and then moves on." Pole was scrolling down a document. "Turner Senior sits on the board of a couple of companies… one of which is a large US pharmaceutical company."

"It might be a bit of a leap, but those people will know a lot about drug production… legal, that's for sure, but perhaps illegal too."

Pole finished reading the document in silence. He rolled his chair away from the computer to face his DS.

"Both Turners were part of a group that pushed for allowing opium production in Afghanistan to be used for medical purposes. I can't recall the details, but the idea pissed off a lot of people in the London drug squad. The idea might have been a good one, trying to channel the Afghan production into something legal, but the truth of the matter is that the Afghan government doesn't have enough resources to police production."

Andy nodded with a smile on his face. "I remember… they said it could drive production up as well as price and would be a disaster."

"I'm glad you recall that too… check how involved the two Turners were."

Andy was about to leave.

"Hang on… I have another request, if you don't mind."

"Fire away." Andy was keenly waiting.

"We have Turner's schedule to China… and we assume he stayed in Beijing. Could you find out whether this is the case? He spent a week there every time he visited. It would give him plenty of time to do a little sightseeing…"

Andy pulled a face. "China is a bit of a difficult nut to crack."

Pole heard some voices approaching, putting an end to the recall of what he'd learned so far. He recognised Turner's PA. The other voice was male and sounded irritated yet contained.

The young woman hurried into her boss's office, flustered. She brought more glasses and a bottle of water which she left on the coffee table in the sofa area, and retreated without a word.

A man that looked in his late 30s, lightly tanned and with an immaculate haircut, walked in. Jared Turner extended a hand to Pole, who stood up.

The grip was light but firm.

Jared Turner turned towards the door and a second man entered. "This is Dominic Tinker, my solicitor. We have just come from a business meeting in the City and were about to debrief. I hope you won't mind if he joins us."

Pole shrugged. "Not at all…" Pole managed a courteous smile that did not reach his eyes.

* * *

"Mo Cho, your father, I never met him." Licot poured everyone a glass of wine and picked at a bowl of prawn crackers.

Nancy felt relieved, yet a little deflated. She sipped some wine without caring much for its taste.

"But I did meet some people who knew him… young artists."

"How long ago was that?"

"Early 90s. It was soon after the Tiananmen Square massacre. The art world was up in arms, literally. There was talk about retribution but nothing materialised, the uprising was driven to the ground… hopes dashed… democracy, free speech in tatters."

"Of course, it was before Hong Kong reverted to China." Philippe placed a few rice crackers in the palm of his hand.

"Very true… Hong Kong was a hub for those fleeing repression… once again."

"My father spent some time in Hong Kong after the events of Tiananmen Square. I have a few photos that show him there."

Licot drank a little wine and nodded. "Yes, I'm certain he did retreat to Hong Kong for a while. The artist I met told me he had been around for a year or so after the massacre but then…"

"He went back?" Philippe couldn't help asking.

"That's what my artist friend told me. Perhaps in '91 or '92."

Nancy inhaled deeply and held her breath for a moment. She needed to scream… why?

"Was he part of the political elite, part of Deng's close entourage?" Her question was bluntly put.

"You mean, did he support the government and the People's Communist Party?"

Nancy nodded. "Was he a traitor? He is pictured with Deng Xiao Ping. There is also a picture of Deng with artists at the 1989 China Vanguard event in Beijing."

Licot nibbled at one of his crackers. "I came across that photo when I was doing my research in 1994. That's when I decided to find out more about your father."

"My family and Deng's are both from the Sichuan province. It's totally possible they knew each other. Deng was my grandfather's age and they belonged to the same social class," Nancy said.

Licot looked surprised. "Very good, that is also what I gathered from the artists I interviewed. Your father knew Deng. For a while, I think he trusted his political judgement."

"Deng was the reason why he returned to China in the first place," Nancy said.

"Mo Cho was already strongly portraying his political convictions in his work. He might have regretted the way the Communist Party dealt with artists during the Cultural Revolution, but he still believed in the ideals of communism."

"Did he not realise the Communist Party did what it did because there was no place for freedom and democracy in their ideology?" Nancy's voice hardened.

Licot smiled kindly. "Perhaps not when he returned, but I believe Tiananmen Square changed all that."

"So why go back?" Philippe gave Nancy a worried look. He seemed worried he was interfering in a very personal matter.

"Did he think he could change things all on his own?" Licot placed his hand on her arm.

Her hand had clenched her glass so hard he feared she would break it.

She placed it on the table. "Apologies."

"Nothing to apologise about." Licot's warm voice was soothing. He paused for a moment, considering his answer. "As I said earlier, I never met your father. But he was a determined man, defending what he believed was right... freedom of expression, freedom to be who you are. He somehow reminded me of Ai WeiWei."

"Are you being kind to me?" Nancy couldn't help asking.

"No, I assure you I am not. Based on all the things I heard then and the pieces of his art I also saw at the time... his art was a means to an end." Licot nodded. "Hence the Beijing event."

"This is almost too good to be true..." Nancy stood up and walked to the large window overlooking the hills. "Or perhaps I don't like the implications of what that means?"

"He was a dedicated artist and people liked him... he followed his vocation, come what may."

"Even sacrificing his family?" Nancy had managed to speak with little anger.

"Perhaps it was not a sacrifice for him. You and your mother were safe, after all."

She had never considered this aspect. Her father had ensured they were both safe, creating an environment in Paris where they were surrounded by friends and supporters.

"The messages of his work were unambiguous and critical. He had hoped at one time that it would make a difference. When the uprising came, and its subsequent suppression, everything collapsed around him."

"So why not return to Europe, or at least stay in Hong Kong?" Nancy had returned to her seat.

"Sometimes you have to carry the fight right to the door of your opponents," Licot said gently.

Nancy closed her eyes. "Even if it means losing your life?"

"Perhaps... I do not know what happened to him after he returned. The artists who spoke to me became vague about his whereabouts."

"They may not have wanted to tell you..." Philippe shook his head. "... To protect him."

Licot said nothing but locked eyes with Nancy. The conversation would be continued, but only on a one-to-one basis.

# Chapter Thirty-One

The light looked faint and he thought he saw movement, or was it the reverberations of Kowloon nightlife that gave him that impression? Jack took another swig of the second beer he had just bought. The night was turning chilly and he would have to decide whether he was going to spend the night at the YMCA or return to the Mandarin Oriental.

He rose to his feet, still surveying the window through which he thought he had spotted some activity.

There it was again… A faint glow, most probably the beam of a torch.

"Second floor, fifth window from the left," Jack murmured.

He shouldered his rucksack, took a last swig of beer and moved swiftly towards the hotel entrance.

He slowed his pace a fraction as he walked through the lobby. A couple of young men came out of the lift, loud and boisterous. Jack stopped the doors from closing with his foot. Predictably, the lift had been programmed not to stop at the floors that were being renovated. Jack alighted at the seventh floor, went into his room and turned to the floor plan showing the fire exits. He was not far from one of them. Jack walked out of his room again, turned left. The exit was a few doors away from the end of the corridor. He inspected the door frame, then the push bar that opened the door itself. There seemed to be no alarm linked to the door. He ran his eyes along the walls. This place had no need for high security.

Jack pushed the bar. The door resisted a little and then gave way. The cold air that rushed in smelt stale and damp. There was no handle on the other side of the door. Once on the stairwell, there was only one way to go... down and out.

Jack took a ballpen out of his rucksack. He crushed the plastic casing with his foot, chose a splinter of the right size and pushed it into the latch bolt. The piece retreated into the frame. As long as it held, the exit door would remain open. Jack lodged another piece at the bottom of the door leaving it with the groove facing out to provide a handle.

The beam of his small torch illuminated concrete stairs that looked surprisingly clean. When he reached the second floor, Jack inspected the door that led to the unoccupied rooms. He smiled briefly. The latch had been pushed back with heavy-duty duct tape, and a long piece of wood was sticking out, creating a handle. He pulled the door open slowly and it responded without any resistance.

Jack stepped into the corridor, switching off his torch. He waited a short moment for his eyes to become accustomed to his surroundings. Despite the lack of electricity, he could see the outline of the corridor fairly well. Doors had been left open along it. Jack started at a slow pace towards the room in which he had seen the movement of a light. The rest of the floor was silent, without signs of any occupation.

When Jack reached the room, he waited for a moment and then walked in. The room had been gutted of its carpets and bathroom fittings. Jack stopped abruptly. A beam of light had just appeared in the corridor, a door had opened at the far end and someone was moving towards the exit.

The exit door opened and closed. The sound of footsteps climbing down faded away. Jack waited for a minute before moving around again. His eyes surveyed the contents of the room. There was little there... a small calor gas heater, on which an old kettle sat, and a grocery bag half full. A sleeping bag had been stretched out where the wardrobe would have been.

Jack moved to the bathroom. A black rubbish bag had been pushed into the corner.

Whoever was living here had not been there long. The smell of rubbish had not yet permeated the room. The floor did not bear the hallmarks of squalor that came with living rough.

There was nothing in the room that gave away the identity of the squatter. Jack ran his torch beam around the concrete floor of the

312

room without success and returned to the bathroom. The various pipes carrying water and waste had been sealed. Jack tried to open them without success. The seal was solid and had not been tampered with. The large tiles in the bathroom had not yet been removed. Perhaps the answer was below them?

He tested the floor with the toe of his shoe; a couple of tiles were loose. Jack crouched, took a Swiss army knife out of his pocket, opened a blade and started lifting one of the tiles. It came up easily, revealing a small cache... bank notes folded into one neat roll, a couple of USB keys, a blue document the size of a man's wallet.

Randy Zhang, clean shaven and with a serious expression, was staring out at Jack from the pages of his American passport. Jack put back the bank notes and the passport. He pocketed the USB keys and replaced the tile.

He returned to the room to choose where he would be best placed to wait for Randy.

* * *

"You're positive?" It was not a question, more an affirmation of what he had heard. Pole had endured a frustrating interview with Turner Junior, CEO of Viro-Tech Therapeutics.

"There was nothing left on that computer... files that might be important have been erased." Andy was sitting on the back of Pole's bike, speaking through a shared helmet intercom.

"But you took the computer and hard drive anyway?" Pole asked, making his way through dense traffic.

"Yes, it's on its way to Scotland Yard as we speak."

"Will you be able to find anything?"

"Perhaps, it depends how thorough they have been with cleaning up Wilson's account. If it comes to it, I'll ask for help from our tech team, but the Viro-Tech guys are pros, so it will take some time."

"They were expecting a visit. Turner was ready with his answers..." Pole slowed down the Ducati to let a car through the junction that led to the Embankment. He throttled up, making his way swiftly through traffic.

"Did someone warn them then?" Andy's body was leaning into the turns of the bike.

"No." Pole was making good progress towards Scotland Yard. "Ollie Wilson's assault was the trigger point. Either because it sent a warning to them or…"

"…because they knew about it in advance." Andy finished his boss's sentence.

Pole gave the thumbs-up, removing one hand from the handlebar. Andy stiffened a little. "I've not had time to make any inroads into Turner's Chinese visits. I've got some ideas about how to get the information, though."

Pole this time only nodded, accelerating to go through an amber light. They were almost there. "Before that, find out more about the group that was pushing to make poppy production legal in Afghanistan."

Pole rolled his helmet underneath his desk and checked his watch. It was gone 2.30pm in London, 10.30pm in Hong Kong. Time to make a personal call.

He would not be using a burner phone inside Scotland Yard again. He hesitated, then picked up his smartphone, sat at his desk and dialled her number.

"It's good to hear from you, Jonathan." Nancy's voice was a little croaky and tired.

"And me you, *mon coeur*, you sound tired."

"It's been rather busy since I arrived, but it's all been worth it. Is Ferguson very pissed off?"

Pole laughed. "You can say that again… I think I'm going to spend a considerable amount of time in the doghouse as far as he is concerned. Marsh is being more circumspect, as you can imagine."

"You can tell Ferguson about my father… I had some rather… disturbing news." Nancy gave Pole a summary of all she had learned. "I think Licot knows a lot more than he has told me already, but he won't speak in front of Philippe."

"Do you trust him?"

"Who, Licot?" Nancy was moving around the room. Pole heard a door being opened, liquid being poured into a glass. "I'm being

314

cautious, but, yes, I do. He lives in an ultra-secure building with other people who seek to protect themselves as much as he does."

"Who are these other people?"

"Other lecturers, lawyers… my guess is that they are the sort of people who are likely to be liberals, possibly politically engaged."

"That would make sense… artistic rebellion is something that French academics like him would appreciate and understand."

"Unless he has been planted there by the Chinese government… which is a possibility… remote, but not to be ignored."

"I'll see what I can find out about him."

"Through Scotland Yard this time, please?" Nancy did not want Pole to become more indebted to MI6 on her behalf.

"Yes, Andy can do a bit of digging around for you. He'll enjoy that."

"Yvonne Butler left a message on my phone. I need to call her. She was rather vague, which is unlike her."

"More information from her contact?"

"I feel like Ariadne. I'm following the thread that someone has left for me to find, and I think I'm getting closer to the goal."

Pole made a quick mental calculation. If the goal was to find her father alive, he would be 77. He could still be alive.

"It would be crazy for me to think my father is still alive. He disappeared in 1992 or thereabouts, according to Licot. People disappear there, never to be seen again, and they are rarely kept alive even in some godforsaken prison…" Pole could not argue with that.

"Which brings me to my question… what do you think the goal is?" Pole asked.

"I'm still in the dark when it comes to that." Nancy's irritation grew in her voice, giving it a tense ring. "But I think Licot is part of the answer."

"When are you meeting him again?"

"He gave me his card. I'll call him tomorrow morning. My sense is that he will make himself available."

"What about Amy?"

"Same answer as we received in London, I'm afraid. There is zero interest in finding out what has happened to her. As far as the Hong Kong police are concerned, it's suicide, end of story."

"The embassy should get involved."

"That's what Philippe is trying to do… but I gather the embassy is being a little slow to respond."

"She's not been kidnapped and there is no dead body… suicide is going to look very credible."

"Yes, unfortunately."

Pole held back. Despite Nancy's reluctance to talk about his MI6 contact he felt increasingly sure he should mention the CIA interest in her.

"Did you have time to look at the Ollie Wilson documents I sent you?" Pole said.

"They're all pointing in one direction. Ollie was convinced Turner was involved in some technology transfer to China that became the condition for closing some commercial deal. It may even be that the deal Viro-Tech is trying to close is completely legal… after all, they own the technology they have developed. I think it was more an ethical issue."

Pole was impressed at the speed with which Nancy had managed to read and assimilate the documentation he had forwarded to her the previous day.

"Do you mean that, although Viro-Tech were entitled to make the transfer, Ollie felt they shouldn't?"

"That's my theory. These transfers have been going on for some years between the private sector and China. Tech companies, both large and small, want a slice of the action in the very large market of 1.4 billion Chinese people. Companies are quite happy, if I can call it that, to let China have a piece of their technology. Whether it is under licence or not makes no difference, once China has it they will appropriate the technology and use it as they see fit."

"I knew it happened but didn't realise it happened on such a large scale."

"As far as the US and Europe are concerned… it does."

"But why seek to eliminate Ollie, in that case?"

"Perhaps the biotechnology involved is too contentious to export, or perhaps it's all about illegal drugs after all."

"You're not serious?" Pole baulked at the idea.

"I'm glad you reacted like that... I don't buy the illegal drug idea either, but I can't find the missing link that transforms a legitimate agreement, albeit an unethical one, into something completely illegal."

"I visited their premises. Turner was extremely well prepared for my questions."

"So, the CEO was expecting your visit."

"Almost certainly... it didn't yield much apart from the fact that the company had cleaned Ollie Wilson's laptop rather thoroughly. What would make the technology they were working on off-limits?" Pole was thinking aloud.

Nancy took a moment. "State or military appropriation... if that technology became of national interest, then the lab that developed it would not be able to dispose of it freely."

Pole tapped his fingers a few times on his desk. She needed to know.

"And the CIA might like to know where the technology was going..." Pole said.

"Do you mean... both agencies are involved now?" Nancy couldn't contain a laugh. "I took early retirement to lead a peaceful life... serves me right."

* * *

Pole's mobile phone was engaged. Cora hung up as it was about to switch to voicemail.

Branning shook his head. "You can do it... just leave a message."

Cora sat back in the old leather chair. She brought the phone to her chin and tapped it a few times.

"I don't know why, but I keep remembering coming out of Ollie's hospital room, and then out of the lift, and seeing the same nurse leaving at the same time as me."

"When was that?"

"Yesterday, and again this morning." Cora sat up, bringing her knees up to her chest... thinking. "I almost missed the lift, but I managed to press the call button quickly enough. The door reopened. I stepped in. I didn't notice the people there... my mind was on Ollie... and I pushed my way back to the rear of the lift. I don't know why."

Cora thought for a moment. "Then when we arrived on the ground floor, I noticed her... I kept thinking there was something familiar about her... but she was a nurse, and I don't know anyone who is."

"Then that's another good reason to call Inspector Pole." He tapped gently on the arm of the chair on which Cora had put her mobile.

She tried again and this time Pole picked up. He sounded distracted, perhaps too busy to listen to what she had to say. "I hope I'm not troubling you."

"Of course, not... what can I do for you?" His tone changed, more focused and considerate. He wanted to hear what she had to say. Cora explained in as much detail as she could about her encounters.

It sounded feeble when she told the story and she felt embarrassed. But she could hear the rustle of paper. Inspector Pole was taking notes. When she finished, he confirmed the times of the encounters with the nurse. "I'll make sure someone in my team checks the CCTV cameras at UCH and in the surrounding area outside."

Cora thanked him. Branning grimaced and moved his hand to encourage her to keep talking. "Go on," he mouthed as she hesitated.

Pole was no longer in a hurry. He seemed to hear the hesitation and gave her time to gather her thoughts.

"I was wondering... I know it's evidence and the lab still need to finish their work in my apartment..."

"But..." Pole's voice sounded amused. "...you'd like to get something out of there."

Cora blinked. Branning gave her an approving smile. "That would be really brilliant."

"OK... and how are you proposing to get in there with a large gaping hole in the middle of the floor?"

"Well... you know I am a performance artist."

"I know that very well... I've been to a few of your shows."

"Oh..." Cora was not sure whether she was pleased or concerned. "Then you will know that I could... use my ropes and abseil down the window at the back of the flat. I've done that before." It sounded worse than it was. "When I was rehearsing that is."

"What does DS Branning say?"

318

Cora handed the phone to him. He cleared his throat and gave Pole his considered opinion. "I believe she can do it, sir."

Branning handed the phone back to Cora.

"I want to know the details of how you are going to go about it. All of it. And I'll speak to the builders too. I want to know whether it is safe to stand at the far end of the room." Pole was not indulging her. He must have gathered there was something that she felt it was important to retrieve.

Cora leaped out of the chair. She no longer had to sit on her hands and do nothing. "I'll get a detailed plan to you ASAP, Jonathan..." She stopped herself... Had she been too friendly?

"Good to hear it... and I mean it... all the details, step-by-step."

\* \* \*

"I'm fine." A voice reverberated across the empty space. Jack had not heard the door open. Perhaps he had dozed off. "I'm sorry I haven't called you for a while... but I'm good. I'm really busy at work you know."

From the bathroom, Jack could hear the shuffling of feet. Randy Zhang had crossed to the far end of the room.

Jack cast a quick glance through the crack created by the bathroom door opening. He could just about make out Randy but could hear clearly his end of the conversation. He must have called his parents to reassure them.

Jack slid through the opening of the bathroom door. He reached the corner that the corridor wall made with the main room and waited.

Randy hung up but stayed where he was. The entire length of the room separated them. If there had to be a fight, Jack would rather maximise the surprise effect.

After a short moment, Randy walked back to the corner of the room where his small calor gas stove stood. He was rifling through the bag of food he had brought with him. This was close enough.

Jack stepped out from his hiding place into the open. "Randy... I just want to talk about Ollie Wilson."

Randy had been crouching to start cooking some food. He muffled a cry and fell backwards, pushing himself up to move as fast

319

as he could out of Jack's reach. He lunged towards his sleeping bag and retrieved a kitchen knife from underneath it.

Jack opened his hands wide and lifted them at the level of his shoulders.

"I'm not armed… I am the person Ollie contacted about his suspicions regarding Viro-Tech."

Randy moved in a semi-circle, slowly, hoping to reach the door.

"I saw the documents Ollie was trying to send to you. They never reached you, because you had left your flat by that time."

"What were they?" Randy's voice shook as he asked the question.

"Four documents, two papers written by Ollie, one on AMR bacteria. The other on the impact of deforestation on the spread of viruses. One paper from the Gates Foundation and Turner's meeting schedule in China."

"That just means you've intercepted his mail."

"That's true, but Ollie told me about his suspicions regarding the technology Viro-Tech was selling to China." It was not exactly what had happened, but Jack needed Randy to drop his knife.

"Why should I trust you… look where that led Ollie."

"Because I'm CIA and your best chance of getting out of Hong Kong alive."

# Chapter Thirty-Two

The water was getting a little tepid. Nancy stretched out her arm, opened the tap and let the heat of the hot water spread around her body. She had switched off the light in the bathroom, enjoying the breath-taking view from the window.

The glass extended from floor to ceiling, three panels that overlooked Victoria Pier and beyond it the Harbour. It was almost impossible for anyone to see into the bathroom, but she still felt a little self-conscious to be walking around completely naked.

The call with Pole had been much easier than she thought it would be. There was a job to do, and their common interest in achieving that had brought them together again. The time for a conversation about trust would come later. She was glad Pole had not demanded that of her just yet.

The bedroom was quiet... no background music. This trip was not a holiday. Although she recognised the need to rest, she also felt she needed to remain alert. Too many people had been hurt or killed for her not to recognise that she was fighting an opponent that would stop at nothing. Getting to the truth about her father's fate might upset certain people. Trying to get to the truth about what happened to Ollie Wilson had already made waves...

It was gone 10pm on the bathroom clock. Nancy stood up gingerly, wrapped herself in an extra-large, ultra soft towel and stepped onto the marble floor. She would order room service and solve the dinner problem that way.

She moved to the spacious bedroom, with its deep carpets and panels of exotic wood on the walls. The sitting area had been built like an extension, jutting out of the room, to give access to the splendid views.

Her suitcase was propped open on the folding stand, still not unpacked. She rummaged through it and found a light shantung top and trousers she slipped into. She yawned; the time lag was beginning to catch up with her.

She placed her order of chicken Caesar salad and tea – something very few hotels managed to do badly – and started unpacking. She just needed to stay awake until she had eaten her dinner.

A soft rattle at the door made her stop. She consulted the alarm clock on the bedside table… less than 15 minutes… this seemed very quick, but then again it was the Mandarin Oriental, the most luxurious hotel in Hong Kong. She moved swiftly towards the door and was about to speak when she froze. The soft noise she had heard was not that of a trolley being arranged, but that of the door handle being moved gently up and down.

She ran to the door and slid the chain bolt into its track. Nancy looked through the security peephole and saw a man was standing at the door… middle aged, bald, with dry leathery skin… Chinese.

Nancy looked around for a weapon. There were a few glass bottles in the minibar fridge, but she doubted there would be enough to stop a determined assailant. She ran back into the main room, grabbed her mobile. Only five per cent of her battery left, she cursed. Why had she not started charging it earlier?

She ran back to the door. The handle moved again. She called reception.

"This is room 578… someone is at my door, trying to break in."

The receptionist did not ask her to repeat herself. The usual pleasant *hello* was replaced by a focused *security is on its way*.

Nancy dropped her mobile into her pocket, dashed back to the bedroom and grabbed the letter opener… an accessory she thought no hotel room would ever bother with. The door opened as she was running back to it, restrained only by the chain she had secured a few moments earlier.

A small, yet muscly hand was moving up the wooden panel, feeling for the bolt at the end of the chain. Nancy braced herself, and with as much strength as she could muster, stabbed the fingers that were exploring the door.

The man yelped and withdrew his hand immediately.

She tried to slam the door shut again with her shoulder, but a metal object had been moved between the door and its frame.

The man pushed as hard as he could, trying to yank the door open.

The sound of a body slamming against the wood made Nancy brace herself even harder.

The assailant threw his body once more against the door in an attempt to break the security chain.

Nancy braced herself against the door. Her body shook at his second attempt. The chain groaned as the screws fastening the sliding track almost gave way. Another thrust against the door and the chain would come loose.

* * *

Since his motorbike ride, Andy had been firing on all cylinders, Pole had noticed with amusement. Andy had delegated the review of the hospital CCTV footage to a new promising recruit. Mandy had impressed Pole with her IT expertise, and tracing an individual was exactly what she needed to hone her skills. The hospital had been a little reluctant, but the supervisor Mandy had spoken to had been much more amenable when she mentioned the Ollie Wilson case. It was attempted murder, and the person who had committed this terrible act might still be in the hospital, possibly disguised as a nurse.

Andy and Mandy gave an approving nod… Well put.

He sat up and poked his head over his computer screen. "How are you getting on?"

"I've traced the nurse we've been talking about. She entered the lift on the floor above the one on which Ollie Wilson's room is situated. I'm following her out of the hospital and into the underground. So far so good."

"And after that you'll check where she came from?"

Mandy frowned. "Really? I would never have thought of it."

"Right… yeah… course, you got it."

Andy delved back into his own work. Tracking down the working group that had suggested the liberalisation of opium production in Afghanistan. Andy had broadened his search to the US and a name had cropped up that Pole would be very interested in. Jared Turner Senior had chaired a committee there until it had been dismantled in 2012.

The report they had requested had been critical. The conclusion was that if the opium production in Afghanistan was sold to legal drug producers, it would inevitably increase the cultivation of opium poppies and push the price up. The Afghan government did not have the means to police the entire territory and control the crops. The Taliban warlords were in power, and this was not likely to change any time soon.

Andy was awaiting information from Interpol on Turner Senior. His colleagues there had assured him he would receive a swift reply. He would call back in a couple of hours if nothing came before then.

"Bugger." Mandy's voice came out loud and clear.

"You've lost her?" he said without rising from his desk.

"Yeah… there must be a blind spot or something at the station. I can't find her anywhere."

"And would the station you're talking about be Balham by any chance?"

Mandy sprang up from her chair. "Wow… How on earth did you know that?"

"That's not the only blind spot in London… but it's the one used by the other people we tried to track down and lost on the Wilson case."

"Well then." Mandy moved around to come and sit on Andy's desk. "She's got to be part of the gang."

He lifted his head, closing one eye. "Send the file to me. I've got an idea."


Pole was returning from yet another meeting with a frustrated Superintendent Marsh and Commander Ferguson.

The Ollie Wilson search had yielded very little.

The informal joint inquiry with the counter-terrorist squad was going nowhere.

324

Ms Wu had a very good excuse for going to Hong Kong… and booking two tickets in her own name was odd, but nothing reprehensible.

Ferguson tried to argue that she might have changed the name on the other ticket at the last minute, but he was clutching at straws. Still, the squad was on Pole's back, and he could feel the heat.

Pole needed progress. The squad would still be on his back, but not Marsh. Marsh would be convinced the Wilson case was a high-profile case. He too was being grilled by the head of the Counter Terrorist Squad and it was not pleasant. He would use the Wilson case to fend them off as well.

Pole walked into the open-plan office. He could already tell Andy was onto something important. He was half standing… still working but surveying the entrance to the room. When he saw Pole he waved, excited.

"What is it that you found that is so exciting then?"

"You remember I told you the jogger was a woman?"

It took Pole a few seconds to recall the encounter between Cora and the jogger along the Regent's Canal towpath. He nodded.

"And you remember I also thought the biker who…" Andy was trying to put it diplomatically.

"…ran over Nancy?" Pole suggested.

"Exactly… was also a woman? Now Mandy's found the nurse Cora had noticed coming out of the hospital lift."

"And it was the same person?" Pole smiled.

Andy snapped his fingers. "And – wait for this – she alighted at Balham tube station!"

"Part of the Russian crowd then?"

"Possibly… well… very probable. I don't think it can be a coincidence."

"Neither do I. What else?"

"Mandy tracked her back inside UCH. She walked around a few floors doing nothing much, checking here and there. But she never went into any of the staff rooms. She changed out of her uniform in one of the public toilets."

"And you've tracked that person back out?"

"We have… that's how we came up with Balham."

"You're the best." Pole gave his DS a friendly tap over the shoulder. "Where is Mandy?"

"Not sure… but I'll be sure to tell her you think she's done really well when she comes back."

"Now that we know Balham is the woman we are tracking's contact point, let's speak to the local guys… they may know how to track her down."

"On it, Guv."

"Is there someone you know in that neck of the woods?"

"Not sure…"

"Let's try to keep this discreet… If this gang is as well connected as we suspect, they have eyes and ears everywhere."

* * *

"I'll tell you all that I know and all that Ollie told me." Jack was still holding his hands up at the level of his shoulders.

In the low light of the room, he could make out Randy's face, covered in sweat. His grip on the knife was so tight his knuckles had turned white. He had no idea how to fight with such a weapon, but Jack did not fancy tackling him… unless he tried to have a go at him.

"You could still be working for them." Randy's voice was hoarse. "Why don't I tell you anyway, and then you can decide."

Jack lowered his hands in a slow deliberate gesture. "Do you mind if I move to the other end of the room and sit down?" Jack followed his words by moving backwards in slow motion. Randy cast an eye towards the door. No one else was coming. He seemed to relax a little, still holding the knife up as he moved to the opposite wall and leaned against it.

Jack told him as much as he could. The way Ollie had contacted him through the embassy. How he had promised to send information to Jack but never managed to. The call from London telling him Ollie had disappeared… The suspicions about illegal drugs.

Jack told Randy about his visit to Professor Park at Harvard Medical School.

"Ollie would never do drugs again. He had a difficult patch at uni, that's all."

"But evidence is not stacking up in his favour in the UK."

326

"That's a set-up."

"Who by?"

"I don't know." Randy slid slowly down the wall. "Possibly the same people who tried to silence him in the first place."

"Viro-Tech Therapeutics?"

"This may sound odd, but I still can't believe Jared would do that." Randy shook his head. "Ollie's girlfriend always told him he was too naive. I guess I was too."

A faint noise silenced both men instantly. It was coming from the floor below them. Jack stood up and moved towards Randy, indicating he should stay down. They both remained quiet. The noise stopped for a moment and started again.

This time Randy stood up and Jack did not stop him. "Take the passport and money you've hidden in the bathroom but leave the rest here."

Randy froze.

"We need to leave now..."

Randy shook himself. He moved to the bathroom, and retrieved his possessions, carefully replacing the loose tiles.

The echoing sound below kept coming and going... someone was investigating the room underneath them.

Jack moved to the door, opened it a small crack and listened again. Their floor was still silent, though perhaps not for long. Jack nodded towards the exit, treading noiselessly. Randy followed without question. Jack opened the fire exit door and listened. There was only silence and darkness. The stairwell was visible only in the light from the open door. Once the door was shut, they would be in total darkness.

"This is what we are going to do," Jack whispered over his shoulder. "I'm not going to use my torch, but we are going to go up in the dark, using the banister as a guide."

"Why are we going up?" Randy asked.

"I kept the door open on the seventh floor." Randy shut the door reluctantly behind them.

Jack and Randy had just started to climb the stairs when they saw a beam of light below them and that it was moving up fast. They had almost reached the fourth floor. The door to one of the floors below opened and the light disappeared. Randy's pursuers hadn't yet sussed out that Randy was on the move.

Only three floors to go. Jack accelerated the pace. Randy followed. He tripped and contained a yelp. Voices could now be heard from below. The door had opened again, and steps were pounding up towards them. "Come on." Jack let Randy go first. He lit the torch so that they could see better and started running towards their escape route. There were now shouts and the steps below them speeded up.

The beam of light that guided them was unsteady yet enabled them to climb two steps at a time.

The others were gaining ground and their own light was shining up the staircase. It was almost upon them.

The seventh-floor door was now visible. Randy opened the door. Jack shoved Randy by the shoulder and pushed him through the doorway. He yanked the piece of plastic that kept the door open. As it slammed shut, someone crashed against it.

It wouldn't be long though before they manage to force it open. Randy and Jack ran for the lift, pushing past a group of men who had just come out of it.

"Where to now?" Randy was breathless, his face ashen with fear.

"Back to Central."

They reached the ground floor. Jack didn't pretend to be calm. He ran through the lobby, followed by Randy. The receptionists and guests stopped to watch the two men dash out. Jack didn't care.

Outside, he pushed Randy into the first cab he saw.

"Mandarin Oriental," he said as soon as he had shut the cab's door.

"The night ferry is quicker." The driver was reluctant to leave Kowloon. Jack took a $100 note out of his rucksack.

"Double this if you reach Central in 30 minutes."

The driver floored the accelerator.

\* \* \*

Cora's plan was on his desk. Pole was impressed. He had seen some of her performances in which the young woman defied gravity and hung in the air, in a choreography that was both aesthetic and dangerous.

She'd come up with a way to harness ropes from the beam that stretched across the entire structure of her flat. It was clever and it should work. Pole had hoped she would take a little more time to consider her plan, but she was keen, and she wanted answers.

Pole went through the Wilson file again. He had kept the name of the fire brigade's senior officer who led the team on the day the fire broke out at Cora's flat. Perhaps she could still be of help.

"Are you serious?" Senior Officer Rachel Lord's voice dropped a little when he explained it to her.

"Completely serious... or rather, she is. She's an experienced performance artist."

"She does that sort of stuff? For a living?" Senior Officer Lord sounded almost impressed.

"That's right... but your people do some pretty daring things too."

"Only when we have to, though..."

"Well, she's a very successful artist... and she produces some rather wonderful watercolours too."

"I'd rather she stuck to the... watercolours."

"If we don't help her, she's going to do it on her own anyway."

"I can't really give you a professional opinion, Inspector Pole. I would be..."

"I'm not expecting you to. I just want you to take a look and tell me whether there's anything that doesn't make sense." Pole hesitated. "Someone like you who knows the ropes, if I can put it that way, and has much knowledge of working in buildings that have been ravaged by fire."

"I could perhaps..." Lord was thinking. "I could perhaps drive by and have a talk with her. I'm finishing my shift in an hour."

Pole thanked Senior Officer Lord and called Cora to tell her that this was his condition. Senior Officer Lord would go through the plan with her. If she thought it was safe, Cora had the go-ahead.

Andy popped his head through the door just as Pole finished his call.

"An extract from a report by the Commission in charge of co-ordinating the world medical production, the International Narcotics Control Board. The local advocate fighting to liberate the production in Afghanistan is... Jared Turner Senior." Andy had opened the document so that Pole could read the relevant passage. He traced the name with his finger and stabbed at it. "Turner Senior is really keen on this. And he had visited Afghanistan a lot, before and since the report's publication."

Pole read the report extract. "This gives us an indication, but not confirmation. There's still a large gap at this end connecting the Turners with a Russian gang."

"Agreed... but Mandy and I are looking into Turner Senior more closely."

Pole was playing with an old rubber band he had found on the floor of his office.

"What we need... is someone who will talk," he said.

Andy leaned back in his chair.

"The only person we have at the moment is that woman/biker/ nurse from Balham. Knowing the reputation these gangs have for dealing with snitches, I'm not sure anyone will want to talk to us."

"Cora has been discreet. She hasn't spoken to anyone else about the nurse. Not even her friends."

"That's what Branning said."

Pole scratched his goatee. "We are going to tell people that Ollie has woken up and ask Cora to go along with the story... that he is recovering."

Andy nodded in approval. "A good old-fashioned trap."

"Why not?" Pole grinned briefly. "You'll be at the hospital, I'll be there too, and Mandy can join us, disguised as a nurse."

"I can set up an alert to inform us when this woman enters Balham tube... I think." Andy tapped his fingers a few times on his upper lip. "Yes, I think I have got enough on her to set up a programme and monitor her."

"That's worth trying in any case. We'll have a team at the hospital no matter what, to give us a decent amount of warning."

Andy was already standing up. Pole shot a hand forward to stop him. "Can someone else do the monitoring for you?"

"You mean... once I've set up the programme? Yes, sure."

"Good, I'd like you on site at the hospital. I'm a known face there but you're not."

"Be great to be part of that." Andy ran a hand over his left cheek. "Although I recall the last time I was posted to a hospital, I ended up needing treatment there myself."

"I certainly won't forget that." Pole's mind flashed back to the case. Andy had been assaulted whilst guarding a key witness and he'd needed quite a few stiches.

"That's OK, Guv... I've toughened up considerably since then. Up to date on my self-defence these days." Andy took up a mock defensive position and tried to look fierce.

No matter what Andy did, he always looked like a nice guy. Pole approved. No one would suspect he was ready to throw a punch if he needed to.

# Chapter Thirty-Three

"Go away." Nancy was determined not to sound scared. Even if the receptionist had heard her before her phone went dead, the security guard would not arrive on time.

The door had become still again. The man on the other side had not given up, but was bracing himself for another harder push.

Nancy looked around in despair. She moved away from the door. Perhaps if he crashed into it expecting resistance, finding none, he would overshoot and fall into the room. She might then have time to run for it.

Her back bumped into something solid and unexpected. A small fire extinguisher was fixed to the wall.

She tried to yank it out of its holder. It resisted her first attempt, came out at the second and, without thinking, she hurled it towards the door as it crashed open. The extinguisher flew from her hands. The impact was fierce. She heard the crack of bones on impact. The body of the Chinese man she'd seen through the pip hole crashed backwards into the corridor.

Nancy leaned down towards the extinguisher. She retrieved it from the floor and waited. The door had busrt open and slammed back, now ajar. She waited for a few seconds, ready to fight again. Hurried knocks startled her.

"Ms Wu... are you alright... may we come in?"

She hesitated. But no, the man she had just slammed in the face would not sound so polite.

"I'm fine." She approached the door still holding her weapon, and pulled it fully open with her foot.

Two security guards stood in front of her. She looked into the corridor. There was blood on the carpet. The man she had just hit had disappeared. Nancy slumped against the frame of the battered door.

One of the security guards called the hotel manager. Nancy surveyed the damage, still leaning against the wall. There was no way she could remain in this room.

Nancy gave a quick account of what had happened to the manager when he arrived. Already two maids had appeared to help Nancy pack her suitcase. The police had been called and Nancy's attempt not to attract attention had just failed.

"We will move you into one of our suites. There is one available just a few floors up with the same view. You will be very comfortable there and..." The woman hesitated. "...there is additional security. We have selected a suite that is made available for high-profile clients or public figures that require additional protection."

Nancy thanked her. "I'm very grateful." She would have been worried if the manager had taken her at her word. A secure door and a video camera at the entrance might be a good addition after all, if she were to get any sleep that night.

It was almost midnight when Nancy closed the door of her new suite. The place was more luxurious than her room, but she was not in the mood to enjoy it.

The police officer who came had been professional, taking notes, asking the right questions. She had convincingly told them she was on a short break in Hong Kong, a place where she had often done business as a lawyer. Mentioning her profession had the desired effect, prompting a mixture of concern and respect.

She stood in the middle of the vast lounge-cum-dining-room overlooking the Bay. It was no longer just a bedroom the Mandarin had provided her with; it was a small apartment. Her head was aching, and her body clock had been tricked into telling her it was no longer time to go to bed. The adrenaline still coursing through her veins after the attack wasn't helping either. She'd moved from suitably tired and relaxed to being wired up by the adrenaline of fear.

She thought about calling Pole, but he would know something was up. He didn't need the additional burden at the moment.

Nancy moved to the small bar that looked well stocked. She decided against anything stronger than a cup of tea. She chose a simple chamomile from the large selection of teas offered by the hotel. Her phone was now fully charged. She checked her messages. There was nothing of importance. Nancy picked up the mug and settled onto the sofa. She stood up again to check she had activated the security at the door, and returned to drink her tea, gazing absentmindedly at the view.

A new email had just come through, it was from Cora. Nancy read it, sipping her tea, and smiled. Now she had an excuse to call Pole that wouldn't mean talking to him about the assault.

\* \* \*

The security guards were not at the door and the doorman looked unusually distracted. Jack wondered how he could get a scruffy looking Randy through the door of the five-star luxury Mandarin hotel. Randy assured him his T-shirt was only a few days old and that his frayed jeans were the latest fashion in Hong Kong.

He must have been right.

They walked through the lobby without anybody querying Randy's presence. Jack chose a couple of seats in a corner from where he could survey the scene. He had heard the word 'police' as they passed the check-in desk and he wanted to make sure the Mandarin would not be swarming with cops asking the wrong questions.

Randy was anxious too. He didn't particularly trust the police but seemed happy enough to be following Jack's lead for the time being.

Jack sat down facing the lobby whilst Randy sat opposite him. He ordered two Scotches and Randy nodded. He was not fussed as long as it helped soothe his nerves.

"Why don't you tell me your side of the story?" Jack picked up his glass and took a mouthful.

"To start with, Ollie and I simply disagreed with Viro-Tech transferring technology to China for further development, on ethical grounds, even though there was nothing illegal about it. Other companies get a lucrative deal with China because they are prepared to agree to a technology transfer. At the end of the day, they are private companies, financed in the private sector, doing what they like with their own research and development." Randy drained half his whisky and began to look a lot calmer. "US government barely knows what R&D the private sector is developing, let alone its impact on national security."

"I gathered that." Jack kept an eye on the far end of the large reception area. A couple of policemen had arrived and were moving towards the lifts.

"I worked with Ollie on the same piece of research. He was building the programme that would gather all the data I needed to validate our findings. Our research concentrated on how the human body protects itself against certain viruses, in particular pulmonary infections like bird flu. It's really interesting to understand what it would take to create a universal vaccine for pulmonary diseases… you know the RNA-based vaccination idea is not that new in concept, but Ollie and I had found a new way of delivering the instructions to the human immune system through lipid nanoparticles and…" Randy stopped himself. "Sorry… I get carried away when I start talking shop."

"That's alright. I've done a crash course on what you and Ollie were studying at Harvard."

"We stumbled over this piece of research from another lab that had never been fully exploited. This RNA-vaccine is incredible… you can map a virus RNA sequence, assemble a vaccine and start testing on mice a week later…"

"You mean it would take only a week to come up with a vaccine that can work on humans, even if it is a novel virus?" Jack's attention had slid towards reception. He redirected his attention to what Randy was saying.

"That's a bit of a simplification, but yes, that's the general idea. You can do in one month what may take a year or more and this gives you a platform too."

"What do you mean?"

"It means you don't have to reinvent the process for a new virus… you simply update the RNA sequence, or even combine different viruses' sequences altogether."

"Is it legal?"

"That's legal as long as you don't use it in combination with the development of a man-made virus, and that's where the conversation became more complicated… we were only at the beginning of our research, trying to come to some conclusion about that."

"Did you speak to Turner about it?"

Randy squirmed at the mention of his former boss. "He was on our backs because of our apparent lack of progress, so we eventually spoke to him about the preliminary results of our research."

"And he saw an opportunity?"

"He has been working on a very high-profile project. He would not tell us what it was, but it involved regular trips to China. Then he wanted to know everything about the potential of what we had discovered. He had some applications in mind for it, but he never told us what they were."

"But you and Ollie did some further research and came up with your own conclusions."

"Jared seems a nice guy when you first meet him, but he is also a tough businessman. Ollie thought he might want to approach the military with the idea… after all, the US army is always looking for ways to enhance its soldiers' resistance to disease whilst engaged in combat. So, you can imagine the importance of what that would mean, to make their soldiers immune to viruses deployed in a biological attack."

"But you didn't buy it."

"It's not that we didn't buy it. Turner made no effort to contact the military. Ollie eventually got into his diary… he is a wizard with encryption you know…" Randy emptied his glass, and the alcohol was doing the trick. "Turner spoke to his father instead."

"About what? I know his father is on the board of a large US pharmaceutical company. Why the interest?" Jack asked.

"Cutting edge biotechnological agent production in China. He and his father have already created a company to do that and entered into partnership with the US pharma you just mentioned." Randy slumped back in his chair. "But still, that's not illegal. Although that may depend on whether there is a conflict of interest. But as long as all parties are well compensated, I doubt anybody will stop the Turners." Randy looked at his glass, somewhat forlorn. Jack ordered two refills.

"The point is, as long as the technology remains in the private sector, they can transfer it to whoever they wish, including China."

Jack recalled a passage in the McCain report he had just read. The transfer of technology from the private sector, proceeding unchecked or even openly tolerated by both the US and Europe, had enabled China to leapfrog the rest of the world, cutting the time and cost of the research process by many years. China now had an advantage over the US in many technological fields.

"Did you or Ollie say anything to Turner?" The two glasses of Scotch had arrived. Randy took his, cradling it in both hands for a moment.

"We didn't for a while. Until Ollie discovered that Jared was going regularly to Sichuan in China." Randy took a gulp. "That's when we realised that he had already committed to transferring our technology. In exchange, he was being shown the site of the factory... I mean the newly formed company's factory that would be producing the drugs he and his father had in mind."

"Which drugs would those be?"

"Antidepressants, opiates... lots of the types of medication sold to the US in large quantities... But we also suspected they had the intention of producing more complex drugs at a fraction of the price they otherwise would cost if produced in the US..."

"And that increased the dependency the US has on China when it comes to its supply chain."

"That's right... but Jared didn't care. Sichuan is a new area for development as far as China is concerned. There are plenty of qualified people but not enough jobs for them."

"Can't they go somewhere else to find a job?"

Randy shook his head. "Not under Chinese rules. You're stuck in the region or province in which you were born and trained. If you move anywhere else, you become an illegal worker."

"So, the Chinese government was being generous with the terms of the deal."

"That's right... Ollie spoke to a friend of his. He didn't mention her name but she had been doing some research about China. From what he said, she was looking for her father, an artist who disappeared quite a few years ago. He came from Chengdu, the capital of Sichuan province. She was hoping to find out what had happened to him."

Jack gazed at the glass in his hand, swirling the amber liquid around.

"Did she find anything?"

"I don't think so, but Ollie thought she might be able to help us once he explained what was happening. However, he never got the chance."

Randy looked exhausted all of a sudden. Jack's time zone hopping was also catching up with him. The two police officers had reappeared. They spoke to the receptionist who looked nervous. It seemed it was not the end of the affair.

"Wait a minute."

Randy looked puzzled, still nursing his glass.

"I just need to ask the receptionist something."

Jack moved without hurrying to the reception desk. "I've lost my room card. I hope there has been no issue with the hotel security. I saw two policemen leaving just now."

The receptionist straightened up. "The incident is under control, sir. No need to be alarmed."

"I'm on floor five."

"That's OK. We are only concerned about floor eleven."

"Good to know." Jack was issued with a new card. He returned to the corner of the lounge in which Randy was still sitting.

"Let's go to my room. We can decide tomorrow if the US consulate is a safe enough place for you to stay."

A flash of concern came over Randy's face.

Jack smiled. "You're safe at least until tomorrow and in any case... you are my guest. You get the bed and I get the bathtub. A much better deal for you than the hard floor of the YMCA."

\* \* \*

"Your text said you had news," Pole said.

"Yep..." Harris was calling him from his car and the reception was breaking up. "My CIA contact has located Randy Zhang."

"In one piece?"

338

"Very funny... but yes. He confirmed Turner Junior and Senior are doing a deal with China but one that we may not be able to stop."

Pole grunted. He had walked away from his office, in need of a breather and a cup of tea. It was not uncommon for him to think about cases during his search for a cup of good brew. This time he had gone a little farther away from the Yard. The Café Conte was rather full of tourists, but Pole had managed to find a single armchair at the back of the long room.

"Just as Marsh was starting to bite," Pole added.

"Hang on." Harris paused and the reception became clearer. "The biotech Ollie and Randy were developing is something they thought they should present to the US government."

"You mean it needed to be controlled because of its potential ramifications?" Pole asked.

"That's the gist of it... my contact couldn't be more specific but I'm due to speak to him tomorrow morning... well, his morning, my midnight."

"I'll get things going at my end. It might be that we don't need the Chinese connection after all."

"I'm all ears. What have you found?" Harris asked.

"Not yet substantiated by evidence, but the Turners have a connection with the production of opium in Afghanistan."

"A Russian connection?" Harris grew serious. "Afghanistan is my area of expertise. What do you need?"

"The name of the cartel that operates in Herat province. The drug squad is finding it pretty difficult to pin them down."

"I'm not surprised... ex KGB or FSB... you don't find them... they find you. They are untraceable, at least not with simple police resources... No offence," Harris said.

"None taken. I've got a pretty good team and they've gotten nowhere."

"Do I feel perhaps... an exception?" Harris had returned to his joyful self.

"A recent addition to their team. Perhaps expendable... I'm working on that." Pole nodded as though Harris could see him.

"Call me back at the end of the day. You'll have your answer about Afghanistan."

"Will do." Pole scanned the room. No one was looking in his direction. He felt happy to continue. "Now about the burner phone... I need to get Ferguson off my back."

"And Ms Wu's. I'm aware of that." Harris's voice had grown serious once more. "We've created a trace of calls that leads to the right address. The one we stormed 10 months ago. Your team should be able to pick it up without a problem."

"That's a little slim if you intend to get Ferguson off my back."

"Pole. I know my job. It would be slim as you say." Harris interrupted his conversation but came back on. "Give me another day and you'll have the record of a purchase of that particular burner phone in a shop near the address the C-T squad stormed in North London."

"Much better."

"Again, your team should be able find this, although it'll be a bit trickier to detect."

"You mean some unregulated vendor?"

"That's right... But the shop concerned is next to a CCTV camera."

Pole switched off his burner phone, replaced it in his pocket and picked up a second one. He had just missed a call from Nancy.

* * *

Cora went for a walk with DS Branning. She had never thought she would enjoy the company of a copper, but Branning had become a comforting presence.

She just wanted to think things through without interruption.

Pole was right. The only way to flush out the people behind the savage attacks on Ollie was to lie about his medical condition. She had agreed. She would do it. But the prospect of having to look excited and happy about a positive development when there was none made her stomach churn.

They were walking along the canal, away from the flat, away from the lock where she had been followed and intimidated.

The weather was cold but windless. The sun had started to set, and yet there was still enough light for the towpath to look peaceful, almost pleasant.

Branning was quietly smoking his cigarette.

"I presume the hospital will have to agree to the plan," Cora asked.

"Yes. Inspector Pole will speak to the registrar. But it won't be disclosed to many more people. The fewer the better."

"What about the nurse I noticed?"

"She isn't on the staff, as I mentioned. That was well done, you know, spotting her." Branning nodded in rhythm with his pace.

"How soon will it happen?" Cora shivered.

"If it all stacks up… tomorrow." Branning stopped to step on his cigarette butt. "You know… you can always say no. There is nothing wrong with not wanting to lie about a loved one's condition."

Cora was taken aback by the comment. She thought she needed to comply. She could see Pole's plan had some real merits. But her heart was still in so much pain that she wasn't sure she could act the part convincingly. She'd been told it could be months before Ollie recovered or perhaps he'd never recover at all.

She stopped at a bench sheltered by some evergreen bushes and slumped onto it. Branning took his cigarette pack out of his pocket, had second thoughts, and replaced it.

"I'm not sure I have the… strength to go ahead with it." Cora let her head fall into her hands, elbows on knees.

"Inspector Pole will understand… it's possible that he can do this without your input."

Branning sat down next to Cora, not too close, but close enough; she sensed he understood the emotional turmoil she was going through.

Her eyes felt sore with tears, and she stayed still, face hidden for a long moment. Branning simply waited, not impatient, just a companionable presence.

"No… Ollie deserves the truth. If I don't do it, Inspector Pole's plan won't work so well."

Branning pulled out a small packet of Kleenex from his jacket pocket. She noticed it had a floral design. He handed it to her.

"Nothing wrong about being sad."

"But everything wrong about allowing sadness to get in the way of justice," Cora said.

# Chapter Thirty-Four

"Suffering from jet lag?" Pole teased Nancy.

"Wide awake whenI should be fast asleep." Nancy was glad Pole hadn't asked about her evening.

"How is Hong Kong?"

"Just as I remembered it. Some places never change, and yet, I can feel a different energy… I can't quite put my finger on it yet." Nancy would have ventured into an explanation but, not now when all she needed was to hear Pole's voice. "Central has always been a packed island. Just as well that Hong Kong decided long ago to create acres of National Park to preserve the forest." Nancy stretched over the sofa. "Perhaps a few new buildings to replace the old… And yet, the House of 1000 Assholes is still standing."

Pole chuckled. "Is that a joke?"

"Not at all… it's called Jardine House. Almost opposite the Mandarin Oriental. It was the first skyscraper to be built on the island back in the 1970s. I had a client whose office was there. It looks very much like any other tall building, but the windows are round, like an asshole. It was supposed to be a distinct feature that would make it more attractive for prospective tenants."

"Who gave it the nickname… the Chinese?"

"No, pretty much everybody, visitors, expats… it's a little crude but affectionate nevertheless."

"Round windows… Is that a little Feng Shui?"

"*Bien vu*, Jonathan." Nancy chuckled. "The round windows were meant to resemble portholes, and the sun or moon… so wealth and heaven if we're talking Feng Shui."

They continued chatting for a little while. Nancy felt the tension in her back gradually easing. Pole's reassuring voice was working its magic.

Nancy stifled a yawn. She had almost forgotten why she was calling him.

"I had an email from Cora. She sounded pleased that she had spoken to you about a person she noticed at the hospital."

"The nurse that is not a nurse... a good observation. She had noticed the woman and decided she should mention it."

Pole ran through the information Andy and Mandy had gathered. Nancy looked around, wide awake again. She needed her yellow pad.

"It's time to turn the tables on those bastards," Pole said.

"The trap is a good idea, but..." Nancy was thinking. "Is Cora OK with this? I don't mean to say she doesn't approve, but she needs to be ready to pull it off."

Pole remained silent for a moment. "I should have thought about that. I won't press her. I can manage without her if she decides it's too much."

"Perhaps you need to give her a little more time to get used to the idea."

"That's why I miss you not being around. No one to bounce ideas off."

"I miss that too, Jonathan. I miss all of it, in fact." Nancy tightened the bathrobe closer around her.

"But we need to see this through." Pole's focus on actions rather than recriminations made her miss him even more.

She was about to tell him about Professor Licot, but Pole beat her to it with more news.

"The agencies have found Randy Zhang."

"Alive?"

"Yes, and able to tell us what he and Ollie were suspicious about."

"Turner Junior is not going to be happy about that."

"As much as I'd love to go and put some handcuffs around the wrists of the Viro-Tech CEO, it won't be on the strength of Randy's evidence I'm afraid, *mon coeur*."

\* \* \*

Senior Officer Rachel Lord had gone around the building twice. She had promised Pole she would survey the state of the structure before

Cora's attempt at abseiling down the walls of her flat and Cora had agreed.

Cora ran towards Officer Lord as soon as she entered her building's small yard.

"So sorry, I went for a quick walk... to clear my mind..."

Lord smiled. "That's no problem. I've just surveyed the building a couple of times thoroughly. The external structure held up pretty well after the fire."

"And it helped that the windows had metal frames rather than wood." Cora jerked her head towards her apartment.

"I read your plan... that's a bit daring for a member of the public."

Cora smirked. "You haven't seen what I can do..."

"I was about to say that you are not the run-of-the-mill member of the public though. I've seen your videos and... well... I'm impressed."

"So, it's OK with you?" Cora beamed.

"Not so fast, young lady. I need to see your equipment and how you are going to gain access to the beams in the flat."

"I'll show you."

Cora led the way. DS Branning had stopped at the gate of the small courtyard. He was giving her space to speak to the person she needed to convince.

She called Pole to tell him she was going ahead. Pole gave her a don't-do-anything-stupid type of reply.

"Anyway, it's been dry for a couple of days. I'll be fine," she said by way of conclusion. She handed the phone to Senior Officer Lord.

"The equipment is in good condition. I've checked everything myself."

"That's very good of you, officer... I presume she's determined to go through with it?"

"You've got that right, Inspector. She won't take no for an answer."

As the equipment had been laid outside her apartment, Cora strapped the harness around her torso and secured the leg straps.

Cora moved up on the emergency stairwell that hugged the back of the building. The metal structure echoed to the sound of her pounding feet, vibrations coursing along its frame.

Cora dragged herself and the coiled ropes to the landing on the outside stairs that was closest to the window she wanted to access. The glass had been blackened by smoke, but she knew exactly where the window locks were.

She turned to look down at her small audience of friends and well-wishers: Johnny, Charlie, Branning and Senior Officer Lord. She gave a confident little nod. Beth was on the landing with her, ready to hand Cora her equipment.

Everyone nodded back and held their breath whilst Cora stepped onto the banister. The weather had been dry all day. The next two days were forecast to be rainy and uncertain. It had to be now.

She felt around in one of the pockets of the harness and took out a small hammer. She broke the glass with a precise knock, cleared the fragments with her gloved hand and found the catch immediately. The window opened.

Cora pushed up the bottom section. She heaved herself onto the frame of the staircase and held the position for what seemed an eternity. With a supple move she landed on the windowsill. She was inside.

Beth threw the ropes to her. Cora arranged them at her feet. She selected one and tied it to one of the D-rings of the harness in a secure knot. She jumped inside her flat and disappeared out of view.

Cora secured the other side of the rope she had fastened to another D-ring on her harness to the hooks and pullies she had had made specially for her performance rehearsals.

The lingering smell of soot and melted plastic made her cough a few times. She stopped for a short moment... focus was essential.

She surveyed the landscape below her. A lot of the debris and damaged furniture had been removed. The props, however, had not been touched. They were covered in smoke residue, but they had not been displaced by the fire.

Cora heaved herself below the beam, swung her body a few times and landed onto the windowsill again.

Beth had jumped on the banister too and threw the other rope towards her friend. Cora returned to the main beam. She secured the second rope to different hooks and pulleys. She sat across the beam for a short moment, planning her descent. The floor where she had decided to land looked solid.

Cora started to slide slowly downwards. She touched down using her right foot... testing the solidity of the floor she had just reached. It felt strong and she rested her foot on the ground, gradually letting the full weight of her body transfer to her foot. The wood held firm.

Cora secured the rope through another D-ring on her harness. If the floor gave way, she would have time to pull herself up.

Her props had been stored by performance event. Some of the heavy pieces were lying at the bottom, but none of these provided an opportunity to hide anything within them.

Cora tried to remember Ollie's words. He had joked that some of the long tubes she was using to build a structure, around which she would perform some complex aerobatics, were ideal to secretly stash away documents.

*It's like an old cypher.* Cora had found his comment a little strange at the time, but not taken any notice.

She displaced a large sheet of plastic. The dust rose to her nose, and she started to cough uncontrollably. She hadn't brought water with her... a mistake. She calmed herself, controlling her breathing. She wiped away the perspiration that had gathered on her forehead with her arm and carried on shifting the smaller metal pieces which appeared more promising.

Each of the tubes was hollow so that they could be joined together in different configurations. Cora started to inspect each one meticulously. After 15 minutes, the pile of props was mounting on one side, so far nothing. She stopped for a moment.

Perhaps she was simply grasping at straws.

She almost kicked the pile of metal that resembled a small pyramid. Tears had gathered in the corners of her eyes and she wiped them ferociously against the shoulder of her T-shirt.

Her eyes moved slowly around the space. All the things that had made the flat home had gone. She gritted her teeth. "For Ollie..."

She resumed the task, going through each piece, starting now on the smaller tubes. One of the props did not match the others. By the look of it, it had never been part of the set she had calibrated herself, but seemed to have been more of a reject, a piece of metal she had discarded when cutting the props to size.

Cora's heart pounded in her chest. An odd piece out, inconspicuous to the untrained eye, but glaringly obvious to her, since she had invented the structure. Cora bent forward in a sudden movement and pulled out the piece of metal from where it had been placed at the bottom of the pile.

The rest of the props that had been stored on top of it came crashing down on her.

* * *

"I have spoken to the hospital." Pole dragged an old chair on casters over to Andy's desk. "The registrar has agreed to what we suggested. His head nurse will be in the loop and that's it."

"We have three plain clothes officers already briefed. The other PC on duty will take over as agreed."

"Sounds good."

"Where will you be, Guv?"

"I'll be outside the hospital…" Pole nodded. "I can't be anywhere near Ollie's room, otherwise I fear it will deter our woman suspect."

"She doesn't know me, so I plan to be in the reception area with my laptop… I can control the camera we have installed in Ollie's room from there."

"And I'll be there too." Mandy popped up from behind the partition screen that separated her desk from Andy's.

"Very good." Pole gave them both an approving smile. "I couldn't hope for a better team."

"Mandy's got really good self-defence training, too." Andy's cheeks turned a little pink.

"Even better. How many times have you been on a live operation, Mandy?"

"Only once, sir, but it was rather tough."

Pole eyed Andy sideways. "It'll be fine. If we stick to the plan, it will work out."

"I've been chased by Commander Ferguson again." Andy changed the subject suddenly.

Pole's attention switched abruptly.

"He asked whether you could call him about Ms Wu?" Andy carried on.

Pole clenched his fist and released it. "I did tell him I would call as soon as I had the time." He controlled his anger. No need to take it out on Andy. He was on his side.

Pole disappeared into his office, closed the door and sat down heavily in his chair.

"Shit." He ran his hand through his hair and paused.

Ferguson was worse than a dog with a bone. He would not let it rest until he had found what he was looking for.

Pole hesitated. Harris had given him the OK. The link between the terrorist, who had attempted to eliminate a key witness, and the SFO prosecutor in the Mark Phelps case, had been planted. The rest would follow.

Still, it would mean lying to his DS, so as to lead him towards the planted evidence.

A knock at the door interrupted his train of thought. He considered ignoring it but Andy was gesturing he needed to come in.

Pole waved him in. "Superintendent Marsh is trying to get hold of you."

Pole rolled his eyes. He was about to dial reluctantly, then stopped.

Perhaps The Super could be of assistance for once.

Pole walked to the top floor of the building and appeared at Marsh's office unannounced.

"Hello, Denise."

"Well… hello, Inspector Pole…" Denise pulled her glasses away from her face and raised an eyebrow. It was not like him to show up out of the blue.

"I'm sure he is, as ever, fiendishly busy, but…"

"As it happens, he wants to see you, so I'll let him know. He has a call in 15 minutes, but I can delay for a bit if need be."

Denise disappeared into Marsh's office and as predicted, she opened the door and ushered him in.

"Pole, you, unannounced." Marsh seem to expect something juicy and rubbed his hands together in anticipation.

"I just wanted to run an idea past you, sir. It's about Ferguson and the inquiry."

Marsh grimaced and waved Pole towards his desk.

He sat down, pretended he was gathering his thoughts about a difficult situation.

"I think Commander Ferguson's team might have missed something important."

Marsh straightened up. He was all ears.

"There is one location that his people do not seem to have checked and that is the area surrounding the place his team stormed 10 months ago."

Marsh frowned. "I don't follow."

"Commander Ferguson is intent on finding someone to blame for MI6 having advance knowledge of the terrorist cell's location. But that doesn't include gathering any form of evidence to substantiate that."

"I'm sure Ferguson is aware of that. He's one of the best in the squad."

"I've worked with Ferguson enough to know how determined he can be, but, in the case of this inquiry, he's perhaps a little too keen."

"What do you have in mind?" Marsh couldn't see where he was going.

"Is it not possible that the person who made the calls from the vicinity of the Scotland Yard building, or near Ms Wu's flat, was a member of the terrorist cell? After all, they were targeting people on the Mark Phelps case."

A knot closed Pole's throat. Lying to save his skin was not what he was accustomed to and yet...

Marsh grabbed one of his Montblanc pens and started rolling it around his fingers.

"That is a good point. Have you spoken to him about it?"

"No, sir. His team was the one who came up with the burner phone issue and I don't want to be seen to influence matters by pointing the finger."

Marsh's eyes grew a little wider. Inspector Pole was being political... a one-off.

"What do you suggest?"

"You might perhaps have a conversation with Commander Ferguson's superior?"

Marsh rolled his eyes. Pole's political acumen had lasted less than a second.

"That would go down like a lead balloon." Marsh pushed his back into his armchair. "However, I could perhaps have the conversation with Ferguson myself."

"That would be excellent, sir." Pole smiled amiably. Marsh was sometimes too predictable. It almost took the fun out of it.

"Fine, let me see what I can do." Marsh looked as if he had just had a brilliant idea.

Pole started to stand up. Marsh waved him back down. "Now, how about Ms Wu?"

* * *

The deafening noise was replaced by silence.

Then a voice calling her made her try to open her eyes.

"Cora… Cora…"

She felt someone heaving her body up.

The dust and soot were coming up in thick clouds. Cora started coughing.

Someone was coughing too.

"Put a cloth over your mouth," Rachel Lord shouted. "Close your eyes if you can." Cora's head movement and coughing had become more muffled.

"Get me some water," Senior Officer Lord shouted. "A bottle, quick."

Using one arm, Cora was slowly making her way up the rope she had tied around her harness. Her face emerged from the settling dust.

She was covered in grime, but she held in her left hand a piece of metal pipe. Senior Officer Lord held her hand out and managed to get hold of the rope. She hauled Cora back towards the inner windowsill. "Are you alright? You gave us a fright." She helped her to settle on the window ledge, unscrewed the bottle cap and handed it over to her. Cora took a long pull, spluttered out a bit of water and coughed.

350

"I'm sorry," she managed to utter with a croaky voice.

Senior Officer Lord climbed outside. Cora moved her legs out too, untied the rope from the harness, and jumped onto the staircase landing.

She showed them the piece of pipe she had retrieved from her props.

"Is that it?" Johnny had joined the small party on the landing.

Cora didn't reply. One end of the pipe had been hammered down so that it was almost flat. The other was sealed with a piece of metal.

Cora tried to ease it off with her fingers but found she had little grip.

She felt anger and anxiety rising in her belly. She turned around.

She had no tools available to pull off the cap.

She slammed the piece of metal on the ground with such force, everyone stepped back.

The cap flew off and out sprang a purple-coloured USB key.

# Chapter Thirty-Five

"Good morning, Ms Wu… this is your morning wake up call," the female voice chimed. "Have a very nice day."

Nancy barely managed a thank you. For a short moment she couldn't quite recall where she was.

It was 7.30am. She was in Hong Kong and had a long day ahead of her.

Her breakfast would be arriving at 8am. She had no time to lose. When the waitress rang the doorbell of the suite, Nancy was ready.

She had chosen a pair of plain light jeans, a navy T-shirt, a pair of sports shoes, but could not resist the appeal of their designer label.

She went to the door, checked first the person waiting on the other side through the small camera screen that had been mounted inside the suite. It was the same young woman who had helped her with the move to her new room. Perhaps the hotel had thought that a familiar face would help to put her at ease.

She shook her head. The poor girl must have had little sleep in between her two shifts. Still, Nancy was grateful for the thought.

The young woman was laying the table for Nancy in the living room, when Nancy's phone rang. Licot's name flashed on the screen. She pressed the reply button and moved to the bedroom.

"Professor Licot, how good of you to call me back."

"I have a full day today, but I thought we needed to talk. My first lecture starts at 10.30am. I could stop at your hotel for a chat before I continue to the academy."

"Give me half an hour. I'll be ready by then."

Nancy returned to the living area. Breakfast had been arranged tastefully on the table… French pastries, exotic fruit salad and a pot of excellent Keemun tea. She poured a cup and moved to the large window overlooking the bay.

The water of the Bay had assumed its daytime colours, an attractive green with splashes of light blue weaving in and out of it. The ferries had started their regular journey between the various islands and the mainland, leaving behind them a white trace of foam. Nancy tried to picture the rest of the island and recalled that Hong Kong territory covered 18 districts, nine in the new territories; Kowloon had five and Hong Kong Island four.

*The boat is small. It reeks of fish. She and her friend have been holding their noses with their thumb and first finger. It's yet another game. Their mothers have told them to be quiet in a tone of voice they have not heard before.*

*They stop pulling silly faces and huddle together at the back of the skiff.*

*The fisherman who agreed to take them across asks for more money just as they are about to board. Children are not welcome on this passage to freedom. They don't always keep quiet when asked to…*

*Nancy's father is bargaining, telling the man that the two little girls are well behaved and will be as good as gold. But gold is exactly what the fisherman needs. She can see a strange light in his eyes… she doesn't know what it means but it scares her. She huddles with her friend even closer.*

*The fisherman says something to her father she can't hear, and he shouts, "Never." The old man shrugs. He needs the money right now if the girls are to cross with the adults.*

*Nancy's father moves to where his wife is sitting. Nancy doesn't understand that the cost will mean parting with almost all they have left. Her mother hands over a wad of green bills. Nancy has never seen these before.*

*The boat leaves the small creek after her father and his friends have changed into old clothes. They resemble smugglers. The two little girls would like to make fun of them but their fathers' faces are too sombre to invite a tease.*

*The sun has gone up. The wind is helping the boat out onto the sea. Nancy is excited. She's never been on a boat trip before.*

The telephone ringing made her jump. Images of a past long gone, that for a moment felt so close, vanished. The hotel manager was on the phone making sure she was happy with her new room.

She was of course delighted, she reassured her. And she hoped calling the police last night had not caused too many problems. The hotel manager sighed. They were coming back today to investigate further.

* * *

The US consulate on Garden Road was not yet open. Jack rang the Consul's mobile with little success. Randy had slept without interruption. Jack had not been so successful. He had improvised a bed on the floor of the bedroom's small corridor. But despite the thickness of the carpet, sleeping on the ground was no longer what he was used to. Jack showered quickly and checked Randy was still asleep. The email he had drafted in the middle of the night, when he had woken, had not been sent yet. He read it again with a fresher head and changed a few details. As noiselessly as he could, he made himself a cup of coffee, gave the message a final read, and pressed the send button.

Hunter was almost certainly in one of his end-of-day debriefs, which gave Jack a couple of hours' reprieve.

Jack's phone buzzed as he settled against the wall of the corridor. He moved to the bathroom to take the call.

"Where are you?" Hunter's voice revealed nothing.

"Still at the Mandarin Oriental."

"Is that guy Randy with you?"

"Yes, sir."

"American citizen from what I gather."

Jack took a few seconds. Hunter had done his homework. "That's correct, sir."

"Get him to the consulate... I sent a request for extraction."

"Thank you, sir. The story is starting to make sense..."

"Perhaps." Hunter cut him short. "But Viro-Tech remains a private company. It has its headquarters in the UK; it has some American, British and Asian investors, so unless they come to offer their services to the US government, there is little we can do."

354

"I'm sure MI6 will be ready to help."

"Yet again, this is an independent British company. The UK government may take an interest in their research, but I think the Brits at the moment are more interested in drumming up tech business to rival Silicon Valley than digging into the business of a private company."

There was little Jack could add to that.

"Look Jack, I will take care of Randy Zhang. He is still in danger, so I will make sure he returns to the US safely. But nothing has changed. I need something that is actionable, here, in the US…"

Jack leaned against the bathroom sink, shaking his head. "Does it have something to do with the agreement between the Chinese and the US, where they are trying to come to terms about medical research and co-operation? Turner Junior is meant to broker the agreement, so I understand that he may be off limits because of that… at least for the time being."

Hunter's silence lasted for a long moment. "I'm not going to ask you where you got that information from…"

"Does it matter anyway, sir? If it's true, let me work behind the scenes until we can properly assess how valid Ollie Wilson and Randy Zhang's claims are. We can't keep allowing a private company to transfer technology to China, simply to do business there."

"I too have read the McCain report." Hunter surprised Jack. "It's a delicate balance at the moment. The Obama administration is aware of the issue and prepared to take action, but we need China's co-operation when it comes to epidemic containment."

"I could debrief my contact at MI6."

"It won't make any difference. The Brits and the Europeans need this deal to go through as much as we do. Bill Gates has done a good job on making governments aware of the need to protect against a new pandemic. For once, everyone seems to be in agreement. You still have 48 hours… actually 36 hours, to find something compelling against Viro-Tech. Otherwise, I want you home."

The phone went dead. "Shit… that can't be right."

"What's that?" Randy had woken up and stood, looking dishevelled, at the door of the bathroom.

"Some mixed up flight details." Jack managed to smile to Randy. "But the good news is… the US consulate is sending you home under protection."

* * *

"Let's take a little stroll," Professor Licot suggested with an amiable smile. Nancy briefly hesitated. But, of course, the Mandarin Oriental was too obvious a place for a discreet conversation.

They left the hotel by descending a few steps to arrive at street level. Licot led the way, making idle conversation about the next lecture he was about to give, and the growing interest in contemporary art in Hong Kong.

They walked one block, arriving at a flight of stairs with access to the hanging corridors Hong Kong was famous for. Whenever monsoon struck, these were used regularly by residents to avoid the street, where they could be swept away by torrential rain in an instant.

Nancy recalled one of those occasions. It had been terrifying to see the water lashing at her windows and the rain filling up the streets to almost waist level.

Licot courteously moved aside to let her climb the staircase ahead of him. She stopped at the top. Licot indicated they should turn left and they followed the network of corridors which connected above the road system.

She had no idea where she was and for a short moment wondered whether she should follow Licot so readily. He must have sensed her unease.

"We're almost there. It's much more pleasant to take the corridors, and more discreet too."

"I'm not sure I would be able to tell if someone was trailing me. The corridors are still very busy."

"But I would." Professor Licot smiled.

Nancy raised an eyebrow but said nothing. Licot stepped ahead as they exited to rejoin ground level. They arrived in a part of Hong Kong that looked modern. Tall buildings that were, however, no match for the skyscrapers rising to over 20 or 30 floors in the most recently built areas.

"It's the part of Hong Kong that was built in the early 60s. It looked fancy then but things have changed dramatically."

The streets were much narrower. The square façades of the buildings constructed from large concrete blocks had been rendered unevenly. Some had been freshly painted in light blue or green colours. Others had their external render peeling off.

Nancy noted the name of the street, Stratton Street. That turned into a small lane, the stones of its walls green with moss and the paving slippery from the lack of sun.

Professor Licot entered a small tea shop. He walked straight through the crowd of regular customers minding their own business. He turned into a small private room at the back.

"Here we are. We'll be safe to have our chat here."

Licot took a seat at the table large enough for eight. Nancy sat opposite. Tea materialised within a few minutes.

"If you like Chinese tea, this in my opinion is the best... aged pu-erh tea."

"Aged for 27 years..." Nancy grinned. "I haven't had this for a very long time."

Professor Licot waited a moment, poured some tea into his cup and raised it to his nose. "Perfect..."

He poured Nancy a cup. "I'm sorry I couldn't speak in front of Philippe yesterday."

"Don't apologise." Nancy took her cup in both hands to warm her fingers. "I don't want him to be involved in something that is becoming... well... more dangerous by the minute, it seems."

Licot nodded. "It's dangerous for many parties." He drank some tea, grunted in approval, and continued.

"I must repeat that I don't know what happened to your father when he went back to China. The artists I knew told me they lost touch with him very suddenly."

"But I presume you know more about the circumstances of his return." Nancy took a sip as well. She closed her eyes... the tea was deliciously aromatic and smooth.

"The answers you are looking for are no longer in Hong Kong." Licot hesitated. "You'll have to go to mainland China to find them."

Nancy put down her cup slowly. She had been expecting as much, but now that Licot had told her, the old enemy had reappeared... fighting the dragon once more.

"What is your involvement in all this, Professor Licot? I need to know a little more from you, if you don't mind, before I contemplate embarking on a trip back to a country I left..." She was looking for the right word. "Left in a way no one should ever have to leave the country where they were born."

"That's fair, which is why we are here." Licot had almost finished his cup. He topped up Nancy's cup before helping himself to more tea. "Hong Kong has long been a place of transit for people who seek to escape the mainland... It was very much so whilst it remained a British colony, of course, but the transfer of Hong Kong to China has made things more complicated."

"Hong Kong has a special status though..."

"Exactly, and we are using this to help people reach freedom if they are threatened in mainland China."

Nancy pulled back a little, seeing Licot with a fresh eye. "Are you telling me you're part of a network that smuggles people to the free world?"

Licot smiled. "Who would suspect a boring middle-aged Professor of Contemporary Art? Academics have sometimes a bad reputation for supporting liberal views, but the days of the Cultural Revolution are long gone and I don't profess radical ideas."

"I presume your network straddles mainland China and Hong Kong?"

"That's right, but I would rather not discuss the details."

"How long has the network existed?"

"Over 20 years..."

"Did my father use the network to get out of Hong Kong? Is that how you knew him?"

"I think you're slightly mistaking the nature of his involvement. He created that network. He knew what it took to make that journey. He had done it twice already."

Nancy bit her lip. She stood up slowly and walked over to the window that overlooked a small courtyard. She wished she was in the middle of nowhere, so that she could scream.

Licot waited patiently until she had managed to quell her emotions. "I'm sorry," Nancy said.

"Don't be... it's a lot to take in after so many years."

"Where in China must I go?"

"Chengdu, Sichuan province."

* * *

"The content of my USB keys should help you, but it won't be enough." Randy was sitting in yet another bedroom. This time within the US consulate compound. Jack looked at the devices. He'd made a copy that he handed over to Randy.

"What would I find in there?"

"All the research that I did on the project that Ollie and I worked on. It's enough to give you the details of how far I went in the mapping of the viruses we were studying. How they invade the human body, and how to trigger the human immune system against them."

"Enough to convince the military that it can be used for bio-attacks or super soldier creation?"

"Not quite. The work that covered that aspect was researched by Ollie, which is the reason why he wanted to talk to you."

Jack couldn't disguise his irritation; evidence seemed to be slipping thought his hands every time he thought he was making progress.

"Apologies... Viro-Tech splits our work and controls our ability to exchange information... at least when it comes to controversial research. It's not always helpful but they are trying to protect the technology, or at least that was the reason given to us."

"What would Ollie have seen that was worrying him?"

"The way to engineer genetic manipulation. He was very good at building complex information systems to manipulate all the data that is required to understand the genetics of viruses, and how they interact with the human body. He extended that expertise to understanding and mapping how human genetics could be modified to fight virus-induced diseases."

Jack looked at his watch. It was already 10.30am and he had made little progress with his attempt to convince Hunter he had something concrete against Viro-Tech.

"Would Ollie have tried to save data in the same way as you did?"

"I'm sure he would have done. We both started talking about the issues we faced a couple of months back, because we knew we could trust each other."

"But he did not confirm that he had done so to you?"

"We discussed preserving the data. But it was complicated to speak, and Ollie was concerned he was being followed. I guess he was right." Randy slumped against the headrest of the bed. He pulled an old tissue from his back pocket and blew his nose.

"I'm sorry, pal... I didn't mean to upset you." Jack grabbed a chair and came to sit next to Randy.

"I know. It's just been a tough few months for a guy like me. I'm a biotech researcher... not a marine."

"And you've done really well. But is there anything else that could help me bring down this bastard Turner?"

"Perhaps... perhaps... Ollie got the feeling Turner wanted to export the lab research to China. I don't know where that lab would be located but Ollie was certain that that was the only way Viro-Tech could get away with their development plans."

Jack nodded. "How big would that lab have to be?"

"Could be part of a bigger complex, but it would require the right specialist equipment... still I don't know where that place could be."

It didn't matter now. Jack knew where to look... Jared Turner had been making regular trips to one distinct location in China for the past few months.

# Chapter Thirty-Six

His Ducati was parked at the side of one of the hospital's buildings. Pole moved closer to the bike rack and parked in such a way that he could drive off quickly. Cora had done an excellent job at relaying the news. Ollie had woken up from his coma. It was unexpected, but the doctors were very positive about his progress. Even Branning was convinced. The discovery of the USB key had perhaps helped Cora to feel the joy she might otherwise have found difficult to summon.

The registrar at UCH had also been most helpful. He called Cora at the time agreed beforehand. She played the game of surprise, and then of delight.

Pole rested the bike on its stand and leaned against it. He kept his helmet on. The intercom headset within it was connected to Andy's radio. Everyone was in position: Andy in the hospital lobby, Mandy on the ward where Ollie was.

Cora had planned a visit as soon as the ward was open, it was almost time. She had told as many friends as she could manage. She was hoping to visit him and speak to him in the morning.

None of her friends had been told the truth: neither Johnny, Beth nor Nat. All of them had taken to their Facebook page and other social media accounts to share the good news.

Pole checked his watch again. Branning had just called in. They were on their way. Cora would be walking through the hospital doors within 20 minutes. Pole moved to the corner of the street. If something was to happen, it would be now. A couple of women matching the description of the woman they were tracking had entered the entrance to the tube at Balham an hour ago. His headset crackled a little as Andy's voice came through.

"The nurses are changing shift."

"Who is inside Ollie's room at the moment?"

"No one... PC William has stepped away as agreed." Mandy's voice was low. "I'm two doors away and I have a good view of the corridor that leads to his room."

"I have some movement..." Andy's voice interrupted. "I see a tall woman that matches the description entering the building... she's wearing a biker jacket and a rucksack. She's just taking off her helmet." Andy closed his laptop, stood up and made his way to the bank of lifts. The doors closed before he could reach them without arousing suspicion. The woman had already stepped in, and disappeared behind the closing doors.

"She's going down to the basement."

"Mandy – did you get that?" Pole's voice sounded a little fuzzy. "I have... is there anywhere she can change down there?"

"Probably the toilets... From what I could see she is blonde with a short bob... but she may change her hairstyle."

More people came out of another lift. Andy hesitated. "I'm staying put on the ground floor."

They all remained quiet for a long 10 minutes. Pole checked his mobile a few times. The woman needed time to change clothes and would need to wait for all the people who might have seen her entering a cubicle to have left.

"A new nurse is coming my way." Mandy's voice was the first to break the silence.

The registrar had provided Pole and his team with photos of the female staff who would be coming on duty for the morning shift. No one had called in sick; there would be no new faces on the ward.

"Damn... it's one of the regular nurses."

"Patience. She'll turn up." Pole's voice pacified everyone. He was not so sure himself. It had to work, but it was still a gamble.

Branning's voice came in to confirm that he and Cora were now on Euston Road, approaching the UCH building.

"Come on..." Pole mumbled.

"Sir... most of the nurses have arrived... all regulars."

"Shit... this is cutting it fine. She's got to act now, otherwise it will be too late."

"She's here... she hasn't changed her hair... blonde, short bob, really tall... and not on the registrar's list."

Pole could hear Mandy moving around. "She's gone towards the nurses' room... No, she just walked past it."

Mandy kept up her commentary. "I can't see her now, so either she has gone into one of the patient's rooms or... the medication room."

Pole moved back to his bike. "Is there any way you can get closer to the medication room?"

"It's at the far end of the corridor. If I do, I'll lose sight of Ollie's room."

"What now?"

"Nothing... I can't see her anywhere..."

Branning's voice interrupted. "We're just walking out of the car park and entering the reception area."

"Just hold back a little, Branning, we have movement near Ollie's room." Pole cut in. "Mandy?... PC William?"

"Yes, sir," Officer William responded.

"Can you see Ollie Wilson's room?"

"I can't... I'm standing away at the moment, as instructed."

"Has Mandy moved back towards the room?"

"I can't see her, sir."

"DS Branning, where are you?"

"We are just entering the building, but we can delay going up."

"Get there right now... Mandy is in trouble."

Branning didn't answer. His large frame sprang into action. He placed his foot between the doors of the next lift about to leave for the upper floors.

"Mandy... do you read?"

"PC William... go back to Ollie's room. Check he's OK."

"I can get there too, Guv." Andy had started to move towards the lift as soon as he heard Branning's instructions.

"Sorry, Andy... you stay put. We can't let her escape this time."

"Mandy..." Branning's voice was anxious. "Are you OK?"

"Sorry, sir… she must have been hiding… she's got into Ollie's room."

The sound of broken glass and metal resounded in Pole's ear. Someone was running. It had to be Branning.

PC William's intercom had gone dead too.

Pole hesitated. He could ask Andy to join them, but he needed him to identify the woman.

"Branning, do you need backup?"

"Stay where you are!" Branning was shouting. "You don't need to do this… I said…"

Movement, broken glass… people thrashing around, voices grunting in the effort of a fight. A body crashing down… the sound of footsteps running away and fading in the distance.

"Andy… she's getting away." Pole straddled his bike and fired it up. "She won't be taking the lift or going through the main door… where is the emergency exit from Ollie's wing?"

"At the back of the building… retrace your steps and turn right into Grafton Way."

"Branning is down. Take over the co-ordination inside the hospital… I'm going after her."

Pole turned the bike in one sweep against the oncoming traffic. He accelerated, cars sounding their horns at him. He moved into Grafton Way at full speed. There were a couple of bikes parked at the back of the building.

A tall woman wearing a nurse's uniform ran towards them. She had thrown away her wig and blonde curls were loose down her back. She had picked up her biker jacket, ready for escape. Her helmet was secured on the handlebar of her bike. With a controlled move she freed it and slammed it on her head.

She straddled the bike just as Pole had only a hundred yards to reach her.

She noticed his Ducati rushing towards her. She throttled up and launched back down the street taking a sharp left into the one-way system.

Her bike only just missed a bus that braked to avoid her. Pole accelerated too, driving against the flow of traffic.

364

She was driving down Tottenham Court Road against oncoming cars. This was complete madness. Pole had no choice but to follow. She swerved between lorries and buses with surprising ease. Pole's Ducati was less manoeuvrable, or perhaps he had less experience of escaping pursuit and he lost ground.

The crossroads between Tottenham Court Road and Oxford Street was approaching fast. From a distance Pole could see the lights had turned amber, within a few seconds traffic would start flowing across her path... there was no way through.

The woman throttled up.

"Shit... she won't make it." But Pole accelerated too. He would have to brake soon if he was to miss the cars that were about to drive across his path.

"No..." Pole shouted despite himself. Two buses following one another moved across swiftly. Her bike span round, attempting to squeeze into the small gap between the two vehicles. She avoided the first, attempted a U-turn to avoid the second... too late.

Pole applied the brakes as hard as he could without risking being thrown over the handlebars. He too had waited too long. Pole threw himself off the bike, rolling onto his side, a human spinning ball.

* * *

Licot had agreed to take Nancy to Sichuan. He hadn't been sure whether it could be arranged so quickly, but it seemed whoever his contact was, their network had managed to help with the formalities.

"I usually deal with people coming out here, and I visit regularly on my own account as well when I lecture, so an extra trip shouldn't raise too much suspicion."

"And what is my storyline?"

"You're a collector – which you are – and I am introducing you to new emerging local artists, with a view to purchasing some pieces."

"Very plausible..."

"As long as they don't ask why in Sichuan and not in Beijing... it will be fine."

"And as long as they don't connect me with my father... I get it."

"They will, but it will take a few days. You haven't set foot in China since you left, so we have a bit of extra leeway."

"I'm happy for you to pretend you didn't know I was his daughter."

"Trust me, if they make the connection, they'll soon locate the articles I've written about him. Anyway, no need to panic... yet."

"Are you certain you need to come with me?"

"Positive... and I haven't been to Sichuan for a while."

"Very well... I'll meet you at Hong Kong International Airport tomorrow, at 7am."

Nancy stood up from the seat she had chosen in the hotel's lobby to make her call. She had half a day to get ready for a trip back to a country she had not visited for over 40 years. She reached her suite, flashed the key card in front of the electronic eye of the door and pushed open its heavy wooden panel.

The maid had drawn the curtains open across the spectacular views of Hong Kong Bay.

Nancy dropped her rucksack in the corridor and strode towards the windows.

A large hand fell over her mouth and an arm wrapped itself around her torso.

"Please, don't scream... I need to speak to you... about Viro-Tech."

Nancy slammed her elbow into the man's stomach. He grunted but only eased off his hold slowly. She freed herself in a sharp move. "Who the bloody hell are you?" Nancy's voice shook with anger.

She scanned the room for a possible weapon.

"We have a common acquaintance and a common target..." The man raised his hands to show he was not armed.

"I'm listening." Nancy retreated towards the bar where she had spotted a few heavy bottles that might do nicely, if she had to put up a fight.

"Inspector Jonathan Pole and Jared Turner." Nancy frowned and ran a critical eye over him.

"I've seen you before... you were on the flight from Heathrow to Hong Kong."

"That's right." He gave her an appreciative nod. "Well spotted."

"Flattery will get you nowhere... you could have picked up those names from a multitude of sources, not necessarily friendly to me."

"Perhaps Inspector Pole has mentioned a British connection in a particular agency..."

The man's bluntness surprised her. "Yet again... no real evidence you are connected even loosely to that agency." Nancy wondered whether the price MI6 would be asking for the information she had received was due.

"You're looking for your father who disappeared 30 years ago on a trip back to mainland China. You have been given information by a couple of contacts at MI6."

"And there is no free lunch, of course?"

The man smiled. "There never is in this business, but at least I can tell you a lot more about the Ollie Wilson case. Randy Zhang is now safely on his way back to the US."

"That's not going to go down very well with Jared Turner." Nancy relaxed a fraction.

"He won't discover that just yet. Still, we haven't got enough to nail him for what he's done... We need... I need harder evidence before my government agrees to grab this guy."

"Viro-Tech is a private company... so unless you can show there is..." Nancy stopped, pondered for a moment and shot Jack a sideways look. "You want to force the US and UK governments to recognise that the research Ollie and Randy were doing is of national interest... in other words, no longer suitable for transfer to an external power."

It was the man's turn to look surprised. "I'm... impressed."

"I have represented very many different types of interests in my career, Mr...?"

"Jack."

"Jack... and I'm pretty good at getting to the crux of a matter quickly."

Jack nodded. "So I've been told... but it's good to see it first-hand."

Nancy straightened up and gave up the idea of throwing a bottle of Scotch or two at Jack. She indicated they should sit down.

"What do you need from me?"

"I believe you are on your way to Sichuan."

Nancy paused on her way to the couch. "Do I need to be concerned that agencies around the globe are aware of my travel arrangements?"

"Nope. You're not being tracked by the Chinese... of that I am pretty certain."

Nancy breathed in slowly. This was not entirely reassuring but it would have to do.

"The only way we are going to convince our respective governments to take the implications of the Viro-Tech research seriously is to find out details about their planned operation in China."

Nancy sat down opposite Jack.

"In case you hadn't noticed, I'm not taking a scenic tour round that country. I am in and out as quickly as possible and I am certainly not going to Beijing. The only place I intend to go to is Chengdu," she said.

"And Chengdu is exactly the place we are looking at."

* * *

His entire body screamed in pain. He could hear through his helmet someone speaking to him. Pole sat up and raised his visor. He nodded to the man who had crouched near him, trying to help. The comms with his team were shattered. He stood up on unsteady legs.

"Perhaps you should wait until the ambulance arrives."

"I need to check that woman." Pole staggered to the scene of the crash. His bike was now trapped underneath the front of one of the buses and the woman's bike had lodged itself underneath the other bus. Pole hobbled as quickly as he could over to the place where her bike was now immobile.

A crowd of pedestrians were assembled around a body that had rolled near the kerb, lying on the ground motionless.

Pole took out his police ID and asked people to give way. She was on her back, her jacket had been turned almost inside out and the nurse's uniform was in shreds.

Pole knew better than to try to remove the helmet, but he slid up the visor. He shook his head in disbelief. There was Cora's friend, Nat, looking pale and lifeless.

The sound of two ambulances made him stand up. The paramedics rushed towards them. A small Asian man took Nat's pulse. "She's alive but the pulse is faint."

"Where are you taking her? UCH?"

"That's the closest."

How ironic. She was being taken back to the very hospital they had come from.


A police car had arrived to cordon off the area. Pole spoke to the officer in charge and asked for a lift back to rejoin his team.

"Andy... I'm on my way back."

"Mandy and PC William are OK, but DS Branning is in a bad way."

"Nat Price is barely alive." Pole took his DS through the chase.

They were coming back to UCH, directly to A&E.

When Pole arrived back on Ollie's ward, Andy was holding a tea for both Mandy and PC William. They looked a little bruised but otherwise alright.

"Branning?" Pole's voice shook a little.

"They are operating... the scalpel she used to fight him off made a large gash in his neck... very close to the jugular artery."

"Half an inch and he would have..." Mandy let the phrase hang. "How about you, Guv?"

"Just a few bruises... nothing to worry about. The ambulance team checked me over."

"They brought her in 25 minutes before you arrived." Mandy took a sip of tea. "They wouldn't say anything about her condition."

"I tried to confirm her ID." Andy looked a little off himself.

"No need... As I told you, I'm absolutely certain it is Nat Price."

"How do you know?"

"She is... was... one of Cora's closest friends."

Those holding teas concentrated on their drinks, and Pole turned around to find the vending machine. "Where is Cora in all of this?"

"I've sent her back home with a police escort."

Pole was about to ask how Cora had taken the news they had caught the suspect, when a senior nurse came out of the operating theatre.

"How is he doing?" Pole moved towards him.

"Not out of the woods yet."

"Any news about the woman?"

"They are running a CT scan."

"Is she conscious?" Pole couldn't quite believe she had survived.

"She is, although we have given her something to calm her down. Amazing after the battering she's taken."

"You need to show me where you've taken her."

"Sorry, but that information is for medical personnel only." Pole took out his ID again.

"Sorry, but she is incredibly dangerous, and the reason why one of my officers is on the operating table at the moment," Pole said.

The nurse went pale and moved the heavy translucent plastic door aside. "I'll show you where she is."

Pole nodded to Andy to follow them.

# Chapter Thirty-Seven

"I am finding the answers to some of my questions… Father always seemed a mysterious and complex person. I dismissed it as just the memory of a child, but perhaps I was right." Nancy had sent a long voice message to Pole. She had tried to call him at 2pm London time, hoping he would be busy. She didn't want to have to lie to him about the Sichuan trip. She had spent the rest of the day planning her trip, thinking about how she would be able to help Jack in his request.

It was time to get as much rest as possible. The next 48 hours would be gruelling. But the thought of not knowing how Pole was, kept her awake more than the trip to Sichuan. She had made up her mind about her return. There was no more room for prevarication or fear.

She drifted into sleep, but thoughts kept pulling her back to consciousness. Her father, if he had survived, would be 78 years old. What would she do if he stood there in front of her? She moved around to find a more comfortable position. She would know tomorrow.

Nancy had woken up early and made herself ready for her trip. The limo was now gliding along the highway to the airport. A small bag and rucksack were all she had packed. She had decided on a simple pair of jeans, a white T-shirt, a dark blue leather jacket but kept her designer trainers.

Licot was already at the airport when she arrived. He handed over her ticket and her passport with a temporary Chinese visa. It was good for 30 days, but she didn't intend to spend more than two days on the mainland.

"Who are we flying with?"

"First leg of the journey, Cathay Pacific... then an internal flight, with Air China."

"How about the transfer between the international and local terminals at Shanghai?" Nancy was reading the details of the flight.

"Not really a problem... you're not arriving at Shanghai International. It's considered an internal flight."

Nancy nodded. They started queuing for the check in. The line of people waiting for passport control was short. Nancy followed Licot, her heart banging against her rib cage. In a few moments she would be one step closer to setting foot back on Chinese ground.

Licot turned back and smiled. His relaxed manner gave her confidence.

The first part of the flight very much resembled any other international flight Nancy had taken. She was prepared for a staggering difference in quality when it came to the internal flight, but the Air China Airbus was comfortably kitted out. Licot had chosen business class. He was travelling with a wealthy client and that choice made sense. There were very few women on the flight, and most of the male passengers were sporting the requisite dark suit and white shirt.

Nancy had picked up a non-contentious book to read during the flight, but she couldn't focus on the pages. She was only a few hours away from the place where she'd been born so many years ago. Glimpses of her grandfather's garden kept coming back. The colour of the flowers, the glitter of the water in the pond... and the distinct smell of Sichuan pepper trees.

Nancy unclipped her seat belt, stood up and made her way to the bathroom. She didn't want to remember the past just yet. She splashed some water on her face gently... "Take it one step at a time," she murmured.

"When we disembark, we'll take a taxi to a little restaurant..." Licot announced as the plane was preparing for landing.

Nancy nodded. The seat belt sign came on. She was not a nervous flier, but this time she clutched the armrests with both hands.

The photos she had kept of her childhood sprang before her eyes, tearing her between anger and hope.

The gentle bump of the aircraft told her they had landed. The plane taxied for a few hundred yards and came to a stop.

Passengers were standing up. She slid into her leather jacket, making herself ready to step into a country she should have called hers.

* * *

The ICU room looked disturbingly familiar. Pole had spent a little too much time on the ward for his liking in recent days. He approached the bed on which Natalie Price was lying. Despite the protests of the nurse, he had fitted Nat with a set of handcuffs. One around her wrist, the other locked over the metal frame of the bed.

"This is not a prison," the nurse muttered.

"Perhaps not, but one of my officers is having his neck sewn back together because of what this woman did. Although he will pull through and that's a relief, I wouldn't want that to happen to you."

This did the trick. The young man retreated into the corridor without a word.

Pole had spoken to the specialist who'd carried out Natalie's brain scan. It was miraculous that she had no brain damage, or even a broken bone, despite the force of the crash. The doctor had allowed Pole to spend just a few minutes with her. She had been drifting in and out of sleep, but the medication the paramedics had given her was slowly wearing off.

Pole took a chair and sat down next to her bed.

Her eyelids fluttered a few times. She was awake. Her restrained hand had moved a few times. Natalie knew she was in handcuffs.

"If you can hear me, listen carefully, Natalie.' Pole bent forward a little to deliver his message. "I have enough evidence to link you to the intimidation of Cora Wong on the Regent's Canal seven days ago, the attempted murder of Ollie Wilson four days ago and, of course, today's attempt which resulted in three of my officers being hurt, one of them now in a critical condition. This is not only going to send you to jail for a very long time, but it's also going to piss off your Russian handlers. And, as you know, they are not the sort of people who tolerate failure."

Natalie's face had changed from relaxed to frozen.

"The Russian or Bratva is not a forgiving gang, and you just failed them not once, but twice. I doubt you will complete your prison term, or that you will even live to come to trial," Pole said, dismissively.

Natalie opened her eyes wide. The hatred in them had changed their colour to the harshest of blues.

"I'm not talking, if that is what you have in mind." Her speech was a little slurred, but she was fully conscious.

"You've not been listening…" Pole moved closer to the bed, ignoring the venom in her tone. "I don't need you to own up to what you've done. I have plenty of evidence to send you to jail for a very, very long time. What I am prepared to do, however, is to offer you a deal."

"I don't need a deal. I need a lawyer."

"I'll get you a lawyer, if you like, but once I make the call there will be no turning back." Pole's voice kept an eerie calm. "At the moment you've just been brought into ICU, looking all but dead. The fact that you have escaped unscathed is almost a miracle."

"Lucky me."

"But if I get you onto the witness protection programme, I'll make sure you vanish today. You will become witness X. You'll be given a new identity, and can even move country, if that is what you want. Natalie Price will have died of her injuries after a terrible motorbike crash."

Silence filled the room. Pole didn't move. His eyes rested lightly on her face. Fear had crept slowly into her expression.

"I know you do drugs, a lot of it… Cocaine and heroin are expensive habits that you can get rid of. It's now or never, Natalie." Pole moved his head slightly to look at his watch. "I'm going to get a coffee and when I come back, you can give me your answer." He stood up in a slow and deliberate motion.

"Sod off." Natalie turned her head towards the wall.

* * *

"They've just left for Chengdu," Jack said as he found a seat in the first floor of the internet kiosk at Hong Kong airport. Harris should have been sound asleep at 1.30am London time, but he had been expecting Jack's call.

"How long have you got?" Harris asked.

"Till tomorrow night… but since there is no non-stop flight leaving for New York after the deadline expires, I'll be on the 3.40pm American Airlines flight the following day."

374

"Unless Hunter shoves you onto a military plane that just happens to be flying by."

"That's always a possibility, but I guess he would've done it by now if he had been that pissed off. He is interested in the intel, he just can't tell me that yet."

"On that subject." Harris was moving around the room. Jack imagined him brewing himself yet another cup of tea… the remedy for all ills, according to his British friend. "I was wondering which one of us was going to broach the subject first, but I suppose it will be me this time."

"You mean, why are the US and the UK governments tiptoeing so much around Turner father and son?"

"Yep… the word at MI6 is that a co-operation agreement between China and some other countries is due to be signed in the next few days."

"Hunter hasn't confirmed the date, but he is being pricklier than usual… if that is at all possible."

"DCI Pole is doing pretty well in building a case against Viro-Tech and Turner Junior. It would be a shame if he had to be told not to proceed."

"Turner Senior has been backed up by some top-level politicians and senior businesspeople in the US."

"Turner Junior doesn't seem to be as formidable as Turner Senior in the UK, but it doesn't mean daddy won't interfere."

"Pole has got his hands on the USB key that we presume was hidden by Ollie Wilson…"

Jack interrupted his friend. "Randy has also stored data that should help to confirm that what they were developing could have lethal implications."

"Wilson's USB key has been through a fire though. There was little left on the device… apart from a line of code… that's it."

"How well equipped is Scotland Yard to retrieve that sort of information?"

"You mean they're not the FBI… but you might be surprised how good at it they are."

Jack shook his head, as though Harris could see him. "I didn't mean it that way. But some additional help with complex technology could be a bonus."

"If there is something there… they'll find it."

"But could you get me the line of code?"

"Possibly… what do you have in mind?"

"What if it is not a piece of code?"

\* \* \*

A row of yellow-and-black taxis had formed along the taxi stand outside Chengdu airport. Nancy looked around at the crowd that seemed to be moving as one. People speaking loudly on their phones, jostling for position wherever they went or bumping into one another without noticing.

Licot gently took her arm and guided her towards one of the cabs. The driver took a quick look at his passengers, sizing them up. Chengdu was a large city, but not one that many foreign tourists visited.

Professor Licot gave instructions in Chinese, and the man was surprised to understand what he was saying straight away.

Nancy's sense of discomfort had just risen a notch. She hadn't understood any of it, and would certainly not have been able to converse with the driver. A lump lodged itself in her throat. If her father were still alive, she would have to speak to him in English – or perhaps French – if he still remembered how.

The car turned abruptly into traffic and joined the throng of other vehicles leaving the airport. They soon came to a flyover that arched towards the east and rose in the air to overlook the suburbs of Chengdu. Endless rows of mid-height buildings, perhaps 12 or 14 storeys tall, kept coming like well-arranged dominoes. The uniformity of construction was staggering, the same rectangular shapes, pinkish-grey stone and small, white-painted balconies. Though the city was leafier than she had imagined it would be.

The car veered right at one of the side exit roads, driving straight towards the lower ground. It turned right again to join another motorway. This time the surroundings looked more industrial, large buildings with sprawling car parks and rows of cars awaiting their drivers' journey home.

Licot said nothing. Nancy also felt no need to talk. The reacquaintance with her own country was more bemusement than shock.

The driver asked a question. Licot replied. Again, he didn't offer to translate. She didn't ask him to.

The vehicle slowed down as they were about to cross a bridge and Nancy edged her body towards the window to take a glance at the river. She tried to remember whether her grandfather's house had even been close to one. The area they were moving through now was a mix of residential, small industrial... shops had started to appear. More people were going about their business. It could have been a typical UK high street... A few restaurants, food stores, electrical goods shops, and the entrance to a building that looked like a covered market. The car slowed to a standstill, took a quick U-turn and stopped in front of a tea house. Licot paid and thanked the driver. Nancy got out of the cab. They both waited for a moment before they spoke.

"Where are we?" Nancy had tried to memorise the journey, but she doubted she would find her way back even if she tried.

"It's a residential area, not very well off and where we are going to stick out like a sore thumb if we don't hurry."

They walked through a few backstreets. Nancy felt helpless for a moment. She tried to shake herself out of it by concentrating on her surroundings. It was not too late to go back.

Licot got out his mobile and made a call.

Within a few minutes a car appeared, an old battered Citroën. The driver didn't get out. The journey started again towards an area that looked poorer and older. The car finally stopped in front of a squalid building that resembled a factory and, to Nancy's amazement, she recognised a word on the sign above the entrance – 'noodle'. She closed her eyes, making an effort to recall its Chinese pronunciation.

*Miantiao...*

Licot smiled at her. "That's right. It's a noodle factory."

They walked along the lane that led round to the back of the building towards a smaller construction that looked like a canteen.

The place was empty as they entered. Licot moved confidently towards a smaller room at the back. Nancy took her time, cautious and yet intrigued by the smell of the food that pervaded the place.

There were three cups of tea arranged on the small table at the centre of the room. They were expected.

Nancy felt weak and she leaned with one hand against the wall. Licot didn't seem to notice. He looked at his watch, took his mobile out of his inner jacket pocket and called. "*Women daole,*" Licot said in Chinese.

They had arrived and the person meeting them now knew.

Nancy made an effort to walk to the table, every step felt as though she was walking through deep sand.

The back door opened and someone walked in, stopping after a few steps.

Nancy drew her hand to her mouth… impossible.

\* \* \*

"The nurse told me you could drink a little tea." Pole placed a cup on Nat's bedside table.

"I'm not changing my mind."

Pole shrugged. "Suit yourself." He continued drinking his coffee. Natalie's jaw had clenched so hard he could hear the sound of her grinding teeth. "In a few moments you're going to need your fix. The hospital deal with junkies all the time, but they still need to have authorisation to administer methadone… so it's going to take a while, a long while."

"So what…"

"And then… I will take over and it can take a bit of time to get that authorisation too… the police system can be a bit congested at times."

"I'm not well enough to be discharged."

"Unfortunately, for you… your scan has just come back and you are as good as new, except for a few bruises. A bit of good luck for both of us."

"Shame you didn't end up under the wheels of that bloody bus."

"Well, I didn't." Pole had almost finished his cup. "I have only a little coffee left to drink. I'll finish it. Then you can tell me what you want to do."

Natalie closed her eyes and yanked on the handcuff.

Pole kept concentrating on his drink. He took a final sip, stood up and dumped the cup in the wastebin.

"The Bratva don't forgive. And even if you're the girlfriend of one of these guys, that will make zero difference... you are expendable and, more importantly, you failed, big time." Pole spoke whilst moving slowly towards the door.

He gave a final look over his shoulder. Rage on her face made her otherwise attractive features bulge. She threw her free hand over her face, the other stopped on its course by the restriction of the cuff.

"Time's up, Natalie. You die, one way or another. You speak to me... you get to be reborn. You stay silent... well, you know the deal." Pole placed his hand on the door to pull it open.

"What do you want to know?"

"Who is the man behind all this?"

Natalie's head turned towards the wall. "Turner."

"How do you know it's him?"

"Because it's rare for the Bratva to do contract killing outside the gang world... that's not their business."

"So, your boss... or boyfriend... what is he called?" Pole had moved to the seat he had occupied earlier, next to her bed.

"Dimitri..." Natalie murmured.

"Dimitri what?"

"Rezmikov..."

"Rezmikov asked you to do this as a favour to Turner because they are in business together?"

Natalie nodded.

"Opium from Afghanistan, Herat province... turned into heroin that floods the European market." Tears started pouring from Natalie's eyes.

"I want him, Natalie..."

"Yes..." Her voice shuddered.

"The problem, Natalie, is that it is your word against Turner's, and if we protect you as witness X, the department is still going to need to disclose your testimony."

Natalie mumbled a few words that Pole couldn't make out.

"I didn't get that," Pole snapped.

"I have proof." She pressed the palm of her free hand against both her eyes in turn, drying her tears. "I made some recordings on my phone, just in case..."

"That's much better... and where are these recordings?"

"Still in a mailbox I created on purpose."

Pole rose slowly. "If the content is as promising as you say... we have a deal."

# Chapter Thirty-Eight

The light cheek bones, the unmistakable slant of the almond eyes, the distinctive button nose… these were features Nancy recognised instantly. But it was not her father that stood in front of her, it was a young woman in her early 30s. She had walked in without a word and she was standing motionless a few feet away from Nancy.

Her calm was impressive. It seemed she knew the shock she had triggered was immense and that Nancy needed a moment, perhaps a long moment to accept who she was, to accept Nancy had a half-sister.

Nancy's mind had gone blank. Of all the outcomes she anticipated, this one she had not envisaged. She was unprepared. If her mind had gone limp, her emotions were raging… pain, anger, betrayal, but somehow hope, joy, had crept in amongst them.

The young woman still hadn't moved and the expression in her eyes was kind. Nancy thought she had seen a flicker of hope too.

Nancy took a step forward, her legs leaden. She wanted to ask a question… struggled to find the Chinese for it. She tried to remember. The effort required was enormous.

"Who are you? *Ni shi shei*?" She repeated the Chinese, not certain her pronunciation was correct.

The woman broke into a smile and that smile squeezed Nancy's heart. If she was in doubt, the handsome smile took it away instantly. "My name is Mingmei," she nodded. Her English was accented but Nancy could tell she was fluent.

"But you are…?" Nancy couldn't quite bring herself to ask the right question.

Mingmei nodded again. She had taken a step forward, towards the table that separated them. Nancy had also closed the gap.

She could take one final step, sit at the table and hear her newly found sister's story, or she could just walk out, fly back to Hong Kong, to London, to the life she had led until now in complete ignorance.

But the veil had been lifted. She wanted to know the truth. No matter how hurtful that truth might be. Nancy wanted the courage to hear about her father who had always been in her eyes so righteous.

Pain and anger tore at her for a short moment and yet…

Nancy took the final step slowly. She moved the chair away from the table, lifting it in a measured movement, and took a seat to listen.

She had lost count of the number of cups of tea she had drunk. Nancy listened, pausing, asking very few questions. The sun was now low on the horizon and the room was getting dark. Mingmei stood up and switched on the light; a single tube, fixed to the ceiling, flickered and finally came to life. They both squinted and smiled.

"Where are you staying?"

"Professor Licot has booked a room for me at the Shangri La Hotel in the centre of Chengdu."

"It's a good choice… quite a few tourists are there. It's the most popular for visitors from abroad."

Nancy felt odd suddenly. Mingmei was working in a factory that produced food and by all accounts didn't seem to be very wealthy. She was at the other end of the spectrum and had booked a hotel room for her in a five-star hotel.

"It's OK." Mingmei smiled. "I'm comfortable… it doesn't look like it here, but the business is doing well and it's the perfect cover."

"How long have you been running this operation… I mean helping people leave China?"

"Since Father disappeared… there were a few months when I didn't know whether I would be able to cope." Mingmei's voice trailed off as she recalled that time. "But Father had already managed to put together a couple of safe routes, as well as gather people on the ground, ready to help."

"And what can I do to help? I must be able to contribute some-how."

Her sister tilted her head. "I'm not sure yet... I need to think."

"Of course, I wouldn't want to endanger your operation."

They both fell silent for a moment.

"It's probably not a good idea if I come back here to visit. Licot and I need to meet a few artists before I leave for Hong Kong again... although..." Nancy hesitated. "I could extend my stay."

"Don't do that. The government will want to know why, and it might look suspicious.... Anything that is a deviation will look suspicious to the authorities in this country."

"There is still so much to talk about."

Mingmei inhaled slowly and gave a short exhale. "I too want to talk some more... but I also need to keep you safe."

Nancy shook her head. "Safe is not what I do but I take your point. I can't blow my cover on my first visit."

Mingmei didn't quite understand.

"I mean... I need to be able to come back again." Nancy felt ex-hausted, but she now had another task she needed to prepare for, before returning to Hong Kong. "And I also have to pay a visit to a business that is of interest to a case I'm working on."

"You investigate criminal cases?" Her sister's face looked puzzled, perhaps even concerned.

"I'm not the police... But that's who I sometimes help."

"But why are you interested in a business in China?"

Nancy wondered whether she had said too much.

"It's a biotech company," she finally admitted.

Mingmei pulled a face. "Industrial espionage... There's a lot of that in China."

Her frankness emboldened Nancy. "It's also linked to an attempted murder."

"What is the address?"

"Century City International..."

"There are quite a few biotech labs there. It's part of a huge complex of offices, a research centre."

"So, it won't be a large factory?"

"No… something smaller, but it could be…" She was looking for the right word. "…very high profile."

"That sounds even more interesting… I need to take a look."

"How are you going to do that?" Mingmei frowned.

"Not sure yet… I'll need a trustworthy driver to start with."

Mingmei poured a final cup of tea. "Let me help."

\* \* \*

"She did a really good job of covering her back." Andy had finished accessing the email account onto which Natalie had downloaded her evidence. "It's not very secure, but I suppose if she thought no one suspected her…"

Pole leaned against Andy's desk.

"But she captured some key conversations. Instructions from her minder, discussions with Turner… It's all very good quality, too." Andy continued as he was going through the list of recordings.

Pole grinned. "That bastard is going to have to talk."

Andy looked preoccupied.

"What's wrong? These are excellent results." Pole raised his eyebrows, surprised.

"I know, Guv, but this single piece of coding from the USB Cora gave us is still bugging me."

Pole shook his head. "And she risked a lot to get it… I understand." He tapped his fingers on the partition separating Andy's desk from his neighbour's. "One thing at a time though. Natalie's piece of evidence is going to make a big difference, and it's enough to bring him in."

Andy pursed his lips. He was not yet ready to admit defeat.

Pole checked the clock on the wall. Ferguson had been quiet, so had Marsh. He was not sure whether this was a good or a bad thing, but he would not try to find out.

Pole left the building to return to the Café Conte near Trafalgar Square. The weather was cold yet sunny. His breath came out in small clouds as he increased his pace. Nancy's text had been reassuring, although he would have much preferred hearing from her directly.

His favourite table had just been vacated by a young woman with a large laptop and a set of bright yellow headphones. She smiled as Pole approached. Pole returned the smile and left his coat on the chair. He ordered, waited and collected his beverage, finally moving back to the table.

Pole took his time to sip his caffe latte with an extra shot. The room was full of the usual crowd – young people on their laptops, two women having a catch-up and a couple having early lunch.

His burner phone was still turned off. He turned on his work smartphone as well as his own mobile.

"Pole… How far have you got?" Harris asked.

"The name of the Bratva boss did the trick… the future doesn't look so rosy for Turner Junior."

"May not be as bad as that." Harris thought for a moment before continuing. "He has a rather large ace up his sleeve."

Pole paused his cup in mid-air before it reached his lips. "What do you mean? He's on record asking for Ollie Wilson to be dealt with."

"That sounds very compelling, but…"

Pole interrupted. "Don't tell me it is some operative you need to indulge."

"Not me… not even the CIA."

"Stop speaking in riddles, otherwise I'm presenting the evidence and getting a warrant."

"Turner is central to an agreement that is about to be signed between China, the US and Europe." Harris's voice had grown serious.

Pole mumbled a string of swear words.

"Couldn't agree more with you, mate. Timing is essential… Nab him too early and he will use it to protect himself and might even ask for a deal of some sort to exonerate himself."

Pole had been about to shoot Harris down for telling him how to do his job, but Harris was right. It was a waiting game.

"When is this goddamn agreement going to be signed then?"

"Actually, it's a rather good agreement… but in answer to your question, Turner is in Beijing at the moment."

"For how long?"

"How long is a piece of string." Harris interrupted. "These things can take days even if the text has been well hammered… but I'd say a good week."

"I need to show Marsh progress though…"

"Don't worry. Someone in the UK government is having a conversation with Marsh, perhaps as we speak. Don't be surprised if Marsh doesn't sound so keen suddenly for you to make headway with the case."

Pole didn't say anything, unconvinced.

"Perhaps you could use the time to cross the 't's and dot the 'i's on the Wilson case. And before you tell me to mind my own business…" Harris's voice had regained some of its cockiness. "You may even want to take a trip abroad."

"Should I be asking why?"

"Yes, you should. Ms Wu has just left on a trip to mainland China…"

A kick in the gut could not have winded Pole more. Harris waited at the end of the phone.

"Look… she's with the chap we have been monitoring for some time. He understands China very well. He will be a good guide."

"Is it about her father?" Pole managed to ask.

"It is…"

"Do I detect a but?"

"Chengdu is the city of her ancestors, and that matters as far as the search for a father is concerned, but it also is…"

"…the place Viro-Tech is growing its lab presence."

"Correct."

* * *

A knock at the door startled Nancy.

Licot poked his head in. "How are we doing?" His placid face couldn't hide his happiness. They had been talking for more than two hours and now he had to interrupt, but Mingmei had been right to take the risk.

"Could you give us another few minutes please?" Nancy smiled at him. Licot nodded and disappeared back outside.

386

"Are you certain? It's got nothing to do with your organisation, or even the people you're trying to save," Nancy said.

Mingmei shook her head. "Nancy..." The name was pronounced perfectly. She had rehearsed it for a while. "You know nothing about this city, and from what I can tell, you don't remember much of your Chinese. How are you going to find the place?"

"I know... no excuse to have let my Chinese lapse." Nancy didn't mind the comment.

"I was not trying to... make you feel bad. I simply know you can't do this discreetly unless you're with someone who knows the streets of Chengdu."

Nancy smiled at the proper pronunciation of the city she was born in... a long vowel at the end and the voice raising up.

"Let's say I agree." Nancy turned serious again. "But I have to see the place for myself."

"You sound like... Miss Marple..." Mingmei grinned.

"Now, young lady... I may be a single woman, and rather sharp when it comes to observation, but the comparison stops there!"

Mingmei kept her grin. "Of course... Sis." Her grin disappeared as soon as it came, but Nancy smiled back.

"Half-sis would not sound as much fun..."

Mingmei beamed at her half-sister for a short moment.

She became serious again. "There are cameras all over Century City."

Nancy stood up, hands on hips, thinking. "OK... I need your expertise but... I will take the risk of getting caught investigating this lab."

\* \* \*

"We have to make Turner feel secure. Otherwise, he will delay the signing of this agreement until he has come up with a plan." Jack was on a call to Harris.

"Pole has already sussed that one out. One of the key witnesses is being moved to a witness protection programme."

"Why should Turner not have wind of this?"

"Because that witness is supposed to have died in a bike crash."

"I get it."

"Any news on your front?" Harris was fidgeting at the other end of the line.

"I've looked at the line of code you sent me. I think it's a password. I ran it past my crypto team and they came to the same conclusion. How about you?"

"I'm a little too much on the fringes of the China Project to start asking questions."

"And you're confident this guy Pole and his team are up to the task?"

"They are surprisingly sharp when it comes to tech matters... but I might give them the heads-up on your suggestion." Harris batted a question from left field. "Have you asked Ms Wu for help?"

Jack smiled. Harris knew him too well. "I thought I could do with someone going to exactly the place I wished I could go myself. She has been a resourceful person and she's got the grit for the task."

"Hands off though... if she's going to become a spook, I spotted her first."

"Maybe, or do you already have some plans for her? I can't help thinking that MI6 providing her with information is no free lunch." It was time for Jack to turn the tables on Harris.

And it was Harris's turn to smile. Jack could hear it in his voice. "Let's say that the person she's going to meet in China is of interest to us, and I hope that they will get on with each other."

"A contact in mainland China. I see the attraction." Jack moved to the window of the room in the US consulate. It looked onto the inner courtyard of the building, protected from any eavesdropping.

"Back to Turner though. Will Scotland Yard be prepared to slow down and not act too soon?"

"The Superintendent who is Pole's superior is a political animal. If he's told by the Home Office to stand down his people, he will."

"And Pole?"

"He knows how to be patient when he knows he will get what he wants... and he does want to nab Turner very badly."

"Sounds hopeful... Shame I still have Hunter on my back. I only have a little less than 24 hours."

"Even if Ms Wu comes back with some good data on Viro-Tech?"

"That's what I'm counting on... my ticket to Washington is a flexible one."

* * *

Marsh had left a message for Pole.

Pole went straight to the top floor, to his boss's corner office.

"He is in a foul mood," warned his PA.

"That's OK, Denise, so am I." Pole hadn't bothered to straighten his tie. At least it was his casual clothes that had been ruined by the early morning bike accident.

"Sir..." Pole walked over to Marsh's desk, pulled out a chair and sat down.

"Pole..." Marsh spread his fingers across his desk. He seemed to have prepared for the conversation with Pole, and yet now was hesitating. "I'm not going to beat around the bush about this one... you've got to lay off Turner Junior."

Pole clenched his jaw and cast a dark eye towards Marsh. "We're tantalisingly close, sir."

"I know you are. I've read your report... but... I..." Marsh pursed his lips. "I've been leaned on."

"May I ask by whom?"

Marsh glared back at Pole. "You may ask, and I may not answer."

"There are only a few people who could do that... MOD, SIS... Home Office?"

Marsh shuffled his collection of pens around on his desk. "That's right, one of those."

"Is it permanent?"

"I have a feeling there is a deal that needs to be concluded... but it could take some time."

Pole reconsidered. "That's alright, sir. It'll give me time to polish up the evidence my team is assembling on the gentleman."

Marsh perked up. "You've got more?"

"The woman we were chasing and arrested has agreed to testify, and she's now being moved into the witness protection programme. She has given us conclusive evidence in the form of recordings incriminating Turner Junior. We will establish incontrovertibly that it is his voice and the recordings haven't been tampered with."

"Excellent." Marsh straightened up in his chair. There was still hope for a high-profile success.

"We've also looked into the USB key retrieved from Ollie Wilson's flat. My team has come up with an idea about its content."

"I thought it was a line of code."

"They think it may be a password," Pole said.

"So, when the time comes, we'll be ready to pounce." Marsh could not hide his glee.

"The minute Turner Junior loses his… protected asset status."

"That'll make the wait more bearable. In the meantime, I presume we need to make Turner feel secure?"

Pole nodded, surprised.

"So what… I too was a copper once." Marsh was pleased with the effect.

"Of course, sir… and talking about strategy, have you spoken to Ferguson?"

"I have indeed. He could see my point, although he still argued that the burner phone could have been used by someone from the Met."

"He needs to get on with finding out who bought the phone rather than trying to make his argument stick." Pole felt a pang of sympathy for Ferguson. His instinct was right, although perhaps now slightly misplaced.

"Any suggestions?" Marsh leaned forward.

"I've asked my DS, Todd, to map all the places which may be selling burner phones illegally around the area of interest, and then check with the CCTV coverage. If this woman went into one of those shops, we'll have it on record."

"Leave the rest to me."

Pole nodded his approval. "One final request, sir."

Marsh looked pleased and ready to accept anything Pole was about to ask.

"I'll be flying to Hong Kong tonight."

"You mean…?" Marsh looked concerned.

"Yes… Ms Wu is in trouble I fear, and she needs my help."

# Chapter Thirty-Nine

The name of the underground station was written on a piece of paper. Licot had frowned at the idea of letting Nancy go on her own, but she had assured him she would be fine.

She only needed to change trains once, and Mingmei would wait for her at the intersection of the two lines.

In the sea of faces, Nancy feared she might struggle to recognise her sister. She had found the underground station easily, though. Chengdu was built along straight roads that seemed to stretch endlessly and met other roads at neat square junctions. Tall buildings and skyscrapers lined the streets, block after block. Nancy was reminded that China was a country of 1.4 billion inhabitants. Space was at a premium in big cities.

Other passengers on the underground had stared at her, but the clothes she had chosen and the way she had arranged her hair avoided their curiosity becoming unwanted attention.

Nancy slowed her pace and spotted the benches that lay at regular intervals along the large corridors. She was about to choose one to sit down on and wait, when a hand squeezed her shoulder.

Mingmei had changed into dark trousers, a dark rollneck sweater and an unzipped biker jacket. Her smile squeezed once more Nancy's heart.

"You found it OK?"

"Easy… just two lines to deal with."

"Not like Hong Kong or Shanghai…" She nudged Nancy forward. "We've got to move quickly. People are leaving work, and this will be the ideal time to try and get into the offices."

They emerged from Century City station after a 15-minute tube ride. The underground steps came out onto a concourse in front of a lake that glittered in the glow of artificial lights. The semi-circular construction on the other side of the lake startled Nancy. It was a massive building, almost resembling a dam. Its white concave façade and slanted roof were intended to make a powerful statement… it was modern… it was imposing.

Nancy stopped for a moment and Mingmei indulged her. "It's a mix of offices, tech labs and shops… very fancy."

"But that can't be where the pharmaceutical companies operate?"

"No, science city is outside Chengdu. It's a gated park, very well protected."

"What about here?"

"CCTV cameras everywhere, security teams doing the rounds… unless you know how to avoid them. Follow me."

They left the lake and its luxurious surroundings, moving round the back of the semi-circle. Tall towers were spaced at regular intervals on the opposite side of the crescent, constructions of metal and concrete.

Mingmei followed closely the line of small shrubs that had been growing along the opposite side of the crescent, designed to hide the maintenance exits. She took a couple of blue cleaners' overalls, with a logo on their backs, out of her rucksack.

"They're for the maintenance staff." She also handed Nancy a cap to put on her head. "This way."

An army of people were at work, moving dustbins, shifting large crates containing linen, and supplies.

One of the vans had been left unattended for a moment. Mingmei took a pile of towels. She told Nancy to do the same and they marched towards the back doors of the building. They needed a badge to enter but the flow of staff meant that the door was left open for most of the time.

Nancy walked in following her sister. They went to the place where the towels were kept. The Holiday Inn Century City accommodated hundreds of tourists and businesspeople every day. They entered one of the service lifts. No one noticed them and now they were on their way to the ninth floor.

Mingmei spoke seldom to Nancy – only one word when needed – Nancy would reply with a nod.

A woman joined the lift at the fifth floor. She eyed the two women a little too long for comfort but exited on floor seven.

Floor nine was quiet. Mingmei had managed to pick up a bucket and mop, and Nancy a cleaning cloth.

They looked around. A security guard was stationed at the end of the corridor, checking his emails on his mobile or watching a film. He hadn't yet noticed them.

"We haven't got badges," Nancy murmured.

Mingmei shook her head. She was about to walk to the guard to let him know they had been summoned by someone inside the lab to clear up a mess in the kitchen, when the lift doors pinged open again.

A woman walked out. She didn't seem to be a member of staff. She was carrying a heavy bag and, ignoring the two women, walked straight to the guard. The man's face lit up. He took the bag and started removing boxes from it. The food smelt delicious, and by the time Mingmei and Nancy had reached his desk, he had already opened one of the boxes and prepared his chopsticks.

"We've been told to come up to clean a mess someone made in the kitchen."

The man barely looked at them, leaned sideways and pressed a button. The door opened… they were in.

"How did you know?" Nancy asked when they were out of earshot.

"At this time of the night this is what people all over the country are doing… most of the lab staff have gone home, so it's time for dinner."

The offices were brand new. Nancy could smell that the rugs had been laid recently and the paint on the walls was fresh. There were three doors down the corridor that resembled air locks. Mingmei noticed that one of the cleaners was finishing cleaning one of the internal corridors, where the access was guarded by one of the airlocks. Mingmei repeated her story.

There was a spillage in one of the kitchens and they must tend to it. Nancy couldn't quite follow what her sister was saying, but the woman shrugged and let them get on with their job.

The offices were locked, but there was a large central open area, in which people worked or had a chat and relaxed. Nancy walked over to the vending machines, pressed a button and waited.

"Good idea," Mingmei said.

She ordered a couple of cups of coffee, moved towards the kitchen and spilled them on the floor. Mingmei took her bucket and went to fetch some water. Nancy grabbed paper towels and dropped them over the spilled liquid.

Each office's wall was comprised of a dense frosted glass panel. There were high security locks and ID pads on each of the doors which required digital identification. It was impossible to see inside. Nancy took a couple of pictures with the phone Jack had given her.

She moved towards the airlock at the far end. She could hear Mingmei wrestling with the bucket. Without a security pass Nancy couldn't get into the part of the office that held what she was looking for. A shadow appeared on the other side of the frosted glass revolving doors. Nancy pulled back to join Mingmei near the vending machines.

The revolving doors rotated quickly, and she was almost face-to-face with a clean-shaven man in a white coat and spectacles. He glared at her and asked a question.

Mingmei dumped her bucket and joined Nancy.

She responded, bowing her head. Nancy gathered she was trying to tell him that Nancy was dumb. The man asked something else. Mingmei gestured towards the spillage in the coffee area.

He wanted to see it. They walked over, and he looked at the mess, exasperated.

He was about to let the matter go, but then took out his security badge and asked a question. Nancy had stepped back a little. She had spotted an old-fashioned sweet dispenser stocked with retro gumballs and painted red, China's favourite colour.

Nancy turned around swiftly. The conversation with Mingmei was getting more fraught and the man had taken his mobile out. Nancy lifted the machine. The metal felt dense and heavy. The man looked in her direction with anger. What was this idiot doing?

Nancy slammed the dispenser against the side of his head without letting go of it. The crush of bones was sickening. The man fell to his knees. She slammed the machine once more against his skull. He collapsed in a heap, unconscious.

Her sister's mouth opened into an "o". She could hardly believe what Nancy had just done.

"Let's drag him into the ladies and tie him up. I'll use his pass to get into the lab."

Mingmei shook her head. "And I thought I needed to protect you." She started to unbuckle his belt and shushed Nancy away. She would deal with him alone.

Nancy was in luck. The man had not locked his office door, as he must have intended to return swiftly.

The research space she entered was split into two. One part contained desks, chairs and a series of computer screens and keyboards, the other part was isolated by a thick glass wall, where machines intended for testing and analysis were still running.

There were rows of bottles containing liquid, glass cases with gloved access so that pathogens were isolated and couldn't cause contamination. There were also microscopes which could be operated in isolation. Sophisticated ventilation shafts prevented the escape of germs and other lethal substances.

Nancy took pictures of the entire installation as Jack had instructed her to do. She shifted her focus to the computers. Some of them had not been turned off and registered routine data. The keyboard was a regular English one. She tried to scroll for more information. She recognised the description of a molecular structure. She took more pictures.

She had been inside for less than 10 minutes. The maximum time she had decided was safe. Someone was moving outside the office. She could see the shape of a body at the second entrance to the lab. Nancy dropped to the floor and started crawling towards the exit door. She was still unnoticed.

The lab door shut behind the scientist. Nancy half stood up, opened the door and ran towards the air lock. She shoved the pass over the electronic eye. And pushed the revolving door frantically.

Mingmei was waiting for her. "He's started to come around. Only a few minutes and he'll start crying for help."

Both women took a bucket and walked out of the main air lock, looking busy. Mingmei thanked the guard and bowed a few times. Nancy followed awkwardly.

He had almost finished his dinner. As they reached the lift, he asked for something and this was one word that Nancy recognised.

Security pass.

Mingmei froze. Nancy turned around and dangled the pass she had just stolen. The lift had arrived. The guard said something but they both hurried into the lift and pressed the button for the basement.

"Take off your cleaning coat and cap." Mingmei was doing this as she spoke. She dumped the uniform in her cleaning bucket. She loosened her hair. Nancy couldn't help noticing how long it was. The lift arrived in the basement.

They walked out as a number of people started to shout. Mingmei joined in and pointed in the opposite direction… "That way."

Both women left through the exit at a measured pace. The weather had turned cold, but it was not chilly air that made Nancy shiver. It was a close shave.

As soon as the women started to mix with the crowd of staff coming and going through the various service entrances, they ran for their lives.

Mingmei led the way. Nancy followed close behind. They ducked, left, right, left, through a number of narrow streets that separated the towers arranged along them. It would have been easy to lose track of where they were but her sister looked back several times to make sure Nancy was following.

Out of breath they stopped near a cluster of trees and collapsed on a bench. There was a strip of water in front of them. It looked like yet another artificial lake that looped around a manmade island.

Mingmei took her phone out of her jacket pocket and when the call went through, simply said that they were ready. She got up, still a little breathless. Nancy stood up too and they started walking along a pavement lined with trees and flowerbeds.

They walked into a small square, bordered by large flowerbeds. A car approached and Mingmei's phone rang three times, stopped, then rang three times again.

"Your car has arrived." She went forward in the direction of the car headlights.

"You're not coming?" Nancy asked.

Mingmei cocked her head. "It's better if we're not seen leaving this place together."

The two women faced each other awkwardly. "Remember what I said... I want to help."

Her sister didn't reply for a moment. Then she made the first move, closing her arms around Nancy in a firm hug.

"He said you would come one day... he was right."

* * *

Pole asked the stewardess to call him when the gate was about to close. He had left a message for Andy to call him back. His DS had stepped into the breach without hesitation, to Pole's delight.

Marsh had not tried to stop him. The Super had once more rearranged the set of Montblanc pens on his desk, cleared his throat and told Pole he understood the urgency.

Ferguson might still try to stop him but there were only 10 minutes to go before the gate closed, another 20 to take off... Pole wondered whether Ferguson would try to get the plane to turn back. The evidence was a little slim and Marsh's blessing made a difference.

Pole's phone rang.

"Andy..." Pole cast an eye towards the stewardess. She looked his way and nodded. He still had a moment.

"Guv, we've got a breakthrough."

"Shoot."

"The line of code or rather, what we thought might be a code or a password, is something entirely different... it's a flattened line of messenger RNA."

Pole's mind went blank. "Enlighten me please. I know what DNA is... obviously. It's the long molecule that contains the biological instructions that makes a living thing unique..."

"Spot on, Guv... RNA is sort of the same. It also plays an essential role in gene expression but it's not as powerful as DNA."

"Right…"

"The point is that it's the genetic base for viruses… viruses are not alive as such. But they can replicate and that's why they make a person ill. The way they replicate is encoded into their RNA."

"Now I follow… What gave you the idea?"

"It's not mine, it's Mandy's." Andy was saying something to someone else in the office. Pole could picture him moving from one screen to another, gathering his data. "She suggested viewing the string of numbers and letters in 3D… and there it was, a single strand helix, with an additional formula that seemed to target a part of this RNA with something called LNPs… I mean lipid nanoparticles… they are like small droplets of fat in which the messenger RNA is packaged."

"So, we now have a bit of this RNA, from which particular virus?"

"We haven't discovered that yet. We need access to a proper biotech lab… so I called Yvonne."

"Good man… any idea why the additional formula is linked to LNPs though."

"From what we can gather, it teaches the immune system to respond to an invasion and stops the virus' process of replication."

"Would it be the same sort of response a vaccine would seek to elicit in the body?"

Andy gave it some thought. "That's got to be right… but I need to check it out."

"Yvonne might have a view on this and if she doesn't, she'll know who to ask."

"Anything else, Guv?"

"I've got news from the US consulate in Hong Kong. Randy Zhang is on his way to the US."

"He just decided to present himself to the consulate?" This was a good question.

"Granted… a little odd, but he has indicated he is willing to speak to us."

"I'll ask Mandy to deal with that. She's really hot on that stuff."

"You mean biotech I presume?" Pole smiled at his reflection in the large window of the airport boarding lounge. The airline staff waved at him. It was time. "Got to go. I'll call you as soon as I land in Hong Kong."

Pole killed the call, swapped his phone, grabbing his burner phone as he was walking towards the ramp that led to the plane. He mouthed a thank you to the stewardess who had been patiently waiting for him. She returned a smile.

Pole walked at a measured pace. They were waiting for him but he had a call placed. "Harris... I'm boarding a plane in less than a minute. The formula that was on Ollie Wilson's USB key is not a password. It refers to the genetic code of a virus and the way to disrupt its replication."

Pole's mobile was buzzing in his pocket as he spoke to Harris. Ferguson's number appeared. "Got to go, Harris... Just make sure Randy knows. I'll wager that is our missing link."

Pole pressed the red button on his other mobile. Ferguson would have to wait until his return.

* * *

The stewardess offered Nancy some tea. "*Xie xie.*" At least she could say thank you in Chinese.

The scene of the previous night replayed in her mind in a continuous loop. The intrusion into the lab, their escape, her sister's hug and the words she uttered then.

"He said you would come one day... he was right."

Nancy still couldn't reconcile what this prediction her father made so many years ago meant to her and what it said about her father's faith in her.

Air turbulence started to shake the plane. The contents of the cup she had been holding distractedly spilt onto her leg. She swore under a breath and wiped away the liquid with a paper napkin.

Professor Licot was reading his book. The seats in club class were comfortable and he had left Nancy to decide to talk if she wished. He knew there was a lot she needed to think about on her way back to Hong Kong. He hadn't asked Nancy about her evening with Mingmei, and she was grateful for that.

It was almost 7pm when they landed in Shanghai. The transit to the international airport took only a few minutes. Passport Control was a little tense for Nancy. The officer asked a few questions. She talked about meeting artists and gallerists.

- Had she bought anything?
- No
- Why not?
- Too many good people, difficult to choose… she would come back.

The officer looked at her with a combination of coolness and dislike. Still, she looked the part… designer jeans, expensive leather jacket, brand new trainers. He let her through.

Nancy took a seat for the final leg of the journey on the Cathay Pacific flight to Hong Kong. Her body relaxed in one go. She noticed how tense her shoulders had been since she'd arrived in Chengdu. Her back felt like a block of wood. She would indulge in a long soak in a warm bath as soon as she reached her hotel.

As the aircraft took off the relief faded. She had left behind someone she had barely gotten to know and yet had started to care for.

After the plane had been in the air for a few minutes, it banked left over the China Sea. Nancy looked through the window. There were a few spots of lights on the vast dark expense… fishermen trying to scrape a living.

*The boat's rocking has become scary. She and her friend have burrowed underneath the tarpaulin the fisherman insists they stay under. Her mother has wrapped her arms tightly around her.*

*There is a loud smack from the bow every time the waves hit the front of the boat. The fisherman is fighting the ocean as best he can, but the boat is too small and there are too many people for such a small craft.*

*The struggle with the sea has been going on for hours. She can't tell how long but she wants it to stop. Her stomach is somersaulting, and she feels almost sick, but not quite.*

*Her friend is not as fortunate. She has been throwing up and her mother is trying to hold a small bucket to catch the bile her daughter brings up.*

*The wind increases abruptly. It changes direction all of a sudden. They have reached another part of the coast that leads to freedom.*

The boat too has veered, and the waves are now slapping against its starboard hull. The women can't help but cry in fear. It feels as though the boat will be engulfed by the waves any moment.

Voices have risen. The three men are arguing. Nancy can't understand but she can hear her father shouting. It's not simply an argument. It's much more than that... outrage... horror. She has never heard his voice sound like that before.

The other man has started to beg. Nancy never thought a grown-up could do that.

The fisherman yanks the tarpaulin from over their heads. He is dripping wet from the rain. He looks at the two girls and their mothers, but before he can say anything, a crash of thunder makes everyone jump.

Nancy's father has fired a gunshot in the air. She doesn't know where the gun has come from, but her father is aiming it at the fisherman's chest.

He returns to the wheel, cursing... they will all drown.

Each wave is a challenge. Everyone is soaked to the bone and Nancy starts shivering.

Her mother replaces the canvas over them as best she can.

The boat's rocking eases off but her mother's body tenses. There are some lights far away on the horizon.

The two fathers have seen these too. No one wants to believe it yet.

The fisherman sniggers as the passengers' hopes are dashed... There is a good reason why their destination is called Big Wave Bay.

The next wave that slams into the boat throws the two men off balance. The fisherman seizes his chance. He tries to grab the gun from her father. They struggle for only an instant and the gun discharge resounds around the small ship. The old man falls on his side. Her father's friend leaps forward. The fisherman mustn't die.

Nancy's father grabs the wheel. The land is so close and yet so far. The old man whispers a few words.

Her father holds the boat as steady as he can. The waves swell underneath it and their direction has changed again. The boat dips and rises. It is a straight run to the shore if they can maintain the course.

Nancy's friend has stopped being sick, but she looks very pale.

*The boat is almost there. Nancy's father is still holding the wheel. He cuts the engine. As he does, a wave no one has seen coming slams into the skiff, rolling it over like a dice and its occupants with it.*

Nancy gazed through the window of the aircraft. She could see neither the stars nor the dark sea below. She only saw one image.

Those waves that pushed them to the shore.

The body of a child, lifeless on the sands of Big Wave Bay.

# Chapter Forty

Pole rose from the seat he has chosen in the arrivals hall of Hong Kong airport. He paced up and down a few times. Nancy's flight had landed. He had only had a couple of hours' rest in his hotel room, but he felt alert.

Harris had been surprisingly forthcoming. Someone didn't want Nancy in Hong Kong, and now that she was returning from Chengdu, she had become a greater problem.

It may no longer be intimidation. Pole stretched his long limbs and rolled his shoulders. The effects of the bike accident still affected his body and a few bruises had started to appear.

The opaque glass doors of the arrivals gate started to open. People were walking through; friends and family were coming forward to greet them. A couple of limo drivers in dark suits with name boards were waiting too.

Pole surveyed them carefully. They were the most obvious candidates, although perhaps a little too obvious. He had spotted another man of medium height, in a heavy leather jacket. He looked American. Pole didn't know why he thought that.

The glimpse of a silhouette moving towards the doors made Pole stop.

Nancy emerged, an older gentleman at her side. She said a few words to him and they shook hands. She waited for an instant, a single bag at her side, deciding what to do next. Pole recognised her expression. She wanted to be left alone.

Not this time though. A smile creeped onto his lips. He took a few steps towards her and waited.

She felt someone looking at her and looked in their direction. She dropped her bag; not yet quite sure she was right. But she was and Nancy started walking towards Pole with a smile that matched his.

The flash of steel propelled Pole forward. Pole's sudden movement made Nancy turn around. She swung her rucksack in front of her, but it afforded pitiful protection as a gunman ran towards them... The sight of a weapon made a couple of people scream, and the mass scramble shielded Nancy for a few seconds. Pole had almost reached her.

The rugby tackle from the American came from nowhere. The assailant toppled to the ground. He rolled on his side and a left kick propelled his gun away. He jumped to his feet and he and the American were now facing each other. Pole had swung round in front of Nancy, and now that she was behind him, he joined the fray. He picked up the gun as the two other men circled each other slowly. A knife came out. Pole placed the firearm in the waistband of his trousers and took off his leather jacket, rolling it in one quick movement around his left forearm. He wouldn't use a firearm, come what may, and hoped the rolled leather afforded some protection against the sharpness of a blade.

The American was in a defensive position, hands raised. He started moving in on the assailant as Pole was doing the same.

The blade cut the air a few times. Both Pole and the American managed to avoid it. The man tried again but his opponents were skilled in combat, and he realised he was about to be overwhelmed.

He cast a glance towards the exit doors. He threw his knife with force at Pole who ducked, but not quite fast enough. The blade sliced a gash in his upper arm.

The man was now running towards the rows of seats that stood between him and the exit. He jumped the rows one after the other, gaining ground towards the automatic doors. The American followed with equal agility. The doors opened into the night. They were gone.

Pole's hand was compressing his wound. Nancy had shaken herself into action. She found a scarf in her rucksack, wrapping it around his arm. "You need a doctor."

Pole shook his head. "I need to find him first."

Pole was already halfway to the doors. Nancy followed. When they came out, it was almost over. The chase had taken both men onto

404

the multi-lane exit roads where large buses pick up speed as they leave the terminal. The American had caught up with the gunman. The only way to escape was to cross the busy road.

The man dashed across near a bend in the road. A large bus emerged without warning. The man lost his balance, his arms whirling in the air and nothing to stop his fall... the American stepped back and watched, as the man fell.

Nancy couldn't help but close her eyes. The squealing brakes of the bus drowned out the thud of body against metal. Pole was about to cross over but the American was already walking back towards them.

"The police will be here shortly," Jack said, "You should go."

Nancy nodded. She plunged a hand deep into her rucksack and handed over the sim card of a phone. He returned her nod and walked back towards the road where people had gathered to help or merely to watch.

Pole took Nancy by the hand. They retrieved her bag from the arrivals hall and jumped into a taxi just as the first police car arrived.

"His name is..." Nancy said, turning to Pole.

"I know who he is," Pole interrupted with a smile. Nancy sighed and leaned her head against his shoulder. This was home.

* * *

The morning was coming to an end. Nancy and Pole had walked since breakfast all the way to Sky Court on top of the Peak, where they met Licot for a coffee before taking a cab to their next destination.

Licot had a surprise waiting for them. He had discussed with Nancy on the way back from Chengdu... Amy was alive and well. She had first thought she'd misunderstood him. But she had learned in the few days she'd spent with him to trust him.

Licot was not keeping her against her will. He was offering the young woman protection against possible unwanted attention. Licot thought Amy had made herself vulnerable by investigating what had happened to Nancy's father. Things were changing in Hong Kong and showing too much interest in well-known dissidents was not a welcome occupation.

Nancy had dropped by Philippe's Hong Kong gallery to tell him the news. They had agreed to meet Licot for a coffee and a reunion they had never hoped would come so swiftly.

But Amy was there, looking well if a little nervous. They had hugged each other, holding back a few tears. They would all soon be on their way to London. Pole and Nancy had left Licot's flat for the last part of their journey, whilst the others were still enjoying their morning. Nancy had bought the bunch of roses at the Mandarin Oriental and carried them all the way.

Nancy walked to the edge of the water and removed her shoes. She unravelled the loose piece of string that held the flowers together.

She entered the water, hardly noticing the coolness of the waves that lapped her shins. She dropped the flowers one by one into the sea, watching them drift away from the shore... all seven of them.

Tears rolled freely onto her cheeks. The soft breeze would dry them soon.

When the last of the roses had floated away, Nancy stepped back onto the beach, lighting three sticks of incense she stuck in the sand.

Pole had found a place to sit at the top of Big Wave Bay, waiting... he was in no hurry. Nancy made her way back towards him. When she reached him, he stood up and wrapped his arms around her, kissing the top of her head and resting his chin on it.

"You don't need to rush, you know."

Nancy nodded. "I'm ready to move on... I lost a friend. I gained a sister..."

"And a cause to fight for."

She lifted her head, with an amused yet surprised smile. "I can't hide anything from you."

"You've done plenty of that, I believe."

Nancy slid her arm around his waist and started walking. "There were certain things I needed to do on my own."

"Such as doing a little bit of moonlighting for the CIA in Chengdu?"

"I was not on my own."

"So, you said..."

They had reached the lane that led back to the road. Pole's mobile was ringing. It was a message. He must have lost reception whilst sitting on the beach.

Pole listened and broke into a grin. "The Chinese and US governments have signed their co-operation agreement. Turner is on his way back to the US... The CIA is assembling a welcome committee."

They stayed silent for a moment, savouring the news.

"So where to now?" Pole asked, his voice warm and mellow.

Nancy grabbed his hand and started running.

"Let's explore the island and enjoy our free time before life throws up another impossible mystery."

Dear Reader,

I hope you have enjoyed BLOOD DRAGON as much as I have enjoyed writing it!

Nancy's story carries on alongside Pole in her latest adventure SON AND CRUSADER

SON AND CRUSADER
mybook.to/apXFqK

Or, perhaps you would like to know more about Nancy's journey. How it all began with Pole and who the mysterious Henry Crowne is.

Delve into the HENRY CROWNE PAYING THE PRICE series to discover who Nancy and Pole are, with

COLLAPSE:
mybook.to/COLLAPSE

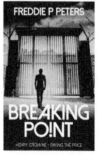

BREAKING POINT:
mybook.to/BREAKINGPOINT

Or

NO TURNING BACK:
mybook.to/NOTURNINGBACK

HENRY CROWNE PAYING
THE PRICE, BOOKS 1–3:
mybook.to/HCPTPBKS1-3

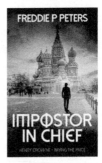

SPY SHADOWS:
mybook.to/SPYSHADOWS

IMPOSTOR IN CHIEF
mybook.to/IMPOSTORINCHIEF

RED RENEGADE
mybook.to/Env1F

Or check out the latest book on pre-order in the NANCY WU CRIME
THRILLER series:

Don't forget you can get access to the genesis of BLOOD DRAGON as well as chapters or receive information about the next book in the series.

Join Freddie's book club at www.freddieppeters.com

Perhaps I can now ask for a small favour? Please take a few minutes to write a review on Amazon, Goodreads or BookBub. Thank you so very much!

Looking forward to connecting with you…

Freddie

# Acknowledgements

It takes many people to write and publish a book… for their generosity and support I want to say thank you.

Cressida Downing, my editor, for her no-nonsense approach and relentless enthusiasm for books… mine in particular. Ryan O'Hara, for his expertise in design and for producing a super book cover. To Helen Janacek for more than thorough copy-editing, Danny Lyle for his typesetting and project management and Vicki Vrint for a bilingual spell-checking equal to none. Helena Halme, an author in her own right, for giving me her help in marketing my books.

To the friends who have patiently read, reread and advised: Alison Thorne, Elisabeth Gaunt, Geraldine Kelly, Malcolm Fortune, Tim Watts, Gaye Murdock, Kathy Vanderhook, Kat Clarke, and Jeff and Jourine Moore.

Finally, a special thanks to ARCADE Gallery for providing plenty of fantastic contemporary art, and inspiration.

Printed in Great Britain
by Amazon

38378566R00235